Skubalon Storm

SECESSION, GOD & COUNTRY
IN A POSSIBLE WORLD

R. Merald Ayer

Milwood Books
Austin, Texas

ISBN 978-0-692-17773-0 (Paperback)
ISBN 978-0-692-18514-8 (eBook)

Cover artwork by Karen O'Halloran.
Cover design by Kathy Hill.

Skubalon Storm/R. Merald Ayer —1st edition.
www.skubalonstorm.com

Milwood Books
milwoodbooks@skubalonstorm.com

R. Merald Ayer
merald@skubalonstorm.com

To my brothers,
Michael Sage and Michael Michalik.
R.I.P.

Inspiration

THE GOOD BOOK, PHILIPPIANS 3:8. KING JAMES VERSION. LEGACY ALT-PROTESTANT

Yea doubtless, and I count all things but loss for the excellency of the knowledge of Christ Jesus my Lord, for whom I have suffered the loss of all things and count them but skubalon, that I may win Christ.

BETTER BOOK INNOVATED WORD. BOB THE RAP-EEST 12:69. CHURCH OF THE P-FREE SABBATH

Dawg, ain't nothing like hangin' with Word.
Innovated. Consecrated. Heavy-weighted.
I been through some–SAA!–times,
    but that don't mean skubalon.
I got my Big. Feel me?

SHIH BUHHARI, 5:58:200. ABU HURAIRA. LEGACY WAY-BACK ISLAM

The Prophet said, "Bring me stones in order to clean my private parts, and do not bring any bones or animal skubalon."

THE FOURTH TELLER, PRE-UR III.

Zounds! I'Faith, foretold is a skubalon storm on the Great Walk. Alackaday, it must whither here now, millennia before the twinkle of its mother's eye. God's Me! The Great Walk Stand must never be.

THE DISAPPEARED. RABBI SCHOLAR ODEDE JÄGER, C. 2026. LEGACY ALT-JUDAISM

You're so full of skubalon. You know that, right?

Contents

Preambulum

DREADFUL ANNUM

HAD MASSACHUSETTS GOVERNOR JOHN HANCOCK not died in October 1793 A.D., he would have uttered these words two months later on New Year's Eve, to those gathered in his Charter Street home in Boston, moments before the eight-foot Baldwin and Storrs grandfather clock struck midnight.

"My dear fellows, we are come to the dawning of 1794, not one moment too soon, you will most assuredly agree. For the year of our Lord and Savior 1793, the mystics prophesied *not* the severed head of King Louis XIV, the French pronouncement of war upon our now-distant British cousins, or the 5,000 good Philadelphians now-perished by the ravishes of yellow fever.

Who among you predicted, even in jest, that the French Reign of Terror would rule the day and yet pale in the wake of recent volcanic terrors wrought upon the Japanese people where the strong and weak alike were powerless to outdistance the thick orange-black lava that would have them? No one! No one dared forecast that God would visit upon our world all of these calamities since last we gathered here to welcome in a hopeful new year."

Were he able, by the presence of a 12-week space-time warp, John Hancock would certainly have added to his list of tragedies during 1793: "and poor John Hancock is dead!"

"Oh, dreadful annum!" he would have continued. "You are the Almighty's loving and vengeful offer of salvation, compelling man to embrace his desolate past, as his only course to–"

Bong! Bong! Bong! The clock striking midnight would have interrupted the good governor's rather lengthy speech, prompting a well-deserved celebration of 1794, the blessed New Year. 'Tis a pity though because, had the governor a few more moments, he would have shared his thoughts on the upcoming election season, the Cumberland County incident and, of course, the burgeoning matzo trade in the distant climes of the Orient.

BOOK ONE

Insanus in medio.

In the crazy middle.

Secession Interruptus l:l.l   **April 21, 2027 A.D.**

MOMENTS BEFORE THE OFFICIAL ANNOUNCEMENT that Texas would secede from the United States, Governor Peter Phelt received notification that his state had been unceremoniously expelled from the Union. Just like that.

The official document of expulsion, issued by the U.S. Government Printing Office, was shorter than the Gettysburg address, but borrowed liberally from same, the governor thought. It read:

> *Eight score and eighteen years ago our fathers brought forth into this great Union, the noble Texas, unique among that young nation of states, having won its own independence at the Battle of San Jacinto on this day in 1836. Bound to their hearts, the Texian spirit conveyed into our union a boastfulness conceived in liberty, and dedicated to the proposition that all of these states united might one day be as great as Texas, but probably not.*
>
> *Now we are engaged in a great un-civil discourse, testing whether that nation, or any nation so conceived and so dedicated, can thus endure. We are long met on the battlefields of that dissertation, day after tedious day, having to bear upon our persons endless pronouncements of "Texas this" and "Texas that."*
>
> *Therefore, with this proclamation, these 49 states do forever vacate Texas, that monotonous inanity which has*

contaminated the very essence of itself and our once-beloved Texian brothers. It is altogether fitting and proper that we should do this.

The world will little note, nor long remember how we suffered endless Texian entrustments proclaiming their own glorious provenance and destiny, but it can never forget what we did here this day to preserve the Union.

The governor had waited too long to make the secession announcement, gauging international grain markets, quelling the nerves of the Red River border caucus, and pandering to his whiny lieutenant governor who would be escorted out of the new Republic of Texas upon Governor Phelt's order.

But there would be no glorious secession and Texas would not leave the so-called "United States" on its own terms. Washington had won this day, but it was an insignificant victory, Phelt encouraged himself. Texas was now a sovereign nation; it was strong and would weather the day's setback and any other attacks the federalists mounted in the future.

From the south steps of the Texas Capitol, Governor Phelt looked across the lush green acres where Texas heroes and their battles are immortalized in granite and bronze on either side of the Great Walk. He'd imagined the perfect spot for what would have been the 2027 Texas Secession monument on the unoccupied southwest corner of the grounds, just across 11th Street from the Governor's—no, the President's—Mansion.

It was on this very spot that Governor Phelt and Texas had so naturally embraced each other in 1996. The Phelt family, relocating from Goshen, Alabama to Indianapolis that summer, had decided to make their pilgrimage to Texas to honor Peter's great-great-great-uncle thrice removed, Antonio Cruz de Mantanzas. According to Dr. Jake Phelt, the governor's father, Private Cruz had fought beside colonels Boone and Crockett during the Battle of the Alamo, and was among those selected by General Travis to steal away under the cover of darkness to seek reinforcements for the doomed garrison.

Young Peter was thrilled by the story and it had kept him awake nights imagining life on the Texas frontier. He forsook Dr. Seuss at bedtime, favoring stories about Texas' struggle for independence, and asked for books on the Alamo and a Bowie knife for his birthday that year.

"The greatest regret of your Uncle Antonio's life was that he failed his commander, General Travis. He couldn't find any Texians to ride with him back to the Alamo. Can you imagine how you would feel," Dr. Phelt asked young Peter, "if all your friends were about to die but there was nothing you could do to help them?"

Peter didn't answer, but cuddled against his father in the big chair as they watched an old videotaped episode of *Combat!* in which Sergeant Chip Saunders bayonets a German soldier because he's a German soldier. "Dirty Kraut," the sergeant mutters, wiping his blade.

"Even though your uncle was just a private, everyone was depending on him, right buddy?" Dr. Phelt squeezed his son.

"What would you have done, Daddy?"

"I would do for God and country whatever I could, and live to fight another day. Just like Uncle Antonio did, right buddy?"

"Yeah!" answered the boy eagerly.

"And what he did he do next?" his father asked.

Peter recited the rest of the story he'd heard many times before. "Two months later he fought gallantly in the Battle of San Jacinto, securing independence for Texas!"

"That's right, son."

Although Peter would never know, later that year, Private Cruz was again called upon to fight gallantly, this time against twenty renegade Texians who wanted his land. To them, he was just another Mexican squatter, a deserter from Santa Ana's defeated army for all they knew. This time Antonio was not rewarded with the independence of Texas, but with his own agonizing suffocation at the end of a rope as his family watched.

A cool northerly breeze had averted another ozone action day and cleansed the skies just enough to see twelve blocks down Congress Avenue where the Rick Perry Bridge crossed the parched Colorado River. Standing on the steps of the capitol, Governor Phelt was comforted by the tale of his great-great-great-uncle, a brave Texian who had served his country and enjoyed thereafter the bounty of a grateful nation. Governor Phelt himself was the proud legacy of Private Cruz; the new Republic of Texas would be the governor's.

Church I:2.1 2025th Year of Some People's Lords (Y.O.S.P.L.)

"THE LEGACY SUFI-DISAMBIGUATION-ISTS will face the Alt-Legacy Bahá'í in the finals of the 2025 Softball Intramural Tournament at two o'clock today! Arse-kicking blessings to all!" The echoed announcement filled the ecumenicon, as the 65,000-strong Church of the P-Free Sabbath faithful readied themselves.

"And finally, next week's Legacy Dianic Wicca sermon has been rescheduled for two months ago," the announcer paused for a smattering of laughter and applause for the Wicca's time-bending antics.

The lights dimmed slowly to black as the congregation cheered, and then hushed itself for the pre-sermon advisory. "_lease note that _astor Yates may use the term "fucking-A" during this morning's sermon. Cover your children's ears if that is your tradition."

It was exactly 42 minutes after the hour. Three stories below the main stage, Pastor Brother Arlen Bob Yates stepped onto an elevator platform supporting the massive wrap-around obsidian pulpit that would emerge from center stage and then rise another 25 feet, seemingly suspended in mid-air.

Pastor Yates positioned himself in the pulpit, adjusted his white gown and earpiece, and listened to Brother Director Cardu cue his ascension. As the pulpit rose silently through and above the stage floor, longtime congregants knew what to expect. The uninitiated, however, were momentarily blinded by a cross-shaped burst of white light that vanished as quickly as it appeared. As their eyes slowly readjusted to the darkness, a resonant image of the same cross watermarked their vision with soft tenors of green and blue followed by subtle burnt orange.

The colors wandered through the spectrum to settle on a soft, comforting white. As their eyes relaxed into the image, the center square of the cross faded to black. Newcomers squinted to see a white-robed, Lilliputian-size Pastor Yates.

The cross slowly disappeared as the tiny Yates grew larger. The crowd cheered, some wiping tears from their eyes caused by joyous exultation or minor optical damage, as the now full-sized pastor smiled broadly and raised his arms to the masses, posing as the background for thousands of selfies as phones flashed.

Yates stole a glimpse of himself on the 6-D, 50 million-pixel megatron screen suspended 90 feet above the center of his modern-day coliseum that was the Church of the P-Free Sabbath. His was indoors and had more seats than the Roman's version, but both employed the latest technologies of the day, provided top-shelf entertainment, and gave the people exactly what they wanted.

The first row of the ecumenicon's second balcony had a bird's-eye view of the horseshoe-shaped stage that gracefully embraced the expansive ground-floor seating area. The superstructure of the main altar soared the 200 feet necessary to join it with the uppermost support beams of the CPFS cathedral, though the details of the high construction were lost in magnificent frescos that reimagined the church's storied past.

"Man, you cain't hardly beat the show these Legacy Alt-_rotestants _ut on, can ya?" a youthful Legacy Jesus-Freak yelled to his new best friend, Mustafa. "This is fucking turmeric!"

"Oh, yes," beamed the 114-year-old man, born in Palestine when it was still part of the Ottoman Empire. "Yes! Veddy good business!"

"Welcome sisters, brothers and others to another mother-of-a-worldwide celebration of Innovated Word!" shouted "_astor Yates, as he was referred to on P-Free Sabbath days. "Welcome! I love you!" He reached out his arms. "Sing with me now! Let us join as one, singing _ray on _oor Sinner!"

He stood before a standing-room-only crowd, a 5.7 Nielsen-Putin rating, and Word knows how many online sinners waiting to hear his sermon, a sacred Alt-Protestant message tailored for each one of them and their problem at that very moment. As always, his words would fit them perfectly, like clothes off the good rack, and smell like the currency-millions they would collectively PayPal to his church this morning.

As the predictable post-hymn cheering and hugging commenced, Pastor Yates glanced up at the sixth-floor media booth on the rear wall of the ecumenicon and listened to the stage directions in his tiny earphone.

"Camera one, when you lose light, _an left and down slightly," Director Brother Cardu said. "Ready camera two, with your close-u_ of _astor, ready mic, ready cue." Yates broadened his smile, and extended both arms out to the masses, his masses. "Camera two, mic, cue."

"Ready camera three, _an left, audience, rear stadium level six," Brother Cardu said, "and three, cue." As the camera panned the nosebleed section, the giant screen was filled with the faces of the P-Free ecumenica, the "Earth-family party boat," as Yates was fond of saying. "Our 'ark' with two-of-everybody and all the in-betweens!"

For some, being in this sanctuary was the fulfillment of a lifelong dream. It was a singular moment, a pilgrimage no less significant than those to Mother Ganges, Mecca or Graceland. For others, it was a shuttle ride from the nearby P-Free City of Light where thousands of church members lived. For all, their love for this church and Pastor Brother Yates was boundless, and they gave of it freely.

In exchange, he ministered to their every need. The church's worldwide network of no-wrong-door social services offered food and rental assistance, a federally-funded charter school with out-loud prayers every morning, free bus rides to the white-collar and black prisons on visiting days, and plenty of old-school Dora the Explorer stickers for the kids. There was free and ample parking at the church or, if you preferred, no-tip valet service. The people liked that.

The keystone of all CPFS legacy faiths was their doctrinal assurance that you can "Repent Whenever." The details and application of this promise varied widely among the legacies; about half had a life-limited guarantee that is, you must repent before death. Others extended the option to atone until after the demise of one's mortal coil, within a reasonable time frame, of course.

The phrase "Repent Whenever" was copyrighted and trademarked within an inch of its life and faithfully placed below every written reference to "Church of the P-Free Sabbath." The marketing department regularly focus-grouped the "Repent Whenever" slogan to revalidate its impact, and make sure that pious, early-adopting adherents weren't getting touchy about the fact that their eternal reward would be the same as some old fart who had a last-minute conversion.

No wonder this place is packed, Yates thought, surveying the crowd. Who the hell wouldn't ante up a couple hours on Monday morning and a little insurance offering to the collection plate for that kind of deal? Repent whenever, and you're in.

It was all right there, chapter and verse in the *CPFS Better Book*, along with "The one who will enter the After, is the person who places their faith in the Innovated Word and Its Blood shed just west of the Trans-Canada Highway, blah, blah, blah."

When writing the passage years before, Yates included the "blah, blah, blah" for the young folks. To them it was an implicit promise from the church and Pastor Yates that sermons wouldn't last forever and a handy spiritual tool with which to remind their parents to please get to the point.

"Blah, blah, blah, Mom," 13-year-old Marisa Manky had quoted scripture to her mother on the way to church that very morning. "I know every boy will turn into a horny bastard in eighth grade. What's your point?"

"Who will enter into the After?" intoned Pastor Yates from the pulpit.

"The _erson who _laces their faith in the Innovated Word and Its Blood shed just west of the Trans-Canada Highway blah, blah, blah!" responded his flock in unison.

"Who?" encouraged Yates.

"The _erson who _laces their faith in the Innovated Word and Its Blood shed just west of the Trans-Canada Highway blah, blah, blah!" repeated the crowd.

"And *when* must we _lace our faith in Word?" he baited them.

"Whenever we want to!" they eagerly responded in a singular voice.

"W*hen* must we _lace our faith in Word?" he repeated into the microphone, no Ps to pop.

"Whenever!"

"When?" leading them into the familiar cadence of every Legacy Alt-Protestant sermon.

"Ever!" they cried out.

"When?" he demanded.

"Ever!"

"When?"

"Ever!"

Pastor Yates continued the exercise, mesmerizing all in the cavernous sanctuary and the P-Free ecumenica worldwide.

With each prompt, they all thrust their arms toward the After to accent the roaring chant.

"When?" he yelled.

"Ever! When? Ever!" The throng asked and answered itself. "Ever! When? Ever!"

Pastor Brother Yates smiled broadly. He closed his eyes and swayed to the chant's rhythmic side-to-side with his best Stevie Wonder. He wrapped both arms around himself, offering the embrace to his followers. Gazing toward the After and the megatron screen, he watched himself raise both arms to the adoring crowd thinking, *we're definitely breaking $25 mil today.*

Birth 1:3.1   December 16, 1984 A.D.

As PLANNED BY A GOD named "God" moments before enjoying a Swanson TV dinner on the eighth day of creation, the Indianapolis Colts played the New England Patriots on December 16, 1984.

Many sports historians believe it was Robert Irsay, the money-grubbing Colts owner (their words, not God's), who'd moved his team away from Baltimore the previous year. That, of course, is patently absurd. It was God who moved the Baltimore Colts to Indianapolis in 1983 so that the team would not distract the soon-to-be fathers of Arlen Robert Yates and Peter Phelt from duties associated with the births of their sons. Had there been a Baltimore Colts game in Baltimore on December 16, the two men would have gone to the stadium and ended up too schnoozled to make it to Baltimore Memorial Hospital in time for their respective blessed events. And that just wouldn't do.

Alas, the almighty hand of God was thwarted by man's free will that day. As it turned out, Mr. Yates and Dr. Phelt found themselves in the none-too-fashionable Caspar's Bar near the abandoned Baltimore Colts stadium listening to the game on a grimy turquoise-colored radio that featured two once-white dials now yellowed with time. The game was on television somewhere but not in Baltimore, thanks to that son of a bitch Irsay. Adding insult to injury, they had to listen to the distant, crackly broadcast of a Patriots play-by-play announcer. Nursing their drinks, the expectant fathers studied every detail of the dingy radio as the hapless Indianapolis Colts played to a 13-point deficit at halftime.

"Serves those bastards right," said Dr. Phelt, looking around the empty bar. "Looks like it's just you and me, buddy. You ready for another? I'm buying." Mr. Yates had barely noticed the man sitting two stools down.

"Thank you, I probably shouldn't," Mr. Yates said. "My wife's in labor at Memorial."

"Hey, go figure, mine is too!" Dr. Phelt said. "That's worth at least one shot. Bartend!"

"Well, alright. Thank you," nodded Mr. Yates. "I'm Benjamin Yates."

"Good to meet you, Benny-boy. Jake—Jake Phelt."

The Colt's rallied in the third quarter with a field goal and a touchdown.

"I don't even know if I want 'em to win any more," Jake said, draining his glass.

"You need another?" interrupted the bartender.

"Make it a double. The same for him," answered Jake.

Benjamin Yates stared at the radio. "Okay, but I have to go after this one." They stayed long enough to hear the Patriots kick a fourth-quarter field goal even though they didn't need it.

"C'mon brother, we gotta book it to the hospital," Jake said, slapping Yates on the back. "Don't know about your wife, but mine will be rip me a new one if she thinks I wasn't there when the baby popped out."

"Jesus," said Benjamin Yates, holding his forehead; it had decided to start pounding right now and not wait for its hangover.

"It's alright. That's the last game of the season, Benny. The nightmare's over," said Jake, helping him off the stool. "You got a car?"

"No, thank God," answered Yates. "I couldn't drive anyway."

"Brother, you are one cheap date; you only had four drinks. C'mon, we can hoof it to the hospital, it's not that far."

Secession Interruptus 1:1.2   April 21, 2027 A.D.

FOR SECURITY REASONS, THEY CONVENED in a nondescript meeting room in the old State Insurance Building on the southeast corner of the Texas Capitol grounds. Nonetheless, the set-up was the same as the regular cabinet meeting room. The governor's chair was in the middle of the long table with Secretary of State Cyrana Johnson on his left and Chief of Staff Mary Levi on the right. From there on, it was musical chairs.

The meeting was to have been a solemn historical event held in the governor's formal meeting room on the second floor of the capitol, open to the press and documented for posterity. It would have been the first meeting of Cabinet of the President of the Republic of Texas. That might happen later but for now the senior leadership team needed a secure room to freely discuss the summary dismissal of Texas from the United States.

"So what if they kicked us out? What the hell does it matter, now??" Mary Levi said, glancing at the speaker phone in the center of the table. "We're out and that's that, right General?"

Attorney General Flip Griff-Raff's voice crackled over the teleconference line from his Bastrop Federal Correctional Institution cell. The facility, 30 miles away, had received many four-star ratings including this review from prisoner Jock Stack: *Not bad. Do your time and shut up.* Griff-Raff had followed that advice for the past seven years, hoping for an early release from the Texas Pardons and Paroles Board. Why parole had proved so elusive was a mystery to the A.G. Surely the board understood that he'd more than paid his debt to society and had always been a loyal servant of Texas as the champion against countless federal encroachments on state's rights; he was famous, a meme. Didn't they know the bogus charges were conjured by the evil feds? And, in any case, what's a little securities fraud among friends?

"I'm sure there's a work-around on this," answered Griff-Raff.

"A work-around? Levi asked. "We are the Republic of Texas, a new nation. What's there to work around?" She'd not intended to deploy her slightly-annoyed-but-principled voice this early in the meeting and reminded herself that she should afford Griff-Raff whatever deference she could muster.

"My team's working 24-7 on uh, moving forward, but–"

"But what?!" challenged Chief Levi.

"Well, it's just that, uh...we're not Texans anymore." Griff-Raff said. Everyone stared at the phone. "And we'll be 'Texas' again"

Church 1:2.2   April 22, 2027 Y.O.S.P.L.

THE CHURCH OF THE P-FREE SABBATH main boardroom was paneled ceiling to floor with donated hand-hewn Carpathian Elm burl. During the construction of the room, the P-Free Sabbath Singers' guitar player and former state employee, Mister Johnny Filbert, humbly requested and received a scrap of the priceless wood paneling with which to embellish the headstock of his instrument.

The master luthier who artfully incorporated the thin slice of wood into the instrument's milieu offered to do the work in exchange for a performance by the famous Mister Filbert at his daughter's twelfth birthday party. After the much-publicized birthday concert, the luthier's business soared, the Carpathian Elm-ed headstock increased the value of Johnny's guitar by 600 percent, and all the pricey leftover scraps of paneling were placed on the CPFS web-store for a suggested donation $500 per scrap. Except for the thousands of elm trees that would now be harvested to make cool guitars, everybody was a winner.

"Sisters, bothers! Good morning! I trust everyone is Word-well," Brother Pastor Yates said, striding into the room. "Sister Chief-Chief, please proceed."

"Thank you, Brother Pastor," smiled Sister Chief-Chief TomBigBee, so-named because she was the CPFS Chief of Staff and Chief of the Tribu de Tejas del Alabamian. "In your Big Chief tablets, you'll find today's agenda. As you're locating that, I can confirm that all Executive Board members have approved the minutes of our last meeting, September 13, 2025, except for Brother Janitor's editing of a sentence that dangled a participle, and a recommendation from the Brother that future meeting notes employ an 'active voice.' "

"Thank you, Brother Janitor for that," said Yates. "Your recommendation is being considered by this body, ever mindful that there is a time and place for everything, including the use of passive voice. Sister Chief-Chief, please continue."

"Thank you, Brother Pastor. Do I hear a motion to approve said notes as originally written?" she asked the group.

"So moved," answered Yates.

"Second," said Brother Janitor.

"Very good," said Sister Chief-Chief. The next item is the upcoming Ministers in Chains celebration." The Chief-Chief paused and looked at Yates. "They are such an inspiration, Brother Pastor. I hope we can show their families how much their sacrifice truly means to our community. These ministers are P-Free Sabbath saints, Pastor, for sharing the gospel with prisoners serving hard time."

"Well put, Sister. These individuals heard the Gift of You message and took it to heart in a very special way," Pastor smiled. I understand a few of them had a pretty good time getting into jail to spread the word of Word."

"Oh yes!" Sister Chief-Chief said excitedly. "Brother Donnie stole a 1964 Mustang, mint condition, from the Westlake Hills junk yard and took the joyride of his life in west Texas! He made sure he gave the cops in Pecos a high-speed chase to make sure he got five to seven; he almost killed the mayor, I hear," Sister giggled. "He's in the Lynaugh Unit in Fort Stockton. He's a good man, Pastor Brother."

"Excellent. I know his family is very proud. Do you need us to take any action today on the celebration or is everything in hand?"

"Everything is on schedule. I know you like surprises, so I won't tell you what all we have in store but you're going to love it," she said.

"No doubt," Pastor said. "So, the next item is a report from the Legacies Recruiting Team?"

"Yes, Pastor Brother, the team is in negotiations with the All-faith Flat-Earthers, as you know," said Sister Chief-Chief. "And the induction service for what will be known as the Legacy-Teletubbies is on schedule for next month!"

"Please share our thanks to the team for their work."

"Is the Monday Service survey done, yet?" asked Sister Elder Buffy, moving on to the next item.

"It is, Sister Elder B. Thank you for that question," Sister Chief-Chief responded. "This is the impact study on the recent move of the weekly worship services from Sunday to Monday, and there is some interesting preliminary data."

"Are," said Brother Janitor.

"Excuse me?"

"*Are. Are* some interesting preliminary data. Not *is*," he answered. " 'Data' is the plural of 'datum', therefore–"

"Time and place, Brother Janitor," Pastor jumped in. "Time and place."

"Yes," continued the sister. "There *is* some interesting results. Attendance by haircutters, bar tenders, stagehands and other weekend-workers has increased by nine percent, and millions of other members around the world who normally work Monday through Friday are now taking off all of Monday to attend services. As a result, forty-seven nations have implemented a 32-hour Tuesday through Friday workweek."

"That is incredible news, Sister," said Yates. "And by the way, thank you and Brother Public Relations on the excellent work messaging to the worldwide ecumenica that Monday is now the official CPFS Sabbath day. It will take time, but everyone will get accustomed to not P-ing on Mondays," he said with the requisite gravitas. "But, now we can P in the church on Sundays." Heads nodded around the table. "How's the other survey going Sister?"

"As you know Brother Pastor, this is a study to identify best practices associated with running a church whose name contains religiously-forbidden language or, in our case, the letter 'P.' Many of our members think it's a fundamental problem when we cannot say the full name of the church on our own Sabbath day. Of course, 'Church of the P-Free Sabbath' is a priceless brand," Sister Chief-Chief reminded the elders.

"And?" Pastor Brother asked, chin in hand.

"These results are preliminary, but members overwhelmingly embrace the church's name, body and soul. We also learned that the name has a net-positive impact on the recruitment of legacy and legacy-Alt faiths. And, when members are asked what their favorite letter is, 99 percent respond 'P'."

"That's my favorite letter," offered Brother Director Cardu.

"Favorite letter? Really? Who the hell has a favorite letter, for Word's sake?" asked Sister Finance and Acquisitions, looking around the table as everyone raised their hand. "Is it P?" she asked them with a smile. Pastor Yates' hand went down. "Ah, there's the one percent!" she said pointing to Yates.

Over the laughter, Pastor protested. "Apologies for my sweet wife, Sister F'nA, who obviously has no love of letters; she clearly did not get enough Sesame Street as a child."

Sister Chief-Chief loudly cleared her throat. "Final results on that survey will be available in two months. And, there is one more item, Pastor. There are thousands of questions in the *Ask Whatever the Frig You Wanna Ask* box about the secession, or whatever it was that happened yesterday. The people want to know where the church stands."

Yates leaned forward. "The ecumenica should already know what I think. Word knows, I've told them often enough."

He stood up and looked around the magnificent room. "This is the church of the people and *that* is the state. We care about souls, not borders or governments. We engage our blessed Word. Politicians engage their masters in Austin and Washington." Heads bobbled around the table.

"Brother P.R., please barf out a worldwide message to that effect ASAP."

Birth 1:3.2   December 16, 1984 A.D.

"ROUND AND ROUND YOU GO. Eenie-meenie-minie-mo. Show me where the red ball go!"

Somewhere around Venable Avenue and Barclay Street, Dr. Jake Phelt and Benjamin Yates decided they were lost.

"Over there," Jake said, pointing across the street to a wiry young black man, deftly maneuvering three Dixie cups in a dizzying pattern on a wobbly card table. Every few seconds a little red ball would appear from under one of the cups and then disappear under another.

"Show me ten, I'll give you twenty, find the ball, and you win plenty," the young man said to the empty sidewalk.

"I love these guys. You ever seen a shell game, Benny?" Jake nudged Benjamin Yates as they crossed the street.

"We do not have time for this, Jake." And then to the man, "Excuse me sir, can you tell us how to get to Baltimore Memorial Hospital?" There was no response. Yates looked at Jake and then down the street for someone else to ask.

"Take a hunch, win a bunch." The ball peeked out from under the first cup and returned there. And then, by a remarkable sleight-of-hand or pre-Swanson dinner planning by God, the ball appeared under the third cup.

Mr. Yates raised his voice slightly. "Hello, Mr. uh?

"Perdue, sir. Famularious K. Perdue."

"Excellent, Mr. Perdue, now–"

"Or you can just call me Famularious K."

"Thank you, I don't think we'll be here that long," continued Mr. Yates. "We need to get to the hospital. Can you help us please?"

"Show me ten, I'll give you twenty, find the ball, and you win plenty." The young man resumed his mantra as the ball appeared and disappeared.

"Show me ten, I'll give you twenty, find the ball, and you win plen–"

"Hey buddy," interrupted Jake, "can you answer my friend? We're in kind of a jam here."

Famularious K. looked up and gave the two men a toothy grin. "Take a hunch, win a bunch." As Jake and Mr. Yates looked at each other, he launched back into his cadence, the ball appearing from one cup and a disappearing into another. "Show me ten, I'll give you twenty."

"I certainly will not! It's gambling! Today is the Lord's day, for God's sake," protested Mr. Yates, "I'm not going to pay this man ten dollars for directions to the hospital. It's extortion!"

Jake couldn't help but appreciate the harmless hustle. "C'mon Benny, it's not extortion if you have a chance to double your money, right?"

"You do it then."

"I'm tapped out. It's only ten bucks. C'mon, it's getting late."

"Show me ten, I'll give you twenty." The man glided the three cups around the table like so many hockey pucks on a just-Zambonied rink.

Mr. Yates looked up and down the empty sidewalk, and then at his watch. "Alright, alright. Ten and that's it." He placed the bill on the table.

Without a beat, the man stopped, placed the lone red ball in the center of the table and lifted all three cups so they could see there was no funny business going on. Mr. Yates nodded. After placing one cup over the little red ball, Famularious K. began to move the cups on the table in a figure-eight pattern.

"Round and round you go, red ball you win."

Mr. Yates concentrated on the cups as they picked up speed, flawlessly guided by the man's nimble fingers. The effect was disorienting and the alcohol was doing him no favors. He squinted and realized, he thought, that the cups weren't moving at all; only the hustler's hands were.

"Eenie-meenie-minie-mo."

Yates took off his horned-rimmed glasses long enough to rub his eyes, replaced them securely on his face and looked again at the motion on the table. *Okay. Yes. Wait, the cups are moving now but, yes, there's the ball under that cup!* He kept his eyes glued to the one cup, noticing that it had a slight smudge on its side. The young man continued to braid the cups about the table, the red ball peeking out twice from under the smudged cup.

"Show me where the ball go." Everything had stopped and the man was talking. "Show me where the ball go," he smiled.

"There. Right there!"

"There?" Famularious K. asked pointing to the smudged middle cup?

"There, yes." Mr. Yates said with a little less confidence. "Jake?"

"Sure. There."

The man deftly enveloped the center cup with his hand and, with a slight forward-backward movement, lifted it. No red ball. "I thought the ball was there myself," Famularious K. said, perplexed.

"That can't be. I watched that ball the whole way. Where is it then? Show me where it is!" Mr. Yates was livid.

"I'll tell you where the hospital is, because you paid for that; but you didn't pay to see where the ball is."

"What?!"

"Sorry, sir. You only paid to see where the ball ain't." The man scooped up the ten-dollar bill and put it in his shirt pocket. "Now, go two blocks down that way and take a–"

"Where's the ball!?" yelled Yates.

Famularious K. stopped, glanced down at the two remaining cups and smiled at Mr. Yates. "It's under there somewhere."

"Show me!"

"Yes sir, by all means. In fact, I will show you right now where the ball is, *and* give you back your ten dollars *plus* my twenty dollars."

"What? You make me sick! Why would you want to give me–?" Mr. Yates sputtered, "I do not accept charity from–"

"Of course not, nor would I offer it, sir," said the young man who now had an accent that sounded a lot more like the Beatles than Baltimore con man hustling ten-spots on a shell game. "May I suggest you wager another ten dollars against my thirty? The ball's either here or there. I believe you have a 50-50 chance of winning!"

Mr. Yates looked at Jake and took as encouragement his broad smile. He slapped another ten on the table and pointed at one of the cups. "You think you're pretty smart, don't you buster?"

"Excellent choice, I must say," the hustler said, tilting the cup to show that the ball was not there. Yates made a sudden move to grab the last cup. His hand arrived at the red ball under the third cup just as the hustler lifted it off the table. Yates snatched up the ball and threw it at Famularious K. who, by now, had the second ten-dollar bill in his pocket.

"Go down two blocks and take a left on 33rd. Cheerio!"

Secession Interruptus 1:1.3   April 22, 2027 A.D.

"WHAT DO YOU MEAN WE CAN'T BE TEXAS?" the governor asked. He pronounced "Texas" like only a Texas politician can: hard T, with a "GSH"-sounding X, and a mouthful of "ZS" at the end. TEGSHAZS.

"Rule 134, sir," A.G. Griff-Raff said through the speakerphone. "Last night, Puerto Rico submitted its application to the United Nations to become a new nation-state member."

"What's that got to do with us?" asked Chief of Staff Levi.

"Rule 137. The U.N. Security Council approved the Puerto Rican application right before the feds issued the Texas-expulsion proclamation." Silence. "And, uh..." More silence. "And –."

"And?! And what, for God's sake?!" Levi yelled, expressing the frustration of the other cabinet members.

"Alriiight then," Governor Phelt lingered quite naturally on the long i. "Please. Let's all focus on the task at hand. This is very difficult for all of us." He took a deep breath and paused, looking at the empty chair present at every cabinet meeting, awaiting the return of A.G. Griff-Raff. "Flip," he said to the phone, "can you please tell us what the hell you're talking about?"

"Puerto Rico *is* Texas now, sir. They applied for membership in the U.N. as "Texas" and, per Rule 137, the U.N. Security Council has recommended to the General Assembly that Puerto Rico be admitted to the United Nations as 'Texas.' It's a dang-done deal, sir. Nothin' to be done about it."

"How can that be?" asked Health and Human Services Enterprize Commissioner O'Nathan Obel, who always tried to say something, anything, at each cabinet meeting. "We're Texas!"

"We were Texas, the state," explained Griff-Raff. "But with our expulsion from the United States, we're no longer Texas the state, and we can't be Texas the nation because–

"Because there can't be two nations with the same name," said Secretary of State Johnson.

"Right. Rule 134," crackled the phone.

"Will you stop with the rules, already?!" erupted Chief Levi.

"Governor?" asked Griff-Raff tentatively.

"Yes?"

"You think I'll be able to get out of jail soon?"

"Jesus, Mary and Joseph, will you please?!" spat Levi.

"I'll look into that, sir, but it'll take some time," offered Famulus B. Redux, Director of Prisons, Pharmaceuticals and Economic Development. His was the longest nameplate.

"Sit tiiight, Flip. Director Redux will have a look. Don't you worry 'bout it," Governor Phelt said to the empty chair.

"I believe the U.N. General Assembly still needs to vote on the Puerto Rico issue. It's no "done deal" sir," interjected the Secretary of State, always on point.

"Alriiight. Secretary Johnson will pursue U.N. options, back channel–nothin' public, understood?" Heads nodded around the table as the governor spoke. "General Jane, you and Lil' J., lock down the borders. Secretary Real, I need a report on the markets on my desk by 4 p.m. Anybody got any questions?"

"Yes sir," said Griff-Raff. "I was wondering if–"

"I'm sorry, Flip. You're breaking up," said the governor, as he terminated the call.

Church l:2.3　　2027th Y.O.S.P.L.

WHAT FOLLOWS IS THE collegiate-level version of the sermon delivered by Dr. The Harrises, professor of Pagan-Christian Theology and filial son of Legacy Symbionese Army. Although the letter P is included in the following, it was not spoken during the sermon's delivery.

The text of this sermon is included as an appendix in the latest edition of the *Church of the P-Free Sabbath Better Book*, available in 36 languages and multiple grade-levels wherever finer books are sold. It also appears in Dr. The Harrises most recent work, *Scatology and Eschatology: Digging Deep into the Excrement of Revelation*.

As historical context, Dr. The Harrises sermon was preceded by a delightful presentation by Alt-Rabbi and jazz historian Bleel Numofe on Charlie Parker IV's magnum opus, *Will This Be*

My Last Pair of Shoes? penned on the eve of the most recent presidential assassination.

The Sermon of Dr. The Harrises:

This 'n thus and so.
And so, the So was thus below,
Among, among the So. O tempora, o mores!
Oh, Word know!

Friends, my dear friends. Relax your bodies and calm your thoughts. Close your eyes. Let your arms rest at your side.

Find your neighbor's hand and welcome it into yours as you consider how—not why—King Saul called the dearest of his progeny a "son of a bitch" right before he hurled a spear at him. Those of you who are able, read along with me in *CPFS Better Book*, First Chapter Sammy 20:30.

"Then Saul's anger was stoked up against John Boy, and he said right up into his face, 'Thou son of perverse rebellious woman, do not I know that thou hast chosen unto thine own confusion, thy mother's nakedness?' Think on these words.

Now, I ask you. Is it crystal clear to you from this passage that Saul is calling John Boy a son of a bitch? He does not say it is so many words. Would you have even known to consider the question had I not posed it? I think not!! Can I get a "Hell, naw!" brothers and sisters? Others? Hell, naw!

But it is right there in the *Better Book* for you to read if you are a believer! Why would Word put something in the *Better Book* that cannot be understood by true believers without a religious scholar, such as myself, explaining what it means? Is that meet? "Hell, naw!" Is that right? "Hell, naw!"

But that is Word. Our Word, our One in After.

Each of you holds in your hands the *Better Book*, the sacred text of our Church. Our book is the direct word of Word. You know this.

You know that our Book is not a meaningless tome of tales, long-ago cobbled together in ancient Greek and Hebrew by Alzheimer patients malnourished by a first century, private-pay healthcare system. Ours is not the word of their god, so egregiously pillaged of its precious-little truth by kings and popes. All of you who can see the word of Word in your *Better Books* know this; you know that Word's word comes directly to you.

But if that is true, you must ask, "how is it that I cannot know if King Saul called John Boy a son of a bitch when Word has told me so in our Book? Why can I not understand my Word?"

The answer, of course, is Faith Alone! You know this! Faith! Say it with me. Faith! Shout it out. Faith Alone!

Right now, I want everyone in this glorious sanctuary and at home to place your *Better Book* on your lap and let it fall open to any page.

For those of you with faith abundant in our loving Word, what do you see on that page? You see words–the words of Word, do you not? Yes!

Faith Alone is a gift from Word, and not until it has been tenderly nurtured and allowed to grow and become part of you, will it give you the ability to see the word of Word.

And that is why, for many of you, the *Better Book* is entirely blank. For you, there are no words on the page. But that is as it should be, brothers, sisters, others! Praise Word! This is how Word intended it to be. Faith is earned, and only with faith will the blank pages in your *Better Book* be filled with the words of Word.

It is only through faith that you will understand how Word, in its wisdom, did so compel King Saul to call John Boy a son of a bitch. For those of you staring at blank pages right now, you must have faith that I am telling you the truth. Our truth! Our faith!

And that is Word's message to us today.

Now, I want everyone to look under your seat, because you're all driving home a brand-new Tesla!"

Capstone Dim 1:4.1 April 22, 2027 Y.O.S.P.L.

ID1: Are you certain we're secure?

ID2: Yes, absolutely sure. The text you just sent was routed through the Venereal extreme-vetting facility via 300 subterranean loofahs.

ID1: Sponges?

ID2: Sponges.

ID1: Where's ID3?

ID3: Here.

ID1: Excellent work on rules 134 and 137.

ID3: No problem. Get this—right now, 179 semis are parked outside the governor's mansion, full of beard nets. Fish in a barrel, these people.

ID1: Cyrana Johnson's no fish. Don't be overconfident. We talked about this, I–

ID3: Do you need a second cup of coffee? Valium maybe?

ID1: What about the Morealiens, Two?

ID2: The instructions and payments have been delivered. They're enjoying their mojitos in Michoacán until show time.

ID1: Back-ups?

ID3: Two redundancies on everything for this operation, just like all the others.

ID1: Good.

ID3: Confidence inspiring, eh?

Birth 1:3.3 December 16, 1984 A.D.

"Y'KNOW, CHICK WEBB WORKED here as a kid. And Al Capone got his syphilis treated right in this hospital. Bet you didn't know that, Benny." Jake opened the door for Benjamin Yates.

"Oh yeah, you'd love for me to make a bet on that too, no doubt. Famularious K.–what kind of name is that, anyway?" Yates snarled, still fuming from losing that last ten dollars. They walked through the lobby toward the elevator, "and it was a *right* on 33rd, not a left!"

"Benny, there was no way to win that game. That guy put the ball wherever he wanted it to be, *after* you pointed at a cup. You never had a chance, and that's the truth."

Mr. Yates stopped mid-lobby and faced Jake. "What's the truth have to do with it–and why were you smiling and encouraging me to bet again?"

"It's entertainment, Ben. You make the bet and the guy dazzles you with a cup and ball show. It's that simple." Jake faced Yates and put a hand on each shoulder. "I'm sorry, okay? I shouldn't have done that, but he was so damned good."

Mr. Yates shoulders relaxed a little. "He was, wasn't he?" He took a deep breath as the elevator door opened.

"Benny boy, I'm going find a couple of Mr. Castro's finest, just for you and me to enjoy when all this is over. And then, when the kids are old enough, we'll all to go to Indianapolis and watch the Colts actually win a playoff game!"

At the maternity ward, they were stopped by a stern middle-aged nurse wearing a starched-white, below-the-knee dress with a plain pinafore, presumably to protect her garment from the bloody business of birth. Her heavy black shoes were reminiscent of Marschstiefel jackboots, and put to rest any questions they might have about who was in charge.

"Names?" she asked them not looking up from her clipboard.

"Dr. Phelt and this is Benny Yates," said Jake.

"Benjamin," corrected Mr. Yates.

"Doctor?" The nursed asked.

"Yes, I'm an optometrist, I–"

"Oh." the nurse said dismissively, returning to the clipboard. "Have you already been here?"

"What? No, our wives are giving birth any minute and we–"

"Your wives gave birth two hours ago," she stated with the dispassion of a judge announcing her twentieth guilty verdict of the day. "Go in there. I'll send in your nurse." She turned away from them as the elevator door opened and another father-in-waiting emerged. "Name?" she barked.

"My sweet lord," said Benjamin Yates as they entered the waiting room. "This is my first child. How could I have done this? What's my wife going to think? Oh my god, I've never done anything like–"

"Benny, Benny. Relax. Everything's gonna be fine. We just need to–"

"Mr. Yates?" asked a young nurse behind them. "I'm Nurse Binky."

"Yes, yes. How my wife? Is everything alright?"

"Oh, yes sir, she and your son are doing fine," she beamed. Turns out this was the first baby for both Benjamin Yates and Nurse Binky.

"A son? A son! Oh my god. Thank God."

"Congrats, Benny. Look at you, man. I didn't think you had it in you," Jake said smiling.

"And you are?" asked the nurse.

"Dr. Jake Phelt, my wife is–"

"Oh, yes, she and Mrs. Yates are in the same room." Baby-boy Phelt had been Nurse Binky's second birth. Things were working out pretty good on her first day as a maternity nurse. "You have a son, too!"

"That's righteous, honey. You hear that Benny, we got two boys! Can we see 'em now?

"Oh no. Your sons are resting and uh, your wives are sleeping now," Nurse Binky said, with a little less first-day eagerness.

"Okay," Jake said, "but everything's copasetic, right?"

"Yes. Absolutely. Everybody is fine," she insisted. "It's just that, um–"

"What?" Yates said more loudly than he had intended.

"Well, it's just that they both gave birth over two hours ago. They were asking for you and uhhh–" The "uhhh" hung in the air like a very loud passing of gas at a Quaker meeting.

"Yes?!" the men asked in unison.

Nurse Binky glanced around the room and took a half-step toward them. "Well, it's just that they were upset, very upset, that you weren't here–apparently," she said in a whisper. "And then Mrs. Yates started to worry that something must have happened to you, Mr. Yates. And then Mrs. Phelt said that Mr. Phelt…"

"Doctor Phelt."

"Yes, Dr. Phelt. Mrs. Phelt mentioned that you might have been detained in a saloon." Nurse Binky used her best air quotes around *saloon*. "But then Mrs. Yates said that her husband would never go into a place like that, especially when his precious first-child was being born. Mrs. Phelt then suggested that Mrs. Yates wait until her second or third kid's ready to pop out (more air quotes), and see if she still thinks that. Mrs. Yates started to cry a little, and then a lot. She could barely control herself because–"

Benjamin Yates heard the roar of a Boeing 720 ascending from the new Dulles International Airport on its way to somewhere exotic and carefree. A gorgeous Braniff Airlines stewardess was offering cocktails, hors d'oeuvres and plump little pillows to first-class passengers. Benjamin relaxed into the leather seat and let the vibration of the plane massage his body as Roberta Vasquez, Playboy's November 1984 centerfold, with whom he had spent some time during month nine of the pregnancy, served him a Manhattan, up.

"Would you care for anything else, Mr. Yates?" Miss Vasquez asked, lingering.

"Call me Benny. Please." he insisted to her inviting cleavage.

"Of course, Benny," her ample bosom responded. "Benny."

"Benny! Benny??" Jake's voice, then the nurse's. "Mr. Yates. Are you all right?"

Yates, startled, reached for a chair to steady himself. He sat down and planted his face into his palms. "We have to do something," he mumbled through the flesh.

"What?" asked Jake.

"What are we gonna do? We have to do something, but there's nothing to do!"

"Of course we can do something," insisted Jake. "We just gotta think. We just, we just have to...let's see. How about, maybe...if... we." His words slowed as he silently evaluated a cascade of possible schemes.

"Okay, I got it. We tell them that we met a couple hours ago when we both went to help an old lady who was hit by a bus. We told each other that our wives were having babies, and then –"

"What? Are you in third grade?" snapped Yates, "that's the stupidest story I–"

"Alright, alright, how about this," interrupted Jake. "We were here all along. Whatever hospital-idiot told our wives that we *weren't* here, was wrong! It was all an unfortunate misunderstanding."

"And how the hell do we convince them that we were here all along?" asked Yates, surprised at his very natural use of the H-word, which he hadn't once uttered since he'd banged the hell out of his thumb with a hammer eight years ago.

"I don't know exactly. Let me see," Jake paused. "Okay, we can pull this off, definitely. But we might need a little bit of help." Jake glanced at Nurse Binky.

"Oh no, I can't. Please don't ask me to..." she looked at them with pleading eyes.

"Of course, of course," Jake assured her, glancing at her nametag and noticing the chain around her neck with tiny gold cross.

"I couldn't lie," she insisted.

"Absolutely, of course," he said, "lying is never a good thing. We feel so badly about disappointing our wives and we want to spare them any more pain, you understand." Jake wasn't sure exactly where he was going with this but knew they needed this nurse on their side.

"Yes, I know, especially Mrs. Yates. She's so concerned about Mr. Yates."

Benjamin Yates felt sorry for the young woman; he knew that before all this was over, Jake Phelt would convince her to go into the mothers' room and lie right to their faces. Not just a forgivable little white lie, but a full-blown rewriting of history that no self-respecting god worth their salt could sanction. He'd known Jake just a few hours, but that was plenty of time to know Nurse Binky was no match for him. But, as unsavory as this was to Yates, he needed the nurse just as much as Jake did.

"We understand," said Yates. "I'm no Bible scholar, but I do know my eighth commandment and it's pretty clear about not lying. Well, except for when Rahab lies to protect the Israelite spies–Joshua 2:5 or something like that. And of course, when the Hebrew midwives lied to Pharaoh to save all those precious baby boys, in the name of God."

"Yes, I knew about the midwives but not the other," the nurse said tentatively.

"Right," said Yates, "but y'know, that's just Old Testament stuff."

"Well, we might not follow all the ancient laws but there are lessons to be learned from the Old Testament don't you think?" asked the nurse.

"I guess," said Yates, "the trick of course is to know how to incorporate those lessons into your everyday life." Jake looked on with amazement, as Yates' truth about lying appeared and disappeared like a little red ball in a three-cup hustle.

"You're right," she said, "my priest tells me sometimes, and even a nun once, that–" She stopped talking.

"That what?" asked Yates.

"We'll, just that sometimes I go overboard a little and maybe take things too serious and everything," she explained shyly.

"Oh," he said. The awkward silence that followed was way to long for Jake who was just about ready to blurt out something that would not help close the deal with Nurse Binky.

"I'll do it." she said. They all looked at each other, not knowing that they had changed the course of human history. Across the waiting room, another father also changed the course of human history when he decided to sit down on a brown chair instead of the cream-colored couch.

"Okay," Jake said. "We need to make this convincing."

Secession Interruptus 1:1.4   April 23, 2027 A.D.

"TEXAS" WAS NO MORE. Provisionally admitted as an alien diplomat with no portfolio, Secretary of State Cyrana Johnson spent three around-the-clock days at the United Nations, negotiating to no avail. Griff-Raff was right, it was already a dang-done deal. The General Assembly bestowed upon the former Commonwealth of Puerto Rico, the honor of becoming the 201st member of the United Nations as the "Republic of Texas."

The piece of land that was once Texas, would still be bounded by the Red River to the north and the Rio Grande to the south. The Gulf of México would lap against its shores, fed by the freshwater inflows from the Sabine River. The land would look the same and it would still be over 850 miles from Orange to El Paso; but mentions of the Texas Rangers, Texas two-step and Texas twang would forever require footnotes, and former-Texans would listen differently to David Rodriquez singing so sweetly about his native Texas borderlands. Texas had survived under six nation-flags since the 1500s. Now it must survive under a different name.

It was five a.m.; Governor Phelt sat in Texas Speaker Hamza El Din's capitol apartment, coffee-less, down the hall from the governor's ceremonial office. He'd slept there at the urging of his security team, for the past two days. Had he known the speaker was exclusively a tea drinker, he would never have agreed.

Travelling with Fish and Haircuts Commissioner Huck Luckadoo, the speaker was attending an economic development conference in México to leverage the recent growth of Texas hair and nail salons that also sold double-tusked narwhals. Turns out there's nothing quite like getting a mani-pedi and shape-up surrounded crystal-blue, floor-to-ceiling water tanks filled with frolicking narwhals, all for sale of course. Some customers purchased the giant fish for their home aquariums; others just waited until the narwhal tusks were chain-sawed and wrapped up to go. It was one of several non-traditional pairings of must-have products, touted as part of the richly diverse Texas economy.

Commissioner Luckadoo and the speaker had arrived in Michoacán ten days earlier, fully intending to return to Austin in time for the secession announcement; however, a last minute meet and greet with industrial kingpins, the Famuloso Brothers, delayed their return until all border crossings were closed. A biker from the local Morelian Banditos, who had hopes of establishing a chain of child daycare/firing range facilities throughout Texas, offered Speaker Hamza a clandestine ride across the border, but he demurred.

"No hay problema." responded the biker, handing Hamza a cocktail napkin as they sat in a high-end tequila/chocolate milk bar. "Hook 'em Horns, señor!"

Perturbed, Texas A&M alum Speaker Hamza, took the napkin. It read, "Welcome Mex-Texian brother." It was signed, "La Presidenta de México."

When he looked up from the napkin, the biker was gone. Hamza's phone played *Yellow Rose of Texas*. He grabbed at it, wondering how he would ever replace that ring tone. "This is Speaker Hamza El Din speaking. Yes–. Yes ma'am. Thank you, Señora Presidenta. I'm honored, I... Yes, I would be very pleased to meet with you, but I can't promise...yes, of course. Thank you. Yes, uh, I... Okay. Vaya con Dios, Señora. Mashi, ma'a salama. Yes ma'am. Toodle-oo!"

Birth 1:3.4   **December 16, 1984 A.D.**

Nurse Binky peeked into the new mothers' room.

"Have you heard from my husband?" Elvira Yates asked, loudly enough to rouse the snoring Mrs. Phelt.

"Yes ma'am, I have, and I'm afraid there has been a terrible misunderstanding."

"Is my husband here?" asked Mrs. Phelt.

"Yes, they're both here," explained Nurse Binky. "I'm afraid I misunderstood the nurse from the previous shift to say that neither of your husbands were here. Actually, they've been here all along. They're in with your sons right now!"

Mrs. Phelt spoke first. "You mean to say that—"

The nurse cut her off, worried she would get flustered answering whatever question Mrs. Phelt was about to ask. "Yes ma'am, both are waiting in the nursery for you. If you think you're up to it, I'll send in someone to help you get ready."

"This seems highly irregular," protested Mrs. Yates.

"Oh no, not at all," Nurse Binky lied through her teeth. "We've found it's best to unite the entire family in the nursery— in a setting where the baby feels most comfortable!" She waited 1.5 seconds for a response, smiled and quickly left the room.

Before speaking to the mothers, Nurse Binky had taken Mr. Yates and Dr. Phelt to the nursery receiving area, agreeing that meeting the moms there would avoid an immediate inquisition concerning their whereabouts for the last four hours. From there, each husband would be on his own.

"I'll go see your wives and be right back," she'd reassured them. A few minutes later, the bassinettes were rolled into the room by two nurses. Unceremoniously, one of them scooped out an infant wrapped up in one of those square white, blue and pink cotton baby blankets that would be used by hospitals for the next millennium.

"Yates?" she asked the two.

"Oh. Yes, here," he said extending forklift arms.

"Relax, Dad," the nurse said calmly. "This isn't a load of two-by-fours. Maybe you should just sit on the couch."

Benjamin Yates sat down eagerly. The nurse gently placed his son in one arm, the baby settling into the crook of Dad's elbow. "There you go, that looks good. Make sure his head doesn't fall off," she smiled.

"Nothing like it, eh?" asked Jake. Yates was so consumed with the joy of holding his brand new, beautiful son, he hadn't noticed that Jake was now holding his.

"They look exactly alike," Yates said.

"Well, yeah. They're babies. The all look the same, pretty much." Jake said. "And they all dress alike–that doesn't help matters much."

"I guess," smiled Yates. "I've never seen a brand new one,"

"Yeah, it's something," said Jake. "Say, we got the story straight, right? We met in the elevator on the way up. When we got off, some nurse said our wives were having the babies and it might be an hour or more. We went down for a soda–for just a little while. When we got back, Nurse Binky told us the great news, right? We asked to see the wives but they were sleeping, so we came up here to wait to see the boys. Got it?"

"I think so, but I'm not a very good liar."

"Jeez, not you too?" sighed Jake. "Look, the nurse did her part. She lied and now it's our turn. We'll do fine, just don't volunteer anything that might–"

"Oh my god, he's, he's–" Yates said, looking at the squirming little alien on his lap.

"What?"

"He threw up something," Yates said as the baby arched its back, trying to cry through the white mucus in its mouth. "What should I do?" He stood up with his son still cradled in his arm.

"Burp him!" ordered Jake, "put him on your shoulder and pat his back."

"What? What do you mean? I don't know how to do that," Yates exclaimed thrusting his son at Jake, "you do it!"

"Alright, alright," said Jake, "here, take mine!"

Miraculously, the fathers traded babies without dropping even one of them. Jake put baby-Yates high against his shoulder and patted the baby's back until he burped, depositing a mucous-y mess on his back.

"Oh, thank God. Thank you," said Yates.

"That's what I'm here for buddy. I am a doctor, after all," Jake smiled. "Here, let's see if we can do something about this mess." As he was about to place baby-Yates in the nearest bassinette, the door of the nursery opened.

"They're coming!" Nurse Binky whispered frantically as she took the baby from Jake. "Oh my, what happened to you, sweet boy? Let's clean you up for your mother." She turned to Yates and took his baby too.

"But, that one's–" Yates said with a worried expression.

"Everything's going to be fine. I'll take care of everything," said the nurse as she disappeared into the main nursery.

The two fathers looked through the glass as Nurse Binky placed the identical, wrinkled babies on a large changing table and drew the curtain behind her. The only thing that distinguished them from one another was the barf that she was now cleaning off baby-Yates, who she thought was baby-Phelt. Jake Phelt and Benjamin Yates felt like they were back on the street guessing which cup the ball was under.

"Benjamin?" Yates turned around to see his wife coming through the door in a wheel chair pushed by an orderly. To his surprise, he gasped as he was trying to say "hi!" but the gasp would have none of it. It seized the "hi" and slammed it against the back of his throat, cutting off all incoming air. No more "hi." No more gasp. He put his hand to his chest, trying to get a breath in, eyes wide. He looked back at Jake, then at Mrs. Yates.

He felt two hard slaps on his back and coughed violently, sucking in a resurrecting breath with all his might. He bent forward, catching his breath. He stuck one arm up in the air, the international sign for "I can breathe now. If you hit me on the back again, I'll kill you."

"Are you alright, Benjamin?" Mrs. Yates motioned to the orderly to push her to the couch across the room. "Here, sit down."

"Yes, of course, sweetheart," he said through shallow breaths. "But how are you, for goodness sake? Are you alright? You look so beautiful," he said with tears welling in his eyes. He already regretted lying to her. He wished more than anything that he was kneeling beside his wife's hospital bed right now, confessing to the whole fiasco. If he undertook his penance to his wife today, and it would be over. Forever.

"I'm so sorry, I –" Yates sputtered.

"Here they come!" Jake interrupted as Nurse Binky appeared with the two infants. At the same moment, Mrs. Phelt was rolled into the room. Jake took the baby offered to him by the nurse and walked toward his wife. "I am pleased to introduce you to Master Peter Phelt." Mrs. Phelt took her son from Jake, cradling him in her well-practiced Mom-arm that welcomed his older brother Phillip two years ago.

"If there is a third–and there's not going to be, by the way," she said with a hint of a smile, "you're in solitary confinement in the hospital nursery until that baby is signed, sealed and delivered."

Oblivious to the reunion of Jake and Phyllis Phelt, the Yates family embraced each other in that singular moment reserved for healthy, beautiful first babies and their grateful parents.

"Time to footprint!" said Nurse Binky.

Capstone Dim 1:4.2   April 23, 2027 Y.O.S.P.L.

ID1:   Who the hell's idea was it to meet here?

ID2:   The other didn't work. Not secure.

ID1:   So, extreme vetting didn't work on the sponges?

ID2: Right, they were tainted with nanites, or something like that.

ID1: Were we tagged?

ID2: No. We caught the breech in time.

ID1: Okay, so–talking through glory holes at Big Dick's Adult Video Mega-pleXXX is the solution you came up with?

ID3: It's one of the Gov's faves.

ID1: That's not even funny. He had that thing in Goshen decades ago, but–

ID3: Yeah, he had that thing in Goshen and now we're sitting in cum and Kleenex trying to–

ID1: Alright. Stop. What's the status on our spies?

ID2: Their covers are still intact.

ID1: We still on schedule?

ID3: There's a little hiccup with the financing.

ID2: That tsunami killed 22,000! For Word's sake, you call that a hiccup? It was devastating for the people.

ID1: Will that impact our plans, Three?

ID3: No, the tsunami won't. But I wasn't even talking about the tsunami.

ID1: What then?

ID3: Borneo won the World Cup last weekend. They're still partying.

Secession Interruptus 1:1.5   April 23, 2027 A.D.

"ONE TRILLION UP FRONT, nine percent of all future Mexican oil revenues, and first right-of-refusal on any maquiladora offers from U.S. corporations." Via a secure video link, Speaker Hamza El Din recited the list to the governor, eleven cabinet members and an empty chair.

"The Mexicans are offering that, for what? What are we expected to do?" asked Governor Phelt.

"Within 48 hours we submit our application to the U.N. to become a member-nation as the uh, 'Republic of North México' but–"

"Stop right there," interrupted Railroad Commissioner, Ozmana Zelotes. "First of all, Texas will never be "North" anything as long as I'm alive, and–México? Republic of North México? Don't expect me to vote for any part of this."

"This is not a vote, Z." said the governor. "Hamza, go on please."

"There will be a rider, we insisted on it, to the effect that there is no association between the United Mexican States and uh, the R-N-M, political or otherwise."

"Republic of North México–RNM. Terrific," grumbled Zelotes.

"And why exactly are they paying an arm and a leg for this?" crackled A.G. Griff-Raff.

"The name association alone is priceless for the Mexicans," explained Secretary of State Johnson. "The new map of the world will have México, New México and North México. Yes, 'North' and 'New' aren't part of México, but you give them the same color on a world map and it's a powerful image."

"The U.S. has to have their slimy hands in this," said Zelotes. "They want to stick our noses into the deep shit by forcing us to call ourselves fucking 'México.' And for what? One trillion? I'm not cramming this sharp stick up my ass for anything less than $2 trillion."

"That can probably be arranged," said the Speaker. "They're backed by deep pockets somewhere, the Borneans maybe. Or California? We can probably start the negotiations at ten trillion and settle on seven or eight."

"Jesus, the Mexicans, Borneans, California? Is there anybody *not* in on this?" asked Zelotes.

"I don't think my grandma knows about it," offered Security Director James (Lil' J) Primo, Jr. He was always good for some comic relief, though he rarely had total control over its content or timing. He used the nanosecond between his delivery and the reaction of others, to analyze what had just come out of his mouth, assess possible negative impacts, and develop strategies to minimize them–basic disaster mitigation stuff. God knows, a stress-relieving joke would do the room a lot of good right now and it did reference "grandma" which was always a safe bet. He figured he'd get 50 percent audible chuckles, 20 percent silent smiles and the rest inscrutable facial expressions.

Almost everyone in the room smiled or laughed. Governor Phelt even added, "Sorry, I had to tell mine." His quip got even more of a response; Lil J was always happy to play the governor's straight man.

"We have no money." Treasury Secretary Judy Real didn't bother to look up from her computer. The room was suddenly silent. "Bond-raters have us at 'default imminent with little prospect for recovery.' The Texas Torrential Downpour Fund has been drained in the past three days, and our cash-balance trends aren't even trends–they're vertical lines down to zero."

"What about the Texas Diverted Funds Fund?" asked Governor Phelt with equal measures of anger and disbelief.

"Nothing, sir," Real said. "Zero. And that Pacific typhoon ruined us on the beard net futures deal."

"We have to respond to Mexico immediately, Governor," counseled Griff-Raff. "I recommend we accept the nine percent of all future Mexican oil revenues, and first right of refusal on any maquiladora offers–but no outright payment. It's gotta be a loan, otherwise we look like some third-world backwater taking a handout."

"That does make some sense," said Secretary Real. "We could structure it as a 0 percent loan, with payments of $1 per day in perpetuity."

"Agreed, but not for less than $7 trillion," said the Governor. "Flip, you draw up the loan. Mr. Speaker, can we get this done tonight?"

"Yes sir," said Hamza El Din.

"But, sir. Isn't this a bit hasty?" argued Zelotes. "Yes, we're cash poor right now, but we do have assets—natural resources, human capitol that can be offered as collateral for legitimate loans from our real friends. We have plenty of empty prisons and schools to fill up with whoever, and we still have five or six state parks left, right?" She looked toward Tomasina Thomas, Commissioner for Air, Field and Feast to solicit support, but got only a steeled face and this: "We have four parks left."

"Well, I know we have land to build a couple more nuc-u-lar waste dumps. Those get a big up-front payments and generate cash flow forever, am I right?" Zelotes persisted.

"Nu-CLEE-ar." Tomasina Thomas said with piercing diction.

"What?" shot back Zelotes.

"Watch my lips. It's not nuc-U-lar. It's nu-CLEE –."

In one fluid motion, Zelotes lunged at Thomas. "You bitch!" she yelled.

Before Lil' J could react, Zelotes was stretched across the conference table in a none-too ladylike fashion with her hands around Thomas' neck. In his practiced nanosecond assessment of the situation, Lil' J scanned the room to make sure no devices were documenting the historic bout; the last thing they needed was gone-viral "girl-fight" video like the one from last year's Oklahoma legislative session. He pried Zelotes' hands from Thomas' throat, a little disappointed that the fight hadn't even lasted as long as the Ronda Rousey-Holly Holm fight back in '15. Lil' J liked a good babe brawl, though he much preferred those with a little less clothing and a lot more mud.

His secret enjoyment of the ruckus was interrupted by General Jane Primo, Commander of the Texas National Guard, and Lil' J's mom. She could be a real buzzkill sometimes. She wasn't his boss—they were both Cabinet members—but she gave him orders sometimes, to which he would always stiffen and respond, "Yes, ma'am!" The governor liked that there were family members in his cabinet and often kidded Lil' J about the time he responded to one of his mother's directives with, "Yes, Mom!"

"People!" barked General Primo, standing. "Every one of us must direct his or her personal inner fighting force toward the success of our immediate mission. This is your moment–our moment. What we accomplish in the next 24 hours will change the course of TEGSHAZS history." Lil' J leaned against the wall behind Zelotes, hoping this wasn't going to be a long speech.

"You." General Primo pointed at Lil' J. "Sit the fuck down."

Capstone Dim 1:4.2   April 23, 2027 Y.O.S.P.L.

ID1: 'Republic of North México.' That's brilliant–your idea?
ID3: I thought you'd like it.
ID1: I do.
ID2: And it didn't cost us one peso.
ID1: Speaking of pesos, is the financing ironed out?
ID2: Just a little more time, but we got it covered.
ID1: Good.
ID3: What about our people on the inside?
ID1: What about them?
ID3: We need to get them out.
ID1: Not yet.
ID2: We think they might be compromised.
ID3: The extraction team's ready. I'm going to give the order, immedia–
ID1: NO! Forty-eight hours.
ID3: Twenty- four.
ID1: Thirty-six.
ID2: Are you two, done?!
ID1: Yes, thirty-six hours. That's final.
ID3: Thirty, or I give the order *now*.
ID1: Okay, thirty–fuck you, Three.
ID3: Now you're talkin' big boy.

Secession Interruptus 1:1.6   April 24, 2027 A.D.

"REALLY, A STRANGLEHOLD? JEEMANEESUS!?" Tomasina Thomas said entering her office.

"Pastor doesn't like it when you talk like that," Ozmana Zelotes said, smiling. She approached Tomasina and put a hand on each shoulder. "I kind of liked leaping at you across the table." Her hands gently guided Tomasina's arms behind her back, maneuvering her to the wall. "I wish that twerp Lil' J and his big mama hadn't broken it up." She kissed her neck, whispering, "That was a little hot, yeah?"

"A little," Tomasina smiled as she freed her arms, pulling Zelotes against her for a deep kiss. Zelotes cupped her ass, massaging her skirt up.

"But not that hot, Commissioner," she said breathing heavily, as she gave Zelotes a short kiss and walked to her desk.

"Really? Just a quickie?" Zelotes asked, mischievously. "I'll do you."

"Later, gorgeous," said Tomasina glancing at the wall of windows as she adjusted her clothes. "You played that well though, I must admit. When did you get your message from Capstone?"

"This morning, in my Alpha-Bits. You?"

"I got mine as I was walking into the meeting. A post-it note on the back on the person in front of me. It just read DIVERSION."

"Yeah, we had to keep them from making a quick decision on the Mexican offer. The money's not there yet, evidently," explained Zelotes.

"Are we talking about the Mexican money?"

"I don't know who's financing this–the Borneans, or the Swahilis, or a bunch of Rin Tin Tin-worshipping Alt-Aggies for all I know. The message just said to postpone the cabinet's decision because everything's not in place yet. That's why I was being such an ass about selling the state parks."

"You think?" smiled Tomasina.

"Yeah, and then you, with your "Nu-CLEE-ar," said Zelotes pretending to lunge at her again. "Ahh, that was beautiful. We're good together, baby."

"Pastor would have been proud. Cardu too. 'Be the moment, trust.' " Tomasina relaxed into her $6,000 high-back leather chair with the gold embossed seal of the former State of Texas. There was a soft knock at the door. They froze.

"Commissioners?" came a whisper through the door. And then another knock, a little louder.

Zelotes sprang to her feet, opened the door and grabbed the arm of Health and Human Services Enterprize Commissioner O'Nathan Obel, and pulled him into the room. He was pale and wide-eyed. He looked at them suspiciously. "Is everything, alright?"

"Relax, Ono. It was a diversion," said Tomasina. He looked at her incredulously, or maybe he didn't know what a diversion was.

"It wasn't real," an exasperated Zelotes explained. She was hoping she could fire things up with Tomasina again, but Ono's interruption had thrown cold water on that idea.

"I know what a diversion is," he complained. O'Nathan Obel had nothing against lesbians; in fact his last three girlfriends had become lesbians after dating him. But, whenever there were two or more of them in the same room, it seemed like they were keeping a bunch of secrets from him. He wondered if lesbians joined an underground cabal as soon as they realized they were gay, one with the means to telepathically share information they preferred not to tell the straight people, men especially. While he cared about these particular lesbians as members of the Church of the P-Free Sabbath and respected them as co-conspirators, he sometimes wondered which secret club they would choose if push came to shove. "Diversion from what?"

"From making a quick decision on the Mexican offer, Commissioner," Zelotes said. "We got messages."

"Oh yeah. I got one too," Ono said nonchalantly.

"So, what were you doing in there? Why didn't you create a diversion, or at least help with ours?" asked Tomasina.

"My note wasn't about that," he said. "At least I don't think it was; it was in Braille Esperanto. But it was important, I know that much."

"How do you know if it was important if you don't read–?"

"Because, scrawled at the top in English was 'Important Braille Esperanto Message!' I received two more since then," Ono said. "I found one under my pillow last night and another under a cheese Danish I got at the extension cafeteria this morning. It's amazing. They show up in the strangest places."

"You're right. Capstone Dim is amazing," Tomasina said, trying to take it all in.

"Who?" asked Ono, with the confused expression he had on his face most of the time.

"Capstone Dim," the women answered together. "Brother Pastor Yates and–and whoever else is in the group," Tomasina added.

"So, your notes are from Pastor?"

"They're from Capstone, and that's Pastor."

"How do you know for sure?" Ono asked. The three ping-ponged looks at each other.

"It has to be Pastor, right? Who else could it be?" Tomasina asked.

"How about that note you found in my panties last week? Zelotes said to Tomasina. "Didn't you say that was from Pastor? Or was that from–?"

"I don't know, I–"

"I think we have a mole," said Ono.

"What are you talking about? We're the moles!" Tomasina said, giving Zelotes a secret lesbian look, Ono was pretty sure.

"Look, CPFS spies are everywhere, you know that," Zelotes said. "So, now we know there's one of us making pastries in the capitol cafeteria and making Ono's bed–evidently."

"But what about your panties?" Ono asked Tomasina.

"Don't get my panties all up in a wad for yourself there, Commissioner," she said.

"No, seriously, how on earth did a note get into your underwear without you putting it there, Commissioner Zelotes?" he persisted. "And who's sending them?"

"For Words sake, Ono." Zelotes said. "The note was delivered there, what difference does it matter how? Where's your Faith Alone? Embrace your gifts without question, man. Word provides. Word abides."

"Communication from Pastor is a true gift and these messages are from Pastor–let's not be so paranoid," added Tomasina. "We've all been undercover for what, nine years? Our last word from anyone at the church was in '23. And now we get four communications in 24 hours!"

"The church is finally using us!" said Zelotes. "After suffering as state employees for almost a decade, this is it–it's our turn."

"Of course it is, yes." Ono reassured himself. "But what if my notes aren't from him? What if they're from some "four-legs-good, two-legs-bad" anti-secession, animal-rights faction?"

"Get a grip, Executive Commissioner!" Zelotes said sternly. "The church has project-planned our lives for the past fifteen years, sent us to the finest universities, and paid millions for our campaigns just to make sure we're all in Governor Phelt's cabinet at this pivotal point in history."

"We'll do what is required, just as we did in that meeting." Tomasina said. "All you need to do us keep cool, and get rid of Medicaid once and for all!"

"Alright, alright," he said. "I just that I don't know what's real and what's not anymore. You two were together before we all applied for our first state jobs and you're still together. But I've gotten married and had two kids since then–my family doesn't know anything about me and CPFS. We go to friggin' Tarrytown Baptist Church, for Word sake."

"Man, I had you pegged high Episcopal at least," Zelotes offered. "Maybe even–"

At that moment, a steel object the size of a softball crashed through the window, embedding itself into the far wall, inches away from Ono's head. The three commissioners stood motionless, stunned. O'Nathan Obel, loyal state employee and Executive Commissioner of the Health and Human Services Enterprize, noticed a small piece of paper taped to the shiny projectile. He peeled it off and read it aloud to his esteemed colleagues. "Faith Alone. Keep your shit together."

Secession Interruptus 1:1.7   April 25, 2027 A.D.

For El President Phelt and his fellow Mex-Texians, the establishment of their state had been much more difficult that it had been for the moon-based Tesla Land or the All-Faiths Caliphate of Borneo, both of which were humming along as off-the-grid, self-sufficient nation-states just days after their peaceful transitions to independence. The reason most often cited for their successes was planning. Planning is everything. Project management professionals who live to plan and plan to live will eagerly tell anyone willing to listen that no less than 93% of a project should be spent on planning; that was certainly the case with the Bornean Caliphate and Tesla Land.

Normally, a Texas State Board of Education-approved eighth-grade history book would not waste its valuable ink and paper on topics as distasteful as unions; however, a recent edition dedicated an entire chapter on a group of 19th century English textile workers who fought against new-fangled labor-economizing technologies that threatened to replace them. The leader of the movement was a direct descendent of Tesla Land's founder.

As the textbook explains, "In 1811, the founder's great-great-great-Grandpa Ludd encouraged workers to go on strike, but not because he abhorred technology or cared about the worker. He did so because he had surmised—through his study of linguistics, sociobiology and advanced toy theory—that the outcomes of their labor movement would ripple through the social fabric of western civilization for the next two centuries where it would create the perfect environment for the creation of Tesla Land." Now, that's planning.

Perhaps even more remarkable than the planning for Tesla Land was that of the All-Faiths Caliphate of Borneo. As is recounted in the Qur'an, the angel Gabriella appeared to 10-year-old Muhammad in 580 A.D. At the time, Little Mo, as his friends called him, was enjoying a French espresso in a Mecca bistro wondering why year designations were appended with "A.D."

"After Death—of Christ?" Mo puzzled. "What the —?" It was bugging the hell out of him, not only because he wasn't a Christian but because it just didn't make a whole lot of sense.

The previous week, Mo had learned from his elementary school textbook—approved by the Mecca Board of Education—that B.C. stands for "before Christ" and A.D. stands for "after death." How could the year 1 B.C. have been "before Christ" and A.D. 1 been "after death"? Did this Christ-guy live only for the blink of an eye?

But then Little Mo heard from one of his smarty-pants friends who knew Latin that A.D. stands for "anno domini," which means "in the year of our Lord."

He asked his history teacher about the Latin thing, and the ancient professor whispered to little Mo, "care ye not for calendars, Mohammed, yet rejoice that we won't have to switch to Islam as long as you don't do anything stupid. Remember what Philippians 2:10–11 says: 'That at the name of Jesus every knee should bow, in heaven and on earth and under the earth, and every tongue confess that Jesus Christ is Lord, to the glory of God the Father.' "

"Islam?! Filipinos?! What the hell are you talking about, old man?" Horrified, little Mo, an inveterate agnostic, stomped on the teacher's sandaled foot and never returned to the closeted-Christian's classroom again.

Understandably, when the angel Gabriella tapped Mo on the shoulder thirty years later to reveal the sacred tenets of Islam and Allah's scheme that Mo should be his prophet, he was hesitant. She said he would be the last in the line of the Biblical prophets recruited to call on all people to submit to God.

"Okay," he said. "I like the idea of being a prophet, but what do you mean by 'Biblical'? Does that mean I have to be a Christian?"

"No. You can be whatever you want," she fibbed.

"But am I required to write a gospel in the Bible?" pressed Mo. "Y'know, like a 'Gospel According to Mo'? I won't do that. No way. I'm gonna need my own book deal."

"That's fine," Gaby said. "But you'd have to get your own publisher, I mean we can't –."

"I'll self-publish, that's no problem. So, we're good, then?" Mo pressed.

"Look, we're still working out the details." Gaby felt the situation getting out of hand.

"Working out the details?"

"Yes. That's what I'm told," she answered tentatively. "I mean, that's what I heard."

"Haven't you people planned this out? Like who's who and what's what?" Muhammad asked, exasperated. "I mean are we gonna do the Pope thing? And what about the Jews? They're Biblical, right? Are they in on this, too?

"I would assume so," Gabriella said, uncertain. She thought his were excellent questions.

"Can we still eat pork fritters? Y'know, there's nothing about that in the Ten Commandments."

"I know. We're in discussions on that because–"

"This sounds like a Ponzi scheme to me!"

"What's a Ponzi scheme?" she asked, her curiosity peaked.

"I don't know, but this whole thing seems pretty shaky. I really don't understand what you want me to do?"

"Tell your people about God," she said with conviction, pleased that she could finally answer one of his questions directly.

"Okay. I can do that," he said. "But my god's not Jesus. Wait, is Jesus even a god?"

"No, but–" Gabriella said.

"And I don't like that A.D. thing either. I need you to know that," he said.

"Yeah, about that," she said. "A.D. doesn't stand for 'after death; it's 'anno domini,' which means 'in the year of our Lord.' You're going to have to learn a little Latin if this is going to work. And besides, in the future that will be changed to 'C.E.'– Common Era."

"Thank god," Mo answered, unconvinced.

The angel Gabriella smiled, paid Mo's tab and left the restaurant. He watched as she walked down the street, disappearing into the dusty suq in search of a good deal on frangipani essential oils. Had she sought advice from Mo, he would have referred her to his favorite brother in-law, Moishe, who would have done her a solid on his patented perfume oil called "French Panties Frangipani," well-known as a rejuvenating aphrodisiac.

By bedtime, The Prophet Muhammad had draft-chiseled into his stone tablet his goals, objectives and strategies for next five millennia, among them, "establish an All-Faiths Bornean Caliphate in the year 1426 M.T. (Mo's Time)."

El Presidente Phelt wondered where his plan to create a new nation had gone so wrong, as he looked across the north grounds of the capitol complex at what was just four days ago, the Texas Workforce Commission headquarters. Without any planning at all, that and hundreds of other ill-fated government buildings across La República del Norte de México would be moth-balled in the coming weeks, as the country's debt mounted and any hope of international assistance evaporated.

Secession Interruptus 1:1.8   May 15, 2027 A.D.

EXTRA! EXTRA!

Republic of North México Declares Bankruptcy as Elgin Airlift Begins

El Hombre de Estado de Austin y México

CIUDAD DE AUSTIN–Thousands of starving Austinites watched from behind barricades at the Elgin International Airport as the first Lockheed D-6 Universe cargo plane touched down with its 200-ton payload of natural alkaline artesian water, edamame and food truck replacement parts.

The airlift was initiated after the Republic of North México (RNM) blockaded parts of the south and east Austin that declared independence from the state formerly known as Texas. A spokesperson for the rebellious Austinites thanked the coalition of nations responsible for the airlift, led by the United States and the All-Faiths Caliphate of Borneo.

The daring flight, originating from Aberdeen Proving Ground in Maryland, entered hostile airspace as it crossed the Louisiana border in the dead of night, flying at dangerously low altitudes through narrow flight corridors of the RNM Piney Woods towns of Los Nacogdoches and Cuidad de Lufkin.

Austin declared its independence on April 28, 2027, one day after the Republic was admitted to the United Nations. The new nation, officially the "Republic of North México formerly known as Texas," closed its borders after an embarrassing secession-interruptus occurred when it was expelled from the United States moments before it could actually secede. That had never happened to Texas before.

After clashes erupted on April 29, all road and rail travel to and from the renegade areas of Austin were blockaded on April 30 by former-Texas governor, now-el Presidente Peter Phelt. For several hours, Austinites assumed the blockade was the government's latest attempt to solve downtown traffic congestion and applauded the bold initiative. However, within 48 hours, the affected areas of Austin were faced with growing shortages of food, clothing and craft beer.

As community leaders plead for reason and calm, RNM construction crews continue to build a 30-foot concrete-reinforced wall that will surround the most awesome parts of the 78704 and East Austin by June 1. As sections of the wall are completed, rebels paint murals promoting freedom and independence, and next week's family-friendly Sergei Eisenstein retrospective.

Pastor Brother Arlen Bob Yates, founder of the Church of the P-free Sabbath, told *El Hombre de Estado de Austin y México* that he expects the wall to eventually surround all CPFS facilities including the P-Free City of Light where thousands of church members reside.

"We will soon be cut off from the rest of the physical world. I call on the millions of P-Free Sabbath faithful to pray for your sisters, brothers and others who find themselves on the frontline of this immense conflagration."

In response to the Pastor's remarks, an RNM spokesperson declared, "The Republic of North México will build this wall around the rebels, and they will pay for it!"

Meanwhile, the Dow Jones Industrial Algorithm continued its precipitous climb that began on April 21 when Texas was expelled from the United States. Light, sweet crude oil for June delivery settled up $1.78, at $13.42 a barrel on the New York Mercantile Exchange, the highest settlement since November 2021. Sixty-day delivery on SWORB matzo grains is up 22.5% for the week and 600% for the year, continuing to outdistance historical earnings. Meanwhile, beard net futures on the Dubai Mercantile Exchange, a benchmark for nose-hair nets and all facial hair-control products from maritime southeastern Asia to Israel and Brooklyn, remain at $1.05/kg., down from $300/kg. this time last year.

The First Teller

Pre-Third Dynasty of Ur (Ur III)

During the last decade of the 20th century, the Bell tolled through the dark night, from coast to coast and around the world, with echoes of how the Tellers Tales were stichened together through the millennia to swath in truth and light, the moment of reckon. The first tale was told before the Big Bang banged, but there is no anniversary to mark its telling. It forever was, and always is.

Aadi Vatkr was the First Teller. He was very old when he finally told his story to his great niece, Dvau Vatkr. Aadi always knew that Dvau would become the Second Teller, just as the Annanuski alien knew that Aadi would be the First Teller.

"You will go to the head of the "endless path" in the caves of the Spīn Ghar now," the alien said to 12-year-old Aadi as he watched over his family's small herd of goats, all the time daydreaming about the first breasts he had ever seen. They were those of his cousin, who three days before had mistakenly left ajar the door of the room in which she was changing clothes. Aadi was suddenly engorged with a craving he had no idea how to satisfy; he stared at her for a precious second until she noticed him.

Surely this was something he should be ashamed of, but he wasn't. Nor was she; she smiled, covered her breasts but not really, and gently closed the door. Aadi discovered the joys masturbation that evening and practiced his technique several times throughout the night. What a glorious, sensual world this is, he thought, when he awoke the next morning, and wondered how on earth it had taken him so long to discover this magical feeling. And then he thought excitedly, *what else is out there that I don't know about?*

So, it was in this frame of mind, that Aadi Vatkr readily accepted the sudden appearance of the stranger with instructions to go to the Spīn Ghar caves. More magic, he thought. He looked at the alien standing before him and listened to its words, though they seemed to have arrived in his mind without bothering to enter through his ears.

"When you arrive, follow the first line of scroll-eating Baluchistan ants you see. They will lead you to a scroll. But you must hurry to arrive before–"

"They eat the entire scroll you wish me to retrieve?!" Aadi heard himself ask the alien.

"That's right," the Annanuski said.

"How do I get to the Spīn Ghar?"

"It's always best to start at the beginning. Which is right here," the alien said. "Alright then."

"Alright then?"

"I'm sorry," apologized the alien. "Doesn't your species say 'alright then' to signify that the conversation is ended?"

"Sure we do, but–the conversation is over? That's all you got?" There was a moment of silence as the alien, questioning its command of the colloquial, confirmed its understanding of the question.

"Yes, that is everything I have," Aadi heard in his head.

"But what happens if I–?" Aadi tried to ask this out loud for emphasis, but was only able to transmit his question telepathically.

"Just follow the scroll-eating Baluchistan ants," the Annanuski said. "Follow the scroll-eating Baluchistan ants. Alright then." Aadi's mind was silent. Countless years later, Dorothy of Kansas would receive an equally unsatisfying answer from her own alien, Glinda, the Good Witch of the South.

Three days later Aadi Vatkr arrived at the foothills of the Safēd Kōh Mountains, 50,000 goat-lengths west of the Khyber Pass. Scanning the snow-capped peaks for any sign of a path that would lead to the high, hidden caves, he felt the tiny footsteps of thousands of scroll-eating Baluchistan ants on his sandaled feet.

"God dammit!!" Aadi yelled (he had no idea what the words meant; he normally used the expletive, 'barnacles.') The ants did not speak to him—because this subspecies of scroll-eating Baluchistan ants didn't talk, but Aadi knew he must follow their column until he reached the scroll.

For days, he travelled as fast as he could, following the path set by the ants, up and down impossibly steep grades of naked limestone, through deep, narrow canyons and, inexplicably, twice around a large, red deodar cedar tree in the ants' path. Aadi rested infrequently; he must arrive at the scroll before it was devoured by the ant-guides showing him the way. When he wasn't thinking about his cousin's nipples, he wondered if the ants appreciated the irony of the situation, assuming it was, in fact, ironic; he thought it might be.

On the seventh day, the Baluchistan ants led Aadi to a non-descript opening in the side of the umpteenth mountain he had climbed. It was barely a goat-length tall and half that wide. As soon as he was fully in the cave, he looked back to its entrance, but it was gone. He extended his arms into the darkness and felt nothing. *This must be what it's like to be blind*, he thought; not like his gramaji who could still see shadows, but empty-socket blind.

He'd stood motionless, and then saw the thin incandescent red thread at his feet leading into the cave. He smiled at his iridescent ant guides and followed their track making sure not to step on them. "Follow the scroll-eating Baluchistan ants," the Annanuski's voice reminded him.

The stream of rose-colored light rounded a corner into an immense cavern lit by quadra-tetra-bazillions of the luminous ants covering every nook and cranny of the chamber, except for a small pedestal in the middle. Aadi shielded his eyes from the brilliance and then, as his vision adjusted, surveyed the spectacle. Atop the pedestal was what he thought must be the scroll. Earlier, he'd tried to tell the alien that he didn't know what a scroll was, but heard only the conversation-stopping "alright then."

Looking closely, he saw that the pedestal itself was made up of tiny pieces of scroll material. Were those the half-eaten scrolls of past tellers who had arrived too late? Was the one intact scroll on top the one he sought, or had *he* arrived too late as well? "In any case," he said, listening to himself, "how will I get to that scroll without being eaten by those damn ants?" They weren't biting him now, but they sure weren't going to let him take their feast without a fight.

"Faith," he heard the Annanuski say. *Great, another word I've never heard of*, thought Aadi. He stood on the perimeter of the cavern, separated from the scroll by 15 goat-lengths of ravenous Baluchistan ants.

"Faith." The alien's calm voice eased his apprehension and fear; he breathed in deeply and with the exhale, bent down and removed his sandals. "Faith." Aadi took a step forward and the red sea of ants parted, giving him a clear path to the scroll. He marveled at the sight and hurried to collect the prize from the pedestal; whatever this "faith" thing was, he didn't want to press his luck. He left the chamber and followed the line of ants out of the cave.

Adjusting to the afternoon sun, he squinted his way toward the shade of an overhanging cliff. Aadi knew no symbols or glyphs, but he knew the scroll would change his life; it already had. He excitedly loosened the binding around the scroll and then stopped. He wanted to see the scroll revealed all at once, in a flash.

Kneeling, he gathered four stones. With his eyes tightly shut, he rolled out the scroll flat on the ground feeling its length, about twelve hands. He blindly placed a stone on each corner. Aadi rose to his feet and stepped back so he could see the entire scroll when he opened his eyes.

"Unu, di," he counted aloud, "tri!" His eyes sprung open and Aadi Vaktr saw before him, the one thing in this magical world he never expected to see.

BOOK TWO

Ante medium rabidus.

Before the Crazy Middle

Politicians 2:1.1   **December 2025 A.D.**

WAS IT ONLY EIGHTEEN MONTHS ago that Mary Levi talked Representative Peter Phelt into going to that Council of Governments cocktail party right before Thanksgiving?

"You know I hate those after-hours COG functions," said Phelt, who had managed to survive the last Texas State Legislature as the first representative of the newly-created House District 151. "This thing is for serious candidates. Candidates with money...and people," he said hoping the conversation would stop there, but knowing it wouldn't. "I have no money and no people."

They sat in Dallas Love Field awaiting an early morning flight to Austin for the ribbon-cutting at Governor's Mansion to mark its most recent post-arson renovation. Mary engaged her pod with a flare of her nostrils. Her nose folded down from her face on an invisible hinge; tiny mechanical arms emerged, positioning a small screen, four inches in front of her eyes showing every flight departure for the day.

"And it's in Muleshoe, for god's sake. That's a six-hour drive," the representative pressed his case.

"From here, sure," she said calmly. "But we can exchange our tickets for the 9:32 to Lubbock, and drive to Muleshoe in an hour. We can stop at Le Café Crêpe & BBQ in Levelland for some of that high-plains haute cuisine," she smiled. "C'mon.

You shake a few hands at the COG event, drink a local something-or-other, and say a few words maybe. Y'know, test the waters."

"Waters? I don't even have waters."

"No one else does either, Peter. The party's been wandering in the wilderness for years and there's a pantywaist living in the governor's mansion."

"And?" Phelt asked.

"Look, the TP Party chair wants to talk to you," Levi said. "They're interested."

"Interested? Those crack pots? You know what 'TP' stands for, right?"

"Texas People's," she said. "What's wrong with that?"

"Nothing, except that the 'Texas People' were communists in the '60s."

"That was decades ago. It doesn't' mean–"

"They *were* the communists, Levi. Communists! You remember them, right?" he asked. "And then, I seem to recall that the TP Party became the Texas PETA Party in the '80s–"

"And the Toilet Paper Party in the early aughts, I know, I know," Levi said. "And that's the beauty of it–they adapt. They've come full circle. Yeah, the party was a little out there in the '60s and I know you're not a big PETA fan, but that's all behind them. They've cleaned up their act."

"Oh, really?" Phelt asked.

"They have, yes," Levi said emphatically. "That's what the Toilet Paper Party was all about. Cleaning house. Getting rid of the crap. Real *in your face*. Remember?!' "

"Barely, I was only nineteen when all that was going on. I was busy amending for my childhood evildoings," he said.

"I bet you were," she laughed.

"Wait. How do you know so much about the TPs?" he asked.

"I don't know, I–"

"You were in the Toilet Paper Party, weren't you?"

"Yes," she admitted.

"I bet you wrote that slogan of theirs, didn't you? What was it, something like–"

" 'We clean up the shit.' " Levi smiled. "But that was then." She paused for effect and delivered what she hoped would be the deal closer. "We're the Texas People's Party now, Peter. We want you to be the next governor of the State of Texas."

Parents 2:2.1   Years 1991-2 A.D.

"PLEASE ALLOW ME TO INTRODUCE myself," intoned the mellifluous voice on the other end of the line. "Agane. Pastor Famulonomous Agane, Esquire." Its articulation was that of southern Georgia, the hospital administrator surmised. Valdosta, or Okefenokee maybe. The name was a puzzler, though. If only the administrator had one of those picture-phones promised at the 1964 World's Fair, he could fill in the blanks.

Having been raised in Georgia himself, the CEO of Baltimore Memorial Hospital Corporation had a practiced ear for accents from south of the Mason-Dixon Line. He'd attended Emory University School of Medicine for one year but decided he didn't like people enough to be a doctor. Unlike many of his fellow students with a similar disdain for humans and their problems, he dropped out of medical school and became a nameless hospital administrator making twice the salary of most doctors, not to mention this pastor-lawyer on the other end of the line.

"My goodness, a minister *and* an attorney. That's what I call full service!" the administrator pandered.

"I'm calling you about a parishioner-client of mine, who was once in your employ and who is currently contemplating the filing of a preliminary assumpsit against the Baltimore Memorial Hospital Corporation, its subsidiary holdings–and you."

"A what?" asked the administrator. He didn't know what an "assumpsit" was, but he didn't like the sound of it. He pressed the record button on his phone.

"A lawsuit," Agane said.

"Yes, of course." said the administrator. "Tell me, is your parishioner-client also contemplating *not* filing a preliminary, uh, assumpsit?"

"Yes. This individual will not proceed with this course of action if, within the next 72 hours, BMHC notifies the parents of two infants born in your facility in 1984, that their babies are in fact not their own. Furthermore–"

"Oh my God. *Please* tell me this isn't about Binky."

"I'm not at liberty to divulge the name of the person I represent at this time."

"Look," the administrator said, "that woman has badgered me and this hospital since 1985 about those damn kids. If that's what all of this is about, you may want to reconsider your case." It felt good not to be on the defensive and the administrator wasn't going yield his advantage. "We were perfectly within our rights to terminate her employment with BMHC. She's lucky we didn't notify the authorities or file our own lawsuit after she broke in and–"

"But you didn't notify the authorities or file your own lawsuit, did you?" the lawyer reminded him.

"No," said the administrator. The line was silent for several seconds. "Look, Mr. Agane, the boys are happy and healthy, and their parents love them. Clearly, we both have the resources to battle this out in court, but neither Nurse Binky nor my hospital want to go down that road, surely."

"And what conclusion do you draw from that assumption?" asked Agane.

"There's nothing to draw. That *is* my conclusion," said the administrator. "We let those poor families be. It's the kindest thing to do for those boys."

"I imagine that would also be very kind to Baltimore Memorial Hospital Corporation. It would certainly help you avoid several other civil suits, a colossal loss of public trust *and* a criminal fraud investigation, I would think. But what do I know?" asked the lawyer.

"And what exactly does Monica Binky lose if we *do not* tell the families?" shot back the administrator. "What is so precious to her that she would jeopardize the free healthcare BMHC provides to thousands of indigent patients every year? Or the hundreds of jobs that would go away if the hospital was involved in protracted litigation? What on earth could possibly be more important than that?"

"God's truth, sir," answered Agane.

"Binky's truth, you mean!" shouted the administrator.

Pastor Famulonomous Agane, Esquire, responded with the calm resolve. "Sister Binky lied that day to the mothers of those children about their fathers being in the hospital when their sons were born; the fathers, in fact, were *not* in the hospital. That lie led directly to the confusion in the nursery, wherein the babies were given to the wrong parents. Monica Binky is compelled by all that is righteous, to shine the light of truth on her sinful transgression. That is God's truth and that is what will be lost."

The administrator knew that whatever happened in the next 72 hours could define his entire professional career. For seven years he'd successfully presided over this baby-switch cover-up, an accomplishment in which he'd taken much pride. He stared at the phone, recalling that Nurse Binky had taken her own sweet time to bring up the possibility that the boys had been switched. She thought she'd switched them, but it was almost a year until she mentioned it to anybody. By that time, the Yateses had moved to Indianapolis and the Phelts were in Alabama somewhere.

Binky had asked to look at the medical files to see if the parents' and babies' blood types could rule out a switch, but the administrator had done that months before. He knew that both Yateses were Type O and the baby they got was Type A. The baby they took home was not theirs and it was too late to tell the parents, if BMHC had a prayer of avoiding a deluge of devastating lawsuits.

When she broke into the records office and found the medical files she knew was right, but she couldn't photograph the evidence because she, like the administrator, didn't have one of those camera-phones promised at the 1964 World's Fair. The administrator didn't press charges and even offered her a raise and promotion if she would let the whole thing go. Fortunately, he didn't put the offer in writing because attempted bribery turns out to be a Class D felony in the State of Maryland. Even more fortunately for him, Nurse Binky quietly quit her job after that and went to live with a bunch of Branch Davidians in Fuck You, Texas for all he knew.

He realized the Pastor-Lawyer speaking. "Hello? Are you still there?"

"Yes. Yes I am."

"Judging from your response, I think that Sister Binky may have to proceed with a legal remedy," Lawyer Agane said.

"No, no, please. May I suggest we give ourselves 48 hours to arrive at a conclusion that is amenable to all parties?"

"Forty-eight hours would be acceptable," the lawyer responded.

"Good. Thank you." said the administrator, relieved. "I will confer with our people today and contact you at 10 a.m. tomorrow to discuss next steps. Does that sound agreeable?"

"Certainly, but I would prefer to call you if you don't mind."

"Excellent. I'll expect to hear from you then," the administrator responded. "Is there anything else you need, at the moment?"

"Yes," The Pastor-Lawyer said. "I didn't catch your name."

* * *

The 1992 national conference of the Professional Human Resources Association for People Who Need People was held in Atlanta, so a meeting in Georgia was agreed to by the parents. Mr. Yates always took his wife, Elvira, to the week-long event anyway, and the Phelt's home in Goshen, Alabama was only 200 miles. Pastor-Lawyer Agane arranged for them to meet at Soul Harvest Tabernacle, located on S.R. 23, not too far from Flippen, Georgia.

Exactly how to comport oneself at the first of what may be several post-baby-switch meetings was unknown to the parents. Had their sons simply died at birth and been resurrected seven years later, they would at least have had the Bible to provide guidance on how to proceed: go to the cemetery, unearth their sons and clean them up, and start a new religion.

But this was no raising of the dead, and there would be no religion-based guidance. This was the "abject disregard for the mother of your first child," as Mrs. Yates would put it to her husband more than once in the coming months. Mrs. Phelt's go-to phrase was "God dammit, Jake!" And while they both knew their husbands were ultimately responsible for the lie that resulted in the baby-switch, each held in her heart a deep contempt for Nurse Binky, who should never have agreed to say that the fathers were in the hospital when the boys were born.

Binky could have put an end to the lie the moment she was asked to participate in it. If she'd just said 'no,' the wives would have learned about their husbands going to the bar, all hell would have broken loose, and everybody would've gone home with the right baby.

Nurse Binky agreed—it was all her fault. It didn't matter that it was her first day on the job and she wanted to make everything perfect for her very first families. She recalled the moment when Dr. Phelt approached her and asked her to lie. He was a doctor and, after all, it was a simple white lie, a "harmless re-interpretation of the truth that would preserve the harmony of a blessed day," he'd said. But as soon as she lied, she felt sick.

Monica Binky had never lied before—well, except for the time she hurt the family cat while forcing it to hug her. She'd always wanted a real cat that would love her and purr whenever she picked it up—one that wouldn't run away when she wanted to pet it. But it had been her elder sister, Jessica, who got to decide which cat to take home from the pound. Monica hated the cat at first, because she knew Jessica chose the one that Monica didn't like. When they arrived home, Monica got her revenge when her parents said that she could name the cat. Knowing that it would drive her very logical, non-nonsense sister mad, she named it Mittens.

"Mittens?! You retardo, why would you call a solid white cat Mittens? You might as well call it Blacky!" Jessica yelled.

"Okay," Monica smiled at her. "Blacky, it is!" She scooped up Blacky the white cat and took him up to her room. Not ten minutes later, she ran back down the stairs crying, with three vertical scratches on her cheek and a red puncture wound on her earlobe. She made a bee-line toward her mother on the divan.

"Honey, what happened?" her mother asked. Monica was a little too big for her mother's lap, but managed to snuggle her bloody face into her mother's shoulder, weeping. "My goodness sweetie, what happen to your cheek?"

"The cat attacked me, Mama!"

"I'm not going to have a cat like that around the kids!" Mr. Binky said.

"Maybe you just scared it a little. Was that it, Mon? Was the kitty frightened?" her mother asked gently.

"She said it attacked her, for God's sake," her father said angrily. "Did it attack you or not?"

"I was just trying to—"

"Did you hurt that cat, Monica!" her father cross-examined her.

"Stop, it George, please," her mother urged her husband. He ignored her.

"Monica Binky, did you hurt the cat? Yes or no?" Monica was silent. "Fine. Where's the cat now? What's his name?"

"Blacky," Jessica answered dutifully. She turned to Monica. "I guess Blacky doesn't like his name so much, does he?"

Most historians believe that when seven-year-old Monica Binky screamed "bitch!" and scrambled from her mother's warm embrace to attack her sister, it was—not to sound too ominous—a harbinger of things to come for young Miss Binky. The reader has no doubt observed that, in a failed effort to secure the love Monica so dearly craved, she injured the object of her affection (the cat), whereupon she sought out the one whose love she truly desired (her mother) and then abandoned her mother as soon as the opportunity to physically assault her nemesis (her sister) presented itself.

As Monica pummeled her sister, Blacky Binky the white cat came down the stairs, crept along the wall into the kitchen, and left the house via the nice little cat door George Binky had installed in preparation for Blacky's arrival. Instead, it was used for his departure.

Monica Binky was the last to arrive at the parents' meeting. She loved old community churches, the sort where you just pulled off a two-lane country road into the red clay and parked wherever. This one was in bad shape, but still had a row of three unbroken stained-glass windows decorating the side of the building. She walked up the wooden steps and tentatively opened the oversized door. It was dark inside, except for the filtered, colored light. As her eyes adjusted, she took in the sanctuary that seemed much too large to fit into such a small building.

She hadn't noticed from the outside that this was a cruciform church, its cross-shaped architecture creating spaces for family pews in the north transept and an area for baptisms in the south transept. She smiled at the five-sided baptismal font, fondly recalling the radical Christian math cult she'd spent a few weeks with the previous year. For them, the pentagon was a symbol for a symbol, five representing three. The pentagon *is* the Trinity because five is the third primary number. Simple enough, it's just math.

The FBI thought otherwise and designated the math cult an "organization of interest," whereupon the group increased the use of five-sided objects, math-o-logical runes and ancient peace signs into their ceremonies to entertain their new, overanalyzing law enforcement friends who wondered, *did the pentagons really represent The Father, Son and The Holy Ghost, or was it straight-up devil worship? How about those weird peace signs and the Dead Man Rune that appears on the tombstones of Hitler's SS troops—were they another way to mock the cross of Jesus or a legitimate sacrament of the cult's true aspiration for peace?*

And then there were these: $A \otimes B$, $A^\dagger$, and the so-called "golden ratio constant." One FBI agent's smarty-pants kid told her dad that they were just algebraic symbols, but the G-Men weren't buying it.

By force of habit, Monica Binky touched the end of each pew as she walked toward the altar, evoking memories of her "My Church, My Everything" report that was a prerequisite to the rest of one's life, if one was a fourth-grader in Sisters of Charity School for Pretty Good Girls in Mt. Vernon, Maryland. Her report, and those of all who had attended the school since 1830, included no less than five pages on pews alone. As required, the pew section of Monica's "My Church, My Everything" report contained an affirmative statement that pews were seated *in*, not *on*; or is it the other way around? In any case, she received less than an exemplary grade for her work because she opined that, in general, pew kneelers should have thicker cushions.

Pastor-Lawyer Agane smiled as he rose from the large round poker table to greet Monica Binky and offer her one of the seven chairs around the table. As he did, he quickly introduced her to Dr. Phelt, Phyllis Phelt and Benjamin and Elvira Yates, as if they were so many accountants meeting to approve a monthly budget report. She didn't know if the parents and Agane had already met with each other, but she knew she was the odd one out; and frankly, she wasn't entirely sure why she was here, except for the fact that he'd invited her.

When he'd first approached her about telling the parents the truth about their babies, he was very kind. As she explained every detail of the birth day to him, he nodded gently and showed her an expression that made her feel like he'd actually been there, but of course he hadn't. He understood the burden of guilt she bore for lying and her need to tell the truth. Since the births, the one thing that propelled her from one healer or religiosity to the next was her quest for redemption. Agane said that telling the truth was her obligation, not only to the parents, but to herself. She agreed that he would contact the hospital administrator on her behalf, but they'd not seen each other since. He hadn't charged her anything for his services and in fact, sent her some money to make the trip to Flippen.

Lawyer Agane sat down and clasped his hands as if to pray. He scanned each face around the table, lingering to offer each one a reassuring nod. "Thank you all for coming today. I know this is not the most convenient location for you," he began. "I also want to thank you for agreeing to not to bring your personal attorneys to this meeting, and to simply hear me out."

"What is she doing here?" asked Elvira Yates.

"I invited Miss Binky to be with us today," explained Agane. "I thought it would be good for you all to meet and–"

"Well, you got your way. You got what you wanted," interrupted Mrs. Yates. "Your conscience is clear."

"What do you mean, I got my way?" answered Binky, incredulous.

"Why couldn't you just leave us alone?" shot back Mrs. Phelt.

"This wasn't *my* idea. He called–"

"Ladies, gentlemen, please," interjected Agane calmly. "The most important thing is that we are here to make right a very unfortunate set of circumstances." Everyone sat silently. "I know that each of you holds the wellbeing of Peter and Arlen to be of the utmost importance."

"Yeah, but I don't know about this scheme to break it to them slowly," said Jake Phelt. "Are you seriously suggesting that we all live in the same town, and the boys just play and go to school together without knowing? And then, what? We break the news to everybody at the next Fourth of July picnic, for God's sake?

"And what about Peter's–our Peter's–brother?" asked Mrs. Phelt. "He'll be devastated." She patted her eye with a tissue, taking a deep breath. "But, we should do this, shouldn't we? We have to do this, right?"

"Well, yes. I think we all agree that we need to get this out in the open," offered Agane. "But only after Peter and Arlen have known each other for a period of time, as is the recommended approach." He reached into his briefcase for six three-ring binders, giving them to the parents and Binky, who pushed the extra notebook in front of the extra chair. "I took the liberty of copying several research studies indicating that the revelation of life-altering information to children is likely to have more positive outcomes if presented over time."

"Revelation?" frowned Dr. Phelt.

"Yes, I'm sorry. Research jargon does tend to be a bit arcane. The studies simply demonstrate that giving young people time to adjust is a good thing."

Elvira Yates examined the Pastor-Lawyer. He was definitely a hired gun, his services available to the highest bidder; but, who was paying the bill? One thing she knew for sure–this Nurse Binky person couldn't afford him. Other than that, she had no idea what shenanigans were going on.

"It will also give you time to get to know your birth sons and, more importantly, for them to know you," said the lawyer.

"Let's be honest, we really don't have a choice to make here," said Mr. Yates, to the tentative nods of his wife and the Phelts.

"You're right," said Jake Phelt. "On the drive up, we all but decided to make the move to Indianapolis. Maybe live somewhere near the Yateses so the boys can go to the same school."

"That's the easy part, though. I don't want to lose my sweet boy, my Peter. But I–" said Mrs. Phelt haltingly, unable to finish.

"But you all must get to know your natural sons," Agane said. "This is the one way to do that."

"It will be hard," she said. The room was quiet.

Not for the first time in her life, Elvira Yates broke a silence, speaking to Monica Binky. "And I trust we will *never* see you again."

Binky smiled. "I'd sooner poke my eyes out."

Children 2:3.1   **School Years 1996-98, Indianapolis**
             Public Schools (IPS) Calendar

AUGUST 1, 1996

THEY MET THE SUMMER BEFORE middle school at the sand quarry off Keystone Avenue, in a thicket of bushes each boy thought was their own secret hideaway. Arlen squatted on the pebbly shore of the quarry lake, sinking his hands into the expanse of tiny colorful stones. Behind him was his hideout, its small entrance formed by long drooping elderberry shoots laden with fruit. The opening was just big enough for a kid; most grown-ups wouldn't even notice it, much less go inside.

"I'm in here!" threatened a small voice.

Arlen scrambled to his feet. He stared at the bushy entrance.

"I'm just telling you that I'm in here!" said the voice. "I didn't want to scare you or nothin'."

"I'm not scared–are you alone?" asked Arlen.

"Yeah. And I know you're alone too, so don't say you're not!"

"Yeah, I'm alone. So, what? Who are you?"

"Peter. We just moved here."

"You live in there?"

"No, no way," Peter said. "I kind of wish I did though, it's really neat in here." He peeked through the opening. "Is this your place?"

"I come here sometimes, yeah. But it's okay."

"Thanks." Peter said, shimmying his way through the opening. "What is this place anyway? It's not really a lake, is it? It's not like the ones I'm used to. It looks like the moon."

"Yeah, I guess." said Arlen.

"My dad saw the first blast-off to the moon. I mean, he was really there. Did you ever see the moon landing, like on a video?"

"Sure." said Arlen "But, I'm not so sure they really landed on the moon."

"You and my brother are just alike," said Peter shaking his head. "My dad doesn't believe it either, and he even saw 'em blast off!"

"Yeah, well–" A car parked on the shoulder of Keystone Avenue blared its horn. Arlen looked up the clay embankment to the highway and saw his mother stopped in her maroon 1980 Delta 88, lights flashing.

"Arlen Bob Yates!" Elvira Yates yelled in her heads-will-roll teacher-voice. Not even waiting for a response, she yelled again, this time louder than the horn. "Arlen!!"

"Okay, I'm going home now!" he yelled. His mother craned her neck out the window to survey the quarry from her elevated position.

"If you are not in your room by the time I get home," Mrs. Yates boomed, "no TV for one week!" He and Peter looked at each other, in horror.

With a quick "see you later," Arlen ran along the shore to the other side of the quarry and disappeared into the woods. He jumped over a shallow ditch and sprinted up Lincoln Road to Northwood Drive, one block away from his house now. There was no sign of his mother's car, as he veered across the neighbor's back yard, jumped onto his back porch and dashed through the kitchen door.

"Where's the fire, son?" asked Mr. Yates, standing at the sink washing dishes.

"No fire, Dad. Just outside messin' around."

"With Charlie?"

"No, he had to go to the Indiana Dunes with his grandma. He said she's too cheap to take him to a real beach, so they–"

"Don't talk about people like that, son," admonished his father. "Please, that's very rude."

"But he's the one that said it!" Arlen protested.

"I don't care who said it." The car door open and shut outside. "You know your mother would wash your mouth out with soap if she heard you talk like that."

"But–"

"But, nothing. Stop now, please," his father said, almost pleading. He hated arguments, especially those between Arlen and his mother. At times, Mr. Yates was inclined to support his son but couldn't, not against Mrs. Yates. She saw things in black and white and that, he guessed, made it easier to wage unyielding battle on the minutest of points.

"What did he do now?" Mrs. Yates complained, coming in from the garage.

"It's alright," said Mr. Yates.

"Well, it's not alright with me if he's down at that quarry," she said. "Go get the rest of the groceries, Arlen."

She waited until he went outside. "I think he was with that boy."

"What boy, Elvira?"

"Our son," she said.

AUGUST 8, 1996

Naked, he approached her slowly. She was nude, laying prone but alert. She wasn't startled when he touched her thigh, but flinched slightly, anticipating. He softly stroked her buttocks symmetrically, around and then up the small of her back. She extended her arms forward as his body covered hers.

He caressed her upper back, exploring every inch, nuzzling, nibbling. Firmly, he held her around the waist. Suddenly she was supine, and then on her knees facing him. Playfully, she maneuvered and mounted him, assuming the position he'd had on her. She slipped off him onto her stomach and angled her buttocks toward him. From behind, he positioned her on her knees parting her thighs and entered her with ease.

Arlen watched as the two squirrels quickly concluded their mating, wrestled playfully for a few more seconds on the corner of the deck outside his bedroom window, and skittered across the yard and up a huge tulip tree.

"Arlen, Charlie's here!" Elvira Yates yelled from the foyer. "Go on up, honey." Charlie Burris, who'd been friends with Arlen since neither could remember, took the stairs two at a time and burst through the bedroom door.

"Hey, man!" he said, flopping on the lower bunk. "Did you hear about Scott Sheehan?"

"Are you kidding? I was there!" Arlen said. "He peed all over me and my dad, and like twenty other people!" Charlie burst into laughter.

"Yeah," Arlen continued. "The tribe got to the park really late, so we all just got out our bags and went to sleep on this huge concrete slab, like for picnic tables except there weren't any there. It was totally dark. And then a couple hours later, Scott Sheehan gets up and starts sleep walking."

"Yeah?"

"Yeah, and then he stops, pulls down his pants and starts peeing." Arlen said through his own laughter. "And then he circles around, peeing all over the place!"

"Ahhh, man!" exclaimed Charlie.

"Yeah, and Mr. Whiteman got it right in the face, all in his ears and his mouth, too." Arlen continued. Charlie writhed with laugher and rolled off the bed. "He was gagging so much, Dr. Gardener thought he was having a conniption fit!"

"Did he live?" Charlie guffawed.

"Just barely!!" blurted Arlen, gleefully.

"Ah, that's so great. I'd almost join Indian Guides if I could see that again. Why do you like it, anyway?"

"I don't know. It's fun, I guess. It'll end this year, anyway. I'll be too old." Arlen said. "Hey, so what happened to the y'know, the ...."

"The rubber?"

"Yeah. Did you give it back? I mean, did you give the wallet back to that guy?" he asked.

"Yeah, my brother took me over to his house last night after dinner. He was almost as old as your dad," Charlie said. "We just told him that we'd found his wallet down by the quarry and came to give it to him. He wouldn't take it a first but then he came out onto the porch and looked through it, to see if everything was there, I guess."

"Did he find the rubber?"

"No, it wasn't there. My brother took it out, just in case we ended up having to give the wallet back to somebody's mom or something," Charlie explained. "But then it turned out to be that old guy."

"But he took the wallet, right?"

"Sure, but you could tell he knew the rubber was missing. He just looked at us for a second and then gave me twenty dollars."

"Cool!!"

"We have to split it three ways with my brother though. Here's your share." Charlie said.

"Thanks! What happened to the rubber?" asked Arlen.

"I dunno. My brother has it. Why?"

"I just never saw one before."

"Didn't you say you found one in the hiding place at the quarry last year?"

"Yeah, but it was all hard and sandy. I don't even know if it was a rubber or..." Arlen hesitated, "what a rubber is, exactly."

"It's like a balloon you put on your johnson when you do it." Charlie said with great authority.

Arlen wanted to respond, "You put it on your what, when you do what?" Instead, he said, "Oh, right. Yeah."

SEPTEMBER 1, 1996

Clemens Vonnegut Junior High School still smelled great in 1996, even though it was six years old. Not just one clean smell, but a million new-car smells comingling in the wide, high-ceilinged halls and immaculate school rooms.

Five years earlier, Peter's dad had driven all the way to Detroit from Alabama to get a Ford Laser convertible right off the production line; it had a great smell too. The Laser wasn't exactly the 1964 Mustang that Jake Phelt's dad got from Detroit back in his day, but Peter thought it was the coolest car ever. The Laser-scent of his new school reminded Peter of catching air off the small hills on Cherokee Road in Goshen, where his dad would speed up just enough to lift off, to the delighted squeals of his young sons in the back seat. His brother Phillip hadn't notice the pristine smell of the car then or at Vonnegut Junior High School now, but for Peter, coming to this school was as exiting and promising as a new Laser convertible. He made sure not to show it when he walked into homeroom on the first day of sixth grade, but he was thrilled.

"Mister Zintel," Mr. Lockhart, Peter's homeroom-history-gym teacher, announced as the bell rang. He pointed at the front-row desk nearest the door. A lanky boy wearing a pointy-collared, polka-dot shirt and knock-off Beatle boots shuffled to the front and took his seat, resigned to Mr. Lockhart's reverse alphabetical-order seating.

"Miss Yurkovic. Mister Yates." Peter watched as Arlen came forward, smiling at a couple girls and doing a down-low high-five with one boy. He took his seat in the middle of the first row. He turned around to see who would follow him to the front and noticed Peter. He smiled and flashed a double thumbs-up.

After the bell rang, Peter fell in behind Arlen and other students on their way to Mr. Jackson's math class.

"Hey, you found the school. Way to go." smiled Arlen. "Peter, right?"

"Yeah, and you're Arlen," said Peter. "Arlen Bob Yates!!!" he faked-yelled, doing an impression of Arlen's mother at the quarry where they first met.

"Oh, jeeeze," Arlen covered his face. "She's so embarrassing. That's what she calls me when she's mad."

"Mine calls me Mr. Phelt," Peter said. "Just like Lockhart does. What do your friends call you, I mean you got a nick name, like–"

"Like what?"

"I don't know, you could go with your initials," suggested Peter.

"What, A-B-Y?"

"Yeah, but 'Aby,' like a real name."

"Hey, Aby," flirted the girl walking beside Arlen. Peter hadn't noticed her.

" 'Aby.' You like 'Aby?' " Arlen asked her.

"I think it's cute," she said. "Much better than 'Arlen.' "

"And 'Mr. Yates' too," added Peter.

"Yeah, Aby! Remind me to tell Lockhart about my name change tomorrow," he smiled.

Peter, Aby and the girl all took the same bus home that afternoon. There was plenty of room so Peter took the seat behind Aby instead of sitting right next to him. A bunch of girls filled the last few rows and Peter's brother, Phillip, sat in the front with the eighth graders.

"Hey, you want to help me do my paper route today?" Aby asked Peter.

"Darnit! No, I can't. I have to do my homework and then I have to go to stupid cotillion."

"Ahhhghgh!" Aby stabbed himself in the chest with an imaginary dagger. "That's worse than death. Boy, sorry. My parents would probably force me to do that, too, if they knew about it–I don't think they do."

"Yeah, my brother doesn't have to go. I don't know why they think I need to learn the fox trot."

"I don't know, the fox trot is pretty important," teased Aby. "Hey, Faith goes!"

"Who?" asked Peter.

"Faith, the girl we were talking to today after Lockhart's class. Y'know, the one who liked my nickname?"

"Oh, yeah. Is she your girlfriend?" asked Peter.

"No. Mine's Missy. She's not in our homeroom," Aby said, "They're best friends though." He looked over Peter's shoulder to the back of the bus and caught Faith watching them. Aby gave her a big smile and made his eyebrows go up and down, glancing at Peter. Noticing his none-too-subtle matchmaking, Peter was embarrassed but still did something he'd never done before. Maybe it was the influence of the carefree Aby and his friends, or maybe it was just the excitement of being in a new place that caused him to turn around and actually smile at a girl he liked.

It had taken the Phelt family five years to move to Indianapolis. Dr. Phelt's optometry practice in Goshen was, to put it kindly, underperforming, so it wasn't like they could sell it for a tidy profit and get on with the next phase of their lives. More than once he'd been sanctioned by the Alabama Optometry Board for representing himself as an ophthalmologist, offering second opinions on a variety of complex optical maladies and dabbling in this new-fangled LASIK surgery thing. For him, it wasn't so much about the extra money he could earn. It was the simple fact that he could cut on eyes as well as any big-deal cornea surgeon from Montgomery or Mobile, so why shouldn't he?

After the optometry board finally revoked his operating license, he tried to sell his practice but no one was interested because there wasn't a whole lot to buy. No patients, no facilities and no license. A couple of months later, he just closed the doors and walked away. He gave his inventory of vintage John Lennon eyeglasses to the landlord to settle the remaining three months of the lease. He'd borrowed more than ten thousand dollars to stock the wire-rim glasses and other Fab Four memorabilia in his office, anticipating an imminent resurgence of Beatlemania. Unfortunately for him, there was no '90s wave of Beatles nostalgia and another Beatle wouldn't die until 2001. Turns out he should have gone "grunge."

Mrs. Phelt's marriage and family counseling practice had been their primary source of income for many years. In spite of his many ill-advised business decisions and investments, Jake saw the move to Indianapolis as an opportunity to reinvent himself; he wasn't sure exactly what he would do, but in such a big city there were bound to be opportunities.

"I got a good feeling about this, honey," he'd said. Mrs. Phelt recalled him using the same phrase right before investing in several vacation time-share deals instead of buying Apple stock in 1980, and again when he convinced her that a big bet on the New York Mets in the 1986 World Series was a lock. Turns out he should have run screaming from both.

So, Phyllis and Jake Phelt, sons Peter and Phillip, and Buster the cat squeezed into the Ford Laser convertible and headed for Indianapolis, via Texas. With the money from the sale of their house, the Phelts could manage for six months until they found jobs. With her résumé, references and work history, Phyllis would not a have a problem finding employment. Jake, having none of those, looked forward to leaving behind his career as an unappreciated optometrist and beginning the next chapter of his professional life.

Jake was disappointed they hadn't arrived in Texas in time to celebrate Texas Independence Day in March, or even San

Jacinto Day on April 21. He'd hoped that the family would arrive in Washington-on-the-Brazos, Texas to see the reenactment of the signing of the Texas Declaration of Independence, but they had to settle for the Brazosport Elder Players' revival of "The Secret Treaty of Velasco." It was a little further south than they'd intended to go, but it would give them a chance to see the Gulf of México and visit Gonzales, the site of the first skirmish of the Texas Revolution in 1831. Peter and Phillip were amazed at their dad's encyclopedic knowledge of texana. A favorite road-trip game of theirs was to come up with a Texas question he couldn't answer.

"How tall is the Texas Capitol?" Peter quizzed his dad as they crossed the Louisiana-Texas state line into Orange.

"Three hundred and eight feet."

"Governor?"

"Bush."

"State bird?"

"Mockingbird."

"Southern?"

"Nice try," Jake said. "No, it's the northern mockingbird."

"How many counties in Texas?" Phillip asked.

"Is that all you got?" asked Jake. "Two-hundred and fifty-four...one hundred and sixty-two more than Indiana, but we're going there anyway!"

"Why don't we just stay in Texas?" Peter asked.

"High adventure, my sons. New opportunities! Indianapolis 500, the Colts!" Jake said. "Y'know, I hear you can sell newspapers at the 500 on race day and then sneak into the stands to watch the race for free. And the Colts, c'mon! You guys were both born in Baltimore, birthplace of the Colts. And Peter, you were born during the first football season in Baltimore without the Colts—now we can all re-Unitas with them in Indianapolis!" No one else in the car knew that Johnny Unitas was a famous 1960s Colts quarterback, so Jake enjoyed his pun for all of them.

"So, we're moving up there for the race and the Colts?" asked Phillip. Jake started to answer but was pre-empted by his wife.

"No, of course not. It's just time for a change. There are better schools in Indianapolis, your father and I will have many new opportunities, and we'll all have a very good life there," said Mrs. Phelt in the voice she often used with the boys to end an argument, instead of saying out loud, "We don't need to talk about this anymore. Your father's an idiot."

FEBRUARY 4, 1998

Mr. Lockhart sat slumped behind the small teacher's desk in the front of the classroom. Every minute or so, he took a deep breath, snoring softly and then all the sudden, snort! The chair was too small for him; with each splutter, his elbows were dislodged from their armrests by his girth. Sometimes he managed to reposition his arms, but mostly he was content to let them dangle at his sides. Twenty-three sixth graders fidgeted and whispered, each stifling a giggle whenever a snort erupted.

There was a soft knock at the classroom door. And another, slightly louder.

"Snort!" Mr. Lockhart startled and looked at the students in front of him, all of whom looked very serious and unamused. He instinctively touched his chin to make sure he hadn't drooled, as he glanced at the door. He thought he'd heard a knock, but he'd be damned if he was going to get up again and answer a door that hadn't been knocked on. He'd fallen for that trick yesterday when he was interrupted from a nap during his afternoon study hall.

He adjusted his coat and tie, pulling his chair up to the desk. Missy Bradford raised her hand; he looked at her suspiciously, although she wasn't a troublemaker. "May I help you, Miss Bradford?"

"I think there's someone at the door, Mr. Lockhart."

"Thank you, I'm aware of that. Please continue with your work." There was another knock at the door.

"Miss Bradford, will you please answer the door?" She walked toward the door, admired by Aby. Mr. Lockhart was right, she was no troublemaker. In fact, she was a regular Goody Two-Shoes and Aby liked that about her, even though she was his exact opposite.

She opened the door wide. "Hi," she said to a girl with a backpack, instrument case, and a basketball-sized Afro. Missy looked at Mr. Lockhart.

"Yes?" he said to the girl. "May we help you?"

"Yes sir," said the girl. "My name is Cyrana. I'm a new student, and–"

"Miss Johnson, yes." he said closing the empty folder on his desk. "Welcome. You come to us from Texas, do you not?"

"Yes sir," she said with a big smile.

"In that case, you will enjoy sitting next to Mr. Phelt, who is a great fan of your home state," he said pointing to the unoccupied desk next to Peter. Cyrana slid her case under the desk and sat down, nodding at Peter. He grown up with a lot of black kids, but was surprised that his new school only had a few black students, and he didn't have any in his classes. Just as Cyrana was getting out some books, the bell rang and the mad rush to the busses started.

"I'm new here, too," he said to her, standing. "Kind of, anyway. I started at the beginning of the year."

"Yeah, my dad's a doctor and he got a new job at Methodist. We moved from Texas. Where are you from?"

"Alabama," Peter said.

"Really? You don't sound anything like my cousins from Alabama."

"Yeah, I was born in Baltimore and only lived in Alabama for a few years. Maybe that's it."

"Well I got a Texas accent I can teach you if you want," Cyrana smiled. "So, you like living here?"

"Yeah, it's not so bad." Peter smiled. "Hey, this is Missy and Arlen–you can call him Aby. They're not so bad either."

"Y'all are so nice," Cyrana said.

"What did you think, we were going to bite your head off?" joked Aby.

"No, it's just that—"

"Well, Peter, the mystery man, is the only one you gotta worry about. We're not absolutely sure why he's here," Aby said conspiratorially, giving Peter a playful nudge. "He's been here for nine months, and I just found out we were both born in Baltimore."

"Don't listen to him, he's crazy," said Missy as they all walked down the hallway toward the busses. "C'mon. What bus are you on?"

"1836."

"Battle of San Jacinto!" announced Peter.

"That's our bus—mine and Peter's anyway." said Aby.

"Mine's 2027." Missy said.

"Yeah, that's the one that goes to the fancy neighborhood." Aby said.

"Oh yeah, like you live in the ghetto, white boy," Missy stopped and closed her eyes, her last words echoing in her head. "Ahhh. I'm so sorry. Things just fly out of my mouth. My mom says it'll be the end of me. I'm soooo sorry."

Cyrana looked at her and cracked a smile, "Well, he is a white boy, isn't he?"

"Yes."

"Then I think you should call him a white boy." Cyrana grinned. "But don't be calling me that!"

FEBRUARY 5, 1998

The next day Cyrana took her viola to school again even though her mom said the school probably wouldn't have an orchestra. When Mrs. Greenhaw saw Cyrana walk into her third-period music class, she thanked Hathor, Saraswati and other ancient goddesses of music for delivering unto her, a fiddler. She was exactly what Mrs. Greenhaw had prayed for nine months earlier when she began planning her 30th and final musical spectacular, *Fiddler on the Roof.*

Over the years, Mrs. Greenhaw had become the expert on high-entertainment, low-budget junior high school stagecraft, marshalling her all-school extravaganzas with the goal of surpassing the previous year's extravaganza-ness. As tradition dictated, sixth graders acted, sang and danced, seventh graders built and painted scenery flats and props, and the bossy eighth graders were the stage managers and directors. With a pit-orchestras cobbled together from students and musician-parents, her productions had become bona fide, city-wide theatrical happenings. Every year it was a hot ticket, but she always made sure her ex-students were able to attend, especially those coming to see their own children perform.

The fiddler in *Fiddler on the Roof* wasn't the biggest role in the play but it was the one that held it all together, just like Tinkerbell in *Peter Pan.* There's no *Peter Pan* without Tinkerbell; that's why all the parents with way too much time on their hands and Principal Button encouraged Mrs. G. to designate a student to play the fiddler part with a fake violin and taped music.

"The play's only three months away," went the argument. "It would be awfully cute and everybody would love it!"

"No," answered Mrs. Greenhaw, whenever the topic was broached. "Our fiddler will come." Rehearsals came and went, Mrs. G. standing in as the fiddler, playing her own violin as best she could so the crew and actors could work on their cues. But no fiddler came. One parent offered up one of their older children who played violin (badly, as it turned out), and Principal Button even suggested they hire a height-challenged adult fiddler to fill the role.

"Or *you* could play the part," said Mr. Buttons, "I'm certain the children would enjoy that."

"No," answered Mrs. G., "I'm an awful violinist. Our fiddler will come." And finally, she did.

"Hello, young lady. What have we here?" she asked, eyes wide, as Cyrana walked into the classroom.

"My mom said not to bring it, but I–"

"Oh no, not at all! What's your name?"

"Cyrana Johnson, ma'am."

"My, what a beautiful name that is," said Mrs. Greenhaw. And then she asked *the* question. "How long have you been playing your violin, dear?"

"Oh, this is my viola. I just started to play last week."

"Last week?" Mrs. Greenhaw asked with palpable sadness.

"Yes, and I love it," said Cyrana, cheerily. "But I've been playing my violin for six years."

"Oh! Oh my. Yes, yes!" said the music teacher.

Added to her delight at finding a violinist, Mrs. Greenhaw realized her goal to cast all of the parts non-traditionally, sometimes adding characters to the play to accommodate all the children. She cast little sixth-grade girls as strong Jewish men struggling to protect their families in the in Imperial Russia's Pale of Settlement in 1905, and the biggest boys in the class as their wives. Melvin Ackermann played the newly-created role of the Palestinian cop, little Ahmed Mohammad played the lead role of Tevye struggling to preserve Jewish traditions, and Cyrana from Texas would play the fiddler from who knows where.

Mrs. Greenhaw was thrilled with the progress of rehearsals after Cyrana joined the cast. She was a natural on stage and her violin playing was beyond her years. One week before opening night, the full crew and cast had their first full run-through, beginning to end, no stops. "No matter what happens, we continue. Fully, faithfully," Mrs. G. explained.

The stage is pitch black. The sun rises on a small Russian village, the fiddler silhouetted atop a thatched roof, softly playing the main theme. Cyrana sways as she coaxes the melancholy melody from her violin, the evocative ambience for Tevya's first line, perfectly delivered by Ahmed Mohammad.

"The fiddler on the roof," says Tevya, looking up at the fiddler. "Sounds crazy, eh?" The violin swells for five measures and then softens under his next line. "But you might say that every one of us is a fiddler on the roof, trying to scratch out a pleasant simple tune without breaking his neck." They'd repeatedly rehearsed the lighting, staging and timing of these first two minutes of the play and it was perfect. Mrs. Greenhaw, breathed a sigh of satisfaction and relaxed into her seat in the tenth row.

"Think horizontally as you play the opening passage, Cyrana. west to east," advised a calm, powerful voice from the back of the dark theater.

Mrs. Greenhaw stood to see where the interruption came from. Then she heard herself continue the thought. "When you play music, you are moving through time. Through space."

Cyrana stopped playing and Ahmed was silent. Charlie Burris stood up from his spot in the rear of the pit orchestra, maracas and kazoo at the ready. All the children, one by one, silently turned and looked into the back of the theatre beyond Mrs. Greenhaw.

"When you own the stage, you command your destiny," the voice and Mrs. G. said together.

"Exactly!" Charlie exclaimed. The few adults in the theatre were confused. They hadn't heard the voice.

"Sit down please, Charlie," said Mrs. Greenhaw. She'd regained control of her–her what? Her mouth? Her spirit? Had she forgotten her Lithobid this morning, for god's sake? "Uh, let's take it from the top one more time everyone. Thank you. Everyone's doing an excellent job."

"I love when Ms. G. comes out with that kind of stuff," Charlie said after the rehearsal.

"But it's true," said Cryana. "After she said that, I felt like I could almost feel time going through me as I played."

"That's what I mean, yes!" exclaimed Charlie. "It's like everything in the world is in one place, all together, happy.

MAY 28, 1998

On closing night, the ovation for Mrs. G. lasted ten minutes and included an impromptu procession of adoring former students onto the stage. Cradling two large bouquets of flowers and flanked by hundreds of past and present cast and crew, the beaming, teary-eyed music teacher struggled to thank the crowd over the cheers.

She gestured upstage, acknowledging the adoration of decades of students and then, turning back to the audience, raised the bouquets into the air, took two steps forward and disappeared in a spectacular flash of fire and fog.

Parents 2:2.2

JUNE 6, 1998 A.D. (AFTER LUNCH)

"ELVIRA, WE'RE GOING TO have to speak with the Phelts at some point," Benjamin Yates said.

"Why? Why do we have to speak with the Phelts at some point?" Mrs. Yates mocked him.

"Because they've been here for two years already, and the boys are best friends," Mr. Yates offered. "And –"

"And what? Do you recall that they just showed up with no warning whatsoever–no phone call, no nothing? And we haven't heard one word from that sanctimonious pastor-lawyer, or whatever the sweet Jesus he was!"

"You're right, we haven't heard from him," he said. She hated when he was like this, so calm and reasonable. But he isn't being reasonable, she thought. Arlen is his son but here he is, stepping outside the fray of his own life to mediate the proceedings as if he were an impartial observer making sure that everyone is respectful, takes turns speaking, and avoids blaming or attacking. Who does he think he is, Gandhi?

"So, what? Do you want us to have a double-date or maybe a pool party?" she asked. "Oh-oh! We should have a giant birthday party and the boys can share a cake. And you and Jake

Phelt can share the story about how you mixed them up when they were one hour old, and how young Nurse Binky was so helpful all along the way. Lots of sharing–that'll be perfect!"

The Yates had never discussed, even privately, anything about the boys being switched at birth. There was the meeting in Georgia with Nurse Binky and the Phelts six years ago, but the nine-hour drive back to Indianapolis had been in silence. After Elvira announced two summers ago that she had seen Arlen with Peter at the quarry, not another word was spoken about it, not even how she knew that the boy was her natural son.

"And why should we have to take the first step?" she snapped.

JUNE 6, 1998 A.D. (ALSO AFTER LUNCH)

Phyllis Phelt hung the dish towel over the oven handle. "I actually thought they'd come over and say hi when Peter started sixth grade, or at least call. I mean, we haven't heard a word from them since Georgia." She'd expressed a variation of that refrain at least a dozen times since they'd moved to Indianapolis two years ago.

"Yeah," answered Jake, not looking up from the afternoon newspaper. His unspoken refrain was that the topic had been talked to death.

The four had agreed with Pastor-Lawyer Agane that it would be good for the boys to learn the truth only after they'd had a chance to know their natural parents, albeit as the parents of the other boy. Agane had assured them it was the best course of action and was supported by peer-reviewed research. Jake hadn't read any of the research reports and began to suspect that their findings were based more on rats ringing bells for cheese than humans smoothing out the rough edges of a baby-switch.

"Why don't you just go have a beer with him sometime; that would break the ice," Phyllis Phelt suggested.

"I don't even think the guy drinks," Jake said, annoyed.

"What do you mean he doesn't drink? You met in a bar and got drunk together. Isn't that why they have our son and they have ours?"

"Yes, but that was only half the problem. He couldn't handle his–"

"And you were the other half!" she shouted.

"Okay, okay dammit!" Jake yelled. Mid-swig of his Budweiser, he felt the bottle slapped out of his hand. It bounced across and off the table, splashing most of its beer on the wall before smashing into tiny brown shards on the tile floor.

Phyllis, shocked at her own action, sat down across the table from Jake.

"I'm sorry." he said. "But I still don't see why we have to take the first step."

Children 2:3.2   Summer Vacation 1998, IPS Calendar

SUMMER RAINS IN INDIANAPOLIS resurrect frozen winter lawns into luxurious, sensual mattresses where young lovers cuddle and gaze at the stars. Arlen Bob Yates and Peter Phelt could hardly wait until they were old enough to do some serious stargazing with Missy Bradford and Faith Bountiful. For the moment though, the fast-growing, lush green lawns would be their ticket to only a little extra cash.

"Let's go to Mrs. McGillicuddy's house. She paid you five bucks last time, right?" said Peter, pushing the mower up the street.

"Yeah, but she got mad when I cut her lawn in circles. She said that you should go back and forth, and circles makes it grow bad."

"I told you not to cut it in circles. Why did you cut it in circles?"

"I got bored. I hate just going back and forth," Aby explained.

"That's great. Now what are we gonna do?

"I don't know—hey, let's go mow a smiley face in Lockhart's yard!"

"Are you crazy? C'mon, we need to make enough money to take Missy and Faith to the movies with us."

"Okay, okay," Aby acquiesced. "How about that big house up on Westfield Road? Y'know that Jesus-freak place. They got a huge yard and they never mow it."

"My parents would kill me if I crossed Westfield!"

"What about your brother? He can come with us; we'll cross at the light on 86th," insisted Aby.

"No way. They'd still kill me and they'd really kill him!" Peter said. "Look, let's just keep knocking on doors. That's how you got Mrs. McGillicuddy, right?"

By the end of the day, they'd cut three lawns, none of which had been mowed since last fall. Halfway through the first one, they decided to up the price to $7, because it was so gnarly, and they got it. On the next one, when they ask for $10, they received what would be accurately described as a thunderous guffaw; the owner countered with $4 and they settled on $5. They were forced to do the last one for free when Mrs. Yates drove by and reminded Aby that a teacher-friend of hers lived there.

"I'm not sure we're cut out for 'business.' " Peter observed.

"You might be right," Aby said. "Hey, let's go by Faith's house on the way home!"

"What? Just stop by her house? Are you nuts?"

"No, we'll just walk by. Maybe Missy's over there. They might be outside or something. C'mon."

"We can walk by, but we're not stopping or anything," Peter pushed the rattling lawnmower as Aby dragged the rake, occasionally turning it handle-down to pole-vault.

"Okay, let's say you, me, Faith and Missy are onboard the Starship Enterprise, and Captain Picard orders us to transport to a Klingon warbird because we're low on dilithium crystals."

"Do Klingons use dilithium?"

"Sure. All spaceships need dilithium for warp speed," Aby explained.

"Not the Borg."

"Really? Are you sure?

"Sure, I'm sure. I think," Peter smiled. "Anyway so we're all onboard the Klingon ship, and–"

"Missy and me are 'security' and you and Faith are the science officers to make sure we get the right stuff."

"Yeah, we're trying to get to the engine room, but we're lost and then we bump into a bunch of Klingons fighting with each other over some gagh, and–"

"And then," Aby interrupted, "they start chasing us and one of them has a huge Klingon sword–what's it called, again?"

"A bat'leth."

"And you and Faith find the engine room, while Missy and me fight off the Klingons. She's amazing, she's fighting off this big hairy Klingon and I jump up into the air and kick another one into the wall."

"And me and Faith are looking all over the place for the dilithium crystals, but we can't find them anywhere," continued Peter, "and we find a tunnel, a secret compartment, and crawl in–"

"Me and Missy smash the last two Klingons and throw them through this big wall of glass and they fall like a thousand feet into the fiery reactor," Aby added. "And then we hug and jump up and down–and start making out."

"Yeah," smiled Peter. "I can't wait to see what happens with Faith and me in that secret compartment."

* * *

Faith Bountiful's alarm woke her up every summer morning at 5:30 a.m. It was a buzzer, not music. If she didn't get out of bed by 5:32, one of her six sisters with whom she shared a room would give her a little shove, even though they were all younger. For all the girls, it was in and out of the bathroom and seated at the breakfast table no later than 6, finish oatmeal and juice by 6:25, dishes done by 6:45, and in the car at 6:50 for a short drive to the Howdy-Doo! Resurrection Church-sponsored swim team practice at the YWCA.

The pool was bordered by a chain-link fence overgrown with Virginia and Trumpet creeper vines that were finally dense enough to provide the necessary barrier, impenetrable to prying eyes. The Resurrectionists planted them three years ago and only this year were the girls allowed to exchange their loose, full-body swim suits for Speedos, but they had to be black. All the team's swim meets were at the YWCA and only female spectators were allowed. Since third grade, Faith had begged Missy Bradford to join the team which did allow "pious young woman of unquestioned virtue" of other faiths to participate if they followed the rules, but Missy said there was no way she'd swim in one of those sacks. But this summer she joined up, because they were wearing Speedos and so far it was pretty fun, except for the prayers.

When they arrived at the YWCA, Bathsheba, Faith's youngest sister, bounded from the car to give Missy a hug. One thing Missy loved most about having Faith as best friend was her sisters, especially Bath. She was the seventh of seven sisters and the jewel of the family, her father said. At first, Missy figured it was because she was so cute and happy, but Faith told her it was because she was the Seventh. Her mother was a Seventh too, but she had brothers so it wasn't quite so miraculous. Plus, Bath was born seven years after Faith on July 7 at 7:07 a.m. and had seven webbed fingers on each hand. That last part wasn't true, but Faith liked to throw that in as a joke sometimes when she told the "seventh sister" story.

"My mom says having one kid was plenty and she won't have any more," Missy had said.

"Mine had two sets of twins, so I guess it was easier for her to get to seven. She says it's the will of the Risen Savior."

Except for her grandma's funeral, Missy had never been inside a church. Her mother wasn't religious and hadn't been to a church since way before Missy was born. Not going to church was okay, but she sometimes missed casual references to Bible characters or stories, and didn't know some of the rules. When she was three, she was in a day camp at the Y and right before lunch the counselor said, "Who wants to say grace?" She thought it was just another camp game and eagerly raised her hand.

"Okay, Missy. Thank you!" the counselor nodded, putting his hands together. Missy smiled and did the same, as did the other children. "Grace" looked like it was going to be fun, maybe something like Simon Says or Mother May I. She scanned the table and waited for the counselor to explain how to play. "Do you need a little help?"

"Okay," Missy said. That was enough to cue the rest of the children.

"God is great. God is good. Let us thank him for our food. Amen," the children sing-songed in unison. Camp games usually had better rhymes than "food" and "good," Missy thought, but all the kids seem to like it so she decided to like it too.

Since then, she'd learned a lot more about grace and religion but still didn't have a clue about what the Risen Savior was and why it got to make up the rules. She hadn't asked Faith about it because she wasn't a three-year-old anymore and she didn't want to look stupid, but she still thought about religion a lot more than most kids. For Missy, it was a club she didn't belong to that had fantastical stories about snakes, floods, zombies and giants, secret books with real special paper and golden type, and ladies who have babies without doing whatever it is you do to have babies. Faith even told her once that there's a secret language everybody church speaks when the ghost enters them.

"I guess if your mom has another girl, Bath won't be special anymore," Missy said to Faith once.

"She'll always be the Seventh."

"Yeah, but she'll be seven of eight, right?"

"No. She'll *always* be the Seventh," Faith said with the same gravitas Mr. Rochester must have employed when saying this to Jane Eyre: "whatever you do, don't unlock the door to the room where I've imprisoned my crazy first wife."

Faith knew for sure that Bathsheba would always being the Seventh, but admitted she didn't know everything about God. She said that if she didn't know something, it was because she wasn't supposed to know it–it was God's will. Not knowing everything was okay for religious people.

Missy nodded tentatively.

"It's a lot to think about, but there's always 'faith,'" she assured Missy. "'Faith' lets you believe in anything you want, without any proof."

Missy wondered if "faith" might be a good answer to all those pesky interrogations in science class, but decided to not ask her friend more questions she probably didn't know the answers to. Missy resigned herself to the belief that it was the will of Faith's Howdy-Doo! Resurrectionist god that Missy not know why her friend didn't know everything about their own religion. It was all pretty complicated and Missy thanked *whoever* for this new concept of "faith"–it was definitely going to make life easier.

* * *

"India?"

"Yeah, for two weeks!" Charlie explained. "We went there last summer. My dad does something for work there. My brother hates it, but me and my mom like it."

"I'd love to go there," Cyrana said. "They play the violin in their lap, but they stand it up like a bass fiddle."

"I've seen that! And they have all kinds of finger drums they play in their laps, too."

"Did you hear a sitar?"

"Yeah, lots of times," Charlie said. "My mom took me all over the place and we saw lots of people playing in the streets. And last year we went to a Name Giver, y'know, just for fun."

"A what?"

"A Name Giver. He gives you your real name, like the name that God calls you."

"Wow, what's yours?"

"I can't tell you," Charlie said. "I mean, I shouldn't tell you. It's dumb, but he said I shouldn't tell anybody until I decide if I like it. My mom doesn't even know what it is."

"I never heard of that."

"Yeah, he asked me about my name and where my grandparents came from."

"Where's that?"

"Scotland," Charlie answered. "And then he asked me why I loved India."

"Do you love India?"

"I guess so. But then he asked a bunch of other questions and my mom told him we had to leave. He held me by my arm and whispered my new name."

"Wow," Cyrana said.

"Yeah, he said my new name and then 'Family,' like that was my last name. My mom was a little freaked out by the guy and asked me what he said to me. I told her I couldn't understand him because of his accent."

"C'mon, Charlie. What's your name?"

"I can't tell you. I don't know if I like it yet," he said. "I'll tell you when I decide, but don't tell anybody about this. Especially Aby–he'd tease me to death if he found out I went to a Name Giver."

"Okay," she agreed. "But what does it start with?"

* * *

"You god-damned punks!" Mr. Dunn yelled into the dark, squinting through the soft glow of the porch light. He stood still for ten seconds watching for any movement in the street and then disappeared into the house.

Aby and Peter had had just enough time to duck behind the hedge against the house, after they rang the bell. He'd never come to the door so quickly. Usually they were safely hidden two or three yards away to watch his reaction, well before he opened it.

Barely five feet away from them, the porch door slammed open again and the massive man stomped out with a powerful flashlight in one hand and a leather belt in the other. "Larry, get the hell out here!" he yelled back into the house. "Larry!"

Larry Dunn scampered out of the house. He still wore the white, shit-stained clam-diggers that everyone made ruthless fun of that afternoon; they were playing at a house being built two streets over, next door to the "nigger shack" as Mr. Dunn called it. He'd told Larry, "niggers are moving in there and it doesn't matter if the daddy's a doctor or not. A nigger's a nigger."

Mr. Lawrence Dunn Sr. was a 'home' racist. He kept his views–perfectly compatible with his upbringing in 1950s south Richmond, Virginia–to himself except when he was at home. It was, after all, his castle and he could say whatever the hell he wanted to. He didn't drink, so he never got loaded and started talking about nigger shacks, or "half-dick hebes" for that matter, in public, nor did he mention them while working any of the five very profitable inner-city day care centers he owned.

Mr. Dunn looked down at the boy. "It's *your* friends that keep ringing the goddamn doorbell and you're going to help me put a stop to this once and for all." He shined his light across the yard and into the street.

"They're not my friends, Dad," Larry said, thinking that would be the sensible thing to say; maybe it would get him out of helping his father chase down the doorbell ringers, whoever they were. But, as the words escaped his mouth, he realized he had inadvertently admitted to knowing who they were; if he didn't know who they were, how did he know they weren't his friends? To avoid that question from his father, Larry blurted out, "They called me a nigger!"

Behind the bushes, Aby looked at Peter, mouthing "What?!"

"What?" asked Mr. Dunn, towering over his son.

Larry hesitated, and then double-downed. "They called me a *dirty* nigger." Those were the first and second times he'd said that word out loud. He'd always heard his father use it and for years was confused about exactly what it meant. He knew it was a bad word–like, one of the worst–but then he heard a black high school kid call another black kid a "nigger," and nobody got mad. But then, another time, his dad got real angry at a retard helping him load bricks into their station wagon and called him a "lazy nigger." That man was real dirty and stupid, but he wasn't a nigger as far as Larry could tell; but, maybe lots of people were niggers.

Mr. Dunn summoned what little self-control he possessed, knelt to the boy's eye-level and said, "Don't you ever come to me without bloody fists and tell me that somebody called you a nigger." He stood up and went back in the house, leaving the flashlight and belt at Larry's feet.

Long seconds passed. Peter and Aby looked at each other wondering what to do. Should they try and sneak away now? Aby motioned with his head for Peter to follow him along the base of the house behind the shrubbery, where they could make a break for it. But Peter was frozen. He'd never seen anybody so angry and mean as Mr. Dunn. He thought he might have peed himself a little.

Earlier that day when he and Aby were making fun of Larry for his pants, that isn't all they did. They'd watched as he was pushed from the third story of the house over on Whitewood Drive, next to Cyrana's. The neighbor boys, and some girls even, were playing on a big house under construction that was, for the afternoon, a huge riverboat going down the Mississippi River complete with stowaways, savage Indians on the shore, calamitous storms, drunken gamblers and brawls, lots of brawls.

Larry had arrived late to the adventure. "Can I play?" he called up to the wheelhouse.

"We're already in the middle of the river. Can't you see that?" yelled Captain Peter Phelt.

"Yeah, but I could row out there, like Arlen did yesterday. C'mon, can't I row out?"

Peter leaned over to speak with his second mate, Vernon Purdy, who then went down to the lower deck. He looked at Larry standing next to a pile of dirt and rocks almost as high as the wheelhouse. "You gonna wear those pants?" he scoffed. Larry hated Vernon Purdy.

"Hey, these are special pants to dig for clams. I just got back from Maryland, the eastern shore," Larry earnestly explained, "we caught lots of clams and soft-shell crabs too, and–"

"You can come aboard but you'll have to work in the engine room," Purdy said as he turned and headed back to the upper deck on the third story of the house. Larry boarded the riverboat and went down to basement where some fifth graders were pretending to shovel coal into the boiler powering the great vessel. He would have gotten right to work, but the engine room boss was a fifth grader too. *I should be the boss*, Larry thought. *I'm in seventh grade, after all.* Larry approached the boss and mention nonchalantly that he should probably be the boss now, since he was the oldest.

"Vernon told me I could be the engine room boss today," said the boy.

"And I got dibs on it tomorrow, so you can't be the boss then either," piped up another little squirt in the corner, who looked like a fourth grader to Larry.

Larry took a menacing step toward the boy. "Dibs on tomorrow? Who wants your dang dibs on tomorrow, you little twerp? I'm not even gonna be here tomorrow, because I'll be on the top deck gambling in the casino!" As if they were all promised root beer floats with double scoops if they did it all at once, every boy burst into a unified, mocking laughter that echoed against the walls of the concrete boiler room.

Larry felt like he was going to cry for a second, but got angry instead. He pushed one boy to the ground, shoved the little boss out of his way, and headed up the stairs.

"Here comes the gambler," one of them yelled to the upper deck. Larry bound up the first flight of stairs and then two more, followed by all the engine room boys. He was met at the top by Vernon Purdy.

"Hey, clam digger. I thought you were down in the hole."

"What's a clam digger? That anything like a booger-eater?" shouted the boiler room boss right behind Larry.

"No little man, you got it all wrong. Booger-eaters wear real pants, not their mom's underwear," said Aby from a gambling table in the corner. "Those do look like what his mama was wearing when we were peeking in her window last week, don't you think?"

Larry lunged at Aby but was tripped to the floor by Vernon Purdy. "You're gonna get your mama's underwear dirty, booger-eater," he chided.

"You're the booger-eater!" Larry yelled, getting up. "And my mom doesn't even wear underwear. I mean ..." Everyone on the deck laughed and hurled wisecracks as they surrounded him. Larry instinctively tried to break through the ring, but was pushed back toward the center with enough force to reach the other side.

"Let's give the young lad a break. He's had punishment enough for his bad behavior," Captain Phelt said from outside the circle. Even though he was still kind of new to the neighborhood, most of the boys liked him to be the captain because he was pretty fair and sounded like a real captain sometimes. "Alright crew, back to work!" By this time, everyone was on the upper deck watching.

"But this one's a real trouble maker, Captain," Vernon Purdy protested. "He might even be fugitive, or a Libyan bomber!" The entire crew shouted in agreement. Sensing the possibility of a mutiny–not the first, by the way–Purdy added, "and you know what we do with cowards like this one!" He led the rush at Larry.

"Stop, everybody back to work! I'll take care of this!" Captain Phelt yelled, but was drowned out by the gang of boys who had already picked up Larry by his shoulders and legs. They carried him over to the edge of the three-story house with only a two-by-four framed wall, and stood him up, facing the drop-off.

"You want a blindfold or do you want to walk the plank like a man?" snarled Vernon Purdy.

Through his tears, Larry muttered something about being sorry. He rubbed his eyes and looked down at the huge pile of dirt that was eight feet down and six feet away. If he could jump to the far side of the pile he might role safely down the other side; if not, he'd end up tumbling down the nearside of the 20-foot hill into the structure's concrete slab.

"What's your poison, A-rab?" Purdy asked the condemned prisoner.

"What's an A-rab?" whispered one third grader to another, who answered, "it's like that movie, Aladdin. Y'know, the magic lamp."

"But we liked him, right?" asked the first boy.

"You gonna walk the plank or do you want to be pushed off?" yelled Purdy, grabbing Larry by the collar, pretending to push him off right then.

"Hey, c'mon Vernon, let him go," yelled Peter from the back of the crowd.

"Yeah, let 'em go," Aby echoed. He maneuvered toward the edge of the house but there were still several boys between him and Larry. He looked down and saw Cyrana and Missy watching from the sidewalk.

"Shut up! This is mutiny on the high seas!" yelled Vernon Purdy to the cheers of the crew. He maneuvered Larry three feet away from precipice and moved behind him, holding his shoulders. "You better help yourself with a big jump, boy."

Horrified, Larry heard the countdown. "Five! Four! Three!" Fearing Vernon Purdy would trip him as he tried to get a good jump, he squirmed away from him and took a desperate leap off the three-story house. His adrenalin lifted him up and out enough to get him over the chasm created by the side of the house and the steep incline of the dirt pile. Realizing he would overshoot the pile, Larry frantically backstroked the air. He was too high to drag his feet across the top of the heap, and his flight continued to the far side of the heap. Terrified, he shut his eyes so tightly that his face cramped.

He braced for the fall and opened his eyes just enough to see that he'd hardly moved at all; he was still above the pile, floating through the air in slow motion. Larry whished that he'd actually read that Jules Verne story about time travel. He'd checked it off on his summer reading list, but had only skimmed it. He remembered something about when time slows down, so does everything else. But this wasn't that; he was the only one in slow motion. It was like Evel Knievel getting run over by his own motorcycle after he jumped thirteen Pepsi delivery trucks. Larry had seen a video from years ago where Evel was on Wide World of Sports, being interviewed from the hospital and talking about making the jump and losing control of his Harley-Davidson. He flew over the handlebars and hit the ground just in time to feel his own motorcycle smash into his back. He said it all happened in very slow motion.

Larry saw himself lose altitude. He'd cleared the first pile of dirt and rubble, and was six feet away from landing on a fresh load of sand. He couldn't believe his good luck, because he never had good luck. He landed in a crouch, ready to roll off the forgiving surface. As he hit, time resumed its normal pace and Larry tumbled violently off the sand right into a shallow pool of sun-warmed sludge that was the construction workers' designated crapper.

Missy and Cyrana ran up to him to see if he was okay. He lay there silently for a few seconds and began to cry softly. "Are you okay?" asked Missy. Larry sniffled and nodded yes, as Vernon and his crew laughed at him from the house.

"Don't let 'em see you cry," said Cyrana, reaching for his arm. "C'mon, stand up." Larry jerked away from her and stood up, trying to rub the shit off his neck and clothes.

"Get away from me. What do you know?" Larry shouted. With a limp, he walked to the street and turned toward the shouting boys. "What do any of you know?"

From behind the bushes, Aby and Peter looked up at Larry Dunn standing on his porch. His doorbell was rung tonight because it was Mr. Dunn's, not because it was his. They always got the reaction they sought from Mr. Dunn: he came out, looked around, said a cuss-word, and went back in. That's all they wanted. Larry bent down and picked up the belt and flashlight at his feet, and went back inside.

They waited for thirty seconds and then bolted from behind the bushes, across the neighbor's yard. They slowed down when they were four houses away to look back and make sure they weren't being followed.

"Jesus," said Aby, "do you believe that guy? I think he would've killed us if he'd gotten half a chance!"

"That's it for me. No more doorbell ringing," said Peter, still breathing hard.

"Me neither. I'm done," Aby agreed. "At least for tonight."

"Larry's dad makes my dad look like a pussycat, I–" Over his own words, Peter realized he was hearing the beating breath of Mr. Dunn, fast and measured. They looked around to see the giant man running toward them, flat hands thrusting with every short stride. He sped under a streetlight, now just one house away, and came at them like a cheetah. At that moment, each boy assumed they would be eaten.

"Split up! Run!" Aby yelled, as he pushed Peter toward the dark yard of the nearest house and then ran as fast as he could up the street. "Go!"

Mr. Dunn didn't even look in Peter's direction. His momentum carried him after Aby, gaining on him until Aby veered left onto Weyburn Road, cutting across the darkness of the corner lot. Mr. Dunn lost sight of him and slowed his pace for a few seconds, but then saw him appear again. He rounded the corner just as Aby turned to look at him and then disappeared behind a tall hedge between two yards.

Mr. Dunn slowed to a walk and then stopped in the middle of the street. "Yates," he said through gritted teeth.

Politicians 2:1.2   December 1, 2025 A.D.

If gubernatorial-aspirant Peter Phelt was going to Muleshoe to schmooze county judges and elected officials, he'd have to make a courtesy stop in Horsesock first. After all, it was his town. He'd established and incorporated it in 2016, and was mayor during its first four years.

Ever since its acceptance into the Texas Municipal League, the City of Horsesock had dominated the Muleshoe-Lazbuddie corridor, as west Texas' economic powerhouse. And just two years after receiving its $400 million economic development grant from the State of Texas, Phelt's petroleum-byproduct manufacturing company was employing its required target of 12.5 people.

After his election to the Texas Air, Field and Feast Commission in 2020, he'd put his holdings into a blind trust, but that didn't stop his manufacturing enterprise from spawning 250 Texas-based retail outlets, each selling football helmets, denture adhesive, surfboards and Gummy Bevos...petroleum-based products all.

"You're great on paper, Peter," Levi said as they drove north on Route 385 from Levelland to Horsesock. "Now all we have to do is to show them the person. The High Plains pioneer, the entrepreneur, the principled policy maker."

"You do recall I authored exactly one bill last session and it didn't even get out of committee, right?"

"But it was a good bill. A little ahead of its time, maybe."

"Requiring cities to remove dead homeless people from the street within 24 hours is 'a little ahead of its time?' " he asked incredulously.

"No, not at all. You know it has nothing to do with that. Your bill failed because it was about local control. When you were 'Mayor' Phelt, did you like the state always telling you what to do?"

"Absolutely not, unless it was about things like picking up dead people off the street or giving kids a decent education. I didn't mind that at all–Horsesock did those things because it was good policy, not to mention the right thing to do. If it takes a state law to force other communities to do the same, I'm for it." Peter had made that argument to his legislative colleagues during the session countless times. He looked at Levi and realized she'd deftly led the conversation to exactly this point.

"And *that's* principled policy making," she said. "Doing what's right and what makes sense for the people of Texas."

"Jousting at windmills. That's all that is," Peter said, looking out at one of the few producing cotton fields left in Lamb County. "Look at that. Over the last decade, we've practically drained the Ogallala Aquifer dry, and we're on the verge of a shooting war with Nebraska over water rights. With all that, you'd think there would have been be at least one meaningful statewide water conservation bill passed, wouldn't you?"

"I would, indeed. Thank you for making my point that we need you to run for governor." she said. "Look, you've taken the first step."

"By what, going to a damn Council of Governments meeting in Muleshoe?"

"No. By realizing that none of this gets fixed without *you*."

"I didn't say I was the only one," he protested.

"Then who? Name me one person from any of the parties who has one-tenth the policy chops and integrity you have." Peter was silent. "There's no one and you know it," she said.

"Alright," Peter said. "But I'll need a whole bunch of Lammes chocolate-caramels, if we're gonna get this thing done."

"In there, Governor."

Peter opened the glove compartment. "How the hell did you –?"

"Lucky guess," Levi said as she lowered her window and waved her arms wildly in the wind. "The next governor of the State of Texas is coming to Muleshoe, y'all! Yee-haw!" She was a damn good knee-driver, it turns out.

"There'll be bunch of Texas People's Party members, but they won't identify themselves as such," Levi said as they pulled into town. We'll meet with the chair later at the Muleshoe Quorum Club."

"Texas 'Peter' Party." Peter Phelt said in his most sinister voice. "That's what we'll call it after I seize control. Bwahahaha!"

Levi smiled. "That's fine with me. We're about due for another name change."

* * *

The Quorum Club had weathered planks for walls, opaque windows with top hinges and a rusted sheet metal roof that rattled in the wind; an upside-down mule shoe hung above the door. On the side of the building were a dozen or so vehicles parked like so many pick-up sticks, a gas pump with no hose and a shiny Tesla charging station. It was the only structure for miles, and there are a lot of miles in this part of the country.

The Council of Governments cocktail party was going strong, thanks to Bailey County residents who had recently voted to allow liquor sales in the last dry county in Texas–

except for Haskell County which was still "part wet," defined in the Title 16, Part 3 of the Texas Drinkin' Code as "kinda like being half-pregnant, but not really."

There was a bona fide buzz as Peter made his way through the crowd, greeting old friends and foes from his days as Mayor of Horsesock. Not that he didn't feel buzz-worthy, but he was surprised. Among the local luminaries making sure they were seen greeting him was Aural County Judge Alfric Jac, the father of the Southern Methodist University debutant responsible for Peter's first lusty trek to west Texas.

"Our prodigal son, come to claim his birthright!" Judge Jac proclaimed with cheerful abandon.

If offered a few minutes at the podium, Peter would keep it positive and big-picture, focusing on the great State of Texas as it forged its way into the second quarter of the 21st century blah, blah, blah. He'd evoke memories of inspiring Texas leaders on both sides of the aisle, interspersed with the requisite mentions of Texas as a "Fight to Work" state, and the new mandatory open-carry law requiring all adults to carry a handgun. Minors weren't required to carry but most did, and many parents chose to outfit their toddlers a .380 or 9mm semi-automatic available with a Big Bird, Batman or Barbie pistol grip. Always good for a round of applause, Peter would remind the crowd that he was a co-sponsor of the bill.

And then there was Texas' secession from the United States. It hadn't been on anybody's radar when there was a Texas-friendly president in the early aughts, but all that changed with whatever happened in 2016 and the election of a Tweet-averse, multi-racial, 30-something Congress a few years ago.

Since the federal desegregation of public schools in the 1960s, calls for secession had been the harmless, babblings of far-right and far-left militias, but secession had been top-trending of late. There were rumors that several small parties represented in the Texas Legislature supported secession, among them the Snail Darter Extermination Party, Texas People's Party and the Texas Parties! Party.

Each had their bone to pick with the federal government, or "the U.S." as would-be secessionists referred to it. There was "the U.S." and there was "Texas," as if the separation were a fait accompli. Their telling of recent history cited the spate of lawsuits between the two as evidence of irreconcilable differences.

More than a decade ago, then-Attorney General of Texas Greg Abbott filed a measly 31 federal lawsuits, a number dwarfed by A.G.s ever since, each running on a campaign promise to file more lawsuits than his predecessor. Each candidate made certain to remind the voters they weren't a big-government lover like A.G. Abbott. Current A.G. Flip Griff-Raff had assured voters on the campaign trail that he would file at least one lawsuit a day because he said, "TEGSHAZS is TEGSHAZS. That's what we do." To particularly enthusiastic crowds, Griff-Raff might add, "TEGSHAZS forever! Fornicate everybody else!" When he visited nursing homes, in search of the octogenarian Baby Boomer vote, he would yell very loudly at the residents without Medicare-funded hearing aids, "Texas Rocks!" They liked that.

Once in office, he made good on his promise to file a daily lawsuit and soon learned that losing a federal lawsuit is often better than winning one. After a first-round loss in a suit defending a Texas law prohibiting certain individuals from using the same toothbrush, A.G. Griff-Raff was celebrated as a David-like hero, daring to confront the giant, Goliath. As with much political hyperbole, the metaphor didn't quite work out because David actually won his fight—and, is reported to have regularly shared his toothbrush with his Judean pals, by the way.

Nevertheless, the A.G. won the hearts of Texans that day, and appealed the ruling all the way to the U.S. Supreme Court, gallantly losing the case and the $19.8 million it cost to pursue it. In the wake of the courageous defeat, a statewide poll rated Flip Griff-Raff the best former Attorney General of Texas ever; in second place was The Honorable Honestus Boone. Onomasticians are quick to note however, that respondents preferred the name "Honestus Boone" over "Flip Griff-Raff" by a two-to-one margin.

All Texas lawsuits, successful or not, were nourished by the welcoming and ample bosom of states' rights, the mother's milk of a nascent revolution. Each bold legal action against the U.S. welcomed into the fold, another disengaged group of Texans who would have otherwise remained politically apathetic. Hundreds of thousands flocked to the secession movement in 2024 after a particularly shocking loss to the U.S. Department of Justice. The indignity of the decision brought Texas one step closer to brink of separation, when it was learned that Texas would no longer be allowed to require voters to provide proof of lineage to a Texian combatant of the Alamo, preferably a DNA-verified mustache or pubic hair.

As Peter Phelt stepped onto the jam-packed bandstand the large crowd applauded, its excitement palpable. This was his room; this was his night.

"My friends, let me ask you just one question," he asked as the applause died down. "What is the difference between a Yankee and a carp?" It was an ancient joke, but he knew they'd love it. "One is a bottom-feeding scum-sucker and the other is a fish!" That one, along with plenty of liquor, always brought out the hee-haws and backslapping, and this High Plains crowd did not disappoint.

"Friends," Peter shouted above the ruckus, "I was a young boy struggling to escape from Indiana to *my* Texas, when Governor Bob Bullock admonished us all never to waste a hard-on!" The laughter burst forth, fortissimo, as predictable as if he was conducting a symphony. Its crescendo peaked; he paused perfect interval.

"And I've got a hard-on for Texas!" Again, the boisterous crowd came in on cue, marcato! Rapid crescendo to molto forte! Two beats.

"It's time for Texas to believe again!" Applause, two, three, four.

"It's time to believe that the promise of our future is far greater than the even best of days behind us. It's time to believe again in the potential of private enterprise, free from the shackles of an overbearing federal government. And it's time to truly restore our standing in the world, and renew our faith in freedom!

"The change we seek will never come from Washington, D.C. Over a decade ago we voted in a demagogue—our demagogue, we thought—who ruined the Texas economy and left the entire country on the brink of war with itself and everyone else. But the worse thing he did was to swing open the doors of the U.S. Capitol and the White House for the elite socialists we now have to fight tooth and nail every single day!

"We do not have to accept our current circumstances. We will change them. We are Texans! That's what we do! We roll up our sleeves and we get to work. We fix things. We stand up and proudly proclaim that Washington is not our caretaker. The United States is not our master!"

He waited as the applause waned and the room became stone-cold quiet, except for a Matthew McConaughey adult-diaper commercial on the television behind the bar. Peter nodded at the bartender to turn it off.

"Friends, I can't tell you exactly what the future of Texas and the United States holds, but I do know that there will come a time when this house-divided will not stand." The crowd remained silent, mesmerized by this firebrand. "And when that time comes, we will tear that house down and build a new nation! God bless Texas!"

Matzo 2:4.1   **December 31, 1794 A.D.**

AT THE STROKE OF MIDNIGHT on January 1, 1794 a young Chinese-Irish rabbinical student struggled mightily with her lessons on the cantillation of her beloved Torah. O-Lan O'Leary knew well the differences between the ancient Hebrew Bible characters she had studied for the past three years and the 64 I Ching hexagrams that had been the Aleph-Bet-Chets of her youth, but learning to sing the Torah without confusing the two had thus far, eluded her.

"O-Lan! Come down now, lass, there's much beoir to be served before the night is out," Sorley O'Leary yelled up the stairs from the rowdy ale house. O-Lan closed her books and hurried down, knowing what was at stake for The Crappy Pig, her father's small pub in the Old West End of Boston.

Tonight, the Pig would make twice what it had during the past three months serving Sorley's barley-apple beoir to the rainbow of neighborhood immigrants, including the Chinese, French, Jews and anyone else with sense enough to drink liquor instead of the fever-causing water. Unfortunately, ten times whatever they made tonight wouldn't forestall the creditors, come the New Year.

O-Lan and her father worked finger to bone until the last man stumbled from the pub, just minutes before sunrise. It was a Wednesday and, although it was New Year's Day, neither they nor the rest of the working class expected any respite. Sorley, asleep on a long wooden bench, was abruptly awakened by the clank of the iron door-knocker. Thinking it was a reveler back for more, he opened the door loaded for bear. A small boy stood before him shivering in the bitter cold with a nest of scrolls and papers in his arms.

"A good day to you, sir," he sputtered, as he placed one of the bound scrolls in Sorley's surprised hand and walked away. The winter air rushed into the tavern as he shut the door and unraveled the scroll. O-Lan stood across the room.

"Bloody bastard." He threw the papers to the floor. "That uncle of yours–he's calling in the note."

"He won't close the note, Dadaí."

"He will, lass, he will."

O-Lan cherished her father *and* her Uncle Wang Lung, who had been very kind after her mother's death two years earlier. He'd continued paying for O-Lan to attend rabbinical school and take singing lessons, and always encouraged her to pursue her dreams, just as he had done as an immigrant 35 years ago. He'd arrived in Boston when he was seven, after escaping from a Russian slave ship in Shanghai. He stowed away on another ship bound for the Americas, one packed to the gunnels with delicious food and cakes, whose crew was a very merry band of pranksters. Soon after leaving port, Wang Lung revealed himself to the captain, who cheerfully welcomed him aboard and treated him as if he were his own son during the jolly good voyage to Boston. Of course, none of this was true for anyone save Wang Lung, but it had been his truth for as long as he could remember, and was the story he told the Jewish family that adopted him.

"Young Wang Lung" is how Mozes Blits Huhnerkaufer affectionately referred to his new son. His name, rapidly repeated, served as excellent diction practice for Mozes, who was learning English, his fifth language. It also served to differentiate the boy from the elder Wang Lung, one of the other eleven children Mozes and his wife had rescued from the streets of Boston.

The Huhnerkaufers were third-generation Dutch immigrants and owners of the thriving Huhnerkaufer Shipping Company, Ltd. The family traced its lineage back to a small band of Jews who made landfall at New Amsterdam on the southern edge of Manhattan Island in 1654. They'd arrived from northern Brazil, after being forced out by the colonial power du jour, the Portuguese. The family's history and the story of the

Jewish exodus were told and re-told to the Wang Lungs and all the other Huhnerkaufer children on holy days.

Young Wang Lung and his siblings thrived under the loving care of the Huhnerkaufers, each brother successful in his chosen profession and all the sisters well married, except for his sister Ruth's marriage to Sorley O'Leary. Sorley was a master brewer, many people said, and by all measure, a God-fearing man who loved his family above all else. Unfortunately, he was no business man.

For years, Wang Lung had subsidized the family so that his sister and niece would have a place to live, hoping that Sorley would one day turn the Crappy Pig into a going concern. He'd sold Sorley the building for a quarter of what the property was worth and let him pay it off monthly, though he'd not seen a half-penny from him for over a year. Six months ago, Wang Lung suggested that Sorley and O-Lan live for free in one of his smaller North End properties, so that Wang Lung could sell the prime property where the ale house was located. He would even give Sorley a share of the profits to relocate the Crappy Pig.

Sorley couldn't bear the thought of leaving the house where his daughter was born and his wife died, and refused to discuss it, but Wang Lung couldn't wait any longer; the property was in utter disrepair and losing more of its value every day. He directed his solicitor to foreclose on the property, but to wait until after New Year's Eve.

"He *could* close on us, but he won't." O-Lan said softly.

"You know nothing of this, daughter. What are you talking about?" Sorley asked, exhausted.

"Matzo, Dadaí. Matzo." She looked at her father. "I told Rabbi Shlomo about the Pig and–"

"You what?"

"I'm sorry, Da. I'm so worried about you, and–"

"You had no right!"

"Rabbi said I should have told him sooner."

"I'll take no charity." Sorely was emphatic.

"You'll not have to. He told me the Council is planning to speak with you and Uncle Wang Lung this week. It's business, simple and sure—not charity."

"What business?"

"Matzo," O-Lan said. "That's all Rabbi Shlomo would say, but he said not to fret because we could stay here and run the Pig as long as we wanted to. And we'll never be poor again."

Sorely leaned against the bar, drained. The drudgery of the past years, struggling to make the barest profit, had become almost more than he could bear. He was too tired to fathom how any business with the Jews and Young Wang Lung would bring even a modicum of stability. Nonetheless, he picked up a growler half-filled with stale beoir and wearily raised it toward O-Lan.

"Cheers, daughter" he said to her with a weak smile.

"L'chaim, Da."

* * *

The consensus that Massachusetts native son John Adams would be elected the next President of the United States had encouraged the Boston Urban Rabbinical Provincial (BURP) Council to seek a corporate charter for the establishment of the Far East Massachusetts Matzo Trading Company in November 1793. In addition to being Vice President under George Washington and a pro-business federalist, Mr. Adams lived just a baker's dozen miles away from Boston, in Braintree, and his wife Abigail grew some of the finest, nutrient-rich rye in New England.

In 1785, the orthodox BURP Council issued a re-interpretation of the Halakha, requiring that unleavened Passover matzo be made with five grains: spelt, wheat, oat, rye, and barley. Making matzo with only wheat wasn't going to fly in Beantown anymore. Most rabbis agreed that making kosher matzo with SWORB, as the collection of the grains would come to be known, was a spiritually sound proposition. However, the logistics required for such an enterprise were daunting, and not everyone would agree with the radical change; for those reasons, Rabbi Shlomo at first urged the Council to reject further consideration of the matter.

Rye was grown locally in limited quantities, and wheat, barley and oats were cultivated in the middle states, but "supplies from the south are not to be relied upon" Shlomo told the BURP. The major supply problem, though, was the lack of spelt, a subspecies of wheat grown only in Europe.

More importantly, the new rule prohibited the making of the traditional one-grain Passover matzo, beautiful in its simplicity and beloved by all. True enough, the BURP Council had been held in high esteem by colonial Jews since its founding shortly after the second round of pumpkin pie at the first Thanksgiving in 1621–but the people had their limits.

Within days of the announcement, the north end of Boston erupted in protests against the so-called "BURP SWORB." The demonstrators won a partial victory when the BURP delayed enactment of the new rule "until such time as all the grains necessary for the SWORB matzo were widely available at a fair price in the Commonwealth of Massachusetts."

It was a postponement, but not a forsaking of its goal to realize the vision of the SWORB matzo. The BURP immediately set out to contract with southern farmers and European spelt growers to purchase the necessary grains, but their overtures were rebuffed. The amount of SWORB needed for a single Commonwealth Passover was miniscule and none of the grain merchants would consider an annual contract for anything less than 25 tons, unless the Jews were willing to pay an exorbitant premium. They were not.

Since his initial effort to dissuade the BURP from enacting the new kosher law, Rabbi Shlomo had become the Council's top expert on SWORB. As a result, he was given the task of devising a plan to secure the five grains necessary for Passover matzo at a reasonable cost from reputable grain merchants.

While many of the older Rabbis blamed crooked, greedy grain brokers for not selling SWORB to the BURP, Shlomo knew it was a simple matter of good business. He had come from a family of farmers and, as a young boy, was sent to the market to sell the farm's surplus pumpkins and squash. His father had two rules: *sell everything* and *sell more for less*. He expected Shlomo to return home in the evenings with an empty vegetable cart and cash–not unsold produce. Offering a good discount on large quantities of produce made that possible.

On the day Shlomo recommended to the BURP that they buy 500 tons of SWORB instead of just a few hundred pounds for Passover, he figured the rabbis would use these words to describe him: shtuss, schlub, schlock, schmuck, schmo, shmegege, and shmendrik! He was correct, and they didn't stop with the S-words. From all quarters of the room they called him "meshuggah," or, crazy in the head. What would they do with 500 tons of SWORB as it rotted on the docks?

"Value-added!" he yelled over the chaos. "Value-added products!" The room was quiet as they all wondered what the genem he was talking about. He looked at their blank faces, and answered before they started yelling at him again.

"Okay, let's say there's a farmer growing tomatoes on a very grand river down by México. The farmer ships half of his crop to New Jersey every year, but the shmendrik doesn't have a clue about what they do with all his tomatoes until one day he sees a jar of tasty salsa in the grocery...and it's made in New Jersey...with his tomatoes!" Shlomo had hoped to see at least one BURP-member head nodding, but got nothing.

"Don't you see? If the Mexican farmer had used his tomatoes to make his own products like salsa, catsup and other anti-oxidant superfoods–instead of just selling his crop to some schmuck in New Jersey–he'd be a millionaire!"

"Okay," one rabbi said tentatively.

"And that's what we're going to do with SWORB!" Shlomo explained. "We'll patent our five-grain mixture and it will be the main ingredient for an entire line of crossover kosher products we can sell to everyone! SWORB bakery products, SWORB Danish, lemon SWORB bars!" Most of the rabbis had never had a lemon pastry, but a lemon SWORB bar was sounding pretty good right about now.

"Chocolate SWORB cookies?" one asked.

"Yes!"

"SWORB waffles with chocolate SWORB sauce?"

"Absolutely! And pastas and teas and whatever we can dream up!" Shlomo's voice cracked with excitement. "And most important, we will have plenty SWORB at a good price, for our Passover matzo!!" The rabbis nodded earnestly. "Great, I'll get started on the product test!"

"The what?"

"The product test. We'll develop a value-added SWORB product to test our merchandising model, and develop suppliers, contracts and sales to secondary and tertiary markets. It'll have to be a high-end, *must*-have product that no Gentile, Jew or Wampanoag can do without."

Shlomo reached into his satchel and, with a Vanna White-like flair, uncommon to most rabbinical proceedings, showed the Council a mock-up of what he hoped would be the inaugural product of the Far East Massachusetts Matzo Trading Company.

"Gentlemen, I give you SWORB Artisanal Beoir!"

Sidelock-ed heads around the table nodded approvingly. "That sounds good to me," said a rabbi standing in the rear of the room. "But can't we just call it 'beer?' I mean, 'beoir' is so 17th century."

"SWORB Artisanal Beer it is!" Shlomo agreed. "Do I hear a second?" The room exploded with applause and self-congratulations as the BURP SWORB industrial complex was born amid glorious visions of unleavened sugary pastries, chocolate and beer.

* * *

By the end of 1794, the Crappy Pig was transformed into a state-of-the-art SWORB spirits and beer research facility. Sorley O'Leary was its master brewer and manager of the ale house, which served as a tasting bar with free samples of the latest test-brews and an impressive upscale menu. The elder Wang Lung had successfully negotiated contracts for the five matzo grains from across the world and made a tidy profit, shipping the SWORB to Boston using the vessels of Huhnerkaufer Shipping Company, Ltd. which he had inherited from his parents.

Sorley and O-Lan had vacated the upper floor of the Crappy Pig, which was now used as corporate offices, and lived a block away on Chamber Street. Young Wang Lung sold the property to the BURP, with two provisions insisted upon by the new owners: Wang Lung must sign off on all of Sorley's business decisions and the Crappy Pig must change its name. Sorley readily agreed to Young Wang Lung's supervision, but questioned the need to change the name of the Crappy Pig.

"What on earth for?" Sorley asked.

" 'Tis a fine name for a drinkin' establishment, that," Wang Lung explained in his Mandarin Chinese-Irish brogue. "But the rabbis feel we might want to name it something a little more uh, *refined*. It's a 'rebranding' of sorts." Wang Lung loved the trendy, post-revolutionary corporate terminology of the day.

"*Refined*, ya say?" asked Sorley. "The Crappy Pig was never supposed to be *refined* alehouse, whatever that might be!"

"Now, don't you get your knickers bunched up, Sorely. The BURP is–how do ya say– sensitive to your concerns and is willing to settle on a name that suits you and the lot of them."

"We'll see about that," Sorely muttered to himself.

"What would you think of ..." Wang Lung paused.

"Yeah? What?" Sorely asked impatiently.

"Instead of The Crappy Pig, we'll be callin' it The Skubalon Pig." Wang Lung spread his arms wide, to suggest the grandeur of the name.

"Skubalon Pig? I don't know what that means but I can tell ya it sounds a thousand times *less refined* than a Crappy Pig!"

"That's just it," Wang said. "It means the exact same thing as Crappy Pig, except its right out of the Bible! Skubalon–it means shit!"

"You mean shite?"

"Exactly. Crap, shit, shite, dung–skubalon!" Wang said. "It's got kind of a ring to it, wouldn't you say? Sku-ba-lon Pig! Skubalon Pig!

"Hmmm. Doesn't sound so bad. If you're sure it means shite, I guess I could agree to that."

"You're a good man, Sorley, a good man!" Young Wang Lung put his arm around his brother-in-law and shook his hand vigorously. "Now, let's talk about Borneo."

Church 2:5.1   May 31, 2007 A.D.

IT WAS MAY 31, 2007 when My Town Earth's final episode aired. At the time, MTE was an unassuming two-minute, syndicated radio feature, offered to stations as a promotional add-on to a three-show package. Now, of course, historians credit it with having sown the seeds of one of the world's great religions.

"From around the world and up your nose, it's Arlen Bob Yates with (beat) My Town Earth!" the announcer proclaimed over a bed of jet flyovers, speeding trains and a lush reverb echoing the "MY-TOWN-EARTH!"

Missy and Cyrana were the backbone of MTE, searching the world for the bizarre and sublime, the captivating convolution, or the last deplorable looking for two minutes of fame over the airwaves and forever on MyTownEarth.com. In addition to its stellar guests, media historians attribute the show's success to Arlen's insistence that it be produced as if it were 1984–nothing but 1984 technology, recorded on a Betamax deck, and aired live with no edits. There was still a Ronald Reagan, an evil empire, and a Democrat in the Texas governor's mansion. Why 1984? Because Arlen wanted people to ask: "Why 1984?"

"I don't think it has anything to do with that commie George Orwell," he'd say to confuse the issue and keep it alive–any buzz was good buzz. And then he might say, "maybe it's because that's when the world was born!"

Fans loved the tangible on-air bond between Cardu and Arlen and their singular quest for the truth as they tracked down Tarzanahan of the Irish Aborigines of the Sahara, the Society of Wrestling Nuns, the Boston Common Unusuals, and – who could forget MTE's three-episode pursuit of Bebe Rebozo?

Cardu didn't appear in all episodes (mustn't give the people too much of a good thing), but Missy and Cyrana felt better when he was on-air to smooth out the presentation, politely cut off windbag interviewees, or just be there anytime Arlen needed to say, "Back to you, Cardu!" Unfortunately, he wasn't for this early MTE episode.

MTE#37 – 02151984 Liquid Emporium

INTRO

SFX: **WATER FALLS, BABBLING CREEK UNDER**

YATES: Good day, folks. This is Arlen Bob Yates and today we're taking a look at one of the fastest growing industries in the United States. That's right, you guessed it – liquids! These days you can get just about anything you want in liquid form, and here to tell us more about the latest trends is the number-one liquid merchant of Marietta, Georgia, Friendly Fred Fluid.

FRED: Hello neighbors!! This is Friendly Fred Fluid here at the Liquid Emporium! Y'know, the taxman's comin' and let me tell all you fluid fanatics and liquid lovers that the Fluid Factory Warehouse is overflowing with thousands of must-have products for you and your family! That's right, friends–

YATES: Hey, wait a minute! This isn't a commercial, buster! We came here to do a probing interview and not–

FRED: Oh my, oh my goodness. I do most certainly apologize, friend!

YATES: That's okay. I just–

FRED: Y'know, sometimes I just can't stop myself! I'm just a pure salesman at heart, Arlo.

YATES: Arlen.

FRED: And you know why?

YATES: No.

FRED: I'll tell you why. Because I like people and people like me. You know what kind of people like me, Arlo?

YATES: Uh–

FRED: People like you, like people like me. And you know why people like you, like people like me? Because I treat them like they're my own flesh n' blood. Take this sale at the Liquid Emporium for instance. We're diluting our entire stock with an unbelievable liquidation sale–

YATES: But–

FRED: Everything's gotta go! Even your old favorites like Liquid Mouse, Aqua Lung and a drenching discount on Liquid Ice!

YATES: Liquid Ice?! But that's–

FRED: Absolutely incredible! Isn't it amazing?

YATES: Well–

FRED: Of course, it is! It's astounding! It's the Friendly Fred Fluid's inventory clearance sale! We'll be washed up if the taxman gets here before you do, so come on down to 9676 Water Way.

YATES: Are you quite finished?!

SFX: OUTRO MUSIC FADE UP-UNDER

FRED: Y'know, I'm glad you asked that friend, because at Friendly Fred Fluids Liquid Emporium we're never finished and you know why? I'll tell you why. Because somewhere in the world there's a poor little child switched at birth who simply doesn't have all the liquid products they so desperately need! But here at Friendly Fred Fluids Liquid Emporium...

YATES: Alright. Cut!

FRED: ...we're never finished, friend. And that's why I'm here to tell all you fluid fanatics and liquid lovers...

SFX: **MUSIC UP**

OUTRO

And then there was the "1984" interview of Pastor Peter Pullam of the Nagaswamie Church of the P-Free Sabbath that captured the hearts of MTE listeners. Submitted for your approval, the official transcript of My Town Earth episode #51 – 0901184 Church of the P-Free Sabbath.

MTE#51 – 09011984 Church of the P-Free Sabbath

INTRO

ANNCR: Today on MY TOWN EARTH, hot-breaking news about the Church of the P-Free Sabbath. From Nagaswamie, Texas, Arlen Bob Yates explains.

YATES: We're on the scene, as this incredible story unfolds—the saga of a church in utter turmoil. With me is Pastor Peter Pullum of the Church of the P-Free Sabbath. We have only a few minutes until everyone will stop using the letter "P." Pastor Pullum, can you give us some insight into the problems here.

PULLUM: Well, Mr. Yates, I'm afraid that the young people just don't understand the sanctity of not using the letter P on our Sabbath. It all started with just a few trouble makers, y'know, but then it got way out of hand. We finally had to excommunicate a boy for repeatedly P-ing on the Sabbath.

YATES: I see.

PULLUM: And then the college kids took over the church one time and would not come out. I just knew they were all in the sanctuary, P-ing.

YATES: Oh my! What happened?!

PULLUM: Didn't you hear? We had to call in the National Guard. All the serious journalists covered the story.

YATES: Oh. No, uh, I was sick last week. Very ill.

PULLUM: This happened months ago.

YATES: Well, anyway, uh – that must have been difficult for you, what with the National Guard here on the Sabbath.

PULLUM: Difficult? It's one thing to have our children take over the church, but then to have soldiers P-ing all over town! It was a horrible scene, Mr. Yates.

YATES: I can imagine. And that was the first time the church of the P-Free Sabbath ever had any problems?

PULLUM: Well, occasionally an uninformed tourist attends a service with an extended bladder but–oh, you'll have to excuse me now. The sun has risen.

YATES: That's fine Pastor Pullum, I was going to have to cut this short anyway. I had a couple of beers on the way over and–

LADY PARISHIONER: Good morning –astor –ullam. It's a beautiful day!

PULLUM: Yes, indeed Miss –olly. –retty sunrise! Oh, I'd like to –resent Mr. Arlen Bob uh, that's funny. He was just here. I wonder where he went.

SFX: **TOILET FLUSH**

YATES: Back to you, Cardu!

OUTRO

Arlen knew it wasn't one of his best shows. He'd forgotten to ask his best question ("Why not O instead of P?") and he'd broken the radio host's cardinal rule: take a leak before the show. Still, inexplicably, the episode's impact was immeasurable; more emails and twoils were received on this one MTE episode than all others combined.

One woman wrote: "That was the stupidest show I've ever heard and I really want to join that church!" Another twoiled, "Why didn't you ask him 'why not O?' And, by the way, I really want to join that church!" It was a sentiment held by almost everyone including Arlen. Had he emailed himself after the Church of the P-Free Sabbath episode, he would have written, "I'm totally burnt out on doing My Town Earth, and I really want to join that church."

One week later as the MTE crew was wrapping up a week in Paris covering the International Kiss Tasting Competition, Cardu looked up from a battered road case full of cables and mic stands and said, "I would very much like to join that church."

Missy looked at him expressionless. "I want to join that church, too."

"I'm going back to Oberlin," said Cyrana. Before joining the MTE team, she spent one year in Oberlin College's music program; she wasn't sure she'd end up playing violin for a living but she knew she didn't want to join some whacko, letter-prejudiced cult. The interview with Pastor Pullum had triggered a spiritual yearning in the other three that she could not fathom and wasn't curious about at all. She booked a flight and was in Ohio the following day, glad that the split with her old friends was quick and painless.

Cardu had joined MTE after spending two years at Finna Galen Himlen Retreat studying shamanic methods with Galen Ram Das. He'd decided to study there rather than take the online shamanism course from the University of Phoenix, because "Finna Galen Himlen" was Swedish for "Finding Crazy Heaven." ("University of Phoenix" means nothing in Swedish.) That was perfect for Cardu, because he was on a quest for so crazy a heaven, that it would embrace all righteous beliefs.

"You do understand that the Nagaswamie Church of the P-Free Sabbath doesn't believe in anything," Arlen said to Cardu and Missy on the flight back to Indianapolis from Paris. "Let me rephrase that. They believe in everything."

"Yes," Cardu said in his affected Hindi-Punjabi accent. "And that is the essence of this church: belief in everything is belief in nothing."

"I don't totally understand that, but it makes me feel good—lighter somehow," she said.

"Exactly, it frees your being and opens your mind," Cardu explained.

"More space on the hard drive," Arlen interjected. "It takes much more neural activity to disbelieve something than it does to believe it. If you believe in everything, you'll have more brain power left over for—"

"But how can you believe in opposite things?" she asked.

"You give yourself permission to do so," Cardu said. "It is your life. You may believe whatever you want to believe."

"But it doesn't make any sense. It's not logical."

"You're right, but this is religion. Logic and reason are not relevant." Cardu paused to let that sink in.

"So, that allows the church to tell me not to do a certain thing, even though the church believes in everything—including that it's okay to do whatever I want to do." Missy smiled.

"That is the most convoluted and sublime statement I've ever heard. I'm stealing it for my autobiography," Arlen smiled.

"Missy is correct," Cardu said "The P-Free doctrine replaces all logic with faith—a full-bodied, robust faith allowing you to believe whatever you want to believe. Faith Alone, let us call it."

"But why do they even need a church?" Missy asked.

"Because humans crave the structure of mother church to complete the circle of faith and exact a price for salvation. We do not believe we are worthy of God-love without some payment," he answered.

"And the P-Frees didn't want to go overboard on the cost for salvation," Missy posited.

"Yes. It is truly inspired," Cardu said. "The doctrine of the Nagaswamie Church of the P-Free Sabbath is that God will love you and let you believe in anything just so long as you don't say the letter P on the Sabbath. That's it. That's all you have to do.

"But if you add on Christianity, Wicca, or whatever, you have to follow all their rules too, don't forget," Missy added.

"Alright, this is finally beginning to make sense," Arlen said. "All these pious types are looking for a little insurance, so they hang onto their own religions while joining this umbrella group. If things don't work out with religion number one, no problem; they have a P-Free Sabbath ticket to the After."

"That is the cynical interpretation," Cardu said. "I prefer to consider the possibility that pious people go there because they think it's a beautiful thing to worship God with people of other faiths."

Arlen ignored Cardu. "So, one Sunday of no P-ing and you're in. Now, that's a sweet deal."

Church 2:5.2   August 1, 2008 Y.O.S.P.L.

"PRAISE GOD AND PASTOR Peter Pullam! Arlen twirled his laptop 180 degrees toward Missy and Cardu. "We have six days and 11 hours!"

They looked at the screen, and there it was—the Church of the P-Free Sabbath on was for sale on eBay.

Nagaswamie Church of the P-Free Sabbath

Item condition:	Pretty Good
Time left:	6d 11h Thursday, 8:08AM
Starting bid:	$79,000.99
Shipping:	Free Local Pickup
Item location:	Nagaswamie, Texas, United States
Delivery:	N/A
Payments:	PayPal, NoseGear, BitBanc

Returns: Seller does not offer returns

Guarantee: eBay Guarantee | See details.

"Here you go!" Arlen smiled broadly and nodded.

"Here you go, what?" Missy glanced at the busy screen.

"There's our church. Look!" he clicked on See details.

Items included with purchase:

1. 49 parishioners
2. Universal Life Church Monastery Letter of Good standing for Nagaswamie Church of the P-Free Sabbath
3. 1 box candles—400 ct.
4. 3 acolyte robes
5. 1 cross with processional staff (gold plated, slightly dented)
6. 1 Star of David with processional staff
7. 1 b/w Yin Yang medallion (large, with processional staff)
8. 16 unidentified religions banners, medallions with processional staffs
9. 600 chairs
10. 5,000 religious hymnals, texts, pamphlets, tracts – various sects and sub-sects
11. 1 *Church of the P-Free Sabbath Better Book*
12. 1 altar
13. 2 choir pews, suitable for 10 singers each
14. 25 assorted *No P-ing* signs
15. 1 pipe organ (missing most of the pipes, we think)
16. 1 copy, Dale Carnegie's How to Win Friends and Influence People
17. 1 copy, Zig Ziegler's *See You at the Top*
18. One building. Four-story brick, supported by steel and oak I-beam. Four-layer brick foundation. Hardwood and concrete floors. Metal roof. Some areas of the building need brick repair, but do not affect the overall structure. Seven windows need replacement.
    - Square Footage: 15,000

- Property Address: 418 Northwest East St.
- Lot Size (acres): 2
- State/Province: Texas
- ZIP/Postal Code: 78653
- City: Nagaswamie
- Type: Manufacturing/Industrial/Church
- Year Built: 1900

"Right there's a fine piece of Texas," Arlen smiled.

"You sound like Peter," Missy said.

"Well, occasionally he's right. But, what are you talking about? You both loved Pastor Pullam; you loved that church!"

"It was spring. The bluebonnets were blooming," said Missy. "We were tired and–"

"This is God's country, just west of Austin, right between Webberville and Utley–it's perfect. Statistically, it's one of the safest places in the world–disaster-wise." Arlen said, though he hadn't the faintest notion if that it was true.

"Then by all means, let's buy a church there!" she scoffed.

"Why not? Do you have something better to do?" Arlen asked. I think we could make a go of this!"

"Make a go? What? As a scam?"

"No. As a refuge, a safe place for people to be together, worship, live–be free!"

"Yeah, right."

"You're not being fair, I–"

"I think it would do both of you some good, actually." Cardu looked at Missy. "You are a caregiver or, it is clear that you want to be. You have always been so. These people need you."

"There you go," nodded Arlen, secretly surprised at Cardu's support. "He's right, you know. Pastor Pullam has up and left his flock. Where are all these people who believe in all that crazy stuff going to go? You think there's an ashram or mosque, a sweat lodge or even a synagogue in Nagaswamie? Hell naw!"

"You *are not* a caretaker," Cardu said to Arlen, sternly. "You have never been so."

"C'mon now, there's no need for that. I don't see anything wrong with providing a needed service for an honest day's wage."

"Well, I know one thing for sure," Missy said. "I can't think of anyone but you who is crazy enough and–I'll say it once, but you'll never hear this from me again–*smart* enough to make a going concern out of a dying church with a letter fetish."

"Aw, shucks," Arlen chuckled at the rare compliment from his wife. "What about you, Cardu? You in?"

"Since the day I was born. I always wanted to be in a church that believed in everything–it is so hard to make up one's mind," he smiled.

They looked at each other across the table, incredulous that they had just decided to buy a church and move to Texas, of all places.

"Now, where can we lay our hands on $79K?" Missy wondered aloud.

Arlen raised his eyebrows playfully. "I have a crazy uncle who left me some money."

Church 2:5.2   June 15, 2026 Y.O.S.P.L.

FBI Special Agent Darrow Dunkin was named after Clarence Darrow, not Dunkin' Donuts; not surprisingly, as a law enforcement professional, he was called upon to explain that fact more often than he cared to. Incognito, Agent Dunkin sat on the first row of the second balcony of the Church of the P-Free Sabbath where he had a bird's-eye view of the stage and mezzanine.

Three stories below the main stage, Pastor Yates flashed himself one last toothy grin before boarding the elevator platform that would transport him up, through center stage and then further aloft to his pulpit. He glanced at the teleprompter. Today's sermon was on enhanced tithing, the giving of more than one's money or time. Not that those things weren't important; indeed, they were essential and strongly encouraged with regular commercial interruptions during every service. But today was all about giving above and beyond the green stuff.

"Aby, -lease keep it simple, high-level." Brother Director Cardu had pleaded earlier that morning. "-lease, don't rile them up. There's another agent here today. He's _robably just a re_lacement for the last one, but we're not com_letely sure they're not ram_ing up the surveillance."

"And what do they think they're going to find, sneaking into Word's house like rats, _retending to _ray with our _eo_le?" Pastor had asked. "I'll tell you what they'll find if they don't watch out!" Cardu hated it when he got this way. "They'll find Word! And if they're not careful, Word will love them and Word will embrace them! That's what they'll find!"

From the media booth, Cardu crossed his fingers, a sacred practice of several legacy faiths. "Ready camera two, with your close-u_ of _astor, ready mic, spotlight one, ready cue." Pastor Yates struck a pose, his praying hands raised to the crowd, thanking them. "Camera two, mic, cue." A sudden brilliant light shown on Pastor as his mantis-like image appeared on the megatron, quieting the crowd to a still silence until only the hum of the building itself was heard.

"Tiiii-thing! Tiiii-thing! Oyez, Oyez! Endue thy younghede! The dead are due!!" Pastor Yates cried out, evoking images of a 14th century undertaker calling out for fresh-dead plague victims.

"Tiiii-thing! Tiiii-thing!"

"Ten million innocents died from the Black Death and one of them was her child! Shall we condemn her and countless other 'Christian' mothers for offering their dead children as tithes to the church? Why should we not?! After all, for her, it is the most _recious of tithes to be given."

Agent Darrow Dunkin made a mental note of "Black Death," "we condemn," and "oyez, oyez," all of which were on the list of suspicious catchphrases included in the latest edition of *Terrorism for Dummies*.

"Analects 17:6 reminds us that Confucius may have said, 'Charity is that rational and constant affection which makes us sacrifice ourselves to the human race.' Booyah! The _rophet Mo said, 'your smile for your brother is a charity. Your removal of stones, thorns or bones from the _aths of _eo_le is a charity. Your guidance of a _erson who is lost is a charity.' And I say to you," Pastor Yates continued, "You can get with this, or you can get with that!"

Despite studying the dossier on CPFS, Agent Dunkin was already lost. He thought he was understanding the sermon, until the Pastor utter a "p." Or did he? It really threw him off. And, who was the 'The Rophet Mo?' "

"Friends, you have heard me say it, and you have read it yourselves in *Better Book* Juan 14:1. 'Let not your hearts be troubled. Believe in Word. In my house are many rooms!' Many." Pastor Yates paused for 1.5 seconds for effect. "In my house, there are *many* rooms." Another 1.5.

"Juan 14:1 simultaneously gives us ho_e *and* anguish. Juan tells us that our lives are insignificant; he warns of danger, yet offers immense o__ortunity with his simple message: 'You can get with this, or you can get with that.' " 1.5.

"Are you a thief!?" Pastor Yates boomed. After a full two seconds of silence, he chuckled softly, with a shake of his head. A smattering of awkward applause mixed with pockets of nervous laughter; there was a palpable anxiety throughout the hall. He had everyone–the newcomers, not sure where this was going, and the old-timers who might be a little short on their enhanced tithing–right where he wanted them.

"Mickey 3:8-9!" he yelled, quickening his pace. "Will a _erson rob Word? Yet ye have robbed me! But ye say, 'wherein have we robbed thee?' In tithes and offerings! Ye are cursed in the kingdom, for ye have robbed Word!"

"Three minutes, Brother _astor," Brother Director Cardu said through the earpiece, as babies cried and grandparents adjusted their hearing aids. "Camera one, when you lose light, center stage. Brother Bob, ready. Spotlight center, ready full on Bob. Bell Choir, ready."

"But are you a thief? Pastor Yates continued softly. "Have you stolen from our Word, that which only you can give? Is your life then, insignificant?"

"Ready camera three, _an left, audience, rear stadium level six," Cardu alerted the tech crew. "Camera one, ready. Bob the Rap-eest, ready."

"Yes, you are not only insignificant, but you are worthless in the eyes of Word *until* you give you, yourself to Word. Literally. Give you. Give your *self*." Yates reproached them in a fatherly manner, reminiscent of the occasional admonishment of Downton Abby's Lady Mary by Mr. Carson, the head butler. Pastor Yates gave the cameras a reassuring nod and raised his arms into the air, as he listened to Cardu calmly issue a barrage of directions and cues.

"Brother Bob the Rap-eest, cue. Bell Choir, cue. Spotlight center, cue. Camera one, center stage cue." From speakers under every seats, syncopated bass-bells punched the air as every butt in the house shook. Dozens of bell ringers wildly stomped a 90 beats-per-minute rhythm on the stage deck, as Bob the Rap-eest launched into his trademarked no-apology funk-a-lology.

> *You are YOU.*
> *Word is IT.*
> *You don't wanna be,*
> *SITin' by the*
> *SIDE of your life, SIDE of your life*
> *Wonderin' 'bout the...*

Special Agent Dunkin could barely contain himself. Bob the Rap-eest was number two on the FBI Ten Most Wanted Fugitives list, preceded only by an embezzling magician who kept disappearing from his San Quentin prison cell. While Bob the Rap-eest couldn't hold a candle to the Houdini-like escapes of the magician, he had escaped prison twelve times during the past decade. Within a few months, though, he'd make his whereabouts known to the authorities and off he'd go to his next prison. It was no big thing for an FBI agent to re-capture Bob the Rap-eest these days, but young Agent Dunkin was thrilled to actually see such a celebrated fugitive.

> WHY of your life, WHY of your strife.
> SAAAAAAAAAAAA.
> Livin' just to DIE in your life, DIE in your life.
> SAAAAAAAAAAAA.

Bob accentuated the short half-beats of his rap with yoga-defying twists and turns that put the old-school rappers and hip-hopsters to shame, in a gentrifying sort of way. Since the early '20s, the black and brown rappers had conceded all things hip-hop to the white, yellow and pink rappers, opting instead for phat, 100-year-old blues recorded with whack 20th century garbage-for-mics. Topping the charts on this particular P-Free Sabbath Monday morning was not Bob the Rap-eest, but Son-House-Swae-Lee's *Death Letter Blues* and A$AP Mama Johnson's *I Went Down to the MOPAC*. Off the hook, baby.

As everyone cheered and stomped to the beat, Agent Dunkin made his way to the end of the row toward the stairs. He turned to look back as the roar of the crowd suddenly increased and spotlights shined on hundreds of men and women dressed in prison-issued jumpsuits–dayglow orange, piss-green or black-and-white striped, depending on their origin. He recognized them as the Minsters in Chains, the self-jailed members of the church who committed crimes for the sole purpose of being imprisoned so they could spread the Better Word to inmates across the world.

"YOU, givin' up YOU given up YOU!" Bob the Rap-eest shouted to the crowd as he tore the Velcro fasteners from his colorful shirt and pants and threw them into the tenth row. He stood center stage in the white shirt and white pants he had worn for the past 13 months at the Texas Department of

Criminal Justice Huntsville Unit. He hoped his next incarceration would afford him a more stylish outfit.

"Agent on the move," Brother Director Cardu said to Bob the Rap-eest and Pastor Yates on a dedicated channel. Bob pumped his fist high to welcome the Ministers.

"YOU, givin' up YOU given up YOU!"
"YOU, givin' up YOU given up YOU!"
SAA SAA SAA SAA.

Do Word! Do Word! Do Word! Do Word!
SAAAAAAAAAAAA.

The music was cued down. "These brothers and sisters have given of their entireties, their lives, their everythings to spread the word of Word in the dark dungeons of this cruel world," Yates proclaimed. "See them now! They are among us in this building, worshipping with us today and living as our neighbors in the P-Free City of Light!" The crowd cheered, and looked around the auditorium with anticipation.

"Will all the convicted murderers please light your beams and be recognized!" Five hundred small lights appeared like stars in the darkness of the ecumenicon. "Beautiful!" smiled Pastor Yates. "Okay now. Assault and battery, light your beams! Second-degree assault! Breaking and entering! Jaywalking!"

Agent Dunkin, now on the ground floor, scanned the balconies, horrified to see thousands of former-Ministers in Chains proudly waving their beams into the air.

"Corporate embezzlers! 9/11 terrorists! Graffiti artists! Office supply pilferers! 2023 terrorists! Blessed are you, released now from the shackles of man!" Pastor Yates yelled.

Dunkin suddenly realized he stood in the middle of hundreds of ministers, all waving enthusiastically to the lights around the arena. Disoriented in the chaos, he scanned the perimeter for an escape route. There was no way he was going to arrest Bob the Rap-eest in this place without backup. The noise was deafening. As he squeezed between a walking tattoo and a convicted former-politician guarding a folder of erased emails, the agent felt a tap on his shoulder. He spun around to see Bob the Rap-eest.

"What took you so long, Agent Dunkin?"

Special Agent Dunkin looked at the FBI top-tenner, star struck. Regaining his composure, he clumsily drew his government-issued .60-caliber Glock and aimed it at Bob the Rap-eest.

"FBI! You're under arrest!" Dunkin yelled through the cacophony. Bob took several steps back.

"That's fine," Bob said, "but I don't want to go back to Huntsville. Can we talk about another location?" He smiled, as the ministers formed a generous circle around him and Agent Dunkin. "How about that new SuperMax under Crater Lake?"

"You don't get to pick and choose where you spend the rest of your life, buddy!" Agent Dunkin shouted, adding, "is there really a SuperMax under Crater Lake?"

"You're so right, agent. Nobody really gets to choose anything, or do they?" Bob raised his arms above his head, as the ministers gave him a wide birth. Sensing victory, Dunkin took a step forward, but then realized that Bob was waving his arms in celebration, and not acquiescing to his arrest. With an elegant 360-degree turn, Bob the Rap-eest pumped his fists to the highest rafters, took two steps backward, and disappeared in a spectacular flash of fire and fog.

Children 2:3.3 **School Year 1998, IPS Calendar**

THERE IS AN UNWRITTEN rule among Clemens Vonnegut Junior High eighth-graders that everybody gets a pass on the new clothes they're forced to wear on the first day of school. This is a blessing for boys especially because there is, potentially, no more embarrassing a day.

Skirmishes with parents about first-day clothes typically begin in late July, weeks before Tax-free Saturday, during which parents can save 7.258 percent on an entire school year's wardrobe. The stakes are incredibly high; just a few hours of shopping on that day can determine every item of clothing worn during next nine months.

Among the strategies employed by many a boy to defeat the enemy, is to make sure they are too busy on Tax-Free Saturday to buy school clothes. A successful excuse not to go shopping must be compelling and involve an activity parents feel passionate about, making them beam with pride about their boy's initiative and sense of community purpose. The goal is for a parent to say "That's a wonderful idea, my socially-conscious son. You most certainly don't have to go shopping with me on Tax-Free Saturday to purchase color-coordinated outfits and adult-looking shoes."

"Hey, your mom teaches school in the city, right?" Charlie asked Aby.

"My dad says teachers might go on strike because the city schools really stink," Peter interjected, excitedly. "He thinks they should, so they can get paid more and get more money for the kids, too."

"Yeah, she's a teacher at School 59 in Broad Ripple. She's in the union, too." Aby said. "Look, I'm just trying to get out of having to wear corduroys and stiff shirts all year. What are you talking about?"

"We can make some signs for your mom for when she goes out on strike!"

Peter raised an imaginary strike poster, and marched in place. "And on Tax-Free Saturday we can all go to Broad Ripple and hand out flyers, and do yard signs too!"

"I don't know. It seems like a lot of work," Aby said.

"You got a better idea?"

"I guess not." Aby wasn't totally sold on the idea, but agreed to go along with it, having nothing else to offer.

Peter and Charlie spent the next two weeks coming up with a slogan and designing the perfect strike poster. It was three feet square and had plenty of patriotic red, white and blue. The slogan they decided on was "On Strike for Your Children!!!"

Charlie and Peter would come over to Aby's house the Wednesday before Tax-free day and parade up and down the sidewalk with their signs so that Mrs. Yates could get the full effect. Then Aby would tell her about all the very important work they were planning for Saturday.

Two days before the showing the sign to Mrs. Yates, Aby met them two blocks from his house. It was looking like the strike would happen, so everything was a go. On the corner were Peter, Charlie and a man with thick straight hair pushed behind his ears, long enough to make Aby think he couldn't be Peter's father. Each of them held a poster attached to a long, thin piece of wood.

"Dad, this is Aby!" Peter said.

"Ahh, so this is the famous Aby I've heard so much about," Jake said extending his hand.

Aby shook his hand firmly and recited what had been drilled into him since he was three. "Hello sir, I'm very pleased to meet you." Aby was thankful that his mother had taught him that because adults loved it and made them think he was a good kid, which he was some of the time.

"Peter says you're quite the lady's man."

"No, I didn't!" Peter protested. Aby, of course, thought he was indeed quite the ladies' man, but firmly insisted he was no such thing.

"Methinks he doth protest too much!" Jake teased.

"What is that supposed to mean?" Peter asked.

"The wisdom of the bard, my boy. If someone keeps saying something isn't true, it most definitely *is* true!"

Peter was learning that when his dad was in his teasing mode, it was often best to not respond. He let a few seconds pass and then spoke to Aby. "We figured we'd bring my dad to march with us outside your house so your mom could see how it'll look if a teacher was doing it. He's not a teacher but at least he's an adult. I guarantee your mom's going to love this," Peter had assured Aby.

"Let's see the signs!"

"No way, man," Jake smiled.

"Yeah, we want you to see it with your mom for the first time and be surprised together," Charlie said.

"Okay, I guess that sounds alright," Aby said, not knowing quite what to make of Peter's dad. He obviously knew about the secret plan and wasn't going to make Peter go shopping for school clothes, so that was pretty cool; still, he wasn't like other parents Aby had met.

"Will your dad be around?" asked Jake.

"No, he's at work. I better get going. See you at my house."

"We're right behind you!"

When Aby walked in, Mrs. Yates was in her small reading alcove bordered by a bookcase and a large bay window that looked onto the sidewalk. Each summer she'd spend hundreds of comfy, private hours in its wingback chair reading novels mostly, the thicker the better.

"Hey, Mom!" he said. She was slightly suspicious because he never made a point to so cheerfully say hello, much less ask a follow-up question. "What are you reading?" Now she knew for sure, that something was up.

"Unleavened Bread and You."

"Oh, that sounds good."

"It's a history of matzo."

"Interesting. Who wrote it, Mom?"

Mrs. Yates glanced up at the person speaking to make sure it was her son. He spoke before she could answer.

"Did you hear that?" He opened the curtains. Peter, Charlie and Jake Phelt were on the sidewalk yelling and marching in circles, stabbing the sky with their protest signs. Aby smiled and looked at his mother to gauge her reaction. She had the same confused expression she had two months earlier as she watched the dog next door shaking and playfully tossing into the air, a red and white stuffed animal. And then, to her horror, she realized the toy was her kitten, Fluffy. The revelation was cruel and abrupt; if Fluffy had to be dispatched, she would have much preferred a prolonged death by feline leukemia for her little friend.

Aby looked out the window wide-eyed and was shocked to see that the signs all read, STRIKE YOUR CHILDREN!! He squinted at the signs but they refused to read anything else.

"What–? Who are–? Is that Charlie?" Mrs. Yates finally arrived at a question. "Strike Your Children!? What kind of a sick joke is that?

"I don't know, I–"

"Who's that man with Charlie? And that boy? Is that–?"

"It's–"

"Go turn on the sprinkler!" she yelled.

"What?"

"Go to the garage right this minute and turn on the front sprinklers. Now!"

"But–"

"Arlen Robert Yates! You will do as I say *immediately* or you'll be grounded for eighth grade! I am serious." She was madder than Aby had seen her in maybe forever. "Now!" As the strikers staged their mock demonstration, anticipating Mrs. Yates' gushing gratitude for their efforts to support the noble cause of inner-city teachers, Aby headed to the garage. In the center of the bay window, Elvira Yates stood tall with steely eyes, fists on hips.

Jake Phelt and the boys noticed her and began waving enthusiastically just as the water hit them from every direction with a force that soaked them and their signs before they could escape down the sidewalk. She watched as they collected themselves in front of the neighbor's house, dripping wet. As soon as she was sure they were looking at her, she pulled the curtains shut.

* * *

Membership in the posse was all set for the first day of eighth grade: Aby, Missy, Peter, Faith, Charlie and Cyrana. It wasn't meant to be a boy-girl, boy-girl thing; it just turned out that way. Charlie and Cyrana were more like siblings than anything else, and if Aby and Missy or Peter and Faith paired up on the playground it didn't matter–everyone always had someone to hang out with.

"Nice button-down," Peter said in Aby's direction as the posse walked toward their new homerooms. "Is that a new belt?" This year there would be no observance of the unwritten rule pertaining to first-day clothes. Aby had been grounded since the miserable attempt to get out of Tax-Free Saturday; grounded, except for shopping with his mother, of course. Sparing no expense, they'd purchased seven new shirts, five pairs of pants, four belts, three pairs of shoes, socks, new underwear and a backpack to replace the one that had served double-duty as Fluffy's scratching pad before her unfortunate demise. The day's success was unprecedented, Mrs. Yates calculated. Not only had she saved $30.12, but the space needed in Aby's closet for the new clothes required that all the old jeans, tattered shirts, and stinky shoes would have to go. Tax-Free Saturday was a resounding triumph.

Aby stopped and looked at Peter and Charlie. "I can't believe *you* are mad at *me*! You're the clowns that paraded outside my house with *Strike Your Children* picket signs and made my mom so mad, she bought me enough horrible clothes to last me the rest of my life!"

" 'On Strike for Your Children.' That's what the signs said!" Peter and his dad had spent hours on the signs so they would be perfect. "What? You can't read anymore?"

"Well, whose brainiac idea was it to write the important words in Lilliputian? What happened to the 'on' and the 'for' huh? Even from five feet away you couldn't read them. It was supposed to say 'ON Strike FOR Your Children!' "

"Yeah, I thought that too when I first saw them from cross the garage that day," Charlie confessed.

"Oh, you're always on his side."

"I am not." Charlie thought about it and then said, "So?"

"Why didn't you say something?" asked Peter.

"Because your dad was so excited about them, I figured I was wrong."

"So, whose fault is it?" Aby looked at Peter. "Charlie's or your daddy's, huh?"

"Shut up!" Peter shoved Aby hard into Missy and they stumbled into the lockers.

"Gentlemen." Mr. Lockhart stood guard outside his classroom. "Would it be possible to postpone your brawl until after school?"

"I'm sorry, I didn't mean to do that." Peter turned and walked down the hall.

* * *

There were three eighth-grade homeroom teachers. Cyrana, Aby and Charlie were in Miss Prophet's class; she was by far the best teacher, according to all the ninth graders who had her last year. Her classes were fun, there no busywork, and she'd give a student a hall pass to go the bathroom without the humiliation of a prolonged interrogation of the crossed-legged suspect. Faith and Missy had Frau Krsna, a musty ancient, who reminded staff and students alike of the mythic Valkyrie Brünnhilde, who had given rise to the phrase "it ain't over 'til the fat lady sings."

Peter found himself posse-less under the tutelage of Miss Turnbuckle, author of the *Homeroom Protocols of Conduct* that could have been used just as well, aboard a Sturgeon-class nuclear attack submarine. Although he'd stopped only briefly at his locker on the way to her class, Miss Turnbuckle knew about the pushing incident and told him to sit in the front row, contrary to her own algorithm-derived seating schema.

He realized the bell was ringing; it was the end of class. He'd missed Miss Turnbuckle's twenty-minute first-day rules briefing lost in thought, trying to figure out what had made him push Aby almost to the floor. Aby was being a jerk, but Peter didn't want to get into a real fight with his best friend.

"Peter," Miss Turnbuckle nodded ominously at him as he was leaving the room. She didn't say anything else.

"Yes, ma'am." Peter nodded back and entered the herd of students in the hallway, ping-ponging against one another. Amid the jostling, something nudged the back of his leg. In stride, he glanced back to see Cyrana, violin case in hand.

"How's Turnbuckle?"

"No surprises, she's Turnbuckle," he said. "Prophet?"

"She's great. She just let us talk."

"What did you guys talk about?"

"Stuff that happened over the summer. Oh, did you hear about that guy, Vernon Pretty?"

"Yeah, the one who pushed Larry off the house."

"Oh, that's him; I wasn't sure. Anyway, somebody said that he got arrested for trying to sell oregano to a ninth grader."

"What's oregano?" Peter asked.

"It's like a spice or herb, but it's not illegal or anything."

"When why did he get arrested?"

"Because when the policeman asked to see the marijuana, I mean oregano, Vernon Purdy ran away and then the policeman chased him and had a heart attack, so they arrested him for resisting arrest."

"That doesn't seem fair," Peter said. "Except that it was Vernon."

* * *

"Sock me, c'mon!"

Missy looked around to see where the lunch monitors were and lightly punched Peter's shoulder. Everyone in the posse was at the table except for Aby.

"Harder," Peter said.

"I don't want to, I–"

"I'll do it!" smiled Cyrana.

"It's got to be Missy," Peter said, "so we're even for when I shoved her into the lockers."

"It's as Bible thing," said Charlie, from the other side of the table that stretched half the length of the cafeteria. "An eye for an eye."

"Yeah," Peter said. "My dad's an eye doctor, or he used to be, so I know."

"You're such a dweeb," Charlie smiled. He leaned across the table and punched Peter hard. Cyrana punched him in the other arm. He felt another light punch in the back.

"Okay!" Aby said, squeezing between Peter and Missy. "We're all even, right? End of story?" They all looked at Peter.

"Alright," he said to everyone's relief.

Larry Dunn was standing awkwardly a few feet away, watching them. He was about to turn and walk away when Cyrana noticed him. "Hi Larry!"

"Oh, hi," he said.

"Hey Larry, you want to sit with us?" Missy asked. She couldn't get the image of Larry lying in the construction worker's shithole out of her mind. "C'mon."

Larry tentatively placed his lunch tray next to Charlie's. "My mom says I have to have a square dance party for my birthday," he blurted out. They all politely nodded and glanced at each other.

"That's bogus," said Aby. "If my mom did that, I'd–"

"It might be fun," said Faith, surprising the posse, not to mention Larry Dunn.

"Really?!" They'd never seen Larry even a little happy before, much less the ear-to-ear smile that was now on his face.

"I don't see why not," she said. "This would be a good chance for me to talk my mom into finally buying me some jeans."

"You think your dad will be there?" Peter asked. "I mean like, your mom and dad, and sister 'n' stuff?"

"My dad's going on a trip that whole week, but my mom will be there."

"Yeah, I guess it might be okay. It couldn't be any worse than cotillion." Peter glanced at Faith, who was the only person who knew that he actually loved cotillion. They'd both been going every Tuesday night since the beginning of sixth grade. Her mom insisted she go to learn more about the rituals of the secular world; she didn't want her daughter to become alienated and, God forbid, follow recent spate of teenagers from the Howdy-Doo! Resurrection Church who had recently joined the more radical Howdy-Doody-Doo! Resurrection Church.

"You mean you all might really come?!" Larry asked.

"I'll go if everybody else is going," Aby said. Around the table, one nod led to another.

"So, we should cowboy shirts and like, hats?" Cyrana had never been to a square dance and hoped there might be some fiddle music.

"Sure, that would be great," Larry looked at Cyrana, making sure to keep a big smile on his face.

* * *

Faith's new Levis were starched hard. Her mother had ironed the legs with a forever-crease down the front, creating a sandpapery leg-torture device worthy of the most ardent religious self-flagellant. Getting into them brought tiny tears to Faith's eyes. It was true that her mother had never ironed any of the soft cotton clothes she made for her husband and children, but Faith was not convinced that her mother's lack of ironing experience was the only reason for the almost unbearable chafing she felt with every step. As the posse stood on Larry Dunn's porch, she silently admonished herself for not attending more closely to the most basic Howdy-Doo! tenet: *Watch out! God might give you what you ask for.*

Larry answered the door in his own stiff pants and a brand-new purple cowboy shirt that featured an embroidered greenish-yellowish-brownish rectangle that gave the impression that he'd recently thrown up. The shirt's large mother-of-pearl buttons detracted only slightly from the orange-on-yellow polka-dotted bandana that was knotted snuggly around his neck. He seemed taller than usual because he was, thanks to the two-inch heels on his shiny black cowboy boots and the white Stetson that added another six inches. His mother stood behind him beaming, compounding concerns of the entire posse that Larry might spontaneously combust out of sheer embarrassment.

"Hello, children! Don't you all look so cute?! Say 'hello' Larry, don't be shy! Come in, come in!" Larry mumbled a greeting.

"Hello ma'am, I'm very pleased to meet you." Aby, as always, was the first to speak. "My name is Arlen Yates, ma'am." The posse filed into the house, trying to mimic Aby's practiced introduction, with varying degrees of success.

"And who have we here?" asked Mrs. Dunn as Cyrana entered.

"I'm Cyrana Lewis Johnson, ma'am."

"Oh yes, you were the little fiddler in the play. You are so talented for a, uh, an eighth grader, aren't you?"

"Thank you, ma'am."

"Well, I so enjoyed you playing, honey."

"Thank you very much, ma'am."

"And you're new to the neighborhood, too. How nice for you!"

"Her daddy's a doctor at Methodist Hospital." Mr. Dunn appeared from the kitchen. "You live over on Whitewood, isn't that right?"

Peter looked at Mr. Dunn and then at Aby.

"Yes sir." Cyrana wasn't liking all this attention.

"Well, that's fine. I hope you and your family are enjoying our neighborhood," Mr. Dunn smiled. "And you two fine gentlemen–you are?"

"Hello, sir, I'm very pleased to meet you. My name is Arlen Yates." As soon as he extended his hand to shake, he regretted it. He and Peter had escaped the wrath of Mr. Dunn after ringing his doorbell, but they were still wary. For all Aby knew, Mr. Dunn would crush the tiny bones in his hand until he got a confession out of him right then and there. Mr. Dunn enveloped Aby's hand in his giant paw and gave it a firm, gentle shake.

"I respect a young man with a firm handshake." He turned to Peter, and extended his hand. "You must be–"

"Peter Phelt, sir." Mr. Dunn seemed even larger than Peter remembered.

"You're not from around here either, as I recall."

"We moved from Alabama last year."

"Al-a-ba-ma. I bet you miss it, huh?"

"I guess," Peter said. "But I like it here, too."

"Well, aren't you agreeable? You better watch out or you'll grow up to be a politician, son!"

"Alright, everyone downstairs! The rest of the kids are already here!" said Mrs. Dunn. "There's a table down there to put your presents on. Larry, honey, show them the way."

The paneled basement was the size of the entire house. In the far corner was a ping-pong table and in another, a full bar with eight stools and an oak floor-to-ceiling cabinet with a centerpiece mirror. Among the display of liquor bottles were pictures of A.J. Foyt, Emeline Pigott, and Geronimo. The room was dominated by a built-in two-corner couch with Indianapolis 500-themed cushions, and a large table crowded with presents and a birthday cake festooned with tiny balloons and square-dancing action figures. In the center of the basement, a large parquet dance floor featured multicolored streamers and a mirrored disco ball suspended from the low ceiling.

The posse stood wide-eyed and a little jealous. Some of their dads had done a little work on their basements, maybe walled off the laundry area or set up a work bench for their tools, but this place was amazing. Seeing what was hidden beneath Larry Dunn's house made Charlie Burris wonder what was under all the other houses in the neighborhood, or the world even.

"Well, this is it," Larry said.

Most of the other kids at the party had settled into playing ping-pong, or Uno. Bobby Rappaport and Rhonda Sterling, the only two eighth-graders who had already kissed, locked lips in the corner.

"Here comes my mom!" Larry hard-whispered across the room. The couple listened to the steps coming down the stairs and nonchalantly sat up. Rhonda gave Larry a little wink just like an adult might, he thought. It was funny, she sat in front him in science class, but she still seemed a lot older than he was—maybe because she was already making out.

"Larry, are you and your friends ready to square dance?" This day could not possibly end too soon for Larry Dunn. The basement door opened and Mr. Dunn's big, shiny black boots trotted down the stairs. He strode across the basement with a John Travolta gait, ready to show these youngsters exactly what it meant to be a card-carrying member of the International Association of Square Dance Callers.

Hands on hips, he clog-danced his way to the caller's corner and grabbed the microphone next to a tape deck and speakers. Mrs. Dunn corralled the children into boy-girl groups of four, all the while adoring her twinkle-toed giant of a husband.

All join hands and circle to the south,
get a little moonshine in your mouth!
All join hands and circle up wide,
spread right out like an old cowhide!

Mr. Dunn sustained his marionette-like clogging, encouraging the young dancers to keep up. His wife prodded and jostled them toward their next move.

All join hands in a great big ring,
circle 'round and 'round with the dear little thing,
All jump up and never come down,
swing your pretty girl 'round and 'round.

If three aliens from the planet Tralfamadore suddenly appeared in the Dunn's basement after decades of observing American popular culture, they would agree that this Earthling ritual was precisely what they'd been looking for on Earth: the perfect Hee Haw/Saturday Night Fever hybrid. They would immediately report their findings to their superiors, hoping it would mean they could finally stop watching television.

Each tune on Mr. Dunn's mixtape flowed seamlessly into the next, his every movement anticipating the next variation in tempo as he nodded the upcoming beat to the children song after song. The kids laughed, trying to keep up with his dance directions; he seemed to have an endless supply of two-line calls.

Pull off your shoes, roll up your socks,
swing those girls till you rattle their hocks!
Randy and Andy and Billy and Bob,
want Lucy and corn on the cob."

Faith's Levi's were no longer so uncomfortable, having been danced into submission. She and Peter conspired to hold hands more than was required by Mr. Dunn's call-outs, and sometimes brushed up against each other just a little during the transitions. Feeling the small of Faith's back was thrilling for Peter; Tuesday night cotillions allowed him only two short dances with her and the monitors made sure that "the gentleman's hand is always placed in the middle of the lady's back," and no lower.

Missy and Aby were in another foursome, having an uncontrollable giggling fit. They'd suddenly explode into laughter, losing what little rhythm they'd established since their last outburst. The other two kids in their foursome were very serious about their square dancing, and the boy kept stopping and staring at them with utter disdain. The dramatic pose he struck in the middle of the dance floor made Aby and Missy laugh all the harder.

Here we go, on the heel and toe!
Pickaninny, pickaninny don't be slow!

Missy and Aby cracked up at the word, pickaninny. It reminded them of a Dr. Seuss story they'd read as little kids, and the funny words he made up, like "murky-mooshy" and "grickily gructus."

Swingin' high and swingin' low.
Shuffle on now, and away you go.

After almost an hour, Mr. Dunn clogged onto the dance floor and weaved his way through the children as the music played, dancing with each couple for a few steps. He twirled his wife around, danced across the room and skipped up the basement stairs. To Larry's utter amazement, all the kids were clapping and cheering. "Your dad is so cool, Larry!" Faith said. "My dad wouldn't dance around like that in a million years."

"Yeah, he's something!" Peter wiped the perspiration from his forehead.

"Sodas and snacks, children!" Mrs. Dunn busied herself on the business side of the bar, setting out chips and Cheetos, Larry's favorite ever since he learned that there was a job called "Cheetos Quality Control Inspector." His dad knew one of them from Frankfort who was part of a four-person panel that got to inspect and taste freshly-made Cheetos every four hours. If they didn't taste exactly like the perfect Cheetos sent from Frito-Lay headquarters in Texas, they'd throw them out and go on to the next bag. It was the coolest job in the world, except that you had to wear a beard net.

Peter nudged Larry, "Where's your bathroom? I gotta pee like a derby dog."

"Upstairs. It's on the other side of the kitchen."

Peter took two steps at a time up to the ground floor and opened the door. He was startled to see Mr. Dunn leaning against the kitchen sink, staring at him.

"So, are you the one who thinks my boy's a nigger?" He walked across the room and quietly closed the door behind Peter. If Peter ever used that word, his parents would ground him for life, but there was no way Mr. Dunn would ever believe that.

"I didn't call him that."

"Just like you and Yates don't go around ringing doorbells in the middle of the night?

"I'm sorry, we–"

"So, you don't think he's a nigger?"

"No, of course not! I–"

"Cause there's only one nigger in my house right now, and you brought her." Peter felt the basement door open into his back.

"Oh, sorry. Hi!" Cyrana smiled. "Mrs. Dunn said I could use the bathroom."

"Well you sure can, sweetheart. It's right over there." Mr. Dunn motioned across the room. "The switch is on the left."

"Thank you, sir." Cyrana walked across the room into the bathroom.

"She's a polite one, don't you think?"

The only thing Peter could think about now was tidal wave of urine pounding on the door of his urethra. He recalled that Mr. Dunn had literally scared the piss out him as Aby and he were hiding in the bushes that night. "Yes, she's very polite."

"Where you from in Alabama?"

"Goshen."

"Is that right?"

"Yes, sir, it's halfway to Enterprize from Montgomer–."

"I know exactly where Alabama's Goshen is," Mr. Dunn backed Peter against the door, extended his arm to the wall, and leaned in close enough to whisper. "I also know that you and I will have another conversation, if you haven't learned something here today about niggers and doorbells."

The toilet flushed. Mr. Dunn moved his arm across Peter's back, and walked him to the center of the kitchen as Cyrana came out of the bathroom.

"You're doing some fine promenade twirls, young man! You just make sure you always know what your next step should be, and I think you'll do fine," he counseled Peter with a warm pat on back. "Keep an eye on that Bobby Rappaport–he's really got some moves!"

Mr. Dunn flashed a big smile at Cyrana. "Everything come out okay?"

* * *

Faith and Peter had different classes right before the noon break, so whoever got to the lunch line first would always wait for the other. They liked talking to each other away from the rest of the posse sometimes; the cacophony of the cafeteria surrounded them like a cave where they could be alone for a few minutes until everybody else arrived.

"When I grow up, I'm going to write story about seven sisters who go to a school to become wizards and fight evil with magic." Peter loved it when Faith got real excited about something. She glowed.

"No boys?" Peter clacked the hard-plastic tray on the stainless-steel bars in front of the displayed food, sliding it past the corn and something that reminded him of Exorcist vomit. "Tater tots, please."

"They're too many books about boys. I want to write about girls." Faith always brought her lunch, but her parents did allow her to buy a low-fat milk.

"Yeah, I guess," Peter said. "Alright, hot dogs!"

"It'll be about me and my sisters and Missy too maybe, but that would make eight and it should really be seven. It's a magical number."

"You know magic?"

"Sure, I know a lot about magic. The Bible's full of it."

"Really?" Peter was skeptical, but knew he'd be convinced by Faith who easily quoted the Bible whenever she thought it was needed. She didn't overdo it, but she didn't underdo in either. "Like what?" He popped a tater tot into his mouth when the cafeteria lady wasn't looking.

"Well, seven's a magic number for warlocks and witches, and it's used 735 times in the Bible. Fifty-four times in the Book of Revelation, alone."

"Revelation. That's like, when everything ends and we all go to heaven, right? Two chocolate milks please."

"Skim, please," Fait said. "It's about the Apostle John, who has all these visions about Jesus, who's really angry because most people don't believe in him anymore. Everything that John sees is in the future, like he's time-traveling, so it's really cool. Jesus decides—in the future—to send his arch enemy Satan to punish all the bad Christians." They headed to the back corner of the cafeteria to stake out seats for the rest of the posse. "But 144,000 will be saved, and they'll all fly up into the air, and actually meet Jesus and God."

"Fly into the air?" Peter loved this kind of stuff.

"Yeah. And 144,000 divided by 7 is 20,571.42 and if you add 2, 5, 7, 1, 4 and 2, and divide again by 7, you get three—the Father, Son and Holy Ghost." Faith reached into her lunchbox. "I can't believe I got another cheese sandwich."

"That's amazing. And you believe all that?"

"Sure, it's the best story ever. And there's this part where John sees a dead lamb, but it's really alive, and it has seven eyes and seven horns." Faith looked at her sandwich. "I hate this kind of cheese and she always sneaks some tomato on it. Like, I'm not going to notice?"

"Want a tater tot?" Peter offered without noticing he'd eaten all of them.

"No, thanks. My Sunday school teacher said that seven is the 'foundation of God's Word' just like the letter 'e' is most important letter in English. If you don't have an 'e,' you don't have anything because you couldn't spell a bunch of words. He said that even though 'e' is the fifth letter of the alphabet, if you divide six into the number of letters in the entire alphabet and add the remainder to five, 'e' is actually the seventh letter of the alphabet."

"Wow." Peter was okay at math, but he was having trouble keeping up. He decided this must be algebra or something.

"Hey, we almost couldn't find you!" Aby said, flanked by the posse. The boys sat on one side of the table facing Faith, Missy and Cyrana. "It's Friday! What's everybody doing for the weekend?"

In unison the girls said, "we're having a sleepover."

"Cool, we should do that too," Aby looked at Charlie and Peter. "What do you say?"

"I'm grounded," Charlie said matter-of-factly as he took a big bite out of the veggie burger his mother packed for him. "Yeah, after Larry's party, I just mentioned to my mom that Mr. Dunn seemed 'a little crazy' with his dancing and stuff. I didn't mean anything by it, but then *she* got crazy and said I should never call anyone crazy even if I was just kidding, because they might really be crazy!"

"I think he *is* a little crazy," Cyrana glanced at Peter. "I mean, he seems nice enough, but he's just creepy."

"Yeah," Peter said. "At least we won't have to see him again. I mean he never comes to school stuff or anything."

"I'm staying away from him, that's for sure," she said.

"It's just you and me then, for the sleepover, Aby," Peter said. "But I'm not coming to your house. Speaking about crazy moms, you think yours will let you spend the night at my house?"

"Don't worry about her, I'll be there."

* * *

Peter felt the rush of a high-pitched wave in the core of his abdomen as he lay on the bed. And then another, more intense this time as his body involuntarily rolled with the sensations. For a second, he almost forgot where he was, as the light-headedness and pressure in his penis intensified.

"What would you do next?" Aby asked, embracing his best friend in the bed.

"I don't know," Peter said through his own shallow breathing. "This maybe, if she'd let me."

He gently placed his hand on Aby's hip. The skin was so soft, his fingers nearing the dimple of his friend's ass.

"Me, too," Aby breathed hard against Peter's cheek. "That's exactly what I'd do."

"What's up, guys?" called Jake Phelt, coming up the stairs toward the bedroom. "It's almost 9 o'clock!" he said, opening the door. "*X-Files* is almost on. You two copping out or you still want to watch?"

Under the covers, the two quickly separated and then re-engaged in a wrestling frenzy. Peter rolled off the bed and hit the floor with a thud.

"Way to go, Aby, don't let that sissy push you around!" Jake smile.

"Thanks a lot, Dad," Peter said as he stood, adjusting his pajamas. "Mom home yet?"

"Bridge night. Popcorn's on. Show starts in five."

Peter walked to the closet for his robe and returned to the bed. They could hear Dr. Phelt's footsteps going down the stairs. "You think they do this? Y'know, Missy and Faith?"

Aby laid back in the bed. "You mean pretend like they're time travelling to different planets and goofing around? Why not—they're best friends like us."

"But, y'know..." Peter hesitated.

" 'Y'know' what?" Aby said, springing from the bed.

"Like, me pretending you're Faith, and—"

"Sure, I guess."

"You won't tell anybody, though—not Charlie or anybody—right?"

"Sure. C'mon, let's go get some popcorn!"

* * *

"HAUN! HAUN!" That's what the sound preceding the morning announcements sounded like to Peter. To Aby, it sounded more like "WAUL! WAUL!" For Cyrana it was an A-440 "AOUN." Charlie said it sounded like the Tibetan deep-chant his brother did sometimes for fun.

"HAUN! HAUN!" "Good morning students excelling at Clemens Vonnegut Junior High School! This is your princi-PAL, Mr. Button. On this day in 1944, Lithuanian poet Jurgis Baltrušaitis died and was buried in Montrouge Cemetery in Paris."

In Miss Prophet's homeroom Cyrana glanced at Charlie and Aby, and nodded. All students had to play Mr. Button's *Fake Fact?* game each morning by indicating on their game card whether they thought the "fact" was true or false. The student with the most correct answers at the end of the year won a two-night stay for their entire family at French Lick, courtesy of the P.T.A. After the award ceremony, all students received a signed copy of *Mr. Button's Fake Fact?*, a compendium of the year's truth.

"The menu for today is corn dogs, cottage cheese and peaches. There will be *no* catsup or mustard packets today because of yesterday's incident." Mr. Button paused to let that startling piece of news sink in; he could bring down the hammer when necessary.

"Part four of the 'Just Say No to Everything' presentation will take place at 1 o'clock in the cafeteria for all grades. And no, you may not 'just say no' to attending this event." Eyes rolled eyes throughout the school.

"Tryouts for both girls and boys Vervets double-dodge teams will take place all week during gym classes. Go, Vervets!

And finally, the birthdays for this month are Paul Ackerman–December 5th, Jimmy and Mark Palmer–December 6th, George Kellogg–December 7th..."

Peter cringed, knowing his name would be read at any moment. He liked his birthday okay, but he hated birthday parties and people saying "happy birthday" all day long and making a big deal out of it. He'd been able to keep his birth date secret since the move to Indianapolis, but Mr. Buttons decided that this year he'd start a new tradition, announcing all student birthdays at the beginning of each month. He was big on new traditions.

"Ellie Peters–December 10th, Charlie Burris–December 14th..." Charlie clasped his hands together and shook them above his head as if he'd just won the heavyweight boxing championship. Peter smiled, wishing he felt that way about his birthday.

"Brenda Throckmorton, December 15th, Arlen Yates and Peter Phelt, December 16th." Peter and Aby turned and looked at each other flabbergasted, and simultaneously broke into a Charlie Burris-style celebration.

"Well, that explains why your folks moved to Indianapolis," Aby said as they were all walking to their next class. "So we could party-hardy together on our bodacious birthday!"

Peter was relieved that the burden of the day would be shared with Aby. Even better than that, Peter, Charlie and Aby decided to celebrate all their birthdays on December 16; it was a Friday so it would be perfect. If the whole posse could talk their parents into it, they'd all go to Steak and Shake right after school, see *Stargate* at the Nora Theater, and then hang out at the Y until it closed at 10.

At dinner that night, Aby cheerily made the case for a three-way celebration to his parents; he knew it was going to be a hard sell, especially to his mother. "You'll never guess what great thing happened in school today!"

"Nobody's science project blew up?" Elvira Yates asked with a raised eyebrow and smile. It was rare and a good omen when she made a joke about anything related to school. Aby laughed over-appreciatively.

"No, mom. Peter and I have the same birthday!" Silence. Aby looked at his parents. "We were both born on December 16!"

"Isn't that something?" Mr. Yates finally said.

"Oh my, what a coincidence!" said Elvira. This was it, she thought–the initial unraveling of the secret they'd kept since Pastor-Lawyer Agane first contacted them in 1991. The parents had done nothing to prepare their sons for the truth since the Phelts' move to Indianapolis, and now the boys might find out on their own; Arlen knew he was born in Baltimore and there was no reason to think that Peter didn't know the same.

"And guess what else, Mom?" Elvira held her breath.

"Charlie, Peter and me are all going to have our birthdays on the 16th!"

"That's so great!" his mother said, relieved.

Aby couldn't put his finger on it exactly, but his mother was acting a little strange. She had not corrected his "Charlie, Peter and me" with a stern "and I," and she was being uncommonly agreeable. As far as Aby could recall, she had never thought anything was "so great!" He did consider that this might be a trap, but he decided to go in for the kill just the same.

"So, next Friday, can Charlie and Missy come home with me on the bus, and then we'll walk to Steak and Shake, and then see *Stargate* at the theatre on 86th, and then we'll go to the Y and you can pick me up there at 10?" Pleased that he'd gotten it all out in one breath, Aby nonchalantly herded some peas onto his fork.

"Uh, yes." Elvira said, as Mr. Yates nodded his agreement. "That will be fun for everyone. Yes, good."

* * *

Elvira Yates and Phyllis Phelt were the first parents to arrive at the YWCA on the night of the three-way birthday. Phyllis read the bulletin board in the common room, still bundled in her wool cap, scarf and overcoat. Being a relatively recent transplant from the south, she was still trying to get the swing of winter clothing. It was 29 degrees outside with snow flurries, but many people wore only sweaters or light jackets. Some had hats, but certainly no gloves or big warm coats. Elvira noticed her because Phyllis because she stood out, dressed so sensibly in this frozen tundra.

"Hello, Phyllis." Elvira offered her hand.

"Hello. Elvira." Phyllis took her hand and held it. "I'm happy to see you."

"Me too." Elvira took a deep breath. "Let's sit."

"It's hard to imagine it's been seven years." Phyllis paused, then chuckled. "Jake told about the sprinkler incident."

"Oh, yes. I was very upset, I hope I didn't–"

"Are you kidding? I laughed so hard when he and Peter told the story. He was livid!"

"I'm sorry, I–"

"Well, he deserved it if you ask me! He never thinks, he just does. He's a good man, but impulsive."

"He sounds like Arlen," Elvira said, "the life of the party."

"Exactly." They sat silently for a few seconds.

"Sometimes I think the strangest thing about this, is that our husbands were in the same bar, and we were in the same hospital room." Phyllis said. "I mean, the nurse mixing up Arlen and Peter was a *human* thing, but the rest of it's...I don't know what. We're not all that religious, but it's almost like–"

"Fate?" Elvira suggested.

"Maybe. I don't really believe in fate, but I don't believe in coincidence either."

"So, what are you left with?"

Phyllis hesitated, though she knew precisely what she was left with. It was the same thing all of her clients were left with at the end of a therapy session, or when they walked out of a rehab center, jail or divorce court. "Reality," she said. "It doesn't really matter why we're here–we just are."

"There's no denying that." Elvira did believe in fate and knew that her god had engineered this moment for a reason. That knowledge had lessened the stabbing guilt she'd felt over the years for leaving Baltimore Memorial Hospital without her natural son. Phyllis, on the other hand, did not have the comfort of knowing why she was sitting here with this stranger.

"I'm glad they're best friends," Phyllis said.

"Thank God for that. Left to us, they would never have gotten to know each other."

"And the boys had such a good time spending the night together at the beginning of the year. They should do that again sometime."

"Yes, absolutely," Elvira said.

"I think the boys might be scheming to have a sleepover at your house tonight."

"Well, let's do that, then." Two weeks ago, Elvira's 37.6 trillion cells–she was slightly overweight–would have collided in a fit of chemotaxis, not knowing the details of Arlen's every scheme and secret plan, but that wasn't so important anymore. She had one priority now: help Peter and Arlen forge a strong friendship. "I'll take the boys home from here. Peter can borrow some pajamas and a toothbrush."

* * *

"How's the ice cream?" Elvira cheerily asked into the rearview mirror.

"Good, Mom," Aby looked at Peter and shrugged. He had no idea why his mom was in such a great mood.

"I'm sorry Charlie couldn't come for the sleepover."

"Yeah, his mom's making him pick up litter on the highway by the Bahá'í Center in Zionsville tomorrow morning. He's not sure if it's a litter-thing or a religious-thing, but he has to go anyway."

"Well, volunteering is good and God knows there's too much litter in the world. Do you do anything like that, Peter? Arlen doesn't. Maybe you can inspire him!" Elvira ricocheted a toothy grin at them.

"No ma'am, not really," Peter said. "But my dad's a member of "Hoosiers in the Alamo" and they have a pancake dinner twice a year to raise money for poor kids in south Texas."

"Isn't that interesting? Arlen, isn't that interesting?"

"Yeah, I helped out last time they had it," Peter preempted Aby's wisecrack, whatever it was going to be. "Maybe Arlen could help next time?" Peter nudged Aby to agree.

"Yeah, sure, that would be great." Aby rolled his eyes, though the effect was lost in the darkness of the backseat.

"Here we are," Elvira announced pulling into the driveway. "Mr. Yates will be so happy to see you both!"

By the time the boys were settled in Arlen's bunk beds it was almost midnight.

"That was pretty slick when you moved to the back row of the theatre," Aby said.

"Yeah, but that was Faith's idea, not mine," Peter confessed.

"So, did you kiss her, scaredy cat?"

"No. I don't know, I wanted to—it's just that, I mean, where?

"On the mouth!"

"No stupid, where? Where would I get a chance to do that?"

Aby couldn't believe what he was hearing. He hopped off the top bunk and sat at the foot of Peter's bed. "You were at the movies! In the back row! That's where almost everybody in the world gets their first kiss. You were in the perfect spot!"

"Yeah, yeah, I know. I feel so stupid. I did lean on the armrest and our shoulders were touching. And then I realized she was holding my hand and—"

"And then?"

"And then, nothing. I froze. I didn't know what to do next. I didn't want to just start kissing her. I mean, I did, but...it's just hard to make the next move."

"I get it," Aby said. "I was lucky, I guess. Missy kinda kissed me first, last summer. Neither of us knew what to do next and it was kind of silly. But then we finally did it again after Larry's birthday."

"Really? And you didn't tell me?"

"She made me promise, sorry. But yeah, my mom was giving her a ride home and she had to run into the Safeway, but we stayed in the car, in the back seat. I wanted to kiss her, so I put my arm around her and all the sudden we were kissing! I mean a real lip kissing, and our mouths were open some, and I felt her tongue with my tongue, a little bit."

"Yeah, that's what I want to do," Peter was flush, imagining a moment like that with Faith.

"It was amazing. You'll get there!"

"I know. I had this dream about kissing Faith on Tuesday night. It was so real. I could feel my hands on her shoulders and her mouth. And we just started to kiss, but then I woke up and

I was–I was wet, but it wasn't piss. I didn't wet the bed or anything."

"You had a cum!" Aby explained.

"A what?"

"A cum–man, doesn't your brother tell you anything?"

"No, he's clueless," Peter said. "How do you know all this stuff?"

"Charlie tells me."

"Did he have a cum?"

"Yeah."

"Have you?" Peter pressed.

Aby hesitated. "Yeah, twice."

"Twice? What were you dreaming about?"

"Nothing. You can make yourself have a cum whenever you want!"

Peter felt like he'd just entered a vast hidden playroom of a house he'd lived in forever. "When were yours?"

"The first time was over the summer and then after Larry's party," Aby said.

"That was eons ago! I thought we told each other everything!"

"Sorry, it was just a couple months ago and it's kind of embarrassing, sort of. Jeez, what am I going to say? 'Hey Peter, my johnson got hard, so I got some of my mom's hand cream and stroked it up and down until I had a cum?' "

"Really?" Peter was riveted. "And then the liquid came out, right?" Aby nodded. "How did you know when to stop? Did it hurt when it came out?"

"No, it comes out and then you're done. You don't really want to do it anymore."

"Really?

"Yeah, there's nothing to be afraid of."

Peter tried to take it all in. He remembered he was breathing a little hard when he woke up from the dream about Faith, but was immediately horrified because he thought he'd wet his bed.

Now he understood that the wetness was a cum, so that was okay. And he could have another one whenever he wanted. Still, he was apprehensive.

"Do you just do it in your bed?" he asked Aby.

"Yeah, the first time I didn't have a towel or anything and it got all over the place. But the last time, I used a big towel and it was fine." There was a long silence.

"You want to do it now?" asked Peter. "I mean, not together. You do it in your bunk and I'll do it here."

Aby realized it was going to be impossible to say no to Peter at this point. They weren't being homos or anything, he thought, and he figured that Charlie's brother probably did the same thing with his buddies. "Okay, yeah. If you want to." Aby walked to the bathroom and to get towels and the cream he'd used last time. He tossed a towel at Peter.

"Put out your hand," Aby said. He squirted some lotion into Peter's palm. "That ought to be plenty." He climbed the ladder to the top bunk, laid back and pulled his pajamas to his knees. He put some cream into his palm. From experience, he knew this wouldn't take long.

Without thinking, Aby glanced toward his dresser mirror and saw Peter's reflection. He had already started. As Aby stroked himself, he heard a sudden muffled groan and felt the bed jerk as Peter came. And then he came again, it seemed like. Aby felt his own orgasm come in waves and, for a few seconds, share its rhythm with Peter's own ecstasy. "Ahh!" Peter yelled out.

"Everybody tucked in?" the door opened. The bright light from the hallway was only partially obstructed by Mr. Yates's silhouette. Both naked boys, mid-orgasm, froze their every movement for one-half second. Aby folded himself into the tiniest fetal position he could manage. He heard Peter shift in the lower bunk. After a few seconds, his father quietly shut the door.

"Jesus, Joseph and Mary." Aby whispered. There was no response from below. "Peter? Peter?"

In order, here are the thoughts that popped into Aby's sleepy brain when he woke up the next morning: 1) It's Saturday! 2) Dad caught Peter and me having a cum last night, 3) I wish I was picking up trash with Charlie at the Bahá'í Center right now. Trying not to jostle the bed, he positioned himself to look at the mirror to see if Peter was awake. The bed was neatly made, as if no one had slept there. Aby looked at the clock; it wasn't even 7:30. He hurried down the latter and looked in the bathroom. Nothing.

He dressed and went down the stairs, listening for noises in the kitchen. A chair scooched to the table and a coffee cup was placed on the tile table top, but there were no voices. He embraced his energetic-upbeat-oblivious self and entered. "Good morning!"

"Good morning, sunshine!" His mother turned from the sink and smiled broadly. "Sounds like you and Peter had a great time last night!"

"What?"

Mr. Yates, silent, looked over his coffee cup from the table.

"I mean, yeah." Aby turned toward the living room. "Where's Peter?"

"Early riser. He was up and at 'em over an hour ago," his father said. "He decided to walk home. You want a bagel? Your mother got bagels."

"He's such a nice boy. He said he made the bed, and he brought down the towel he used last night and put it right in the dirty clothes hamper." Elvira kissed Aby on the cheek. "Cinnamon-raisin or plain?"

* * *

There was still a full week before Christmas vacation but there wasn't much schoolwork to do. Tests were over and homeroom periods were extended to four hours, attributable to bureaucratic stratagems understood by nary a student or parent.

Last year, that made sense because preparations for Mrs. Greenhaw's holiday pageant consumed the last two weeks before break, and everyone rehearsed during the long homeroom period; but she was gone now. The only extracurricular activity the new music teacher came up with was a music memory contest, which Cyrana won last week. The rest of the posse entered too but they, as Cyrana teased them, "couldn't tell Twinkle, Twinkle from a Brahms concerto." None of them protested, because they were pretty sure she was correct.

Peter was glad to be stuck in Miss Turnbuckle's homeroom without the posse. He just wanted to get through the last week of classes and go to Alabama for Christmas to visit relatives. He'd tried to act sick on Monday morning, and then again on Tuesday, but his mother had taken his temperature and found it to be 98.6 degrees. Game over.

He was able to convince his dad into taking him to school for a couple days to avoid the morning bus ride with Aby, Missy and Cyrana. He wouldn't mind seeing Cyrana so much, but he cringed at the thought of talking to Aby or Missy.

He sat in the front row of Turnbuckle's class pretending to read, but listening to the incessant self-talk that had consumed his thoughts ever since Friday night. Through the dim light in Aby's room, he'd met Mr. Yates' eyes and, for a second, lay still, naked. He couldn't move. Mr. Yates looked away as Peter then covered himself.

Aby tells Missy everything, Peter said to himself. He tells Charlie everything too. They've been best friends since they were little. Why wouldn't he tell Charlie?

"Ralph!" Miss Turnbuckle interrupted Peter's noisy solitude. "This is your last warning. If you don't stop bothering Janie, you are off to the office, mister. If you have nothing else to do, review chapter three of the Protocols of Conduct manual."

Peter's silent chatter continued. And he told me that he kissed Missy, even though he promised her he wouldn't tell a soul. I'm so stupid. I can't believe I went along with that. Charlie and Aby are probably having a real fine laugh right now.

After homeroom, Peter went to the nurse's office and peeked in the door to make sure she was there. When no one was looking, he put three fingers deep into his mouth and pressed on the back of his tongue. He grabbed the door handle as he leaned into the office and projectile-vomited his trail mix and milk breakfast onto the floor, splattering three snotty sixth-graders who were actually sick. One little princess in a beautiful, Christmassy dress, felt a droplet of vomit on her cheek and immediately added her own breakfast to the slippery floor. The other two kids retched and threatened hurls of their own, but managed to contain their innards, as the nurse came out from the inner office.

Launching into uber-Florence Nightingale mode, she calmed the younger students, produced a mop out of thin air it seemed, and began cleaning the floor. "We're going to have to call your parents to come and take you home, Peter," she said, almost apologizing. "You may not be able to come back for the rest of the week, honey."

Big Dick and the BVM 2:6.1   December 25, 1998 A.D.

PETER LOVED CHRISTMAS IN GOSHEN. He swore he could recall every detail of that first Christmas in 1985 when the Phelts inaugurated the holiday routine they would follow for years. The first Saturday after Thanksgiving, they always visited Aunt K's to fresh-cut a perfect Walter pine from her forest. They decorated it that weekend and started going to Methodist church regularly so they wouldn't stand out so much when they showed up at the packed Christmas Eve service. They always had canned oyster stew before the service and after they got back, Peter and Phillip were allowed to open one small present. On Christmas morning, after all the gifts were opened, Jake Phelt made chorizo and eggs, Battle of San Jacinto-style.

Very little of that would happen this year because Christmas marked eight months since a killer tornado sent to their heavenly reward 20 Alabama Goshenites, and rendered to kindling three churches. As devastating as it was, it was not a unique tragedy; another tornado had wreaked its own havoc on Indiana's Goshen in 1965 on a Palm Sunday 35 year ago.

After hearing of the horrible storm in his Goshen and subsequently learning about Goshen, Indiana, Jake Phelt experienced an added layer of connectedness to their friends and family in Alabama who felt the fury of the storm. It was at times like these that Jake wished—yes, he wished it—that he believed in God, instead of being the conspiracy-theorizing, agnostic Area 51-er who would over-consider anything except the existence of God. He wished he could fathom the sublime grace of the Goshen Methodist minister who lost her 4-year old daughter that day and said, "Do not blame God. God has been with us throughout all of this. God did not make this happen." But he couldn't so, like an eco-tourist observing a Melanesian cargo cult, he compassionately witnessed his community make sense of the disaster and embrace, more than ever, their all-powerful god who neither caused nor prevented it.

The Phelts checked into the Motel 6 in Luverne, ten miles west of Goshen, warmed up two cans of oyster stew on a hotplate and divided them into four Styrofoam cups. Around nine o'clock they dressed up and went to the Land of Goshen Community Grace Church for the Christmas Eve Mosh. Even though it was a little less festive this year, the service was packed and the band rocked.

There would be no presents this year, so everyone slept in on Christmas morning; they decided to contribute what they would have spent on presents to the Crimson Cross rebuilding fund. After Grand Slams at Denny's they visited friends and family and listened to their stories about where they were when the tornado struck. That afternoon, the Phelts and half of Goshen converged at Big Dick's Adult Video Mega-pleXXX to see if the image of the Blessed Virgin Mary would re-appear on the parking-lot side of the building just like it had early Palm Sunday morning in 1984.

The glacial pace of the Vatican Miracle Commission to confirm the miraculous sighting of the Virgin Mary had been a conversation starter among Big Dick's patrons for the past 14 years. But, truth be told—and why not?—most other Goshenites had given up hope that the Roman Catholic Church would ever approve the application and supporting documentation submitted by Pastor Bobby Balaam to the Catholic Dioecesis Birminghamiensis in the spring of 1985. The initial application was immediately returned to him because he'd ignored the Papal Style Guide Encyclical guidance to define the acronym for Blessed Virgin Mary (BVM) upon first usage in each section of the document. Ever-persevering, he re-submitted the application in 1986, this time to the Archidioecesis Mobiliensis. The events leading up to the sighting were summarized thusly by Pastor Bobby in the corrected version:

> After being referred to as "Little Dick" since birth, Ricardo Cabeza Jr. used a substantial inheritance from his father to legally change his name to Big Dick Cabeza in 1973; he then employed his new moniker in the establishment of a chain of Alabamian porno video outlets.

> On April 12, 1984. three days after the grand opening of the Goshen flagship store, a young priest from neighboring Troy—who was saving souls at Big Dick's very early that Sunday morning—saw an image of the Blessed Virgin Mary (BVM) breastfeeding the baby Jesus on an exterior wall of the edifice. Immediately preceding the sighting, the priest was inside the store, undercover as it were, watching a video titled "Ooo Baby, Bless You!" with a busty 20-something breastfeeding the Pope on its cover.

The priest later stated to Vatican investigators: "the Holy Father wasn't wearing his cassock during most of the movie, but I could always tell it was him because of his hat. Do you think I really saw the BVM on the wall? Do you think God wanted to tell *me* something?"

"I do not know, my son," a Cardinal responded. "One cannot hope to fully comprehend the ways of our lord. What was the name of that video again?"

And so began the trials and tribulations to have validated by the Vatican, the sighting of Mary and the baby Jesus on Big Dick's wall. Protestant and Catholic, religious and secular alike prayed for the church's validation because a team of consultants guiding the town's lobbying efforts promised untold riches that would accompany the Vatican's confirmation of a miracle. They pointed to France's Our Lady of Lourdes, where Marian apparitions most certainly appeared in 1858. The first apparition was seen in in Lourdes in February 1858 by Bernadette Soubirous, a 14-year-old peasant girl who told her mother that a "lady" spoke to her in the cave of Massabielle while she was gathering firewood. Similar apparitions of the alleged "lady" were reported on seventeen occasions that year. In just four years Lourdes went from a sleepy village in the south of France to a regional economic powerhouse, and had since become the darling of venerating Popes, millions of pilgrims, and a tourist industry serving their every need.

But none of that had happened with Goshen's Marian apparition. The Archdiocese of Mobile conducted one interview with the priest and then unceremoniously archived Pastor Bobby's application materials.

And that was that, until that Palm Sunday in 1998. Weeks before, Big Dick had hired a sign company to erase all memory of the unfulfilling miracle by installing the initials of his Mega-pleXXX in huge one-foot thick letters on the parking lot wall where the Blessed Virgin Mary had appeared: B D A V M. He'd been counseled by a public relations firm in Montgomery that an acronym emblazoned across the wall was the way to go. Acronyms were "in" and acronyms that didn't spell out an actual word were "even more in," they'd advised. Using the initials for Big Dick's Adult Video Mega-pleXXX was their elegant solution.

He'd intended to do something with the wall for years but hadn't wanted to upset the religious folks in the community, many of whom were his regular customers. But it had been 14 years since the priest saw the image of the Virgin. There were a few believers in town who prayed at the wall every Palm Sunday and Christmas, but most Goshenites had forgotten the sighting, or never believed it in the first place.

The sign contractors worked the day before Palm Sunday, prepping the wall and laying out where exactly each letter would be positioned. They epoxied the gigantic letters in three rows: B D on top, A in the second row, V M on the bottom row. Big Dick admired the craftsmanship as he backed his car away from the wall that night after work. He'd had great hopes that Goshen would be the next Lourdes, but it was clear that it was not to be. He pulled out of the parking lot that night, relieved to be moving into the next apparition-free phase of his life.

Big Dick was sound asleep the next morning when the neighbor's bicycle crashed through the bay window of his den while thousands of objects, large and small, assailed the exterior walls of his three-story stucco. Every shingle was ripped from the roof; through the smashed windows of his home, 112 mile-per-hour winds rushed into his house and his lungs.

The F4 tornado's assault on Big Dick's now over-inflated balloon-of-a-house was four seconds old. For the next eternal two seconds he arched his back, desperately trying to expel the air from his body. The catastrophic internal pressure violently pushed outward against his ribcage and the ceiling and walls of the house. Big Dick wrenched opened his mouth in a silent scream, and widened his eyes in a futile attempt to discharge the agonizing pressure. One-half second before his lungs and house exploded, the brand new sign on the side of his beautiful store flashed through his mind and Big Dick knew everything would be alright.

Eight months later, on Christmas day, the police restricted vehicle traffic from those streets adjacent to Big Dick's Adult Video Mega-pleXXX. The Phelts were fortunate to find paid parking in someone's yard just ten blocks away. The hawkers were out in force, selling t-shirts emblazoned with BVM or BDAVM, with the D and the A crossed out. Another shirt showed two angels removing the D and the A from the side of the parking lot wall. Peter liked the one with a huge tornado carrying Big Dick and the letters A and D away forever. There were decorated neckties, bobble-heads and gimme caps, all intended to recreate the moment when the tornado made a direct hit on Big Dick's Adult Video Mega-pleXXX wall, leaving only the letters B, V and M. At long last, this was confirmation of the miracle–the 1984 apparition of the Blessed Virgin Mary on this sacred ground.

It took the Phelts 30 minutes to get within sight of the wall. A small boy with a widow's peak sat weeping on the curb, his father trying his best to console him.

"I miss Mama," he sobbed.

"She is with us, son," The man picked the boy up and joined the growing crowd inching its way toward Big Dick's parking lot.

"She is, Daddy? Can we see her?"

"Yes, we will see your sainted mother," his father reassured him. It broke Phyllis' heart to hear the man promise, "God is making miracles today."

The wall itself was pockmarked from the battering of the F4 winds, but the Styrofoam B, V and M were unscathed. This seeming anomaly was attributable, by those who gave it no religious meaning, to the fact that inexplicable things are the norm in violent tornadic events.

"Take the Spencer twins, for example," explained the atheist weather man on Channel 24. "When the tornado hit, they were swimming laps in the family pool. A bolt of lightning struck the water, hurling the girls out of the pool and onto the deck. Turns out they were just fine, except that each one was missing an eyebrow. Nobody thought that was a miracle; they just thought it was weird. Why is that wall any different?"

From the perspective of the insurance adjuster who arrived at Big Dick's on the Monday morning after Palm Sunday, the three undamaged letters didn't matter at all; they were simply items the insurer was not obligated to replace. The letters that did matter were the D and the A because they were gone, a verified corporate fact duly noted on the claim form signed by the executor of Big Dick's estate one week later.

The majority of Goshenites who came to Big Dick's immediately after the tornado on Palm Sunday didn't care about the D and the A. They just came to learn why the tornado devastated their town, demolished their churches, and killed their children. Why? As non-Roman Catholics, they'd not experienced the spiritual ecstasy their Catholic neighbors had in 1984 when they learned about the apparition of the Blessed Virgin Mary and, since then, had become dismissive of the young priest's claim. But now, the apparition and the tornado were linked. If there *was* a reason why that the tornado killed 20 Goshen innocents–a reason that would soothe the hearts of those left behind–they would find it on this wall.

Jake felt the dense crowd around him and looked back to see the shoulder-to-shoulder mass of humanity. It moved as one, surging toward the wall. He reached for Phyllis' hand and held it.

"Hold onto your brother, Phillip," he said to his eldest.

The multitude glommed onto itself, leaving each person with barely the space their feet had managed to claim. Bellies and breasts pressed against butts and backs. Jake squeezed Phyllis' hand, looking to make sure it was hers. The wall was like a deep-space black hole, its inexorable gravity quietly sucking in more and more people.

Jake tried but couldn't see how far they were from the edge of the throng. The sun beat down on the crowd, now captive of itself for two hours without water or a miracle.

The quiet was broken by a young woman nearby. She spoke softly, but Phyllis could hear the panic in her voice. "Please, I can't breathe."

And then from the very back, a male voice. "This is bullshit!"

Jake saw a raised fist near to the wall. "Yeah!"

"There's nothing here!" a woman shouted.

"Shut up!"

"You're an idiot! *You* shut up!"

The crowd became erratic, no longer just inching forward, pressing inward. There were jolts from the sides and front, punctuated with accusations amid shouted pleas to "be patient" and "love each other!" From the rear, the splat of a siren broke through the noise; the ocean of people moved forward like a tidal wave, crashing into the wall and echoing back into the throng.

"Go home!"

"Fucking Catholics!" The voice's anger was frightening. Phyllis looked to the front of the crowd, almost against the wall, and saw the boy with the widow's peak perched on the shoulders of the shouting man, who thundered aggrieved obscenities at everyone, anyone. He cursed the triumvirate: God, Big Dick and the Pope. He cursed himself and the emergency workers who didn't even try to remove the ceiling fan blade imbedded in his wife's head that morning. He knew she was dead and knew they needed to go rescue people who still had a chance to live, but neither mattered. There was a fan blade lodged four inches into her skull and her 2-year-old son was screaming at his mother to wake up. He cursed the crowd into silence.

"Daddy?" The boy pointed to the center of the mob where a woman in white hovered above the heads of the people. She had golden hair and lay peacefully on her back.

"Do you see her, Daddy?" The crowd strained to see where the boy was pointing. "Is it an angel?"

The exhausted man looked up at his son. "Yes, it's an angel. It's Mary." He took the boy from his shoulder-perch to hold him in his arms. "It's her. And she'll take care of Mama in heaven."

"She's here!" said a woman close by.

"Where?" asked another.

"She's over there, I think. The white!" someone called out.

"The Blessed Virgin Mary is here!" another cried out.

Over the next six months, the Vatican Miracle Commission would receive testimony from more than 200 people swearing they saw the Blessed Virgin Mary at Big Dick's Adult Video Mega-pleXXX on Christmas Day in 1998. The Phelts saw a stretcher-bound woman in respiratory distress being carefully transported above the heads of the crowd, but they were also deeply moved by the passionate recounting of those who saw Mary. By the time the Papal commission confirmed the apparition at Big Dick's one year later, the Phelts wouldn't be certain at all what they saw that day.

* * *

"What was it like when you saw her?" asked the Seventh.

Faith, her sisters, their parents and grandmother crowded around the Bountiful's large kitchen table staring at Peter. The events at Big Dick's had made the national news on Christmas night and, as soon as Peter arrived back in Indianapolis, he'd received a dinner invitation from Faith.

"Did she say anything?" Bathsheba pressed.

"Give him a chance to speak, Bath," scolded Faith.

Peter looked at Faith. He was so excited when he'd heard her voice on the phone. Her calling was no less a miracle than the

Blessed Virgin Mary in Goshen. Her parents would never allow her to call a boy, except maybe to discuss a miracle. The Phelts had only been home for a few minutes when the phone calls started. Local reporters wanted an interview, clergy wanted to pray with them, and a terminally ill man wanted to touch the hand of one of the Phelts. Phyllis wasn't thrilled that Peter would be grilled about Goshen by the Bountifuls, but let him go anyway.

"No, she didn't say anything." Peter didn't want to lie, but he didn't want to let them down either–but he hadn't seen the Blessed Virgin. He wasn't sure about other people, but he only saw a woman on the stretcher.

"Praise the resurrection. How close were you, son?" Mr. Bountiful leaned forward.

"It's hard to tell, sir. So much was happening, I–"

"Some people say they touched her," Bath said.

"That's true," Peter offered.

"You saw people touch her?"

"Yes, I mean, no. Some people said they touched her."

"Give the boy a rest now, Bathsheba. We can all talk to Peter more later, if he wants." Mrs. Bountiful reached across the table and patted Peter's hand. "Do you need anything else to drink, Peter?"

"No ma'am, I'm fine." He was relieved. "Thank you very much for dinner. It was delicious."

"Thank you dear, for sharing your testimony. Girls, you clean up; let's let Faith and Peter watch some TV. Faith, why don't you take Peter down to the basement?"

The basement was warm and cozy. "You want to watch something?" Faith asked, patting the seat beside her on a big leather couch. "Here, you do it," handing him the remote control.

"Sorry about Bathsheba. She can be a real brat sometimes." Faith smiled and took Peter's hand to show him how the controller worked. She moved a little closer and the blond hairs on his arm stood erect.

"She's alright," he managed to say. He desperately hoped that she didn't want to talk about Goshen any more.

"Did your parents take you out of school early for the break?"

"No. I got a bug or something and left school on Wednesday before break."

"Oh my god, were you in the nurse's office when that kid threw up on everybody?"

"What? No, I just had a headache. What kid?"

"Nobody knows, it was a seventh or eighth grader, I think. All the kids that got barfed on were sixth graders."

This was a sign that things were looking up, Peter thought. Maybe he wouldn't be "the kid who puked on everybody" when they all returned to school. "That sounds pretty bad," he said.

"Yeah." Faith wasn't showing Peter how the remote control worked, she was just holding his hand. She abruptly kissed his cheek lightly and lingered with her face against his. He turned his head and kissed her, but his mouth was dry and he didn't think he did it right. They parted awkwardly. She smiled encouragingly, and Peter touched her face.

"Did you find something to watch?" Mrs. Bountiful called from the top of the stairs. Peter and Faith moved two feet apart.

"Yes, Mother!" Faith grabbed the remote and clicked on the television. The theme to *The Fresh Prince of Bel-Air* boom-boxed through its tiny speakers. They looked at each other and smiled broadly.

"Missy says sometimes you and Aby make up stories about amazing adventures we all go on," she said coyly.

"What?"

"Yeah. They sounded fun!"

"What do you mean? What did she tell you?" His voice had an edge she'd not heard before.

"I don't know. Nothing. I didn't mean anything, I was just–"

"What else did she say?"

"About what, Peter?"

"About anything!" Peter stood up and looked around the room, deciding what to do next.

"Can we come down?" Faith's three youngest sisters asked from the top of the stairs.

"Peter, c'mon." Faith said softly, patting the couch beside her. "Come, sit here with me."

"I should go," he said.

* * *

"Peter!" Aby yelled from the back row of the Bus 2020. "There he is, the holy man of the hour!"

"Hey, Peter!" Cyrana grinned. She was sitting next to Faith but moved so Peter could sit there. He smiled at Faith and sat down. It had been three days since the fiasco at her house, three days beating himself up for being so paranoid and ruining the greatest moment of his life. He couldn't believe he did that to himself. One second he was kissing the most beautiful girl in the world and the next he wasn't–all because of his fear that Aby might tell Missy and Charlie, and Missy might tell Faith, and what if Charlie told Cyrana, blah, blah, blah. It was driving him so crazy, he'd put a thick rubber band on his wrist like his dad did when he was trying to quit smoking. Every time he thought of that night at Aby's, he snapped it hard to remind him to think of something else. It had worked pretty well the last couple of days.

"Hey Cyrana. Is that a new case?" Peter asked, hoping to forestall questions about Goshen or Christmas break. All that was in the past.

"Yeah, here, look!" She opened the large case on her lap. "My dad said we could rent it for a while to see if I like it. It's big enough for my violin *and* my viola."

"I'm not sure I even know the difference, but that's cool."

"She's going to be famous," Faith said reaching back to touch the plush interior. "That's so soft. I love the purple."

"Why rent?!" Aby chimed in. "Maybe Peter can put in a good word with the Virgin Mary and it will be yours!"

Peter tensed up just at Aby's voice, so carefree. He snapped his rubber band, turned around and cheerfully responded, "Sure, I'll do that as soon as I ask her for the power to make you be quiet whenever I want!" Everybody laughed, thank God.

"You wish!" Aby said as he pretended to choke. "That would never work..." he said coughing and gagging, "in a million ...years." He slumped over, silent.

"Hallelujah!" said Cyrana, nudging Faith.

"Hey, there's Missy and Charlie!" Aby said as the bus came to a stop at the at the school's main entrance. Peter snapped his rubber band.

The Bus 2027 kids waited in the freezing logjam of students waiting to shake hands with Mr. Button, who wore his Vonnegut Vervets neck tie, a gift from the P.T.A. on his one-year anniversary as principal. In the windy 23 degrees, he managed a personal greeting to each student.

"Welcome back! It's so great to see everybody ready to go for the New Year! "Good morning, Miss Johnson, I cannot wait to hear you play whatever it is you have in that suitcase! Miss Bountiful--welcome back! Straight A's again this semester?"

"Yes, sir!"

"Greetings, gentlemen!" he said to Peter and Aby. "How about it? Are we going to beat School 59 this year in double-dodge?

"Yes sir, if we end up playing them in the tournament." Peter said.

"Well, your mother might have a thing or two to say about that, am I right, Mr. Yates?"

"She said she has to be neutral, so she'll be rooting for us *and* her own students if we play them," Aby said. "But us mostly!"

"Go Vervets!" said Mr. Button.

Double-dodge wasn't the biggest sport—most of the cool boys played football or basketball—but a lot of kids played it for fun or were on one of the school's intramural teams. Matches are played with five-member teams on a walled-in area half the size of a basketball court. Each team must stay on their side of the court and the game starts when the referee blows the whistle and everybody races from their back wall to grab one of the five balls placed on the midline.

"Then, all heck breaks loose," as Mr. Button once described it. If somebody gets hit and isn't able to catch the ball, they were out. If they catch the ball, the thrower's out. The team with the last player standing wins.

The Marion County junior high school double-dodge tournament was scheduled for the second Saturday in February. Schools had registered in the fall and the brackets were announced before the break. Four groups of teams would play at different sites in the morning and the group winners would compete in the afternoon for the championship. School 59 was in one bracket and the Vonnegut Vervets were in another. Aby really hoped the Vervets would play his mother's school in the afternoon.

Principal Button loved double-dodge and he'd make sure that January was dedicated to Vervets double-dodge. There would be fundraisers for new VD uniforms, special double-dodge modules in history class and double-dodge ice cream served in the cafeteria every Friday.

As noted in his short bio in last year's yearbook:

> *Mr. Button played double-dodge as an army brat, moving from base to base with his family. It was one of the few constants in his life, especially after both of his parents were abducted by a race of lizard-like aliens in 1967. (Students, are you reading this with purpose and intent? Does this seem plausible? Do you even care if this is the truth?)*

Mr. Button always strove to keep the children on their toes, even while reading their yearbooks.

Wherever his career took him, he'd joined the local double-dodge league, and even had a tryout once with the El Paso Corgis semi-pro team. The experience ended his budding double-dodge career because he just wasn't tough enough. At that level, balls fly at 70 miles per hour, and Jedi-like teamwork often results in three players instinctively delivering laser shots at the head of a single player with precision timing. Head injuries are common, as players launch themselves headfirst into brick walls at times to avoid or pursue a ball. Mr. Button sustained a concussion in his first game with the Corgis, which very much impressed his coaches and prospective El Paso team mates. "¡Excelente, Botón!" the head coach said as he patted his ass and sent him back into the game.

Mr. Button recalled running back onto the court but nothing after that, until he awoke in an ambulance with the emergency medical tech asking him, "¿Quién es el presidente, Señor Botón?" Luckily, each of those words was among the 200 Spanish terms he'd learned in preparation for moving to El Paso. "Who is the president?" He looked right into the six eyes of the med tech.

"Afrika Bam-baa-taa is our presh-i-dent" he slurred with a great sense of accomplishment. "Yesh!"

After five days in the hospital, Mr. Button was discharged with a stern warning from the doctor never to play double-dodge again, and box set of the entire discography of Kevin Donovan, AKA Afrika Bambaataa, as a parting gift from the Corgis management.

"HAUN! HAUN!" "Good morning students excelling at Clemens Vonnegut Junior High School and welcome back to school! This is your princi-PAL, Mr. Button. The tallest man in medical history was eight feet tall and wore a size 37 shoe. The menu for today is chicken fried steak on a bun with pickles, blueberries and cauliflower." He paused; everyone in the building knew what was coming next.

"Who loves VD?!" Mr. Button's voice crackled with excitement through every classroom speaker. He listened as the response reverberated through the halls into the open door of his office. "We love VD!"

"Who loves Vervets double-dodge?" he encouraged them.

"We love Vervets double-dodge!"

"One more time! Who loves VD!?" Mr. Button's call-and-response with the entire school reminded Aby of one of the radio preachers his mom listened to sometimes.

"We love VD!"

"Alright! How 'bout 'dem Vervets?!"

"We love VD!"

Mr. Button clicked off the microphone and leaned back in his chair, confident this would be a winning double-dodge season. The girls' and boys' team rosters were all set, and Coach Garth was the non-binary to get the job done. Coach G. and Mr. Button spent a good part of the Christmas break developing team schedules and daily practice drills leading up to the tournament. They had the raw talent; the challenge was to make sure both teams peaked at the right moment.

The girl's first team was led by the Palmer twins, eighth graders with strong, accurate arms. The fastest dodgers on the team were two sixth graders, both named Martha, who were good hurlers for their age, and incredibly difficult to hit with a ball. They would likely be the last Vervets standing in a tough match. With their ability to dodge almost any ball, they could wear down the remaining players on the other team until they let down their guard and "that's when M&M nail 'em," Coach G. would say.

The fifth player on the team was their secret weapon, Soames Finkle, an energetic, wiry seventh grader who handled her wheelchair better than most people handled their bodies. She never came out of the locker room until the final game in a match, when she would roll onto the court, popping wheelies. Opponents didn't know what to make of her. She often threw two or three of them out while they were wondering if it was okay to throw a ball at her.

The boy's team was a work in progress. Peter was a talented double-dodger even though he'd never played in Goshen. He'd picked it up in sixth grade and, along with Aby, was one of the best players in the school, though neither had bothered to try out for the team before. Peter could throw the ball faster, but Aby was always the last one standing. Despite demonstrating little potential in other sports, Aby was a top player because he was a natural dodger. He'd make a spectacular jumping-dodge on one play and dive the opposite direction to the floor on the next. It was impossible to predict his sixth-sense acrobatics. He was a masterful, moving target that drove opponents crazy.

The rest of the team was made up of veteran players, none of whom were willing to give up their spot on the first team to the two interlopers, no matter how good they were. The coach knew that it would take more than Cokes and hotdogs after practice to turn this team into the well-oiled machine they would have to be to win the tournament. Sometimes it was best to let boys and their testosterone take their due course; if the vets wouldn't play nice with the rookies, then they would have to play against them.

On week one of practice, Coach G. told the three best veteran players to choose any two other players to make a practice team. They choose other vets, leaving Aby and Peter to team up with the rest of the players on the second team. The match was on.

The first game lasted thirty seconds, if that. When the whistle blew, Aby and Peter's team sprinted to the center court and snatched up all the balls. The veterans, assuming they could beat the other team to the line, hadn't hustled and found themselves blundering into a barrage of un-catchable balls hurled at their ankles.

The second game was close all the way until it got down to three vets against Aby. He was finally hit by a fluke ball that came off the fingertips of the thrower not at all as intended, fooling Aby. It nicked him on the foot, losing the game for the second team and setting up the deciding game.

It was a tough slog for both teams and came down to Aby and Peter against three on the other team. With the absence of their teammates, the two weaved beautifully, using every inch of the court as if each move had been carefully choreographed. The three veterans were caught off guard when Aby scooped a ball off the floor, tumbled forward, and passed the ball hard across the court toward Peter. Standing three feet away was a tall muscular boy, ball raised above his head, ready to dispatch Peter. Aby's throw hooked, missing Peter's outstretched hands and hitting the other boy in the stomach. He crumpled onto the floor. Aby and Peter ran to the center of the court and met in a huge bear hug.

"You got lucky, homos," spat a veteran player. Peter broke away from the hug as he heard Aby yell back.

"You got something against homos?! HA!" he laughed and put his arm around Peter as they went to the back of their side of the court as the rules called for when a player was hurt. "Can you believe that kid?"

"Why did you have to say that? Now they're gonna think we *are* homos!" Peter glared at him.

"Jeez, it was a joke. Nobody thinks we're homos. It was just a stupid name he called us." Aby said, annoyed. "Hey, let's try that play we've been working on. They'll never see it coming."

"Alright, yeah. Okay, sorry about that." Peter snapped the rubber band on his wrist as they positioned themselves against the back wall.

"Alright, let's go!" Coach G yelled. Each team had two players remaining, so two balls were placed in the center of the court. "Ready?"

The whistle shrieked. From the back wall, Aby sprinted toward middle court line. When he was ten feet away from the balls he lunged forward and slid on his stomach like a puck on wet ice, arms outstretched to the balls. He flipped one ball back for Peter and punched the other along the floor toward his opponent running to grab the ball. Perfect timing. It rolled under the reach of boy who had perfected his technique of taking exactly seven steps from back wall before bending in-stride to pick up a ball in center court. Trouble was, the ball was already at his feet on step six. He tripped over the ball and tumbled to the floor right in front of Aby; he was out. They both looked up at the other veteran player just as he was knocked off his feet by Peter's kill shot to the knees. Game over. Aby and Peter high-fived each other and were met center court by all the veteran players, who grudgingly offered handshakes.

"Can you believe that?" Coach G asked Mr. Button. "It's like a feel-good afterschool special. We'll be right back after this commercial!"

"I believe what I see. What I don't believe is that you actually thought this would work." Mr. Button was loving every minute of this B-movie.

"Believe it, baby!" Coach spanked the principal on the ass and ran out to center court congratulate all the players.

Peter and Aby were named first team co-captains after that and that's the truth; you can't make this stuff up. The next three weeks leading up to the tournament were busy with practice four times a week. Peter was glad for the distraction and had been able to relax a little and be friendlier with Aby. He wasn't as anxious as he was during Christmas break and, with time, felt his paranoia being replaced by a tentative gratitude for Aby not mentioning that night to him, or anyone else, he thought.

* * *

The Phelt phone rang. It was the Thursday night before the double-dodge tournament. Jake had surprised Peter and Phillip with grilled hotdogs and hamburgers, a surprise indeed since it was -8 degrees outside. They watched from the den as their dad lifted the lid of the Weber kettle grill. It bellowed a dense, grey cloud into the frigid wind as fat-fed flames shot up, desperate for oxygen.

"Hello?"

"Phyllis? Hi, this is Elvira, Elvira Yates."

"Hi, Elvira! How are you?"

"We're all doing very well. And you, how is everyone? Peter? Your family?" Elvira caught herself. "Well, there I go, saying something stupid."

"Don't you worry about it. We're all doing fine. Jake's outside getting frostbite and grilling hamburgers."

"Well, that's different."

"That's Jake," Phyllis said.

"Boys will be boys. Listen, we're all pretty excited about the tournament this weekend."

"Yes, the team is looking pretty good. That's all Peter talks about!"

"Arlen, too–he's been badgering me to do something tomorrow after school with, what do they call it, their posse? He said they need to have a pre-victory party to make sure the Vervets win. He is little a con man, that one."

"Genes," Phyllis offered with a chuckle. Elvira laughed out loud; she liked this woman.

"So, I wanted to check with you before I called the other parents. I was thinking dinner tomorrow, early, so everybody can get home and be rested for Saturday. Maybe the kids can all come on the bus to our house after school, and parents can come after work? Around six?"

* * *

Phyllis, Jake and Phillip arrived late on Friday. A very tall black man, impeccably dressed in a three-piece pinstripe suit, starched white shirt and a red power tie, answered the Yates' front door. Bowing deeply at the waist, the humorless man intoned, "May, I help you?" He allowed the Phelts to stand just inside the doorway and that was only because it was so cold out. Normally, the butler would very politely insist that callers to the house remain outside until their identity was confirmed and their purpose stated.

"Why uh, yes," stumbled Phyllis. "We are here to see the Yates, please."

"The whooooo?" owl-ed the man in a deep baritone.

From the living room, Peter and several other kids burst into laughter. Above the uproar, the man smiled broadly, "I'm so sorry. They discovered I do a bad impression of Lurch and forced me to do that! He opened the door wide, exposing the crowd of conspirators. "I'm Cyrano Johnson, Cyrana's father."

"I like this guy!" announced Jake.

"Wasn't that great?" Peter came around the door with the rest of the posse and assorted siblings.

"Dr. Johnson, isn't it?" asked Phyllis shaking his hand.

"Yes, neurology, at Methodist. But I think I make a pretty good butler, too." He put his arm around Cyrana's shoulder. "Cyrana, you know the Phelts, right?"

"Hi Mrs. Phelt. Hi Mr. Phelt."

"Hi, sweetheart," Phyllis was a big fan of Cyrana after her tour de force performance in *Fiddler on the Roof*. "I bet you were in great demand over the holidays, you and that violin of yours."

"Yes ma'am, I played for two pageants and my mom took me down to Monument Circle on a couple of the warmer days to go busking."

"A wandering minstrel! A noble calling, indeed!" Jake declared. "You know, 19th century troubadours often sold elixirs, cures and potions. Methinks this might be a lucrative business opportunity for father and daughter!"

"I would certainly entertain such a proposal," Dr. Johnson smiled. "But Cyrana's set on donating all her earnings to the children's neurology clinic at my hospital, so I think I'm out of luck."

"That's a very nice thing to do," Phyllis said. "Very mature." She shot a glance at her very immature husband. "Is your mother here?"

No, ma'am, she's in Texas taking care of my nini."

"My wife's mother isn't well," Dr. Johnson explained.

"Some butler you are! Our guests still standing in the foyer with their coats on!" Elvira teased, coming in from the kitchen. "Hello, Phyllis!" she said with a welcoming hug. "And this must be older brother Phillip! So nice to meet you, young man." As cordially as possible she smiled and extended her hand to Jake. "Good to see you, Mr. – I'm sorry, Dr. Phelt."

"Are you a physician as well?" Dr. Johnson asked.

Jake pretended not to hear the question. "Jake is fine. Good to see you too, uh –."

"Elvira, please."

"I guess that makes me Cy," said Dr. Johnson. "Now, let's see what we can do about those coats."

The adults gathered in the kitchen. The moms were all acquainted with one another; each one with a husband present introduced him around. To Jake and Phyllis' surprise, there was an impressive selection of beer, wine and spirits. They helped themselves at Elvira's urging as Phillip joined the kids in the living room.

The Bountifuls sat at the kitchen table with Benjamin Yates, posse-moms and a woman Phyllis didn't recognize. Uber Bountiful was topping off the wine glasses of everyone around the table as he delivered the punchline of a rather long joke. "And then Balaam *beats* the donkey, and the donkey –," he said through his own laughter. "And the donkey starts talking!" After several seconds of silence, everyone laughed politely.

"Hey, what do you call a donkey with a Ph.D.? asked Benjamin Yates, clearly not able to hold his liquor any better now than he did in 1984.

"A smart ass!" Jake said from across the room. "Hello, Benny!" Yates looked at Jake, momentarily surprised to see him. Of course, he knew he would be here tonight, but he'd allowed himself to not think about it and instead, enjoy a gin and tonic—or three—until the Phelts arrived.

"Uh, everyone. This is Peter's father, Jake Phelt."

"Hello all! Thanks for set-up there, Benny. Not often you get a chance make your first impression with a punch line."

"Oh, was that a joke?" Melinda Bradford smiled. "Hi, I'm Missy's mother, Melinda. And this is my friend Suzanne."

"Ladies, the pleasure is mine. I have to tell you that Peter had a mad crush on Missy his first day in sixth grade, until he found out that she and Aby were an item, am I right, Benny?"

"I wasn't aware of that." Benjamin Yates. In danger of sobering up, he poured himself another drink.

"Oh yeah, but then he met your girl." Jake slapped Uber Bountiful on the back. "And the rest is history I guess. At least for now!"

"Peter's a nice boy. We like him very much."

"I love it when animals talk in the Bible!" Benjamin Yates blurted out.

"How is the lasagna coming, Ben?" Elvira asked loudly from across the kitchen. "You set the timer, didn't you?"

"Five minutes to go."

"If you love chatty animals, then you'll love the Hindu scriptures and the Quran," Esther Bountiful paused to gauge the reaction of the group. She and Uber were required by their Howdy-Doo! Resurrectionist beliefs to spread their version of the Good Word; proselytizing was the hallmark of the Howdy-Doos, thus the name "Howdy-Doo!" So, they sought out opportunities to mingle in the general population, wholeheartedly embracing whatever non-spiritual customs were necessary to gain the acceptance of non-believers. They would—for a time—become at one with their secular brothers and sisters and, when the opportunity arose, share their truth. Through the years, they had found it necessary to become meth heads, join a Nazi rock band, and even vote for Pat Buchanan in the 1992 presidential primary. Clearly, they were willing to do whatever it took to reach the lost souls of the world.

"Animals communicate and teach lessons in most religions," Esther continued. "In Islam, humans and all creatures praise Allah. And I say, why not? Humans are animals, too. Name any prophet–I bet you he talked to ants or bees or bats or something."

"Dr. Doolittle?" Jake offered with a laugh.

"Not exactly what I had in mind, but that's interesting because that story is about a doctor who shuns human patients in favor of animals because he can better communicate with them than he can with humans." Esther drained her shot glass. "Mmm-boy! That's, how do they say it, 'gnarly!' Whew! Anyway, the Dr. Doolittle story becomes very compelling when you consider it was written by a World War I soldier during a time when humans were not communicating very well at all."

"Wow. You're good." Jake said.

Elvira was the only one to hear the crystalline ping from the plastic timer. She reset it for three minutes, yelling into the living room. "Arlen, did you see your friend Larry at school today?"

"What?" he shouted back.

"Larry, Larry Dunn. Did you see him at school? Come out here, please, so I don't have to scream."

"When are we going to eat?" Aby bounded into the kitchen.

"As soon as your friend Larry and his parents get here. Did you talk to him today?"

"Of course I didn't talk to him! Why are they coming?"

"Because I ran into Mrs. Dunn at the market. They were so nice to invite you and all your friends to Larry's birthday party– I thought we should reciprocate." The doorbell rang. "Cy, would you mind getting that?"

"Is that the Dunns?!" Aby asked.

"As you wish, madam," Dr. Johnson said, as Lurch. He lumbered through the living room to get into character, winking at Peter along the way. Aby came around the corner from the kitchen and froze as Dr. Johnson answered the door with a deep bow.

"May I help you?" With a sweeping gesture of his arm he welcomed Larry Dunn and his parents into the foyer.

"Hello," Mrs. Dunn said with a tentative smile.

"Good evening, madam. You look lovely this evening, if I may say so." Lurch said.

"Is this the Yates' house?" Mr. Dunn glared at his wife, ignoring the butler.

"The whooooo?" inquired Lurch, most sincerely.

"I wasn't talking to you," Mr. Dunn snapped. Cy Johnson was startled, and at once recognized a familiar tone and anger in his words. The only thing missing was the "boy" at the end.

"Mom! The Dunns are here! Hey, Larry!" Aby interjected. All the kids looked on, thinking this should be real funny like it was when the Phelts arrived, but it wasn't. Peter shuddered.

"Hey Mr. Dunn! Uh, this is Dr. Johnson; he does a great Lurch, huh?

"Oh, yes, Lurch!" Francie Dunn looked at her husband glowering at black Lurch. She had admitted to herself long ago that he was a little prejudiced, but he was usually very polite to the blacks in public and she was proud of him for that. His business was based largely on getting along with them and he'd prospered because he was so good at it. She knew it wasn't right, but one time she'd chuckled when she'd overheard him say to Larry, "I could charm a chicken leg off a starvin' nigger." He never joked around like that outside the house, and he even liked some of the parents who dropped their kids off at his federally-funded daycare centers every day. But one thing he would not abide was being the butt of a joke, or being made fun of by anybody, especially a nigger.

Cy Johnson stared at Lawrence Dunn, resigned to accept what was right in front of his face: a modern-day version of every east Texas racist who made sure that he'd stayed on his side of the tracks in Jasper. He'd obeyed his parents and silently endured the oppression and violence of white people–all the white people as far as he could tell, as a child. His Uncle Marooney said they weren't all bad and took Cyrano with him one Saturday to help mow some of their lawns; he was six that summer of 1949. To his astonishment, some of the whites seemed nice; one lady even set out some lemonade in paper cups on the back porch for them. As they were taking their five-minute break, sitting on a decorative pile of loblolly pine logs, Cy looked at the large house and saw a little boy peering out an upstairs window. He looked at his uncle and asked quite innocently, "How come he doesn't mow his own yard?"

"Maybe he will one day, and we won't have to," Uncle Marooney offered, because that's the sort of thing he said to young people to keep their hopes for the future alive; however, at that moment, he was having a little trouble wrapping his own Jim Crow-era brain around that possibility.

Dr. Johnson looked at the man in front of him and for one second, imagined visiting upon him all the rage of his youth, just like his brother had on two white teenagers after they left Uncle Marooney for dead in a ditch, his face beaten so badly he wouldn't open his eyes for three weeks. Even after nine years in prison, Cy's brother never learned the lesson, but Cy had: there's no fighting the Lawrence Dunns of the world on their terms; you defeat them in other ways. He extended his hand to Mrs. Dunn, "Cy Johnson, I'm Cyrana's father. Sorry about the confusion. It's just a little game we were playing earlier."

"Hello, Francie, I'm so glad you could make it!" Elvira said, appearing from the kitchen, oblivious.

"I'm glad we could, too. We don't get out that much; thank you for inviting us."

"Of course! And you've both met Dr. Johnson. He's the life of the party so far!" Elvira was in full-host mode. "Hello, Larry! I can't tell you how much all the kids enjoyed your birthday party. It was so nice of you to invite them. And your square-dancing father!! Oh my, you are a legend, sir!"

"We all had a lot of fun." Mr. Dunn said, managing a smile. The timer pinged at Elvira from the kitchen.

"Okay! Everybody down to the basement!" Her command reminded the Phelts of the tornado drill at the Motel 6 they stayed in over the Christmas break. "We set up big tables so we can all sit together. Take your drinks with you. Everything else is there. Benjamin, can you...? Never mind; I'll get the lasagna. Dunns, please help yourselves to beverages. Larry, get yourself a drink, honey."

A ping-pong table, a huge work bench and two card tables were set up diagonally across the basement, interrupted by an iron pole in the middle of the room, from which hung several "Go, Vervets" flags. With everyone seated, Elvira asked if any of the children would like to say grace. To Aby's relief, the three youngest Bountifuls eagerly raised their hands. He knew he'd be forced to do it if nobody volunteered and, truth be told, he wasn't sure he could get through the entire "God is great, God is good, and we thank him for this food" prayer. Did something come after that or was it okay just to say "amen?" Last time he tried the Lord's Prayer, he remembered the "God is great, God is good" line, but followed it with "now I lay me down to sleep" and got totally lost.

Peter found himself seated between Faith and Mr. Dunn. The love of his young life and the scariest person he knew. He felt an arm around his shoulder.

"Good to see you again, Master Phelt."

"Yes, sir."

"And who do we have here?" Mr. Dunn leaned forward, looking at Faith.

"Faith Bountiful sir. I was at Larry's party."

"Yes indeed! Forgive me!" Mr. Dunn said with a broad smile.

"And these are my sisters. Rachel, Rebekah, Ruth, Delilah, Dinah and Bathsheba."

"Hello, young ladies!" He reached across the table to shake each girl's hand as the mothers around the table complimented Esther Bountiful on her daughters.

"You're sure lucky to have such a pretty girlfriend there, Peter!" Mr. Dunn laughed and slapped him on the back.

Peter blushed and felt a response coming out of his mouth. Remaining silent had not been considered by the mouth, although that may have been the best of its three options—history would tell. The other two possibilities were to answer "I sure am!" or "uh, she's not my girlfriend." Peter glanced at Faith's parents as the mouth spoke.

"Uh, she's not my girlfriend, exactly."

"Not your girlfriend?!" Mr. Dunn asked. There was polite laughter among the adults.

"This salad is excellent, Elvira," Cy said from the far end of the table.

"Well if that pretty one's not your girlfriend, you must not like girls!" Mr. Dunn shoveled in a forkful of lasagna. Peter looked as his plate and did the same; the mouth was stymied.

"He likes girls!" Aby protested. "He's not a homo!"

"Arlen!" Elvira glared across the table. "There's no need for talk like that."

"But he's not a ho—"

"Shut up, Aby!" Peter yelled. The table was silent.

"But you're not. Tell him you're not a homo!"

"Arlen Bob Yates!" Elvira was halfway out of her seat. The room was silent.

Mr. Dunn spoke first. "I sorry, Mrs. Yates. I had no idea this was a touchy subject."

Jake and Phyllis were speechless. What on earth was going on here? Their minds raced. The posse was quiet.

"You are whoever you are, Peter. And that's a beautiful thing," Melinda Bradford took Suzanne's hand under the table. "Don't let anybody change you."

"Mo-om," Missy two-syllabled her mother.

"It's not a touchy subject!" Peter knocked his chair over leaving the table. "Just shut up!" He ran up the basement stairs and slammed the front door on his way out.

When the Phelts arrived home, Peter was on the front stoop, shivering. Phyllis hurried from the car and draped Peter with her long coat.

"C'mon, sweetheart let's go in."

"Man, it's cold." Jake glanced at Peter as he unlocked the front door.

"I'm hungry." Phillip said. "Can I make a peanut butter and jelly?"

"That's a good idea. We have chips. Peter?" Phyllis busied herself getting plates and glasses for milk, as Jake made the sandwiches. They all sat down at the table. Peter took a few bites of his sandwich, occasionally shaking his head in silence as if answering a question or denying an accusation.

"Can I be excused?" Phillip stood and drained his glass.

"Yes," Jake was hoping they could all be excused from this entire night. Peter pushed his chair back.

"Can we talk for a second, please?" Phyllis looked at Peter, hopefully.

"There's nothing to talk about."

"We just want to make sure you're okay."

"I'm fine."

"Can you tell us a little bit about what was going on at dinner?"

"I don't know. It's stupid." Peter fidgeted with the rubber band on his wrist.

"What's stupid, buddy?" Jake asked.

"Everything is! Double-dodge, the Virgin Mary, Larry Dunn, his dad—why did they have to invite him anyway?" Peter wiped tears from his cheek.

"That guy's a jerk, don't listen to him. He doesn't—"

"It's not him. It's me." Peter sobbed, just able to catch his breath. "I'm the stupid one. It's just that he—"

"Mr. Dunn?"

"No! Someone else."

"Did someone do something to you?" Phyllis was holding back her own tears and reached toward Peter.

"No, no! But everybody thinks I'm a queer!"

"No, they don't, buddy." Jake knew those were the words to say, but they weren't true. As soon as Aby said "he's not a homo," everybody thought, for the first time, that he might be. Even Jake.

"They do, too, and it's all Aby's fault! He told all of our friends I was a homo, and then tried to make up for it by saying I wasn't one to Mr. Dunn." Peter pushed further back from the table. "And now everybody thinks I am!"

"Are you?" Jake heard himself ask.

"Jesus, Jake, stop!"

"No!" Peter stomped out of the kitchen. "See, even you think I am!" He took the stairs two at a time up to his bedroom and locked the door.

* * *

All night, he struggled to sleep. He prayed that the light around the curtains was the morning, and not the floodlights from the neighbor's backyard–he couldn't bear the prospect of lapsing back into another chaotic dream. Disembodied voices talking at him. About him. Coach G. shouting, Principal Button announcing true or false facts. Faith's soft cheek. The expression on Mr. Yates face. And Aby. Aby everywhere, cracking wise.

He sat on the edge of the bed. Across the room, his Vervets Double-dodge uniform stood up and faced him; it had no face, and no arms or legs to support it. He rubbed his eyes; it took a silent step forward. He breathed in, and in again as the uniform slowly approached. Its sleeves reached out, outstretched fingers inches from his eyes. He gasped again but his lungs were full. His eyes widened as he wheezed for air. A head appeared from the neck of the uniform. He tried to cry out, but couldn't make a sound. The hands grabbed his skull, its thumbs pressing into his temples; the head grew larger, its angry, evil face bursting into a deafening laughter. "SISSY!" it thundered. "SISSY!"

Peter pushed the thing away, and uniform fell to the floor. He ran to the door, all the while watching the empty, limp uniform. He burst into the hallway, panting. Faith and Aby were standing behind a table displaying colorful swimsuits and beach towels. Faith smiled adoringly, "Would you like to buy a bikini, sir?"

No!" he yelled.

"Are you sure?" asked Aby, earnestly.

Peter banged on his bedroom door. "Let me in! Let me in!"

"Peter, please let me in," Phyllis knocked loudly on Peter's door. "Are you alright?" Jolted awake, he looked at the blank ceiling, disoriented. "Peter, can you open the door?"

"Huh?"

"Open the door, sweetheart."

He opened the door and looked at his mother suspiciously and then around the corner. "What time is it?"

"It's early, not even seven. You can go back to sleep if you want." Phyllis kissed his cheek. "Would you like me to call Coach G. and tell him you're not feeling well? It's okay."

He looked at the uniform on the chair and snapped the rubber band hard on his wrist. "No, I have to get ready to go."

* * *

Both the boy and girl double-dodge teams made it through their two morning matches at Arsenal Technical High School with ease. Coach G. and Mr. Button were self-bedazzled; they knew their teams were good, but they didn't know they were that good. After the matches, both teams boarded the bus back to Vonnegut Junior High with a stop at Waffle House for lunch.

Peter hadn't spoken to anyone all day, except for the necessary chatter during the games. The solitude was good; it helped him focus on the game. Coach G. knew something was up with Peter and Aby, but he didn't intervene; it was a calculated risk, the sort Coach had taken a thousand times. *Let the drama ride,* he thought. *They'll figure out whatever the hell it is, after the game.*

The scene at Vonnegut Junior High was chaotic. The School 59 booster busses clogged the circular drive. Families, players and fans jammed the sidewalks spilling into the road, causing great consternation among the fluorescent-green-clad sixth graders who had been strategically stationed along the sidewalk to prevent exactly that.

Mr. Button busied himself greeting everyone, leaving Coach G. to open the gym doors for the horde of fans, each scrambling for a seat.

"Hello, Coach!" Elvira Yates wore the colors of Public School 59, but Coach knew her true allegiance lay with the Vervets.

"Good luck today!" he yelled through the noise.

The Vervet boys took their seats in the first row to watch the girls' match. The Boston Pops played the "Star-Spangled Banner" through the gym's high speakers, followed by Jim Nabors singing "Back Home in Indiana," and an all-school a capella version of "Go! Fight! Win! Vervets!" Mrs. Greenhaw would have been proud.

Peter looked across the gym floor at the P.S. 59 boys' team. He moved slightly to the left as Aby's arm brushed his during the fight song. He caught the eye of a boy from the other team and stared at him unflinchingly, expressionless. The boy looked away. *If there was a homo on that team, it was definitely that kid,* he thought. Peter snapped his rubber band. He wondered how hard the boy could throw and whether he was even first string. He was probably just a backup.

Peter was startled by the cheers for the girls' teams taking the floor. As they had in the morning matches, the Vervet's Palmer twins orchestrated the attack, calling out plays. The girls anticipated each other's moves and passed the ball with precision. They were one team, not five players. The sixth-grade Marthas each threw out a 59er during the first minute of the game, the twins dispatched one player each, and the wheel-chaired-wonder, Soames Finkle, took care of the final player.

They girls trust each other, Peter thought. That's why they're so good. Aby bumped his arm, standing to cheer the girl's first-game victory. Peter snapped his band. Aby was the one who wanted to pretend they were on adventures with their girlfriends. Was that only four months ago? He was the one who said, "What would you do next?" Peter was stabbed by the memory. Aby was the one who told me I should have a cum. Why hadn't Aby locked his bedroom that night?

The 59ers were ready for the second game. Clearly, they'd decided it was Soames Finkle who threw off their first game. When the whistle blew, their three fastest players ran to the center line. Each scooped up a ball and hurled it at Soames in one grand motion. All three made hard body contact, one against the side of her head. The 59ers lost one player during the assault, but it was worth it. The Vervets had to take a time out to tend to Soames and get her off the floor. When the game resumed, the Vervets couldn't stage any sort of attack and lost the game.

Peter was unmoved by the drama. *How on earth did Coach G. not see that coming?* The opening play had unfolded to Peter in slow motion. As the three 59ers rushed the line, the remaining two staged a clownish dancing diversion; it distracted the Vervets long enough for the 59er to pummel Soames. *Coach should have put the Marthas in center court to disrupt the speedy attackers, and then sic the Palmer twins on the other two 59ers. It's so simple; if you know what's coming next, you can stop it.*

Peter punished his wrist with the rubber band. I should have known Aby would mess everything up last night if he got a chance. Everything was going fine until he yelled, "He's not a homo! Tell him you're not a homo!"

The gym erupted. Peter had missed the rest of the game; the Vervet girls had won the match. Aby and the rest of the Vervet fans were cheering and stomping like maniacs. Peter was disoriented, but didn't lose his train of thought. In the midst of the noise around him, the truth–the actual truth–dawned on him. *It was Aby. He is the homo.* Peter shuttered at the thought of getting so excited when he touched Aby in bed, even if he was pretending that Aby was Faith. *He was touching me, but he wasn't pretending. He was touching me–he wanted to do that. And when the truth was about to come out about him, he sabotaged me and...*

Peter realized he was in the Vervet huddle. Their match was about to start. Coach G. knelt in the middle of the circle, diagramming the first play on a small chalkboard. "Got it?" Peter shook his head and tried to focus.

Aby looked around the circle at the team. "Everything's a challenge," he said with all the life-or-death determination an eighth grader can muster. "To the last Vervet!" he shouted. "We fight!"

"We fight!" the team responded. Peter was rejuvenated by the team and felt the strength of his arms and legs.

"We fight!" Aby roared.

"We fight!" Peter was the loudest to respond.

"We fight!" the team shouted to the delight of their fans, now hungry for a boy-girl clean sweep of the 59ers.

The Vervets ran onto the floor, each boy taking his position against the concrete wall that was the back of their half of the court. Across the gym, the 59ers readied themselves to race for one of the five double-dodge balls placed in center court.

The whistle blew. Aby stayed against the wall while the other four Vervets scrambled to retrieve four of the five balls. The fifth was grabbed by the smallest 59er who immediately threw the ball as hard as he could at the only defenseless Vervet. Against the wall, Aby caught the ball with ease and the boy left the game to the cheers of the home crowd. The Vervets had the 59ers right where they wanted them.

As planned, Aby remained against the back wall as the other four moved toward center court. Each was capable of delivering a kill shot to their mark, ending the game right there. If someone missed, Aby would swoop in and pick him off with his ball. Peter and his frontline teammates cocked their arms, ready to throw their balls at the same instant.

On cue, they all hurled the balls with all their might, except for Peter. At that moment, he turned his back to the 59ers and threw his ball with ungodly force at Aby. From just ten feet away the ball hit Aby's face before he could react, be frightened, or even register that the projectile was coming. It might as well have been a bullet.

"SISSY! You're the one!" Peter walked toward Aby. "SISSY!" he yelled.

The second of the two impacts was the most damaging. The first impact of the ball only broke his nose and pushed two front teeth through his upper lip. The second, when his skull cracked against the concrete, took the light from his eyes. Aby's body slowly slid down the wall to the gym floor, leaving a streak of blood to mark its descent.

The Second Teller:
Part One

Pre-Ur III

"There were no marks on the scroll at all! It was blank," 90-year-old Aadi told the teenage Second Teller, Dvau Vatkr. Her gramaji sat in the corner of the dark room eyeing the old man. Aadi Vatkr was respected well enough, but a young woman meeting a man in his private space–even if he was on his deathbed–was highly irregular.

"I was sent by the Annanuski alien when I was 10 to retrieve this scroll," Aadi said. "It was a glorious journey filled with magic, and–"

The old woman interrupted him with a loud yawn; she had heard variations of the story at every marked-moon celebration over the past eight decades. Aadi slowly sat up in his bed and leaned back on a cushion against the hard mud wall. His hand reached under the covers. "I have something very special for you," he whispered to Dvau Vatkr, eyebrows bobbling. "Would you like to see it?"

GramaJi sprang to her feet and positioned herself between her granddaughter and Aadi Vatkr.

"Relax, my dear cousin," said Aadi, "I wish only to show Dvau Vatkr–and you, of course–this." From beneath the covers he produced the ancient scroll, the scroll that no other person had ever laid eyes on. Most in the clan doubted its existence, but still wondered if they would find it in his hovel after he died. He handed the scroll to the girl, instructing her to unroll it.

Standing over the girl, the woman scoffed. "Look, it is still as blank as you said it was the day you found it! Of what use is an ancient scroll with no marks or etches?"

Dvau Vatkr gasped, transfixed on the scroll. "Don't you see it, GramaJi? It is the most wondrous image." She looked to Aadi Vatkr. "What is this thing, this 'scroll'? I feel like I could crawl into it and walk until the harvest comes."

Aadi leaned forward. "If you want, you can tap on it twice—to the beat of "Mawakti in the Evening, Mawakti in the Night"—to see more."

"You crazy old man, this is nonsense!" said GramaJi. "There is nothing to see on that worthless scroll."

"But don't you see the Torah Bora Mountains?" protested Dvau Vatkr. "And the deep blue land on the horizon?"

"No! What are you talking about?" GramaJi scowled. "There is no such thing as the 'Torah Bora Mountains!' You're too young for this. That old man is tricking you now, just like he tricked me when I was young."

Aadi Vatkr winced and wished that the old woman's memory of that morning so long ago was as pleasant as his. Regaining his composure, he said to Dvau Vatkr, "If you tap the scroll three times, your tale will begin."

"Don't you dare say another word to her!" cried the woman, grabbing at the scroll. "Give me that thing!"

Dvau Vatkr easily kept the scroll from her grandmother's grasp. "It's okay, GramaJi," she pleaded. "Everything will be fine. Please."

"But—" GramaJi protested.

"I'm sorry," Dvau Vatkr said, "but I am the Second Teller." She stood and tapped the scroll three times, took two steps backward and disappeared in a spectacular flash of fire and fog.

In the blink of her duos oculos, Dvau Vatkr found herself in a snowy canyon surrounded by sheer cliffs, the heights of which were obscured by a soaring lodgepole pine forest. She braced herself against the shock of sub-zero air beneath the thin cloth chador she'd worn to visit Aadi Vaktr.

"This will keep you warm, child," a voice reassured her. Dvau Vaktr startled at the large warm pelt that suddenly enveloped her. "But you must keep moving."

"Yes," she said, noticing the chiseled-leather Texas cowboy boots on her feet.

"I'll not have much time to spend with you," said the voice in her head. "Your tale has now begun and it must end at the edge of the blue land on the horizon. You will have your entire life to make the journey, but you will barely make it–if everything goes the way it should. But you already know this, don't you?"

Dvau Vaktr was just about to ask the voice what the handoo it was talking about, when she realized she already knew. As she stood in the snow in her custom-tooled LaReyna Specials with perfect arch support, she also realized that she knew everything that was foretold in the scroll.

"I do," she said silently. "I understand it all, except for one thing."

"Yes, I know," Voice sighed. "There is that."

"What?" Dvau Vatkr asked.

"There is that," repeated Voice.

"What does that mean?" she said aloud this time.

"I mean, er, that there is a 'that,' " stumbled Voice. "That's all I meant."

"Can we just start this part over?" Dvau Vaktr asked calmly, silently now.

"Yes, of course."

"Why, if I know everything," she enunciated each word, "will I just barely make it to edge of the blue land before I die?"

"Oh, that!" answered Voice, relieved. "That's the free-will thing. You'll have lots of choices to make along the way, trials and tribulations, you know, that sort of thing. For the moment, it looks like you'll make it there a little late, but everything will work out fine. Unless, of course, all hell breaks loose."

Dvau Vaktr could hear a smile in Voice's inflection. "Alright, then," she said. "What did you think I was actually talking about?"

"Let's walk," said Voice. Dvau gathered the fur around her and tucked the scroll safely into its conveniently located pelt-pouch. The boots reminded her that they were on her feet and began walking up the hard dirt path alongside the canyon creek.

"I apologize for being a little obtuse before," Voice said after a while. "This is my first time as a 'voice.' In training, they told us that humans really like to put their own spin on the messages they receive from gods, extraterrestrials and burning bushes. They said I should be mysterious, distant. But I don't know if that's really me. I mean, feel like I need to explore my–"

Wow, that's all I need. A messenger trying to find itself, Dvau Vaktr thought. "Can we get back to the scroll, please?" she said aloud.

"Yes, of course," said Voice, all business now. "The Ten Concepts have been revealed to you, as you have said. If you don't mind, let's review."

"Yes, please," agreed, Dvau Vaktr. She felt the scroll do a little jig in her pelt-pocket. She unrolled it but saw nothing. "It's blank. All the marks have disappeared."

"No way," Voice protested.

"Way," said Dvau Vatkr, exasperated. "Look, maybe you need a little more training to figure all this stuff out."

"No, no, wait. Try this." Voice said. "Click your boot heels together three times, and–"

BOOK THREE

Sed creaturae non sunt.

They are but creatures.

Black Shade 3.1.1   April 21, 2047 A.D.

Oaxaca in the spring was always beautiful and April 21, 2047 was no exception. The abbot rocked quietly on the porch, listening to the driverless Uber donkey cart delivered another pilgrim.

He knew well that the September 5, 1999 decision to establish Black Shade in Santa Lucía del Camino had been made not by him, but by You Know Who in 304 A.D. That the official name of the Mexican state in which Black Shade was located was the "Free and Sovereign State of Oaxaca" was icing on the cake. Free and Sovereign. "We were destined to call this liberated, sacred ground our home," the abbot had reminded his flock through the years of Pharaonic-like persecution at the hands of the Americans.

As the first abbot of Black Shade wrote in The Rise and Fall and Rise and Fall of Black Shade, Hollywood-controlling kikes and Texas Film Commission Austin-artsy-farts had quashed all attempts to produce what would have been a blockbuster film recounting the remarkable story of Black Shade and its patron saint, the martyr Lucía. What follows are the original pitch and an excerpt from an un-produced film script, salvaged from the charred remains of the original Black Shade facilities, burned to the ground in 2026 by the Policía Federal Ministerial.

The pitch:

Alright, get this! It's 283 A.D. Lucía's super-rich dad dies when she's five, leaving Mom and Lucía all alone. In 3rd century anywhere, women and children without a man around are skubalon-out-of-luck even if they have dough, so Mom arranges a marriage for Lucy to the youngest son of a wealthy pagan family. Unfortunately, Lucy's made a secret vow to become a nun and when he finds out, the pagan is really pissed off because he wants her inheritance. You're gonna love the ending!

Script excerpt:

INT. BEDROOM – DAY

Lucy's mom is terminally ill.

MOM: Mi querida Lucía, come to the Shrine of the Martyred Saint Agatha with me. I need a miracle!

LUCY: Okay, Mom.

EXT. SHRINE HOTEL – DAY

Lucy sleeps restlessly. Mom is in the other bed without her sleep apnea mask, snoring.

GOD (to Lucy): Because of your youthful and vibrant faith, your mother will be cured and you will be a saint one day, just like Agatha!

LUCY: Awesome.

INT. PORCH – DAY

Mom is cured. She and Lucy relax with masala chai lattes.

LUCY: Mom, you have to donate all of your riches to the poor as thanks for your miraculous good health!

MOM: Sure, I'll do that after I die.

LUCY (in perfect Bible speak): Whatever you give away at death for the Lord's sake, you give because you cannot take it with you. Give now to the true Savior, while you are healthy, whatever you intended to give away at your death.

INT. CHURCH – DAY
Mom leads a caravan of gold and jewels up the church aisle to the altar. The crowd of poor people cheers.

Although the remainder of the script was lost in ashes of the 2026 raid, the rest of the story is well known. When the pagan learns that the riches have been given to the church, he enlists the Governor of Syracuse to help force Lucy to marry him and get back the family wealth from the padres.

The governor sends guards to arrest Lucy, but they cannot physically move her; even when they hitch her to a team of oxen, she doesn't budge. Piles of wood are stacked around her and set afire, but she doesn't burn. Finally, the pagan runs her through with a razor-sharp, sternum-piercing sword, whereupon the governor's soldiers gouge her eyes out.

As all adherents know, it is that last indignity that made Santa Lucía the perfect patron saint of Black Shade. She willingly gave her sight to serve God and in so doing, led countless others to her Lord. This is the very essence of Black Shade, AKA Sombra Negra, and its thousands of followers who literally give of their sight so that others can see God.

Black Shade's Saint Lucy Enucleation Clinic was small, clean and efficient. The staff included one full-time eye surgeon, an anesthesiologist, three psychiatrists and support staff sufficient to remove 50 pairs of eyeballs daily. True enough, numbers were down from the 300 per day in the early aughts; back then, there was a weeks-long waiting list of believers ready to have their eyes removed and donated to poverty-stricken children all over the world.

For the donor, total blindness guaranteed a path to God that was uncluttered by visual distractions. "Darkness will light the way!" promised Black Shade brochures, regularly smuggled across the U.S. border, along with ice-packed eyeballs and the occasional kilo of cocaína to cover expenses.

At the beginning of the century, only corneas could be salvaged and transplanted, wasting significant eyeball tissue. Things had changed in the '20s, as human limbal stem cells were engineered to restore corneas, and total eyeball transplants became commonplace. That was great for little blind kids bumping into walls all over the world, but it forced Black Shade to rework its spiritual business model. It used to be, if you had no eyeballs, you'd be stone-cold blind until you were dead. But it wasn't that way anymore; now you could get new eyeballs, no hay problema!

Black Shade's foundation was its members' unbridled and permanent commitment to serve God. Enucleation was their sacrament: the outward and visible sign of an inward and spiritual grace. The first abbot of Black Shade often recounted how his Episcopal priest had repeated the phrase in preparation for his boyhood confirmation ceremony. Outward and visible sign of an inward and spiritual grace. For Black Shade, it was imperative that the sacrament abide, and the grace of God remain blind.

And so, because it was no longer enough to remove eyeballs that could be replaced, the second Abbot upped the spiritual anti for the new generation of fanatics. The confirmation ceremony for these adherents, coming after their hollow sockets are healed, is no less powerful than that of the Catholic novitiate. Dressed in white, she makes her public vow to the church, thus becoming the bride of Christ and consecrating herself to God until death.

Similarly, as the Black Shade confirmation ceremony nears an end, the abbot invites the group of initiates to the altar. They face the congregation and each one self-administers one drop of a nerve-killing acid into each of their empty sockets to forever blind and bind themselves to God. The abbot and assembled congregation listen as each new devotee quietly embraces the excruciating pain of their wondrous rebirth.

Capstone Light 3.2.1 January 18, 2023 Y.O.S.P.L.

"Welcome to the first meeting of 'Capstone Light' on this, the 18th day of January, 2023rd year of some people's lords." Pastor Yates was uncharacteristically formal as he looked at his oldest friends and co-founders of the Church of the P-Free Sabbath. Brother Director Cardu and Sister Missy Finance & Administration glanced at one another, each assuming his tone was a contrivance to imbue the announcement of some new initiative with the requisite gravitas.

"Thank you," Sister F'nA said.

"You're welcome."

"Will anyone else be joining us?" Cardu asked.

"No, just us. We will announce the formation of Capstone Light as a high-level, long-term strategic planning effort at the next executive meeting."

"I think this is a very good idea, Pastor. Planning for the church is long overdue if I may say," Cardu offered. "But shouldn't we invite some of the other elders to share their thoughts now?"

"There will be time enough for that."

Sister F'nA studied her husband. "Planning for what?"

"Well, actually, this is more of an implementation effort, if you will."

"Okay," Sister said tentatively. "What are we implementing?"

"We had a visitor at our service yesterday, as you know," Pastor said with a practiced indirectness that usually presaged a very long explanation.

"An unannounced visitor from the FBI is certainly not an uncommon event," Cardu said.

"Agent Dunkin was not unannounced. He was 'arranged,' "

"And why would we arrange for an FBI agent to be here, especially on a day celebrating the Ministers in Chains?" Sister F'nA leaned forward.

"Thank you for that question, because it gets to the crux of the matter and the work we have done–and will do–as Capstone Light."

"Have done? We just got here. I thought this was a new group?"

"Yes, about that..." Pastor said, engaging his nose pod. As the small screen emerged from his face, he added, "I'm messaging you a document containing the successful actions of 'Capstone Dark' since 2009. If you don't mind, please–"

"2009?" Cardu and Sister F'nA exclaimed together. "Dark!?"

"I probably should have mentioned it earlier, but–"

"That's 14 years ago–we'd just started the church, for Word's sake," the sister yelled.

"I'm sorry if you question my methods and feel that I've distrusted you, but I had no choice," Pastor stated as if reading a prepared statement at a press conference. "We needed a clandestine vehicle to accomplish certain things. I did not involve you for your own safety–I'm sharing it with you now because I do trust you and I need you. The church needs you."

There was silence as Sister F'nA and Cardu deployed their nose pods and began to read the document.

"You've got be kidding," Sister said with a furious tremor in her voice.

"For security reasons," Pastor instructed, "you will have exactly nine minutes to review the document before it dissolves." The two stared at their pod screens, trying to take in years of clandestine operations directed by Pastor and carried out by strangers.

CAPSTONE DARK: FOUNDATIONS & ACTIONS
September 1, 2009 – January 18, 2023

- **2009-Jan:** CPFS received federal notification of pending tax evasion and fraud charges against Pastor Yates and CPFS Board (and aggravated jaywalking charges against the Pastor).

- **2010-July:** Capstone Dark initiated negotiations with FBI/IRS.

- **2010-Aug:** CPFS agreed to deliver an unnamed high-value fugitive from FBI Top Ten Most Wanted List on January 1, 2011, in exchange for dropping FBI/IRS charges; negotiations to drop the jaywalking charges continued.

- **2011-New Year's Day:** Unnamed high-value fugitive surrendered to FBI to serve 27-year sentence in Crater Lake Super Max.

- **2011-Feb:** FBI/IRS reneged on agreement to drop all CPFS tax evasion charges immediately; charges to remain pending until anonymous prisoner serves entire sentence.

- **2012-Feb:** CPFS high school seniors Ozmana Zelotes, Tomasina Thomas and O'Nathan Obel are recruited to serve as undercover agents. Surveillance of then-high school senior and future FBI Special Agent Darrow Dunkin begins.

- **2016-May:** Ozmana Zelotes and Tomasina Thomas graduate magna cum laude from Smith College and Trinity University, respectively.

- **2015/17:** After flunking out of Ringling Bros. and Barnum & Bailey Nice Clown College, O'Nathan Obel enrolls in Texas A&M, excels as a Yell Leader, and graduates May 2017.

- **2017/19:** Ozmana Zelotes, Tomasina Thomas and O'Nathan Obel attend LBJ School of Public Affairs. Internships secured by CPFS for these individuals include: Thomas: Texas Air, Field and Feast Commission, Washington University Biodegradable Cat Litter Department, Percina Tanasi Advocacy. Zelotes: Travis County District Attorney's Office, Texas Railroad Commission, Texas Young Republicans. Obel: Horsesock Public Health Department, Brietbart "Big Journalism" Summer Scholar, KVET-FM's "Bucky Godbolt Spins the Oldies" radio show.

- **2019:** Ozmana Zelotes, Tomasina Thomas and O'Nathan Obel accept manager-level positions at Texas Railroad Commission, Texas Air, Field and Feast Commission, and Texas Health and Human Services Enterprize, respectively.

- **2022:** Tomasina Thomas elected Texas Air, Field and Feast Commissioner.

The document dissolved. Sister F'nA and Cardu looked at each other as their nose pods folded neatly back into their nasal chambers.

"Just so you know," Pastor said, excited that he could finally share some details of the Capstone Dark project with his colleagues, "Zelotes will be elected Texas Railroad commissioner next year, and our own O'Nathan Obel will accept a gubernatorial appointment as Health and Human Services Enterprize Executive Commissioner in 2027!"

"I don't even know who these people are and, frankly, I could not care less," Sister said, standing.

"Oh, I forgot to mention!" Pastor Yates was oblivious to his wife's anger. "Peter will be re-elected to his Texas house seat next year and he'll announce for governor in 2025–and he'll win!"

Sister shook her head, sighed and sat back down. "You do realize that today is January 18, 2023, don't you?"

"Are we to understand," Cardu asked calmly, "that you have controlled every aspect of Texas state politics–not to mention the IRS, FBI and at least one scary fugitive on the Top Ten list– during the past 14 years and that you can also tell the future?"

"I only know the future because I control the future," Pastor explained matter-of-factly. "There's no magic here."

"Okay. And you did all of this because of some trumped-up tax charges from the IRS in 2009?"

Pastor chuckled and then laughed outright, not meaning to. "I'm sorry, I don't mean make light of your question," he said snorting through three deep coughs. "Damn ragweed. No, no, this has nothing to do with the IRS or any other feds, though I can certainly see why you might think that."

"Alright, I'll bite," Sister said. "If this has nothing to do with the feds, what on earth are you doing?"

"I'm taking over the world." Pastor leaned back in the chair and clasped his hands in his lap. "But we can talk about that later."

Church 3.3.1　　　**August 1, 2018 Y.O.S.P.L.**

"They do not understand it, and that's a problem." Brother Director Cardu had pressed the issue at the last elders meeting. No one, especially Pastor, would want to discuss it again this soon; still, Cardu had asked Sister Chief-Chief to include in on the agenda. This year marked the tenth anniversary of their acquisition of the Church of the P-Free Sabbath. Cardu had hoped it would be a time for reflection and renewal.

The church had grown exponentially since Arlen had outbid all comers on eBay for the church property, building and the rights to all things "P-Free." As the construction of the now-world-famous CPFS ecumenicon began, he'd invested the rest of his inheritance in marketing and a team of financial professionals to leverage federal and state grants and loans, secure foundation grants for the education and health of the ever-growing CPFS flock, and wrangle an annual capital campaign that dwarfed the $25 billion a former U.S. president never managed to cobble together for that border fence thing.

Cardu prayed to many deities for one thing on this anniversary: a pause, a moment to appreciate and truly give thanks for the great movement they had created. A moment to stop, look up at the boundless and beautiful Texas sky, and then start anew.

"Brother Pastor Yates will not want to discuss this again this week, if ever," Sister Chief-Chief TomBigBee. She didn't look up from her Big Chief tablet. "The agenda's set."

Brother Director Cardu leaned back in one of the leather chairs around the long meeting table, momentarily calmed by Word's universe around him. He read the quote from his own Gospel According to Cardu, masterfully carved into the Carpathian elm wall: "It's that way for a reason. I guess that's a good thing." (*CPFS Better Book*, Cardu 3:12). He'd penned that particular chapter in 2014 and had revised it regularly since then. During the past year, there had been so many updates, it was affectionately referred to as "Cardu's Diary."

As he and Sister Chief-Chief waited for the others to arrive, he drew miniscule circles in his own Big Chief tablet.

"I do not know Word, therefore I am." Brother Pastor's words from last week's meeting had still lingered in the room, waiting to be heard again by Cardu.

"You know I love that passage and embrace Word with all my soul, Brother Pastor," Cardu had insisted. "But too many of the people do not understand the *CPFS Better Book*. It is confusing for them. There are too many contradictions. I understand why that is, but–"

"You do not understand why that is!" Pastor Yate's booming accusation startled Cardu and everyone in the room. "If you did, we would not be having this conversation, Brother Director Cardu! You, of all people! Say it with me, Brother: 'Word is unknowable.' "

"Word is unknowable." Cardu repeated the phrase, words he, Sister F'nA and Pastor had written together years ago.

"Again please, Brother–and everyone!" Brother Pastor stood and raised his arms.

"Word is unknowable," the elders repeated in a practiced unison.

"The only way to celebrate our unknowable god is through our baffling religion. Word is unknowable. The church is unknowable. The *CPFS Better Book* incomprehensible." Brother Pastor Yates paused for effect and then asked with his trademarked (literally) smile, "Is that crystal clear?"

Capstone Light 3:2.2   January 18, 2024 Y.O.S.P.L.

"Welcome to the second meeting of Capstone Light on this, the 18th day of January, 2024th year of some people's lords! Is there any old business to discuss?" Pastor asked jauntily.

"What, since the first Capstone Light meeting one year ago?" Sister F'nA snarked.

"Yes, and speaking about the frequency these meetings, I'm thinking the third Wednesday of each year. I –."

"So, you're taking over the world," Sister F'nA stated in a pronounced monotone.

"Excellent! Picking up exactly where we left off last time!"

"That's what I do–pick up the pieces."

"We're taking over the world," Pastor answered, and then added quickly, "slowly, of course."

"And we are?"

"We are both of you, myself of course, Zelotes, Thomas, Obel and a couple of old friends."

"We better order in, because I have at least five hours of questions about Capstone Dark and that document you gave us nine minutes to read last year. I'm sure Brother Cardu has a like amount. My first question would be 'who are these 'couple of old friends?' but I know getting that out of you right off the bat will be like pulling teeth." Sister F'nA opened her Big Chief. "So, let's start with the Three Musketeers–Zelotes, Thomas, Obel. Then we can spend some getting-to-know-you time on Black Shade, and then circle back to extract some truth about your 'old friends.' "

"I'm an open book, ready for the reading," Pastor smiled.

For the rest of the day, Cardu and Sister F'nA interrogated Pastor Yates thoroughly and without humor; they pressed for details and tried to flesh out vague statements, playing good cop/bad cop as needed, and slapping the hell out of Pastor when he refused to respond. That last part isn't true; there was no slapping, though not because it wasn't considered.

Pastor was a master dissembler. His verbal sleight of hand revealed tantalizing half-truth that quickly vanished in confusing caveats and red-herring clarifications. The effect on his interrogators was delayed. Thinking they had a full understanding of one topic, Cardu and Sister F'nA would move on to the next, only to realize Pastor's explanation of the first was nothing more than gibberish.

At the exhausting end of it all, Sister F'nA regretted there was no official record of the conversation to see if they could, at the very least, confirm some un-truths. The next day, Cardu told her that all conference room activities are digitally documented; everything is archived and preserved for posterity.

"Everything?" Sister asked.

"Everything," he answered, avoiding eye contact with her.

"Since when?"

"The beginning."

"I see," she said.

"It is for my eyes only," said Cardu. "The archives will be sealed until the church's Tribulation Jubilee whenever that occurs. And, of course, at that point it won't matter. My only role is that of dispassionate archivist. I make no judgments."

"Right. Okay." She studied Cardu's inscrutable expression and decided to leave it at that. "We have a full transcript of yesterday. Did you bring a copy?"

Cardu glanced over to make sure the door to her office door was closed, reached into his bindle and handed her an inch-thick notebook. "Pastor would have our heads if he knew."

"He's probably arranged for it to burst into flames in nine minutes." Sister thumbed through the pages. "There was nothing about Black Shade in the Capstone Dark document—I threw out their name to him just to see if I got a reaction. I didn't notice anything, did you?"

"No, but that means nothing."

"I can't prove they're involved, but I just have a feeling there's something there. He's got so many Word-damned secrets," she said. "Do you know anything more than rumors about Black Shade?"

"They smuggle eyeballs across the border to donate to poor children. Believers have their own eyes removed and then put acid in their sockets. They believe that darkness illuminates the path to their god. They're Christian-based, only moderately-renegade if you compare them to the Legacy Southern Diocesan Decapitates or the Legacy Nouveau Luths."

"Yes," agreed Sister. "I'm not questioning the practices of our Legacy Faiths, but you have to wonder if Martin Luther would still preach that 'inner repentance is worthless unless it produces outward mortification of the flesh' if he were alive today."

"Yes, I do wonder that."

"In any case, the Decapitates make Black Shade look like a group of pious Sufis venerating Rabi ' a al-Basri over tea in 120 Hisri," Sister said.

"Ha! That's a good one, Sister. So true!"

"There, see? We're not doing so badly; we identified a truth."

"Here are a couple more truths," Cardu smiled. "Our Legacies Recruiting Team has tried to contact Black Shade for years. They're very popular among our membership and many would like to see a 'Legacy Black Shade' as part of CPFS."

"But our members don't really know really anything about Black Shade," Sister said.

"Right, their InterMess presence and social are active, but it's just fluff for potential recruits–wide-eyed innocents, as it were."

"Interesting choice of words there, hombre."

"Couldn't resist," Cardu smiled. "It's odd, though, that Pastor hasn't just jetted down to Oaxaca like he always does with potential Legacies." Remember that time, he–?"

"Don't get me started." Sister cut him off. "Okay, what else we got?"

"I don't know. What about the 'un-named high-value fugitive' from the FBI Top Ten Most Wanted List. How did Pastor convince a top-tenner to go to jail for him?"

"Right. And what did he give in return?" Sister F'nA asked.

"Maybe this is someone from the past; someone who owes him," Cardu speculated. "Wait, do you remember that professor Pastor interviewed on My Town Earth? Y'know, the guy who wrote I'm Okay, You're a Chuckle-headed Mooncalf."

"Right. He begged to be on the show forever to promote his book. Pastor finally agreed and the book sold really well, thanks to the interview."

"Yes, but then he murdered a colleague who debunked his research and published his own book: I Suck, There's No Such Thing as a Chuckle-headed Mooncalf."

"Exactly. Maybe–" Cardu's nose pod unfolded from his face as he spoke. "Here we go. Let's see. Looks like he served a life term for three years, and–"

"And what?"

"And – he works for us!"

"For CPFS?"

"Yes. He's a principal investigator in the R&D Division." Cardu's nose pod folded back into the center of his face. "Okay, so it's not him, but I think we're on the right track–an old acquaintance paying off a debt."

"Maybe, but what on earth did someone do for–or to–Pastor that requires a payment of 12 years under Crater Lake? And who knew there's a Super Max under Crater Lake, anyway?"

"There is, I'm certain," Cardu assured her. "I read there wasn't one in a fake news article."

"Is there any way to find out who this person is? The FBI doesn't have anything older than 24 hours on the InterMess. How are we supposed to see who was on the Top Ten List a dozen years ago? Sister said, exasperated. "They used to keep all that posted for months, but–Word dammit!" she threw her Big Chief tablet across her office. "We just spent an entire day firing questions at Pastor and all we got from it is more questions!"

"That is often the way it is with questions." Cardu felt a mini-lecture on the discovery and evaluation of evidence coming on. "You see, the–"

"You're not going to give me the 'peeling back the onion' talk are you?"

"Caught me."

Sister buried her face in her hands. "Where is Mrs. Greenhaw when you need her?"

Matzo 3.4.1   February 15, 2027 Y.O.S.P.L

"Chag Sameach, my friends!!" Legacy Alt-Jew rabbinical scholar Odede Jäger bellowed to the overflow crowd from the Church of the P-Free Sabbath guest podium. "Happy Passover! May you be blessed with happiness, prosperity, peace and good health on Pesach and always! Happy Passover!"

She was an annual favorite of the CPFS faithful, Legacy Alt-Jew and non-Legacy Alt-Jew alike. On the last day of Passover, CPFS ratings reliably peaked on all media, as long as Odede Jäger took the stage. Pastor Yates and Sister F'nA stood with the rest of the throng to welcome their old friend.

"Today we celebrate the liberation of the Israelites from Egyptian slavery and the freedom of all religions to flourish in the bounteous bosom of the Church of the P-Free Sabbath!" She opened with that line every year and once again, it met with a thunderous response.

"Do you know what Moses screamed at his second-in-command, Famuel, as they watched the Red Sea engulf thousands of Egyptian cavalry and foot soldiers in hot pursuit of the Israelites?" Scholar Jäger asked the crowd as it quieted. Transforming her visage into that of the ancient prophet, she channeled Moses. Spellbound, the congregation watched as the great man himself recreated the moment through her, from the podium.

"Jesus! You forgot the what?" Moses yelled.

"The grain, Master. The grain for the matzo!" said Famuel.

"Please, knock off the 'Master' stuff, will you? Now that we've escaped slavery, we are a free and egalitarian society. No matter how strong we become in future millennia, we shall never become oppressors and no one will call me 'Master,' " he soap-boxed. Regaining his focus, Moses again shouted, "Jesus! You forgot the what?!' "

"Who is Jesus?" asked Famuel, confused.

"Never mind who Jesus is—you forgot what?!"

"I forgot the grain for the matzo you told me not to forget."

"How could you do that? The one thing I asked you to remember was the grain to prepare the matzo for Passover!"

"For what?" Famuel often had to ask Moses what he was talking about.

"Passover! That's how we and future generations will refer to our escape from Egypt," Moses said, exasperated. "Didn't I mention that before?"

"No, Mast—" Famuel racked his brain for a solution to his colossal blunder. "I don't suppose you could re-part the Red Sea and I could pop back over to Egypt and grab the grain?"

"You 'don't suppose' incorrectly," Moses said.

"Is that a no?"

"Yes—no!" Moses lamented that Aramaic was such a difficult language, but that didn't stop him from rejoicing in the countless Israelites who had followed him out of downtown Cairo to make good their escape. They'd travelled east, on ancient Egypt's version of California's Route 1, along the coast to where they were told the Red Sea flowed into the Mediterranean Sea. Things got a little tense when everyone realized that Moses wouldn't have to part the Red Sea because it didn't go that far north; here, all they would have to do is walk along the coast to the Promised Land. Easy peasy.

But the people wanted a parting of the Red Sea! That was why most of them decided to make the trip in the first place. Moses, always thinking on his feet, hurried his people south until they stood on the shores of the Red Sea with a hoard of Pharaonic bad boys in hot pursuit. And there, Moses channeled his favorite actor of all time, Charlton Heston, and damn-well parted that sucker. It was a sight to behold!

Standing on the eastern shore of the Red Sea, Moses forgave Famuel. "Don't worry about leaving the matzo grain behind. I think I just heard Yahweh say something about a brand-new recipe for matzo."

"Awesome," Famuel said, eager to talk about something else. "Y'know, I just gotta say, the people think you've done a terrific job getting us out of Egypt! That was one hell of an exodus."

"One hell of a what?" Moses asked.

"Exodus."

"Oh my god! Thank you, Famuel! I've been tortured about what to call my book about this," Moses was giddy with excitement. "I was thinking about The Great Escape or maybe Houdini and Me, but nothing seemed to click. I just couldn't come up with the right title."

"One Hell of an Exodus does have a certain ring to it." Famuel ventured.

"It does, doesn't it?" Moses agreed. "One Hell of an Exodus. Yes!"

Scholar Jäger paused for effect; she could pause for effect with the best of them. "Now, some folks don't truly appreciate the struggles of the young Moses and the ultimate impact he had on the world. Think of it–here's a kid born in the Land of Goshen in 1391 B.C.; the Pharaoh is killing all male Jewish babies, so his mom puts him in a basket and floats him down the Nile to escape."

"Check it, yo. This next part is bat-shit crazy!" continued Scholar Jäger. She could communicate with the young folks with the best of them, too. "So, he's floating down the Nile which is actually going north–that's a whole other story–and he winds up bumping into Pharaoh's daughter, Thermuthis, who's taking a bath in the river. Long story short, Thermuthis adopts baby Moses because he's so cute, and his natural mom–who's a slave in the Pharaoh's household–ends up nursing him because Thermuthis can't do the nursing thing.

"Do you believe all of this?" the scholar asked. "I mean, we're talking some serious suspension-of-reality to get with this. You feel me?" Another pause. "DO YOU FEEL ME?! Because if you don't feel me, there's no way you're believing what happened next–Moses became the adopted younger brother of Rameses II, the future evil Pharaoh that Moses and the Israelites would end up fleeing in 1446 B.C. I mean, you can't make this stuff up!

"Let's face it, little man Moses floating down the Nile had zero prospects. Zilch, bupkes! But did he kvetch? No, he got to work saving the Israelites, am I right? And how did he do that, I ask you?

"He parted a sea–not just a lake or his hair–and he parted it without having even one environmental impact analysis or public hearing for input! Mazel tov! That's number one.

"Number two: he con-ver-sa-ted with God! Not bad, eh? Enough said.

"Number three: after 40 years in the wilderness–when he was like 100 years–Moses climbed up a mountain and brought back an actual rock with the Ten Commandments on it. And NO," Scholar Jäger added sternly, "there's no such thing as the 11-20 Commandments that Moses forgot to bring down from Mt. Sinai. Haters!"

"We love you, Odede!" yelled someone from the third balcony.

She smiled up into the darkness of arena. "I love you too, bubbala!"

"Do you know what happened when the Ten Commandments were shown to the Israelites?" she continued. "One of the teenagers asked which one of the commandments said they couldn't eat pork chops, hog jowls, and pig feet. Ever the arbiter of truth, Moses answered, 'There is no such commandment.' And he was correct.

" 'You mean we could have been having triple-pig pizza all this time and nobody ever bothered to mention it?' the people asked.

" 'Yes,' said Moses, with great solemnity."

Scholar Jäger became very serious. "In his autobiography, *One Hell of an Exodus*, Moses reflects on this critical point in history, noting it as the Israelites' 'come-to-Yahweh moment.' As every Jew knows, it forever altered the course of Judaism, having laid bare this and other deep divisions among the Jewish diaspora, brought to light by these burning questions:

1) Well, that's just great—now we can have porky pizza but we're stuck in the wilderness. Whattaya gonna to do about that??
2) In the future, when we can only afford *one* streaming service, will it be Netflix or Amazon? How about HBO? (If we have Amazon Prime, many rabbinical scholars pointed out, we'll be able to order a Swine Delight Pizza right to the house with no delivery charges.)
3) So, can we leave this wilderness, already?

"Now, because he was a prophet," she continued, "Moses knew that Famuel would lead half of the Israelites to the South Seas island of Borneo, where the Alt-Israelite sect would thrive as an open society, embracing world travelers, and growing the finest matzo grains on earth. In the year 740 A.D., the Bornean Israelites would welcome to their island paradise thousands of like-minded Muslim food refugees yearning to be free from the tyranny of their own dietary enslavement.

"As for Moses," concluded Scholar Jäger, "he took the rest of the diaspora to the Promised Land to create the nation of Israel! That's another whole other story."

Politicians 3:5.1   September 4, 2026 A.D.

"I understand some of your family members will help out on the campaign. Can you tell us more about that?" asked Ever-even Ivan, intrepid reporter from the multi-million-dollar non-profit news outlet. Brother Director Cardu, Sister F'nA and Pastor Yates watched candidate Phelt's first live campaign press conference on the big screen in the CPFS boardroom.

"Yes, indeed. My brother Phillip Phelt will represent us at some events around the state. He is a great lover of Texas and Texas history, as was my dad, who passed away years ago.

'Family' is very important for me and for all Texans. I'm happy that Phillip will be with me, but my mother, rest her soul —"

"Your real mother?" Ever-even interrupted.

"Excuse me?" Peter shot a nervous glance at Levi, which she had begged him never to do during a press conference. In the boardroom Yates, shot his own glance at Cardu and Sister Missy, but his was different from Peter's.

"Your biological mother, sir."

"That's correct, my mother Phyllis Phelt." Peter instinctively knew when a reporter had something and wasn't just fishing. This one had something, or thought he did. "Next question, please—"

"Thank you everyone," Levi interjected, commandeering the mic. "Representative Phelt needs to board a plane to Marfa. Later today, we'll advise you on the candidate's itinerary and other availabilities." The broadcast was terminated.

Yates watched the faces of Cardu and Sister Missy.

"What was that?" she asked.

"The truth is what that was," Pastor said.

"Wait, what? He was adopted?" Ever since they were kids, Missy had hated it when Aby stingily kept a secret. Sometimes he'd shared a tantalizing piece of it, but you were never sure when you had finally heard the whole truth. "Is this more 'Capstone Dark' crap that happened seventeen years ago?"

"No, it's nothing that I had control of. And it's no big deal yet. For now, it's just a good story."

"Will you please tell us what's going on?" Missy backed her chair away from the table. "If not, I've got work to do." She stood to leave the room.

"Okay," Pastor cleared his throat. "Welcome to the second meeting of Capstone."

"Word Almighty, you are such a nerd," she said. "Why the cloak and dagger? Just give us our secret decoder rings and tin-foil hats, and tell us what you have to say."

"Alright," Pastor said. "Peter's biological mother is actually my mother."

"What the hell are you talking about?" Sister asked. "You're brothers?!"

"No, my biological mother is Peter's mother." He looked at their blank faces. After keeping this particular secret for decades, he couldn't quite believe that now was the time to say out loud, "Peter and I were switched at birth."

"How on earth did that–?" Cardu interrupted himself. "And you didn't tell us? When did you find out? Does Peter know?"

"No, but his campaign is uncovering the facts as we speak. My mother told me the summer after my injury in eighth grade."

"And you didn't tell us? We were your posse! I was–am you're best friend!"

"I'm sorry. I apologize, Charlie." He hadn't called Cardu "Charlie" for years. "I didn't know what do with it. I was still recovering. Missy, you spent all your time with Peter, and you were in India with your mom most of that summer, Charlie–I only saw you a couple times." The three were silent.

"What now?" Sister asked. "Did you feed this to Ever-even Ivan?"

"Not exactly. Let's just say it was arranged for his interest to be piqued by a waiter at the AARP Club Med in Borneo last month. He thinks he knows more than he does; he doesn't know about the switch. Yet."

"It makes sense though, Aby, you being Mr. Phelt's son," Charlie said. "You were both kind of–"

"He was never my dad," Pastor said. "And he's dead anyway."

"Why have you held onto this so long?" Sister asked. "If you wanted to hurt Peter with this, you could have leaked it when he first ran for the Legislature."

"Yes. This really makes no sense." Charlie said.

"And it does make sense that neither of you ever told me exactly what happened that day when Peter knocked me out cold?" Pastor stood up. "Nobody told me that he fired a dodgeball at my head at point-blank range and almost killed me. Nobody told me that I was in a coma for days."

"I should have told you," Charlie offered. "But–"

"I didn't know anything until I got out of the hospital that summer; my mother told me about everything, including the switch. But I kept it all to myself. No big deal, right? You thought I didn't know what happened, but I did–I knew it and thought about it every day." He paused to catch his breath; he walked the length of the table, looking at the floor.

"But then I found God at The Way, right, Charlie?" he continued. "Excuse me, we found God. You and me, sharing everything right down to Deacon Dees baptizing us together in that shit-for-water White River."

"I remember," Charlie said.

"That was so long ago." Sister F'nA offered.

"For me, it was yesterday." Pastor continued. "I was submerged in the water and when Deacon Dees brought me up, it was unimaginably beautiful. I felt the spirit of the Holy Ghost enter me, in every part of my being. You did too, Charlie; I saw it in you. And we hugged each other, sopping wet, and were cheered by our brothers and sisters in The Way. Do you remember what I said to you, Charlie?"

" 'I'm free,' you said. 'I'm free.' "

"Yes. For that one instant, I was free. The freest and safest I would ever be in my life, I thought. I'd embraced the mercy and love of God, and was protected from everything by our blessed Way family–our new posse. It was glorious." Pastor's eyes teared with the memory.

"Yes."

"And how long did the everlasting grace of God last that day for me, or any of us?" Yates dried his eyes. "What was it? Five minutes later, when Deacon Dees introduced the newcomers, there you were." He looked at Missy. "You and Peter. Come to join the family. That was my family! The one place where I felt healed and loved. And safe."

"I've told you before. When we came there that day, we didn't even know that you were a member–"

"I know, I know! But God knew!" Pastor shouted. "God knew." He looked around the room, annoyed that the maintenance crew hadn't replaced those screaming LEDs in the ceiling. He'd specifically told them to find some more of the old-tech, black market soft-white incandescent bulbs he used in his office. The sun had almost blinded him that day as the Deacon laid him back into the White River to be baptized.

Their nose pods simultaneously played the Alice in Chains tune they'd agreed would indicate a top priority alert. Cardu sneezed as the small screen emerged from his nose. It was Sister Chief-Chief.

"Sorry to disturb you Brothers, Sister. Ms. Levi of the Phelt campaign back-channeled us with an urgent meeting request. Santa Rita rig, 4 a.m., tomorrow morning."

"What?" Sister F'nA asked. "The Phelt campaign? Since when are we being 'back-channeled' by the–? I didn't even know we had a back channel."

"A back channel is like a big smelly fart," Sister Chief-Chief offered in a bureaucratic monotone. "There isn't one until there is one."

"Please let them know we'll be there. Thank you, Sister." Pastor's screen folded itself back into his nose as he looked at Cardu and Sister F'nA. "There is a back channel and that's the last secret I'll ever keep from you."

* * *

Santa Rita No. 1, located in Section 2, Block 2 (Reagan County, University of Texas holdings) roared to life on May 28, 1923, spewing oil over the top of its derrick, and covering a 250-

square-yard area around the site. In 1940, the Texas State Historical Association relocated the Santa Rita rig from its original site to the University of Texas campus in Austin, commemorating the ingenuity and perseverance of Texas wildcatters and the emergence of Texas as an economic power to be reckoned with–or "with which to be reckoned," as reported by the New York Times.

It was the perfect spot to have a meeting with a future Texas governor, because the Santa Rita rig was not at all what it seemed. It wasn't the first Texas gusher and it wasn't the biggest crude oil producer by a long shot. Any Midland-Odessa preschooler knows that the first big rig to gush black gold was the Texas and Pacific Abrams No. 1 in 1920, but that fact counts for little in the making of a legend where controlling the narrative is everything.

When they arrived at 3:59 a.m., there was a black Prius stretch limo parked on MLK. The chauffeur approached them before they could get within twenty feet of the car. "Pastor Yates," he stated, "you and your party will follow me, please."

In the small grass triangle, Santa Rita No. 1 pump jack labored in the darkness; it was just for show. Beside it was a wooden structure, seven feet tall with door-width sides; in fact, each of its sides was a door.

"Please enter and close the doors behind you," said the driver. It was a snug fit; they entered and pulled the doors shut. The floor descended slowly into a small room furnished with a loveseat, table and chairs. As they stepped off the platform a voice said, "Welcome to the antechamber." "Antechamber" had been on Pastor's list of words to use in a sermon, but he was waiting for just the right situation. Antechamber: a small room that serves as the entrance to a larger room– a sublime metaphor waiting to teach a worthy lesson, to be sure.

"Pastor Yates, please leave the room," said the voice. Whoever designed this experience, clearly did not share Pastor's concept of an antechamber; the door on the far wall was an exit to an even smaller room. He walked through, and closed it behind him.

The room was damp and musty. Oversized bolts fastened thick, bleeding iron strips across its concrete walls. In one corner was a square table with two chairs; in the center, a refurbished Corliss steam engine that powered the arm of the Santa Rita rig on the ground above. It hissed and clanked erratically until it suddenly ceased all movement. Across the room, Peter stepped out of the shadows; it was all very dramatic and much appreciated by Pastor Yates, the consummate showman.

"The suit is very nice, but you look tired—like someone just told you that my mom is your mom," Pastor said. "I'm sorry, brother. Elvira is definitely an acquired taste and I'm not sure you got enough years left in ya'."

Peter examined Brother Pastor Arlen Bob Yates of the Church of the P-Free Sabbath. He was a worldwide brand, a meme; his likeness was omnipresent on the pop-upz, skymages, full-moon ads and physical billboards where they were still allowed. Added to those and other opportunities to see his smiling face, were the legion of international destination-resorts that bore his name for not an insignificant sum.

"Why are you here?" Peter asked.

"I was under the impression you requested this meeting."

"No. Why did you come to Texas?"

"To be with you," Pastor smiled. Peter didn't. "Truth is, I've been here for over twenty years and I still don't have faintest idea. I might ask you the same thing."

"I was meant to be in Texas," Peter said. "I've loved Texas since I was a child. You know that."

"I know very little for certain," Pastor smiled broadly. "You're not recording this are you?"

"No."

"In that case, I came to Texas to create a mega-church large enough to amass the fortune I would need to destroy you when you were at the pinnacle of your career, because you ruined my life. Naturally, I named my evil empire the Church of the P-free Sabbath. It's pretty simple." Pastor smirked, with the same question-mark face he'd made as a kid after suggesting some crazy scheme to the posse. "What do you think?!"

"I think you haven't changed much," Peter smiled. "Other than that, I don't know what to think."

"Me neither, still trying to figure it all out."

"So the "P-free" doesn't refer to me in any way?"

"No. Man, you're more paranoid than a Texas Democrat. I must say, I'm a little disappointed that you haven't read a little bit more about the church's origins, especially the name."

"Oh, I have," said Peter, "and it's all very enlightening, not to mention a good yarn."

"What is religion if not a good yarn?"

"I did listen to the My Town Earth episode where you and Charlie, sorry, Cardu, interviewed the church's founder. When was that, '05, '06?"

"So you heard that show, but still you wonder if the P is for Peter?"

"Can't always believe everything you hear, right Pastor? I'm just a curious guy."

"You are wise beyond your years, my son," Pastor smiled. "If you're curious, you've come to the right place, because I have all the answers."

"You are such an ass."

"Funny you should mention that. I was thinking of changing my title from Brother Pastor to Your Ass-Holiness, but it was already taken."

"It's got a ring to it, though." Peter paused. "I need your help to contain this story."

"Wow. That's it?" Pastor asked. "I need your help to contain this story? That's all you have to say?"

"I don't have the luxury of time to get all sentimental about this. It's true, right?"

"Without a doubt. Elvira told me about it in '99. My dad corroborated the story."

"There couldn't be a better story to derail my candidacy. Think about it. I'm switched at birth with the boy who turns out to be my best friend, after my parents move the family to Indianapolis. Why move to Indianapolis from Goshen Alabama, if not to continue the crazy sex quadrangle our parents must have had? Who knows? And then, you and I have a falling out and don't talk to each other for decades, but end up potentially being two of the most powerful men in Texas. We've surely kept this a secret to serve nefarious goals, most likely related to the establishment of a one-world government."

"It's not a bad story," Pastor said.

"The conspiracy crews are all over it already. Can you blame them?"

"Nope."

"Look, the Texas People's Party will help defend me against any false facts, accusations, whatever. What they're concerned about is you. You and me. CPFS and the Texas P Party don't exactly see eye to eye on anything–except maybe secession."

"And freedom of religion?" Pastor said without expression. He was still amazed Peter had zero inkling that CPFS was responsible for his election as Texas House District 151 Representative and Air, Field and Feast Commissioner in 2022– not to mention his first electoral success in becoming the honorable Mayor of Horsesock in 2016.

"Yes, of course."

"Who's here with you? In the limo out there." Pastor asked.

"My campaign manager Mary Levi and uh, did you know Cyrana's with the campaign?"

"No, I hadn't heard that," the pastor lied. "That's great."

"Your dad is here, too."

"My–? What the hell is he doing here?" Pastor's surprise was real this time.

"He contacted me yesterday to see if he could help. Maybe make a statement, or something." Peter looked at the speechless pastor, trying to gauge his sincerity. He knew Yates had orchestrated his election wins over the years, so there was no reason to believe that the arrival of Benjamin Yates wasn't also his doing. "He flew in last night. He said he called the CPFS main offices but couldn't get through to you."

"I need a mojito," Pastor said. How did his people not know his father would be in that limousine outside? He made a mental note to re-read Donald Rumsfeld's memoir, *Why Didn't Somebody Tell Me That?*

"The world needs a mojito," Peter said.

Pastor took a slow deep breath, trying to forestall a panic attack. He felt the high-pitched pressure in his chest that always came with not knowing where all the players were and what they were up to. He looked at Peter and cursed himself for revealing a weakness. His mind searched for an out; some way to regain control. It would come eventually, but not now.

Pastor looked at Peter. Maybe he did know that his entire professional career had been orchestrated by the church after all. "How can I help you, Representative Phelt?

Children 3:6.1   February 13, 1999 A.D.

Even the light penetrating his eyelids was blinding. Aby buried his face in the pillow and listened to what he thought were real voices. He turned his head away from the darkness just enough to see Mr. Button, Pastor-Lawyer Famulonomous Agane and Benjamin Yates at the foot of his hospital bed. The three dissolved into the Tin Man, Scarecrow and the Cowardly Lion as everything went dark. He listened to random bits of conversation between periods of silence he first thought were a matter of seconds, but then began to wonder if they were days.

"I just happened to be in town for a parole hearing for the Speedway Bomber, and..."

"Subclinical seizures mostly, but we're observing periodic focal and..."

"SISSY!"

"It looks like Peter will be in there for several weeks, we'll see. No charges filed, yet. But..."

"I love you, sweetheart. All your friends are waiting for you to come back to school, and your dad and I..."

"Myoclonic seizures ... let's increase the Phenobarbital to..."

"Hey, you in there?"

Before the double-dodge tournament, the most pressing issue between the Phelts and Yateses was the baby switch. They'd ignored it until less than two months ago, though they'd had years to tell their sons they were living with the wrong parents. They could have done it with a therapists or they could have mentioned it in passing over breakfast one day and let the chips fall where they may. But none of that happened and now the switch paled in comparison to Peter's "felonious assault on Aby"–at least that's how Elvira referred to it, as she recounted the crime to doctors, nurses and anyone else who would listen. Nurture ruled the day, as Elvira cursed and disavowed her natural son, and Phyllis protected her Peter from school officials and the police.

"My boy is sick," Phyllis told a Washington Township officer. "He needs help." The police agreed to postpone questioning or charging Peter, as long as he was admitted as an in-patient at Larue Carter Mental Hospital.

At the double-dodge tournament that day, the posse ran from the stands onto the court. Peter stared at them blankly, erratically jerking his head "no" as Aby lay motionless on the floor. Faith took a step toward Peter but hesitated, frightened. Charlie tried to go to Aby but was stopped at the circle of adults and teachers surrounding him. Missy put her arm around Faith and they, with Charlie and Cyrana, walked off the court.

"How could Peter do that? That's so awful!" Faith bawled into Missy's shoulder.

"He didn't know what he was doing."

"That's evil!" Faith exploded. "I hate him!"

Had Aby heard the voices as he was lay unconscious on the gym floor surrounded by his parents, Coach and the noisy crowd? Does Faith hate somebody? Faith? Did he see who she was talking about? Who does she hate? He yells at his mother to be silent, for once. I want to hear what they're saying. He couldn't see his friends; his mother badgers him. "Arlen? Arlen? Wake up sweetheart, please." SHUT UP! SHUT! UP! That's in the future—how could I hear that? No. I'm in the future. I am in the future, but—? Please be quiet. Just be quiet.

He bolted upright in his bed, wincing in pain. He felt a strong, comforting arm supporting him, though he didn't whose it was. "We'll take care of you," a woman said.

* * *

Dr. Larue Carter was the founder of the first psychiatric hospital in Indianapolis in 1945. On February 14, 1994, Peter Phelt became the first future-Texas governor to be involuntary committed to the facility. He would successfully secret this fact until releasing it himself during his 2026 Texas gubernatorial campaign, hours before his opponent intended to do the very same. The announcement of the Phelt campaign's hastily developed Texas Mental Health Initiative included the candidate's emotional revelation that he himself had been forced to live with the stigma of a childhood bout with mental illness.

But that will be then, and this was now. (It's okay to re-read the previous sentence, if you need to.) Peter was a patient at "Larue" as they called it. He was locked in a room—for his own safety, they said—with only a bed and a single chair for the family-only, one-at-a-time visitor he was allowed. He slept most of the time for the first few days, waking only to eat what he could and watch his mother fight back tears.

After the first week of blood work, scans, and assessments, he was moved to a room with two beds, but no roommate. He was provided five therapy sessions per week, three meals and two snacks per day, and lots of colorful pills. He was allowed to sleep as late as 7:30 a.m., but his schedule's flexibility ended there. There were three recreation hours each day; during the last, he could have visitors in the common room if he wanted. That every hour of the day was accounted for suited him. Except for the therapy hours, it kept his mind off the fact that he was locked up.

His dad visited daily and told forced, lighthearted yarns and jokes as if they were having a catch in the back yard. After he'd told all of his stories two or three times, he had very little to say and said very little. One time he came in and didn't even say hi; he just sat and then left. The next day he apologized, but did it again the next time.

For weeks, Phyllis didn't ask Peter anything other than "how are you feeling?" and "is the food okay?" If there was an opportunity to ask a non-probing follow-up question she would, but she was skittish. She had missed all the signs of Peter's imminent meltdown and had decided that her years of therapeutic practice were of no use to her in this situation; in fact, they were a liability when it came to Peter.

When she finally asked a different question, it was this: "How do you feel about Mars?"

"Sounds good. There's a vending machine on the second floor." Peter looked at her across the checkerboard.

"No, silly. The planet, not the candy bar." Phyllis was thankful for a moment of lightheartedness.

"Oh, yeah," Peter smiled. "We studied the Mars Observer last fall after it was lost. But there's another one going up in a couple years, right?

"Yes, the Mars Global Surveyor," said Phyllis, happy that he recalled studying the topic at school. She'd gone to see Mr. Button and some of Peter's teachers to see if there were any light assignments he could work on when he was ready. "So, we were thinking of taking a trip to the Johnson Space Center in Houston later in the summer if everything works out. They have a great Mars exhibit and another one on the Mir space station."

"Alright." Peter nodded and jumped three of her checkers. "King me."

* * *

At Vonnegut Junior High, the rest of the school year was tense and confusing. There was no posse and no Peter. And until the last day of school, when Mrs. Yates insisted on showing everyone that nothing could keep her boy down, there was no Aby.

He literally had no say in the matter of returning to school because for a while he was unable to speak, a result of the brain injury he'd suffered. After two weeks in the intensive care unit, his physical health and speech improved and he was moved to the stroke wing of the hospital, where he stayed until the insurance company said he had to move to a rehabilitation facility.

Mrs. Yates unsuccessfully fought the decision, claiming his temporary vision loss and difficulty moving his left leg and arm required that he remain in the hospital. Aby's neurologist, Cy Johnson, didn't support her, explaining that Aby would receive more intensive therapies at the rehab hospital, although he would have to continue wearing a dark covering to protect his eyes. For Aby, getting out of the hospital was the most important thing; if it meant that he had to be in a rehabilitation facility for a while, so be it.

"You look like Zorro, except your blindfold doesn't have eye slits." Charlie and Cyrana sat at a table in a recreation room with Aby. They had gotten a ride with Dr. Johnson, who was checking up on Aby and his other patients at the rehabilitation hospital. It was a quiet Saturday, absent of tough-love therapists and family members loudly encouraging patients to "take one more step."

"Well, you look like a monkey!" Aby laughed.

"Do you wear that thing all day?" Cyrana asked, waving her hand back and forth in front of the thick black blindfold to make sure Aby couldn't see anything. He didn't flinch.

"Yeah, except if I'm in my room with all the lights off, or sleeping. What do you think of my cane?"

"Cool."

"I'm getting pretty good at it and my walking's getting better, too." Aby said. "Hey, so how's old Lockhart doing? Still snoring away the afternoons?"

"I don't know, but he told me to say hi when I told him I was coming to see you. He was the monitor in the cafeteria yesterday," Cyrana said.

"Yeah, tell him I'm doing great." Aby rubbed his eye, underneath the eye cover. "How's Faith? She and her mom stopped by last week, but she didn't stay long."

"She's good," Cyrana glanced at Charlie. "It's weird."

"What's weird?"

"I don't know, she and Missy aren't really friends anymore. She's real quite around school, and Missy doesn't hang out with us so much."

"But she goes to see Peter!" Charlie blurted out.

"Who, Faith?" Aby asked.

"No, Missy! Missy goes to see him! Can you believe that?" Charlie asked.

"Charlie, c'mon," Cyrana said.

"I mean, like you guys really liked each other, right?" He pressed the point with Aby.

"Yeah, but it's okay," said Aby. It was impossible to read his expression with the eye covering. "She's his friend too, I guess."

"Yeah, I guess," Charlie said. "But–"

"Hey, when will you come back to school?" Cyrana interrupted

"Definitely by the end of school, my mom says, just for a visit–" He was interrupted by a voice across the room.

"Hi." Aby recognized Larry Dunn's voice.

"Hey, Larry!"

"Hi. My dad, uh–I wanted to come by and say hi. Your mom said it be would okay."

"Yeah, sure. Thanks for coming!"

Larry crossed the room with a book in his hand, nodding at Cyrana and Charlie. "Oh, sorry."

"About what?" Aby asked.

"Oh, nothing. I just brought you a present but it's a book and–can you even see?"

"Sure, he can see. They're just giving his eyes a rest from all the light and everything," Charlie had been asked countless stupid questions by classmates about Aby since the injury. "He's great, he's gonna be fine. Jeez."

"Oh, good." Larry put the book on the table next to Aby. "It's The Giver. My dad said it got some kind of award and it's about a kid our age, sort of."

"Thanks, that's cool."

"It's not wrapped or anything." Larry looked around the room and shuffled in the silence. "Well, I have to go. My dad's waiting outside."

"Okay, see you later." Aby waved, wondering if real blind people said "goodbye" instead of "see you later."

* * *

"He's going home Monday," Missy said.

"Texas Independence Day," Peter zipped up his jacket. The outside courtyard at Larue was surrounded by the hospital itself, but it was still a blustery 45 degrees. "Well, it's not really. March 3rd is when they signed all the papers and declared independence, but April 21 is when the Texians beat Santa Ana at the Battle of San Jacinto in 1836."

"The who?" Missy asked.

"Texians. It's what people from Texas were called back then."

"Oh." She'd heard Peter go on about Texas before, but was never too interested.

"I wonder if he remembers. I told him about the battle a million times, but he might not remember that Monday is San Jacinto Day."

"So, now it's his Independence Day too, kind of."

"I guess so, yeah." Peter said.

"So, are you still going to Houston this summer?"

"But that wasn't the first Independence Day," Peter said, oblivious to her question. "Part of east Texas declared independence in 1826 but it didn't last. It was called the Republic of Fredonia." Peter chuckled. "My dad got mad at Aby once because he made fun of Fredonia– yeah, these guys called the Marx Brothers made a funny movie about a fake country named Fredonia. Aby loves that movie; he acted out scenes from it, and marched around and sang this one hilarious song about Fredonia going to war. It was real funny, but my dad didn't think so."

"Why, if it was so funny?"

"I don't know. Just because he knows a lot about Texas history and really loves it," Peter explained. "I kind of understand it, I guess."

"Yeah, me too." They sat quietly for a minute.

"So, what else did Aby say?" Peter asked.

"Nothing, I mean, I don't know. Faith told me about him going home. I haven't seen him."

"You haven't seen him? I thought you and Charlie and Cyrana visited him."

"We'll they went to see him. I guess, I–"

"What? Why haven't you?"

"I'm sorry!" Missy's voice cracked. "I'm sorry."

"It's okay, it's fine." Peter said, trying to calm her. She took a tissue from one of Larue's ubiquitous Kleenex boxes and dried her eyes.

"I just hated how everybody looked at you that day you hurt Aby, like you were some kind of monster. Everybody ran to him on the floor, but he wouldn't wake up. And they all stared at you, like you would attack them or something. Even Coach G. looked like he was afraid of you and he's a grown man."

Peter looked at her, aghast. "What? I wouldn't–"

"And then Faith started yelling that she hated you."

Peter's eyes widened, realizing that without anyone telling him exactly what happen that day, he'd unconsciously arrived at the conclusions that he'd had a big seizure or something, and Aby had gotten hurt lunging for a ball. Two separate incidents.

"And then she screamed that you were evil. Your girlfriend called you evil!" Missy stopped abruptly and looked at Peter. "You're just an eighth grader," she said softly. "You can't be evil."

Missy had broken the one condition she'd agreed to when she was allowed to visit Peter: don't talk about that day. Peter's therapist and Phyllis realized this was an impossible request of someone so young, but felt that a visits from friends were essential to his recovery. Missy had been the only one to even ask about Peter, and Phyllis desperately wanted him to know that he hadn't been abandoned by the entire world.

Politicians 3.5.2   September 7, 2026 A.D.

It was early in the gubernatorial campaign and there were already three promising "Peter Phelt" scandals: 1) a clandestine familial connection with the most powerful religious leader in the world, 2) the mouth-watering prospect of a campaign financing/influence scam, and 3) a baby switch. All were fair game at the Labor Day press conference, as candidate Phelt and Church of the P-Free Sabbath Brother-Pastor Yates emerged from the East Austin Communities YMCA to face a parking lot full of reporters.

Nose pods emerged to record and "super-drupal" the event worldwide. As juicy as the political angles were, it was Brother-Pastor Yates who generated the national and global coverage. Arlen nodded to a Madagascar Daily Planet reporter who'd interviewed him last week, and another from the Vatican Press who refused to ever interview him. He never spoke at public events, much preferring the CPFS ecumenicon in Nagaswamie and other church facilities around the world where they could micro-manage every detail. For this event, Ministers in Chains who were between prison sentences, provided undercover security and CPFS-others circulated in the large crowd to initiate applause and/or laughter as needed.

"Good morning ladies and gentlemen! First, I'd like to say happy Labor Day to Texas workers and the families that support them! Texas is a proud Fight-to-Work state! We fight for our jobs and the right to Fight-to-Work! With me today is a man everyone knows, Pastor Brother Arlen Bob Yates from the Church of the P-Free Sabbath, and—"

"Pastor Brother Yates, are you endorsing Representative Phelt for governor? A man yelled from the rear.

"Do you know who your real parents are?"

"We'll get to your questions shortly. If you don't mind, I—" Peter raised his hand to quiet what quickly became a barrage of questions.

"Did you used to date the Pastor Brother's wife?"

"Does the P stand for Peter?"

"Please, excuse me, I'd like to—" shouted Peter.

"Will you become a member of the church, Representative Phelt?"

"Silence!" Yates said in a powerful, piercing voice. And there was silence. "The Representative has a few more remarks before taking your questions. Representative?"

"Yes, thank you. Uh, Pastor Yates and I chose the Austin East Communities YMCA for today's press conference because the people here work day-in and day-out to strengthen and preserve Texas families, and we are pleased to announce that the P Party and the Church of the P-Free Sabbath will be co-sponsoring a new initiative called 'Make Texas Families Great Again.' For too long, our families have suffered, but no more. No more, my friends!

"There is nothing more important than family! In the past few days, there have been many rumors regarding my family, and the citizens of Texas have a right to know about my heritage if I'm going to ask you to make me your governor. Ladies and gentlemen, I'm pleased now, to introduce to you Mr. Benjamin Yates, my natural father and the adoptive parent of Pastor Brother Yates." The elder Yates smiled and stood between his sons.

"What you see here is a family; an uncommon family to be sure, but a family like yours," Phelt said with his arm around Mr. Yates' shoulder. "On the day Pastor Brother Yates and I were born, an unfortunate bureaucratic mistake resulted in two little boys going home with the incorrect parents. But the parents who reared both of us could not have been more loving and kind, and I think I speak for the Pastor, when I say that my life has been blessed!"

Before reporters could yell out a question, he added, "Brother Yates?"

"Thank you. You know, I never had a brother," Yates spoke softly to the crowd. "But when I hear you, Peter, call me your brother, it's very special. I cannot adequately express to everyone how extraordinary I feel right now, because I've never had such a feeling. It is an honor to stand here with our father. His sweet nature abides in you, Peter, as his nurturing has guided me throughout my life."

He put his arm around Benjamin Yates and the three embraced. Peter felt the old man's tears on his cheek and realized the crowd was applauding. Even as he felt his own tears welling up, he marveled at the ease with which Arlen had created such a moment.

"Dad," Arlen said as the clapping died down. "I love you and I want to thank you for being here today. And I want to thank Word for every twist and turn of history since the beginning of time that has led us to this moment. Thank you."

"Thank you, son." Benjamin Yates said, wiping his eyes. "And thank you, Peter, son."

"We have time for a few questions," Peter said, pointing to the rear.

"Pastor Yates, are you endorsing Representative Phelt for governor today?"

"No, I've never supported a political candidate for office. Frankly, I don't enjoy being involved in any aspect of politics."

"Mr. Yates, is Representative Phelt's mother travelling with you?" Benjamin Yates looked to his Pastor-son to answer the question.

"Representative Phelt's natural mother did not make the trip. She is a very private person and will not be giving any interviews." Pastor pointed to a reporter in the back. "Yes?"

"To confirm, both of your natural parents are deceased. Is that correct, Pastor?"

"Yes, sadly they are. I would truly love to embrace them, as any child would his parents. But we should remember, it's the Representative who felt that loss much more than I ever could. Jake and Phyllis Phelt raised and cherished him, and Peter and his brother Phillip loved them dearly." Pastor cleared his throat, bringing a handkerchief to his eyes. Peter suspected the question was a plant.

"Thank you, Brother Yates," Peter said, nodding toward a venerable Austin American-Statesman reporter, noted for toppling more than her share commissioners and politicians. She was old-school, no nose pod for this one. She put her dog, Pugsly, on the ground and flipped back a page in her Big Chief.

"A question for both of you, if I may. Secession—is that a 'when' or an 'if?' "

"I hope to Almighty Word that 'secession' is a 'never'." Pastor answered quickly.

"I, too, hope it's a 'never,' " Phelt answered confidently. "But we must remember that secession is not an end unto itself. Secession is a process, a potential path to greater things. Texas will be greater under my administration and we will achieve that greatness by any means necessary! Thank you all for coming today! Thank you!"

Peter waved and turned abruptly, corralling the Yateses back into the YMCA. The reported jotted down the quote. Pugsly, astride a campaign brochure on the pavement, peed on Representative Phelt's face.

* * *

Peter and the Yateses greeted the YMCA staff who had gathered to watch the press conference from the lobby, and then went into the Cross-Blast Inferno Exer-Space Room for privacy.

"I think that went well," said Mr. Yates. "That was kind of you, Arlen, to acknowledge Peter's and Phillip's loss."

"How did you think it went?" Peter looked at Arlen.

"I think there are opportunities for you to enhance your relationship with the press," Arlen offered.

"Ouch. That bad?"

"Just a suggestion. And, by the way, you'd do well to stop referring to your party as the 'P Party.' The 76 percent of eligible Texas voters who aren't sure what party you represent think that the P stands for Peter. Lousy optics. It's best to stick with 'Texas People's Party.' "

"And just moments ago the good Pastor said 'Frankly, I don't enjoy being involved in any aspect of politics.' "

"But I didn't say I *wasn't*."

"What are you up to? You just schooled me out there, up one side and down the other. You were damn good, I must admit. You had them devouring each morsel you offered and made me look awkward and inept at every turn. You think I'm out of my league? Is that what this was all about? The pastor shows the politician how to run for governor?"

"Okay, you two," interjected Mr. Yates. "I really don't think that—"

"No, it's fine Dad. Peter's right," admitted Arlen. "That's exactly what I did."

"Jesus." Peter kicked over a stack of undulating yoga-metric hypercubes.

"Because I want to help."

"How? You just said that you wouldn't endorse me—not that I would accept your support. And why? Why for God's sake would you support anyone from the P Par ... the Texas People's Party."

"Secession."

"You just categorically rejected secession out there," Peter looked at Arlen, incredulous. "You know what? Thank you for your help on the press conference. I think we've laid the baby-switch issue to rest. I have work to do."

"You're so full of—."

"Arlen, please." Mr. Yates pleaded.

"You're not running for Mayor of Horsesock any more, Peter. This isn't about toothbrush lawsuits against the federal government or finally getting rid of the last public school. And it's not just another redneck rally where you do a secession striptease to win the primary. It's getting serious now. You know that—"

"Terrific—tell me what I know?" Peter shot back.

"You know that whoever wins this election will be the first president of the new Republic of Texas." The three were quiet. Arlen took a seat at the one of the training tables with Mr. Yates.

"Maybe." Peter looked out the window at Pugsly, underfoot the media crews loading their trucks.

"Absolutely. You know better than anyone that Texas has been moving toward secession ever since it joined the Union in 1845."

"We at least agree on that," Peter said.

"I usually don't say things like this but," Arlen smiled, "do you mind if I just get to the point?"

"Please."

"I know you don't believe most of the skubalon Griff-Raff and the P Party believes. That's not you. You care for people, and you–" Arlen looked over his shoulder and around the room. "You believe in a compassionate government that cares for all its people."

"Who's piling up the shit now?"

"You're driven to serve. You can't help it, for whatever reason."

"Do you want to keep psycho-babbling me, or shall I schedule another appointment?" Peter asked curtly.

"No, I'm sorry–look, I want to help you serve. Let's work on this together."

"Why? Why do you come to me now? For years, you and your people have fought us tooth and nail on healthcare, charter schools and everything else including the goddamned snail darter that's been extinct for five years now. Can we stop with the fucking snail darters, already?"

"They'll come back," Arlen couldn't stop himself.

"Jesus, are you able to be serious for more than two minutes? Or real? Or something other than the passive-aggressive jokester you apparently still are after all these years?"

"Maybe you two can discuss this later," Mr. Yates suggested. "This doesn't seem like the right place to–"

"Maybe you're right, Mr. Yates," agreed Peter.

"No, no, wait," said Arlen. "You're right, you're right about that. And you're certainly entitled to ask me "why now?' "

'Well?"

"I'm here for my church and the millions of people who depend on it. The church needs Texas to survive. Any day now the feds will indict me on tax evasion, fraud and I don't know what other trumped-up charges–and seize all the church's assets."

"So, you move." Peter said.

"And where would you suggest we move? To another state? That won't make any difference. Another country? No, they'd tax me and the church to death, if they didn't hang me first."

"So, you're left with what?"

"An independent Republic of Texas. It's our only hope," said Arlen. "Just like it's your only hope to save the real Texas." He paused to gauge the effect of what he thought was a pretty convincing answer to the 'why now' question he knew Peter would ask–the Capstone Light plan depended on Peter believing that CPFS was as fully-invested in secession as he was.

"Your people can't handle the federal charges? My god, I can't even imagine the resources and influence you must have at your disposal."

"We've been fighting them since 2009, Peter–not even two years after we established the Church of the P-free Sabbath," said Arlen, almost pleading. "We're in perpetual negotiations. We give more and more and it's never enough. They make a deal, take what we've offered, and then renege. We've haven't gotten anything from them, except a couple hearing postponements. You wouldn't believe some of the things they have us doing. Check up on it for yourself."

"I will. Don't you worry about that," Peter said.

Children 3:6.2   June 3, 1999 A.D.

As soon as Mr. Dunn spotted them a half-block away from Vonnegut Junior High, he began waving like an island castaway who'd seen a ship on the horizon. He met them at the curb, opening Aby's door as the car rolled to a stop.

"Good morning, son!" Dunn took Aby's arm.

"I'm fine. I don't need any help," Aby said.

Elvira retrieved a white cane from the back seat. "Here, honey."

"Oh. Sorry. I was just–" Dunn sputtered.

"That's very kind of you, Mr. Dunn, but Arlen's doing very well. Dr. Johnson says he won't have to wear the eye covering too much longer and he'll be ready for school by September."

"Well, alright. I'm just so, uh–I want to help any way I can." He watched Aby masterfully maneuver his way to the school's main door. Neither Dunn nor the group of people in the foyer waiting to welcome Aby back knew that he and his dad practiced the car-to-door journey at the school for almost an hour the previous night.

Elvira felt a wave of empathy for Coach G. as she and Aby sat with him in Mr. Button's office; he blamed himself for everything. He thought he understood the players on his teams better than any teacher in the school. He knew about all their little dramas, the cliques, who had a crush on who, and on and on. On the morning of the tournament, he thought something might be going on with Peter because he was so quiet during the first round of games, but he didn't have a clue it had anything to do with Aby. Still, he'd made a point to have lunch with Peter just in case there was anything he wanted to talk about. He'd left Waffle House convinced that everything would be fine. Since the injury, however, he'd accepted the fact that he'd been wrong, too eager to believe everything was copacetic so that the team could get on with winning the tournament.

"So, young man," said Mr. Button, "it looks like you will be in tip-top shape to return to school in the fall!"

"Yes, sir."

"Your folks tell me you're going to Indiana Beach in July. Doing anything else fun?"

"It'll be fun when Bible day-camp ends in three weeks." Arlen shot a smile at his mother. "I mean, y'know, I'll be thankful!"

Coach G. was silent, thanking God for this moment. He cared deeply for this strong, resilient boy who had worked so hard to make it back to school, on this last day of eighth grade.

"Well, we all have a lot to be thankful for," the principal said.

* * *

"I don't remember any of that!" Jake and Phyllis Phelt had never seen Peter cry so hard. His body convulsed with sobs, a stream of tears joining the mucous from his nose.

"I know—we know, sweetheart," Phyllis offered him a box of tissues.

"I don't need that," Peter rose and walked across his small room at Larue, wiping his face on his sleeve.

"You'll remember everything with time," Phyllis said. "And then we'll try to figure out why."

"What do you mean why? Didn't I have a seizure or something, and it made me act crazy?"

"They don't think so," Phyllis said quietly.

"What do they think it was?"

"They don't know right now, but—"

"But what?!"

"But they'll find out," Phyllis tried to reassure Peter. Jake sat on the bed; with a frustrated sigh, he laid back and clasped his hands across his face.

"They'll never find out why," he mumbled.

"Jake, stop!"

"You stop!" He stood up from the bed. "Our son didn't almost kill his best friend because of a seizure or puberty or a chemical imbalance!" Phyllis grabbed him by the collar, pushed him toward the door but he kept talking. "Don't you remember, Peter?!" Jake shouted.

"Stop this! Stop this now!" Phyllis yelled.

"Remember what?" Peter asked.

"On the double-dodge court when Faith called you evil?"

"Shut up!" Phyllis shoved Jake hard against the door banging his head and reminding them all why Peter was in Larue Carter Mental Hospital in the first place. She backed away, shocked at her own anger.

"Behold, young man!" Jake shouted, pointing at his wife. "It is here before you—the evil in all of us. It's in your mother. And in me!" Phyllis looked at him in disbelief, wondering if the right person was locked up in Larue.

Right before three burly attendants burst through door to see what the hell was going on, Jake bellowed at Peter with outstretched arms. "Sinner, repent and cleanse yourself in the presence of Almighty God!" Had the Red Sea been in front of Jake Phelt at that moment, it would surely have parted.

Politicians 3.5.3   November 3, 2026 A.D.

There were no election-night surprises on November 3, 2026, including the significant margin of victory Governor-elect Phelt achieved over multiple candidates fielded by the Snail Darter Extermination Party, the Texas Parties! Party, and the Ex-Houston Mayors Party. Together they received 33 percent, leaving the Texas People's Party with an impressive 67 percent.

Cardu won his bet with Pastor and Sister F'nA on what the winning percentage would be. He said it would be 66; they guessed in the high fifties. He'd managed the entire clandestine effort to elect the governor; by intelligent design, no one but Cardu knew any of the details.

"I hope you kept track of how the hell you pulled this off," Pastor said, almost disappearing into one of the three double-deep plush recliners he'd ordered for the Capstone Light trio to enjoy the victory party—broadcast live from Driskill Hotel—from the safe confines of the CPFS boardroom.

"Don't tell me how, just in case somebody water-boards me," admonished Yates. "But Brother, I gotta say, getting Peter elected governor–with only three percent of Texans actually voting for him–now that is miraculous!!"

He poured himself another shot of Antonio Cruz de Mantanzas Handmade Vodka. "Texans are pathetic. Only five percent of us voted in the most important election in Texas history; the other 95 percent are...are what? What the hell are they doing?"

"Going to church?!" Sister F'nA guffawed, reaching over to slap her husband's leg. Cardu coughed a cloud of smoke and passed the joint to Pastor.

"Going to church, yes!" he howled. "Going to church!" They all laughed uncontrollably until they forgot what they were laughing about.

"Oh, my Word," Sister sighed.

"Indeed," said Pastor, recovering, "My Word."

Cardu was zoned out in his incliner; the other two thought he might be out for the night when he startled himself back to consciousness. "I remember what I wanted to say about how we did it," he said excitedly.

"No Charlie, we really don't want to know how you won the election. Please." Pastor fended off the goofy smile on his face, as he stumbled through the sentence.

"Of course we do!" Sister flashed the toothy grin that Pastor had fallen for in seventh grade.

"Do we? Really?" he asked.

"Ye-es," she teased. "We most certainly want to know how Charlie got Peter from less than ten percent in September up to 67 percent."

Finally able to share a little of his brilliant strategy, Charlie was energized. "Okay, so in the 89th Legislative Session we–"

"Which one was that?" Arlen asked.

"Last year, 2025."

"Oh yeah, thanks. I can never keep those straight, y'know, the every-other-year thing with the legislature. It's almost as complicated as healthcare." His voice began to trail off. "Who knew healthcare was so complicated? It's all pretty heavy."

"Wow," Sister F'nA offered from the stratosphere.

"Should we order in some dumplings and pizza?" someone asked.

"Didn't we do that already?" she wondered aloud. Pastor looked at the plate on his lap, the one with pizza crust and a pool of soy sauce.

Cardu pressed on. "Remember the voter registration lawsuit that Texas lost in 2024 where the state had to stop requiring voters to provide proof-of-lineage to an 1836 resident of Texas with a DNA-verified pubic hair?"

"That's one good thing the feds did this decade," Pastor said.

"Yeah, but the ruling was overturned by presidential executive order, just days before the election. Remember, he was paid off—one of his shell companies received a no-bid contract from Texas Hundred-Dollar Stores to provide all of their matzo-based tampons. Very absorbent, and fashionable!"

"Kabuki!" slurred Pastor. "Artifice, the mendacity!"

"Wow," said Sister F'nA, from the mesosphere now.

"But the whole thing backfired. They thought they were restricting the numbers of people who would be allowed to vote and they were right about that: only 17 percent of Texas residents were eligible to vote. But, here's the ass-kicker."

"I love it when Charlie talks 'Texan,' " Sister observed aloud, about herself.

"Ninety percent of eligible voters are now Mexican immigrants because they're the only ones with DNA tie-backs to 1836! And 90 percent of them voted for Peter because he wants to secede! Why? Because they hate the U.S. even more than they hate the 'Texas' that tried to keep them from voting in the first place!"

Cardu took a deep breath. "So anyway, that's why Peter got 2.9 million votes and everybody else got skubalon," he looked at Sister F'nA. "Don't bogart that joint, my friend."

"I'm glad you waited until we were good and high to explain all of that." She handed him the duby. "Is that the Legacy Rasta Gold?"

"Yeah, it's the election night special," Pastor said. "Nothing but the sweetest bambalacha for my Capstone Light homies."

"Oh shit, is this really an official Capstone Light meeting?" Cardu asked. "I should have worn my embroidered art silk sherwani with churidar in royal blue. Hey, next time, let's try the brownies."

"Brownies!" Pastor attempted to connect with Cardu on a high-five, but failed.

"So, he's elected," Sister said, one foot in the exosphere. Now what?"

"We relax for one evening and enjoy our good works."

Children 3.6.3   September 7, 1999 A.D.

Aby, Charlie, Cyrana, Missy and Faith boarded the bus on the first day of high school, and took the seats they'd sit in for the next nine months. Had they been the only students on the bus it would have been a lopsided ride, with Missy on the right side and the rest on driver's side. Though no one knew it at the time, Peter would never return to balance out the bus. Nonetheless, it was exciting, riding to school with the older students and other ninth-graders from exotic junior high schools feeding into North Central High School.

Aby had waited for this day ever since–when? He couldn't remember. The last thing he recalled clearly was the Vervet pre-game huddle and running onto the court. None of it mattered though somehow, the weirdness between him and Peter. Aby had forgiven him for "stealing his girlfriend," as a lot of the kids said. It's no big deal if Missy likes Peter now, Aby thought. "There are other fish in the sea," he'd heard Mr. Phelt say to Peter's brother when he was jilted once by an older woman—an eighth grader. Yeah, there are tons of other fish in the sea.

He'd wanted to go see Peter but his mother refused to take him. She had no use for Peter anymore, nor did the rest of the diminished posse. Faith was the maddest at Peter and dumped him last February; now, she hardly talked to anybody.

The whole thing reminded Aby of "All My Children," a soap opera he "watched" with his mother after he came home from the hospital. They'd first watched it together when Aby was an infant, before Elvira went back to work full-time. Then and now, the show was her one guilty pleasure, its promiscuous themes anathema to her Christian beliefs. Aby liked soap operas because someone was always dropping a bomb, like the one his mother dropped on him July 3 during a commercial. He remembered because it was the day before July 4th and he'd been promised a trip to Carmel, the suburb where the good fireworks were.

"I love you Arlen, but Phyllis Phelt is your mother."

Aby was still wearing the black eyeshade, but it wasn't necessary to see his mother to gauge the expression on her face. He could tell from her voice that she was serious, although her statement was preposterous.

"It was an accident. We came home with you instead of Peter from the hospital. We didn't find out about the mistake until you were five and then it was too late."

"Tonight, on The Late Show with David Letterman, join Farrah Fawcett..." blared the television, as Aby tried to comprehend his mother's—this woman's—words.

"We thought of giving you go back to the Phelts, and just make a clean break, but we loved you too much."

"If it's got to be clean, it's got to be Tide!" The commercial crowed her words into a corner of the room and muffled them.

"And now, with everything that's happened, we feel closer to you more than ever. We couldn't bear to—"

"Get a little closer with the new and improved Arid Ultra Clear," the cheerful announcer urged.

"Our show's back on," Elvira said. From beneath the black eyeshade, Aby wondered if he'd heard her correctly, amid the last three minutes of "messages from our sponsors." Not daring to ask, he took refuge in the soap opera that was the one constant of his life at that moment, as Erica, Jack, Edmund, Skye, Janet, Trevor, Amanda, and Myrtle alternately consoled and traumatized each other–again.

The bus pulled into the long, bustling drive in front of North Central High School. His vision fully recovered, Aby jumped off the last step of the bus with a familiar sense of his own invincibility; he was moving forward and leaving the drama behind.

* * *

Nobody at school dared asked Larry Dunn why they hadn't yet received their invitation to his October birthday–not because they didn't want to go to another square-dance party, but because he frightened most of them a little. When Aby, Charlie and Cyrana saw him since last summer at the rehab hospital, he was his reliable shy, harmless self; now he was angry and volatile.

During the first week of school, Larry and several other students were asked to solve one of the long-division problems the math teacher had written on the chalkboard. One by one, students went to the front of the class to explain their work to the class. The last problem was Larry's.

With a playful gravitas, the teacher looked at the unfinished work. "And whose problem might this be?" he asked in Larry's direction with a smile.

"It's your mother's fucking problem!" he spat with more venom than a ninth-grader should ever have cause to summon. The teacher looked at him for a couple of seconds without expression and said to Faith across the room, "Miss Bountiful, would you mind solving the problem?" Larry walked out of the classroom, down the hall, and out the front door of the school.

The answer to the math problem was 27, which is the number of years to which Mr. Dunn was sentenced the day before school started. It wouldn't take a civics class to teach Larry that a Class C felony theft conviction will get you two to eight years in Indiana State Prison; add on perjury, conspiracy and generally being an asshole, you're looking at some serious time.

Had Mr. Dunn, alone, embezzled $10 million from his own federally-funded daycare centers, he might have been able to negotiate a plea deal to return the stolen funds, pay a fine and serve a reduced sentence in a cushy white-collar Hoosier prison–French Lick, maybe. Unfortunately, he had employed the it-takes-a-village-to-embezzle-10-million-bucks method. He'd recruited into the conspiracy his accountant and assistant director, their assistants, the cafeteria cashier and the maintenance guy (who turned out to be a kick-ass kickback machine on their building and services contracts and a couple union deals they had with the International Association of Industrial Daycare Professionals).

When two bus drivers and three crossing guards learned of the scheme, Dunn welcomed them into the fold. Dunn knew that even the looser welfare mothers of the children attending his facilities could cough up a nickel for a bus ride or a safe street crossing. Three-hundred kids multiplied by two bus rides and four street crossings per day multiplied by 225 school days per year multiplied by five cents multiplied by ten years adds up.

"Take care of the nickels and the dollars will take care of themselves," Mr. Dunn would encourage the crossing guards each morning. "It would be a darn shame if anything happened to one of these beautiful children."

By the time the feds had enough evidence to make an arrest, the money had disappeared and all of Dunn's co-conspirators were south of the border, in Kentucky. He had planned to smuggle his fortune and family out of the country nine months ago, but then Aby was injured.

Maybe it was his blood on the gym's concrete wall or Mrs. Yates horrified screams. Maybe it was the grace of God offering to Dunn a path to redemption, his very own Jacob Marley moment. Whatever it was, as he'd watched from the stands he felt what he later realized, were compassion and empathy. He felt culpable, as his mind raced to his teasing of Peter the night before about not liking girls.

In the following months, he'd struggled with his need to help fix Aby, in hopes that his guilt would desist. But it was more than that. He was changed, or was changing; he couldn't tell. It was as if he'd awakened from a deep sleep, and was now a good man. It wasn't his decision to be a good man, rather a new reality he had to deal with. But he was also an ex-bad man whose inherent misanthropy had long expressed itself in violence and racism. He was a reformed loathsome addict with no option to return to his old ways.

It was a Friday night in June when three FBI agents rang the doorbell. Out of habit, Mr. Dunn snatched the door open, hoping to catch a doorbell-ringer running up the street. He however, was the only culprit taken into custody that night. Two teenagers making out in the driveway across the street were the only ones to observe the short, handcuffed perp walk to the unmarked Crown Vic, but everybody would know about it by the next day.

> *Mighty burden, mighty burden,*
> *Pick you up, put you back down,*
> *Make you what you are deep down inside.*
>
> *Mighty burden, mighty burden. Sing it!*
> *It's an evil doodley-doo, yeah, they'll pray for you,*
> *'Cause you got a mighty, mighty burden every day.*

Mr. Dunn had come to love spirit-filled Negro blues and hollers since his metamorphosis, and could pluck out his favorites on a guitar, if they were in the key of E. God had surely inspired his own writing of "Mighty Burden" and he sang it out loud when nobody was around. Mostly though, he sang silently to himself for solace and guidance, as he struggled to keep his temper in check and show his family how much he truly loved them.

His conviction was no surprise. The evidence against him was clear, convincing and abundant. His court-appointed attorney advised him to return the money and testify against his co-conspirators but Mr. Dunn's long-lived disdain for the feds abided. He would do nothing to help them, even if it meant harming himself.

"What will we do without you?" Larry sobbed into his dad's shoulder the night before he was sentenced.

"You and your sister and mother will be fine. I've taken care of that. All you need to worry about is—"

"But what do I say if somebody asks where you are?"

"We discussed that, remember?" Mr. Dunn said, tears welling up. "You don't have to tell anybody anything."

"But what about my birthday?" Larry persisted.

"I'll have to miss that this year, but your mother will—"

"But you promised to—"

"It's your mother's fucking problem now!" Mr. Dunn yelled. He stood up from the kitchen table and looked at his family for what he thought might be the last time. "I have to go pack."

The sentencing hearing lasted one hour; its transcript would account for 73 pages of Marion County, Indiana's 1999 state-required archival records. On the less-bureaucratic side, Larry Dunn would remember it as the most confusing and sad hour of his life. Through quiet tears, he grappled to understand the judge's every word but kept getting stuck on nonsensical phrases like "pursuant to," "statutory maximum" and "remanded to the custody of." Finally, there was this from the bench:

> JUDGE: Pursuant to the Sentencing Reform Act of 1984, it is the judgment of this Court that the defendant, Lawrence Dunn Sr. is sentenced to 27 years and one day in custody, to be followed by six years of supervised release, a mandatory assessment of $7,000, and a fine of $12.2 million dollars.

Mr. Dunn glanced back at Larry and winked as if everything had gone exactly the way he'd planned.

> DEFENSE: We request that Mr. Dunn be allowed to voluntarily surrender.
>
> JUDGE: Does the government have an objection?
>
> PROSECUTION: No, Your Honor.
>
> JUDGE: Mr. Dunn will report to the Marion County Sherriff's Office for processing no later than noon on September 8, 1999.
>
> DEFENSE: Thank you, Your Honor.
>
> JUDGE: We're adjourned.

Larry's relief at knowing he'd be able spend a few more days with his dad was dashed as he got into the back seat of car outside the courthouse. Mr. Dunn grabbed a small backpack out of the trunk and walked his wife to the driver's side.

"I love you," He said leaning in to kiss her on the cheek. He looked in the back seat at Larry and his sister. "I'll see you later. I promise."

The Second Teller:
Part Two

Pre-Ur III

With three clicks of her cowboy boots, the writing on the scroll appeared. For posterity's sake, please note that the three "clicks" sounded more like "thunks."

Voice read the Ten Concepts from the scroll:

1. There will be Happy Matzo.

2. The five grains shall be as one.

3. Five grains will be cast down to the earth as mammon; Four Grain will comingle with One Grain in dreadful coition. Five Grain shall beget the sad matzo.

4. But wait! Number 3 is not true; verily, it is fake prophesy.

5. One Grain (with a little help from the other grains) shall immaculately beget the Happy Matzo.

6. The Happy Matzo shall bring forth unto the world, the Cleansing.

7. Place-holder for future Concept, if needed.

8. Tellers and the Fams shall be the guardians of the Happy Matzo and the Cleansing.

9. A great nation of souls shall be delivered.

10. Oklahoma shall be as Canada.

"Want's coition?" Dvau Vatkr asked.

"Look it up," said Voice. "That way, you won't forget what it means."

"Okay," she said. "I really like the last one–it's mysterious!"

"I don't believe you. You don't like it at all, do you? Tell the truth."

"Oh, I do!" she insisted. "It's a great prophecy, but how do I figure out what it means?"

"Not your job," Voice said. "The only thing you need to do is take the scroll to the blue land by the time you drop dead."

"Which is what, another 40 years?"

"Actually, more in the 35-year range–y'know, depending on how much free will you exercise."

"Either way, it shouldn't be a problem getting there in time, right? How far is it?"

"Four million goat lengths," said Voice.

"I think we only count to nine in my culture. Is four million more than nine?"

"It is, a little."

Dvau Vatkr walked up the steep paths of the Hindu Kush until she saw in the distance, countless soaring minarets backlighted by a brilliant sunset.

"That is Kaziristan," Voice said in a monotone. "They'll want you to be queen, but–"

"Wait, what?" Dvau Vatkr asked. "Queen? What?" There was no response. "Hello? Anybody there?"

No response still–and that was the last she ever heard from Voice.

As soon as she crested the next ridge she was met by a raucous crowd of Kaziristanies offering her pine nuts, berries and a drink that smelled like rotten dates. Before she knew it, the adoring, jibber-jabbering Kaziristanies corralled her into a plush sedan chair which was hoisted upon the shoulders of six huge people and carried through the gilded city gates.

"Shahbanu Dvau Vatkr! Shahbanu Dvau Vatkr!" the New Year's Eve-in-Time-Square-sized crowd chanted maniacally. "Shahbanu Dvau Vatkr! Shahbanu Dvau Vatkr!" She held onto the sides of the litter as it pinball-ed against the packed throngs lining the boulevard.

"Shahbanu Dvau Vatkr! Shahbanu Dvau Vatkr!" She pulled back the sedan curtain and tentatively waved at the cheering people, whereupon she was lovingly pelted by offerings of food, teas and spices. The surge of the human mass almost caused the porters to lose control of their precious Shahbanu Dvau Vatkr. She pulled the curtain shut and held it tight as one of the carriers barked an order. The sedan chair lurched forward and quickly picked up speed.

After a few moments, the ride steadied as the cacophony lessened. Dvau Vatkr heard the labored opening of large doors followed by the slowed rhythmic shuffling of her porters. She opened the curtains as her conveyance was lowered to the glistening floor of Shahbanu Dvau Vatkr's royal greeting chamber.

"Our Shahbanu." The woman, ten years Dvau Vatkr's senior, knelt to kiss the tile upon which the new queen would place her blessed feet. Dvau Vatkr stepped out of the sedan and blinked at the splendor, thinking the images would resolve themselves into a reality that was more comprehensible. This was not a dream, she told herself, because she was incapable of creating such beauty, even in deep unconsciousness.

She couldn't quite discern where the ceilings or walls began or ended. The main level and many balconies were crowded with Kaziristanies of all shapes and shades; the one constant among them was the eye-boggling mix of colors and textures they wore. Dvau Vatkr surveyed the quiet gathering, losing sight of this or that person as they disappeared into the equally ornate walls.

"Shahbanu," the woman said softly, rising to her feet. "Will you grace the throne of the people now?" Dvau Vatkr considered Voice's last words: They'll want you to be queen. But−"

"Does that mean I will become the queen?" she asked the woman.

"You are already Queen of Kazⁱᵣⁱstan, my Shahbanu," said the woman. "Your coming was foretold in an ancient scroll delivered to us by a goat-herding girl a thousand years ago."

BOOK FOUR

Ante proximum daret.

Before the next-to-last.

Jake 4:1.1   **December 15, 1997 A.D.**

Dear son,

I'm sure you know by now that it was a biblical parasite that made you evil, just like the one that killed King Ahab and that's now infesting the bitter waters that will kill millions of North Americans in the end times. But, that doesn't mean God doesn't love you, son; on the contrary, it means that God has chosen you! Yes, chosen you to be the harbinger of the world's destruction as foretold in the Book of Revelation. And let's not forget..."

"Holy fuck-me Jesus, Mary and Joe DiMaggio!" Jake crumbled the piece of paper and threw it across his cluttered Motel 3 room; he couldn't afford Motel 6. He'd been holed up on the east side of Indianapolis for six months writing this letter to his son, ever since his last apocalyptic outburst at Larue Carter Mental Hospital. After he'd been removed from Peter's room, and then banished from the hospital forever (unless, of course, he would like to return as a patient), Phyllis Phelt decided to call a lawyer.

"You sound like a friggin' Jehovah's Witness pamphlet!" Jake admonished himself. Speaking aloud to himself was comforting, even when it was hard to hear. "You sound like a madman! But it's all true. You know it's true."

The back and forth with himself continued around the clock on some days. Miss Jane Dubois, the southern hooker who regularly used the room next door, had knocked several times.

"Can y'all please be a little quieter?!" She was very polite. Once, after he hadn't been talking to himself for several days, she knocked on his door and asked, "Y'all okay in there, honey?"

He was beginning to think that he'd never finish the letter, but he had to. It was the only way to tell Peter that he shouldn't feel guilty about hurting Aby, because it was God's plan. A plan that started when they were switched at birth so that they could be raised by non-natural parents or something like that. It was God's–"

"God's what–what is it?" Jake asked himself. "What will you call it?"

"I don't know, His 'intelligent' something,' " he answered defensively.

"Of course it's intelligent. It's God." He hadn't quite worked out all the whys and what-fors–"

"Whys and what-fors are the same thing! Can't you get that through your thick skull?" he cursed himself for being so forgetful. "Whys and what-fors are the same thing!"

Two months earlier, he'd received a restraining order from a Marion County cop. Naturally, he called Phyllis immediately, even though "Call Phyllis" was number one on the list of things Jake wasn't supposed to do. The second was "Kill or Otherwise Inconvenience Phyllis."

"Hello, this is the residence of Phyllis, Phillip and Peter Phelt. We're sorry we can't answer your call. Please leave your name and a short message. Thank you."

"Uh, hi. This is Dad. Hi. I miss you all. Phyl, could you call me back when you get this please? I think I've figured out some stuff that's pretty important. Actually, really important. It'll probably clear up a bunch of the confusion, y'know, about what happened at the hospital. And I was thinking, that maybe–" BEEEEEEP.

"Hello?" Jake redialed the number.

"Hello, this is the residence of Phyllis, Phillip and Peter Phelt. We're sorry we can't answer your call. Please leave your name and a short message. Thank you."

"So, as I was saying, I–hey, did you add salt to the water softener? It probably needs some about now. One of the boys should go with you to Habig's because those bags are awful heavy, and there's no way in the world you'll get them down to the basement by yourself. Anyway, I–" BEEEEEEP.

Jake redialed.

"Hello, this is the residence of Phyllis, Phillip and Peter Phelt. We're sorry we can't answer your call. Please leave your name and a short message. Thank you."

"None of this was Peter's fault!" Jake said quickly. "A scarab beetle bit him and it was all planned out by God way before you even got pregnant and before everything happened in the maternity ward in Baltimore. Don't you see? That wasn't my fault! It was all meant to be. It was fate, goddammit!" BEEEEEEP.

He lay back on the bed and let the receiver fall from his hand. He'd spent months wading through religious texts, and conferring with healers, shamans and a Bahá'í priest who said that Bahá'í was the religious "one-stop shop" and he should have come to him first. He'd read the Cliff's Notes and even committed to memory, the entire title of Charles Darwin's *On the Origin of Species by Means of Natural Selection, or the Preservation of Favoured Races in the Struggle for Life.*

That led him another book with a long title, *The Origin of Consciousness in the Breakdown of the Bicameral Mind,* but found that he had to intersperse doses of *Dilbert* and *The Far Side* to get through the full eight pages he managed to get through. It was almost as difficult to read as the first paragraph of his wife's dissertation.

After he'd skimmed Spinoza and attended a high school revival of *Candide,* he stopped searching for confirmation of the hypothesis he had first postulated that day in Larue Carter, resigned to the realization that there would be no unearthing of deep thinkers to provide the basis for his great spiritual vision.

Over the phone's nagging dial tone, Jake heard the familiar click of high heels outside his door. There was a soft knock, and then another. Through the peephole, he saw a fish-bowled version of an attractive thirty-something woman flashing a smile. He opened the door.

"I'm sorry to bother you, honey," Miss Jane DuBois said. "But my sweet pussy needs a home." Jake looked at her.

"Aren't you the cutest thing?! Look at you all embarrassed, my goodness gracious," Miss Jane said picking up the cat-carrier at her feet. "Can I come in for just a sec, hon?" It was in the low 40s but she wore hot pants and a baggy, sleeveless GO TIDE! shirt that left little to the imagination, but Jake didn't notice.

"Uh, sure." She was right, he thought. He was embarrassed at her sweet pussy joke and didn't know how to respond. He'd always been quick with a clever comeback, but not anymore. He'd been so immersed in himself that he'd forgotten what it felt like to have a laugh with some else.

"Thank you, sweetheart." Miss Jane patted Jake on his cheek like his Aunt Thelma used to. "You know something? I'm in a pickle, and I know we don't know each other, but you seem like a sweet guy. This is Crimson, by the way." She took a tiny kitten out of the carrier and put it into Jake's arms. "Isn't she precious?"

"She is, yes." Jake said.

"Is your friend here?"

"I'm sorry?"

"Y'know, the fella I hear you talking with sometimes," Jane smiled.

"Oh. No, he's not here."

"Well, that's fine. He didn't sound as nice as you, but I know one of you is named Jake. It was kinda hard to figure out who was who, on account of the yellin' 'n all."

"I'm Jake."

"It's a pleasure to meet you Jake. I'm Jane."

"I'm from Alabama, too," Jake said, disengaging Crimson's front claws from his pants.

"I miss it," she confided.

"Yeah. Me too." he said. "I'm going back home, though."

"Well, good for you, Jake. But bad for me, I'm afraid."

"Why is that?"

"Well, I was gonna ask if you would take care of Crimson while I go on a little trip with one of my customers. It'll be a fun trip I guess but, I'll be workin' if you catch my drift."

"I do. When are you getting back?"

"Don't know exactly, but before New Year's, for sure. Don't you worry about it, honey.

"I'm leaving sometime before then, but I'm paid up through the month. I could take care of her. When I leave I'll just make sure she's got plenty of food and water." Supine on Jake's lap, Crimson luxuriated in his gentle belly rubs.

"That would be so nice." Miss Jane leaned over and gave him a kiss on the cheek.

"I'll give you my extra key so you can get in to my room when you get back." They listened to Crimson's purr.

"Thank you, Jake. I might go home too, but not for a while yet." Jane took a deep breath and looked around the room cluttered with boxes, a huge suitcase Jake was living out of, and stacks of and papers and books on the table and chest. "I took a class last semester at IUPUI," she said.

"That's good."

"Yeah, I went to 'Bama for a couple years–more than a couple years ago. I thought I'd try and take one class just to see if I could–I don't know." Her drawl was less pronounced. "The only class I could get into was on the works of Thomas Wolfe. Did you ever read–"

"You Can't Go Home Again? No." Jake interrupted. "And I don't believe anybody who says they did."

"Oh. Are you going home for good, or–"

"For good, one way or the other." They sat silently watching Crimson be a kitten.

"Well, I hope you have a good trip and find what you're looking for," Jane gave Jake a pat on the arm and walked to the door. "Wanna a blowjob for the road?"

* * *

Nine days later, on December 24th, Jake finished three identical letters. Each read:

My dearest son,

I was going to write "your birth was a brilliant North Star, illuminating my path to a life of purpose and joy. On that day, I received the blessing of unconditional love and, with time, came to understand the true meaning of your righteous gift to me."

But then I decided to write, "I'm sorry I fucked up, I really am. Maybe one day, after I forgive myself, you will consider doing the same."

Dad

Jake left the motel mid-morning and dropped the letters to Peter, Phillip, and Arlen in the corner mailbox. He took Stop 11 Road east, past Emerson Avenue, and headed south on I-65 for home.

After midnight, he pulled into the Motel 6 in Luverne, just like he and his family had exactly one year ago. He'd missed the Land of Goshen Christmas Eve Mosh that the boys really enjoyed last year–he wouldn't have gone anyway, he thought. He warmed up a can of oyster stew on a hotplate, as tradition dictated, and clicked on the television to see if he could catch a re-run of the local evening news.

"Reporting from Big Dick's Adult Video Mega-pleXXX, this is Fargol Minkelmin for GOSH-TV," the reported said earnestly. "Back to you." All the stations would have a story about the crowds converging tomorrow on Big Dick's, possibly to witness another miracle. Jake smiled at Fargol Minkelmin, recognizing him from middle school; he looked like he enjoyed his job.

"Way to go, Fargol," Jake said out loud. "Good on you."

He fell asleep on the bed without eating and awoke famished. It was before 5 a.m. when he walked into Denny's; the booth where he, Phyllis and the boys sat last Christmas morning was available, but he took a seat at the bar. He nursed his Grand Slam and coffee for an hour, watching sleepy out-of-towners come and go, some quietly pious, others chatty and boisterous. This was an important day for all the Big Dick pilgrims and for Jake. He was ready for whatever the day would offer.

There were two cars in the side lot when he arrived at the Mega-pleXXX as the sun came up. Jake assumed they were owned not by miracle seekers, but family-less solos looking for a little Christmas Eve companionship on what for them must be the loneliest night of the year. He was wrong.

Parking his car, he saw a young man round the corner from the front of the building walking backwards with a video camera. It was a re-enactment of the young priest who claimed to have seen the first apparition of the Blessed Virgin Mary breastfeeding the baby Jesus on Palm Sunday in 1984. At first, Jake thought it might be some kids making a parody of the original sighting, now verified by the Vatican Miracle Commission, but then he observed the reverence and adherence to the truth with which the documentary was being filmed.

The priest was carrying the video "Ooo Baby, Bless You!" with a woman breastfeeding the Pope on the cover. Jake observed that the robe-clad priest was quite excited about the souls he'd saved that fateful night in 1984. He watched as the two re-shot the coming-around-the-corner scene again, pack up their equipment and drive away.

Jake stared at the wall. The only change since last Christmas was the Vatican Miracle Commission's bronze plaque consecrating Big Dick's parking lot.

Big Dick, BVM and the OMG

When the Blessed Virgin Mary (BVM) gave birth to Her Blessed Son, the miracle was unknown to most earthly beings. It was much the same in 1973 when Big Dick Cabeza established a blessed chain of Alabamian porno outlets, Big Dick's Adult Video Mega-pleXXX (BDAVM).

On Palm Sunday 1998, the mighty hand of God brought forth a reckoning and redemption to the righteous people of Goshen, Alabama. On that day an F-4 tornado brought home to the Bosom of Abraham, twenty Goshenites, and laid waste to three sacred houses of worship. At the same moment, God showed His people that the Blessed Virgin Mary was here present, by removing all that was on this wall except the letters B, V and M.

On Christmas Day that same year, a holy apparition of the BVM appeared in this hallowed parking lot to the cries of "OMG," an acronym standing for "Oh, my God!" This acronym will be used in the future by all God's people as they do something called "texting" on something called a "smart phone."

All of these miracles were foretold by the Scetes Desert Mamas and Papas in 217 A.D. and way before that, by an all-gender beluga whale off the coast of Da Nang.

Consecrated by the Vatican Miracle Commission
February 13, 1999

Jake did not expect a miracle for himself here, today; he was unworthy of the Vatican's god or any other, but felt he needed to be here just the same. It was in this parking lot one year ago that his family last resembled anything like a family. For him things started to fall apart with Peter as soon as they returned to Indianapolis and since then, Jake had lost everything. The most positive interaction he'd had with another human being in the last year had been with Miss Jane DuBois, her buoyant spirit and well wishes for his return home. "You want a blowjob for the road?" He'd thanked her and said no. Thinking of the long road he would soon travel, Jake wished for a second that he'd said yes.

* * *

Tallassee, Tennessee marks the north end of the Tail of the Dragon, the most dangerous road in the United States, his AAA TripTik Travel Planner warned. Jake had joined AAA a few weeks ago to find the perfect spot, and this was it. If things worked out, there would be nothing left of him for Phyllis and the boys to bother with; they could just get on with their lives.

After filling the tank and ten gas cans, he bought a fifth of Old Crow and headed down Route 29 into Deal's Gap. The TripTik said there were 318 curves in next 11-mile stretch, so it shouldn't be a problem to find a suitable sharp curve with a spectacular drop-off; after his six-hour drive from Goshen and he was ready to get it over with. He drove slowly for three miles until he saw the perfect hairpin cutback in the road. The brilliant winter sun setting in the west made the windshield almost opaque; if he ignored the curve and sped up, the car would fly off the equivalent of a twenty-story building and disintegrate on the rocks below in a spectacular explosion.

Jake stopped on the side of the road and placed five opened gas cans inside the car, and three in the trunk. He poured the last two cans over the seats. In the open glove compartment, a small Chock full o' Nuts coffee can was half-full of wooden matches and M80s, the rest of it packed with crumpled newspaper that protruded through a small slit in its plastic lid like a fuse. Jake had tested it a dozen times and found that the newspaper would burn for about 20 seconds before igniting the can's contents. From there, the flames and fireworks would ignite the gas and blow everything to kingdom come, as the car careened over the cliff.

He took a swig of bourbon, and realized he was thinking about what would have happened if that asshole Irsay hadn't moved the Colts from Baltimore to Indianapolis in 1983–maybe things would have been different. He started the car, imagined himself embraced by Phyllis and the boys, and lit the fuse.

* * *

It wasn't until February 2000 that police identified Jake Phelt as the driver of the car.

"It was the fingerprints on a bottle found where the car went off the road. That and a partial VIN–sorry ma'am, that's the Vehicle Identification Number–found by the search and rescue team." Phyllis, Phillip and Peter sat around the kitchen table with a Blount County, Tennessee sheriff's deputy and local Marion County detective. "There wasn't even much of the car left, much less a body, ma'am. Uh, you say there wasn't a note or any communication from your husband before Christmas?"

"Just an occasional phone message during the fall." She wiped a tear from the corner of her eye with a soggy tissue. Peter and Phillip looked at each other. Peter left the table and went to his room to get the letter from his father.

"We each got one of these." He handed the letter to Phyllis. She read it and gave it to the sheriff.

"Why didn't you–" Phyllis stopped and cradled her head in her hands. "Oh, it doesn't matter anymore."

"Why didn't you boys show this to your mother?" the officer asked.

"We didn't think it meant anything. Dad was driving Mom nuts, and–"

"Ma'am? Is that true?"

"We we're going through a divorce," Phyllis said dismissively. "There was a restraining order, but there was never any trouble."

"I see. Is that all?"

"Yes, yes. That's all," she snapped. "Are you about done with the questions?"

"Yes ma'am. We apologize that this has taken so long. One last thing. Are you aware that your husband took out a $5 million life insurance policy on himself last February?"

Dunn 4:.2.1   September 1, 2026 A.D.

Dunn sat on an iron bench, the same one he'd sat on every afternoon for years–he'd lost count of how many. He scratched his chin through his thick beard and, for the third time this week, considered shaving it off. To his left, six black men shot hoops. On his right, a group of swastika-ed whites gathered around three industrial-grade picnic tables. Free weights clanked amid unintelligible conversations.

The prison yard was surrounded by cellblocks 16 and 17, and the outermost stone wall of the 25-acre SuperMax facility situated 500 feet below Crater Lake, Oregon. Most of the time, the inmates forgot they were imprisoned in the Earth instead of on it. The SuperMax environment mirrored current meteorological conditions, projecting a real-time image of the sky above, on the rock ceiling below. Days were days and nights were nights, and the moon and sun took their turns, regulating the circadian rhythms of inmate and guard alike.

"What are you in for?" asked a young voice in front of him. There was a manufactured confidence to this one, Dunn thought. Whoever this asshole was, he was scared shitless–or pretending to be.

Dunn ignored the voice, hoping it would go away but it didn't. It cleared its throat and said tentatively, "Good morning, I–"

"I dunno–what are you in for?" Dunn mocked.

The man looked over his shoulder because that's what inmates do when they're about to tell another con a secret. "You. I'm in here for you."

"I'll beat you brain-dead if you try anything with me, boy."

"No, no—I didn't mean anything like that."

"Go fuck yourself," Dunn said without looking up.

"My name's Bob, Bob the Rap-eest," he said. "Maybe you've heard of me, I—"

In a swift, practiced motion, Dunn swung his tree-trunk leg parallel to the ground at the voice, sending Bob the Rap-eest to the deck.

"Naw, I haven't heard of you but I imagine you'll be mighty popular in here," he said. "Fresh, young, white, and a rapist. That's a quadruple-dip for most of 'em in here."

"I'm not a rapist." Bob groaned. "I'm a rapper. A Rap-eest!"

"Then you're dumber than I thought."

"And it's not just me who's here for you."

"Don't be trying to sweet-talk me now, rapper."

"I have lots of friends here. We want to help you," Bob said.

"That's great, another fuckin' gang to deal with," Dunn sighed. "I'm feeling a little charitable today so, before I beat you deaf and dumb, I'll bite—who is 'we?' " Dunn stood, towering over the rapper. "This better be good."

"Ministers in Chains."

"What did you say?" Dunn's expression softened.

"I'm with Ministers in Chains. We're here to help you escape."

Dunn's eyes filled with tears. He quickly wiped them away, sitting down. It had been more than 15 years since he received instructions on how to pay what he felt was an un-payable debt owed to Arlen Yates, the boy, for causing his blindness, albeit temporary. Dunn still had the Hallmark Tender Notions-Thinking of You card from Pastor Yates, in which was written:

Meet your penance, January 1, 2011 0900 hours.
Grand Central Station, north side of the clock.
Yours, A.B.Y.

It was that simple for Lawrence Dunn; for him, it was God's truth that he was the catalyst for Peter's blinding of Aby. Until that moment at the double-dodge tournament in 1998, he'd never actually witnessed the direct result of his own malice and cruelty. It had never mattered if he was being mean for a purpose or simply because the opportunity presented itself; in all cases, its motivation was his need to control and dominate. He was the cat torturing the tiny gecko on the back porch, the rapist brutalizing a life; his victims were the means to his own passing rejuvenation, nothing else. Why he'd badgered Peter that night, suggesting he was gay, he couldn't recall. He was just doing what he always did: target a vulnerable person, identify their weakness and expose it the world.

"Is my penance over?" Dunn asked.

"Almost," Bob the Rap-eest sat on the bench beside Dunn. "The Ministers will help us escape. After that, there's one more thing you'll need to do. Then you can go home.

"There are Ministers in the SuperMax?"

"Yeah, about 50 self-incarcerated Ministers, plus a couple hundred converts. They've been watching over you since your second week here; sorry about that first week."

"I had no idea, but none of that matters now." said Dunn, revising his reality. "So, you know who I am?"

"You're Mr. Dunn, from Indianapolis," Bob said.

"Is that all?"

"I know that you call a mean square dance." Bob watched as Mr. Dunn again, reorganized his reality.

"Is that in some dossier you have on me?"

"No sir. I learned my first dance steps at Larry's eighth-grade birthday party from you."

"What?"

"I'm Bobby Rap—"

"Bobby Rappaport?"

"Yes sir."

Dunn smiled. "I never forget a good dancer." Bob watched as Dunn connected the rest of the puzzle pieces. "You were in Mrs. Greenhaw's class then, like Larry?"

"Yes." Bob put a hand on Mr. Dunn's shoulder. "Do you want to go home?

"Now?"

"Right now, if you're ready."

"Oh, my god. Sweet Lord." Dunn said. "I'm ready."

Bob stood and nodded at one of the black prisoners on the basketball court and then at a white Aryan. Each suddenly ran at the other full speed; with a deep thud, their powerful bodies collided, both men crumpling to the concrete, dazed. Weapons appeared from every prisoner's garment as the gangs followed their leaders to the center of the yard, roaring fearsome battle cries, chains and shivs at the ready.

"What the hell?!" Dunn shouted.

"Don't worry, it's just a few Ministers having a little fun," Bob yelled over the piercing alarms. "Follow me." They moved along the wall to a secluded nook in the rocks, now completely obscured by tear gas streaming from the air vents. He turned to Dunn. "This will feel pretty strange, but there's nothing to worry about." Dunn nodded, and braced himself.

"Alright, Bobby."

"It works best if I hold your hands like this," Bob yelled over the chaos. They grasped each other's hands firmly in a double-handshake. "You ready?!"

"As I'll ever be," Dunn said.

"Okay, it's just like dancing. Follow my lead!" Bob the Rapeest led Dunn two steps backward, and together they disappeared in a spectacular flash of fire and fog.

Galen and Fafáfa 4:3.1 January 2, 2004 A.D.

Galen Ram Das preferred the hottest spring at Finna Galen Himlen, the earlier in the day the better. It was his time to be alone and quiet, in this intentional community of 100 workers who toiled endlessly and happily to serve its 5,000 annual visitors.

He had learned to live on little or nothing during his two-year odyssey from the Tail of the Dragon to this off-the-grid slice of heaven nestled into the western slopes of Oregon's Cascade Range. If his not being arrested for insurance fraud was any sign, his fake suicide had been successful. He assumed that Phyllis, Peter, Phillip and Arlen received their shares of the $5 million life insurance policy he had purchased just a few days after Peter injured Aby, but there was no way to confirm that without revealing himself.

In the 105-degree hot spring, Galen actively observed the sun rise from the east, as he did each morning. He reached into his bindle for a dog-eared copy of Be Here Now, the seminal work of his namesake, Baba Ram Dass; it had revealed his path to the truth-of-now where Galen no longer thought of insurance pay-outs or rigging his vehicle to career off a Tennessee cliff and explode into a million pieces on a dark New Year's Eve. He was Galen Ram Das, or Crazy Servant of God, and he was home, here, now. He had no past.

Galen had mastered the ability to be in a deep meditative state, and yet be hyper-aware of his physical surroundings. His heightened spatial sentience had been honed by a 90-day blind immersion experience, during which he'd been blindfolded at all times. For the final three weeks of the training week, he'd worn NASA-grade earplugs to simulate deaf-blindness. This new knowledge so inspired him that he included it in the Introduction to Shamanic Journeying class he taught.

He heard her footsteps on the gravel path, about 150 feet away, he reckoned. From the gait and the lightness of her step, she was thin and either still sleepy or mildly depressed.

"Good morning," she said flatly. Sleepy and depressed, Galen thought. He nodded without looking up, hearing that she was disrobing. She entered the natural rock pool without disturbing its gentle rhythm, sustained by the steady gurgle of water from subterranean hot springs. She found her place across from him with her back to the sun, and slid into the hot water. From her barely audible "oh!" Galen heard the surprise on her face and smiled. He opened his eyes to nod his thanks for sharing that moment in her life with him.

"Oh my god! What the hell?" he yelled out. Galen had not spoken a word in 18 months, since he took a vow of silence to mark his induction into the Shamanic Sister-Brotherhood. Is this an otherworld she-demon conjured by an unknown enemy?

Disoriented, somewhere between his this and the rest of the world's that, he observed himself involuntarily reaching for the small blackboard he used to communicate. He pressed the chalk onto the slate, but had nothing to say. This thing before him had jettisoned his every awareness backwards, into the past that he had come to believe no longer existed. His thoughts raced, struggling to understand how this was happening. Why didn't I see this coming? I'm a goddamned shaman for fuck's sake!

"Are you alright?" the woman asked.

"It speaks!" he scrawled on the blackboard and thrust at her.

"What does?" she asked.

"You!" He showed her the blackboard, but his vow of silence had already ended and he realized he wasn't ready to begin another stint quite yet. He let the writing slate fall from his hand and sink to the floor of the pool. "You. You speak."

"Yes," she responded, a little frightened. "I apologize. I'll leave you alone now."

"No-no. Please stay." said Galen. He looked at her, splashed his face with water and rubbed his eyes. He double-double checked that he was on his normal metaphysical space-time continuum, and made sure he wasn't trapped in some whacky, out-of-body mind-fru. In his heart of hearts, he knew she was no demon or evil apparition, and that he was here, and it was now. Still, he strained to prove himself wrong. He needed this to be a demon; otherwise, he was just another earthbound schmuck who'd never outdistanced his past and who might as well give up and crawl back up into Mama's womb.

He recalled something he'd learned in the exorcism module of his Shamanism 101 class two years ago: the exorcist must compel the demon to speak its name. At the time, there weren't any possessed people or demons around so students practiced on a cat; unfortunately, the cat never said its name so they weren't sure if they were doing it right. Nevertheless, Galen gave it his best shot.

"Declare yourself, demon!" He stood up and pointed down at the she-devil to infuse the moment with drama, but quickly sat back down realizing he had a full-on erection. "Fuck! Holy shit! What the–?" he whined. "First you make me break my promise of silence and start cussing like a sailor–and now I got a hard-on! I haven't had a boner for years!"

The woman looked at him, not sure if she should get the hell away from this maniac, or yield to a strong urge to burst into laughter. Across the pool, Galen breathed rapidly and cupped his face in his hands. It felt good, he realized–all of it. It was exhilarating to speak again, emancipating to curse, and electrifying to feel the ole' goop-shooter down there, ready for action. He leaned against the stones, looked up at the sky, and laughed. And laughed. And laughed. The woman watched for a moment and then slowly moved across the pool and up the stone steps. She dressed. Galen kept laughing until she took her first step onto the gravel path.

"My name is Galen, Galen Ram Das. And yours?"

"Clara Barton, Clara Barton Fafáfa."

From the pool, Galen turned to study her face. "My name is Jake Phelt. And yours?" he asked.

The woman scrutinized him. "No. I'm not going back. I'll never go back," she said. "My name is Fafáfa."

Galen & Fafáfa 4:4.1   October 1, 2006 A.D.

"It does matter that Cabeza de Vaca was shipwrecked on the shores of what is now Texas in 1523 before the Rosenbergs were hanged in 1953. Of course, paper-folding flat-timers think the two events happened, excuse me – are happening –at the same moment, forever. Do you agree that we are in the 2006?" The Abbot explored his braille wrist watch. "Do you know what time it is, right now?"

"We don't do time." It was a tiny voice.

The blind Abbot imagined before him a beautiful, nappy-brown-headed, precocious three-year old.

"Very good, that's very good indeed! Now tell me, would you like an ice cream?"

"Yes, please!" the girl said, with a slight Jamaica-Brooklyn-Seoul accent.

"But you already had your ice cream or, you're having it tomorrow–right now? Could all of that be true?"

"I don't think so," the girl answered honestly, though it might jeopardize her chance of getting ice cream out of the old man.

"So, you do 'do time' after all!"

"Yes sir, if you're talking about ice cream," she said.

"Very good, Miss–"

"Bella!" she said proudly, squirming from her mother's lap. "May I have my ice cream now?!"

"Bella," admonished her father.

"Nonsense," the Abbot smiled. "She's earned it, I think. Now, Miss Bella, there's a very nice lady outside of my office who would love to take you to the kitchen for your ice cream."

Bella looked at her mother for approval and then walked toward the office door, wide-eyed.

"She's adorable. Smart, very smart. Is she yours?"

"She's of the world," said Galen Ram Das.

"Of the world," echoed her mother.

"In your faith, what does that signify?" the abbot asked.

"She was conceived in the sperm pool at Finna Galen Himlen, in Oregon."

"I've heard of this," the abbot nodded. "Quite the technological feat. I understand the pool sustains and nourishes the sperm of all comers, so to speak, until they find their way to a welcoming egg. So, the father is–"

"Of the world," the woman repeated.

"We've come to Black Shade to learn about unbridled and fearless faith!" The brash non sequitur burst from Galen just as he'd trans-visioned it would. From the moment Bella was born, Galen and Clara Barton Fafáfa knew they must travel to Santa Lucía del Camino to become disciples of the Abbot of Black Shade for one reason and one reason only–though they couldn't quite pinpoint what that might be.

The abbot stood up from his desk and walked behind their chairs. He was a large man whose flowing burlap robe made him all the more imposing. His sandals creaked as he placed a hand on each of their shoulders.

"And who are you?" the abbot asked them.

"I'm sorry, Abbot, I thought you'd received our letters," Galen fumbled. "We've come from Finna Galen Himlen. I practice shamanic teachings, and–"

"We are travelers." interrupted Fafáfa. "Like you, Abbot."

"Travelers, yes. In your faith, what does that signify?"

"That our journey has not ended."

"Yes. Indeed it has not." The abbot returned to his desk. "You and Bella will thrive here, if you chose to stay."

"Thank you, Abbot," Fafáfa reached to put her hand on Galen's arm with a wide smile. "Blessings upon you. Thank you."

"You are welcome, you may leave now." Without looking up, the abbot busied himself with a stack of papers as they stood to leave. "Oh, one more thing. When I leave this place, you, Clara

Barton Fafáfa, will become Abbot of Black Shade. Until then you will be my FeMaestra and counselor. Galen Ram Das, you will apprentice to replace the current head mono of our Saint Lucy Enucleation Clinic; his eyesight isn't quite what it used to be, I'm told. You'll also provide spiritual technical assistance to the Enucleation Nation–go easy on the shamanic stuff at the beginning." The abbot nodded, dismissing them for a second time as the office door opened.

"I'll show to your dormitory now." The mono behind them could have been a twin of the abbot were he not significantly younger. He, like the other monos and the abbot, wore a burlap sack robe and Birkenstock knock-offs. Galen and Fafáfa rose from their chairs, awkwardly mimicked the bow they'd seen others offer the abbot, and followed the man outside.

"I am Mono 72," he said leading them on a gravel path with many forks, each marked with Spanish and Braille signposts. "You'll be in E342 and E343. Your daughter will stay in the children's quarters and move into the Enucleation Clinic when Abbot determines it is her time. Here, these are yours." He handed each of them a large sack containing a rope belt, sheet and blanket, baking powder, sandals, a blank journal and a carpenter's pencil. "The sacks are your robes. You'll have to cut out the holes for your arms and head."

"Thank you," said Galen. "He's very direct, the abbot."

"He is that. He hates to be idle when there is so much to learn and praise."

Galen and Fafáfa smiled at each other and then at 72. They were home.

Gunfight at Boquillas 4:5.1   September 1, 2026 A.D.

THWACK! Dunn's arms and fingers throbbed from gripping Bobby Rappaport's hands so tightly, for how long he didn't know. Tiny red-orange dust particles painfully invaded his eyes; he squeezed them shut, letting the tears inside do their work.

"Bobby?" Dunn shook Bob the Rap-eest's hands. "Bob, can you hear me?!" Nothing. Where were they? It was dry, hot and sunny, but they were shaded–by a tree or structure of some sort? No. It felt small. Were they in a tent, under a tarp of some sort? He was frustrated, unable to orient himself. Dunn explored the ground with one foot; it was earthen, a floor of a hut? Adobe, that would account for the–.

"HAUN! HAUN!" Bob the Rap-eest HAUN-ed, as his body jerked back to life, breaking his death grip on Mr. Dunn's hands. "Holy Word!! That was one hell of a passage! Sweet Palabra! Where are we?"

"How the hell would I know?" Mr. Dunn. "I can't see a thing."

"Word, what a trip! Let's see here now–" Dunn listened as Bob walked around the room, opening cabinets and drawers. He stomped purposefully on the ground, pausing as the floor's pitch rose. He kicked at the hollow sound. A table, a small one it sounded like, was moved a few feet. Bob opened what must have been a trap door to a cellar. After a few seconds, he dropped the door back to the floor.

"Okay, we may not have much time. I'm not sure how long we were in-passage, but I think we're in the right place. Boquillas, no?"

"Boquillas?! What the–? You're the one who was driving. Go outside, look around, and find out where the hell we are!" Dunn ordered.

"You were here before, right?" Bob asked. "You came through here when you escaped to México the first time, no?"

"Yeah, but no one knows that, but–"

"Larry, right?" Bob said.

"Yes, goddammit! Can we stop with the games? I told Larry about my escape from Indianapolis to Texas in '98. He knows I crossed the Rio Grande here. But why would he tell you about that, for fuck's sake? You're starting to piss me off!"

"Okay, sorry," Bob said calmly. "Look, Pastor Yates needs one more favor from you."

"No, I'm through. I've given him enough." Dunn was resolute.

"I know you given a lot; he knows that too. But there's really no choice at this point." They both heard shuffling outside.

"Oh fud, they're already here," Bob said. "It wasn't supposed to go down like this. C'mon, get down."

Bob tipped over a wooden table and the two took cover. The front door creaked open an inch; a sliver of light divided the room.

"Dad?" Larry's whisper through the door was barely audible.

"Larry?" Dunn moved from behind the table toward his son. He felt Larry's arms on his shoulders, drawing him into a near-suffocating bear hug that he reciprocated. His tears soothed his eyes. "It's so good to see you, son." He'd not allowed himself to feel such deep emotion since his incarceration in 2011. "Nice beard," he said, touching Larry's face and shoulders. "You're all grown up. You look just like me, I bet," he laughed.

"Dad, we–"

"What are you doing here?" Dunn stepped back and looked in Bob's direction. "What's he doing here, Bobby?"

"I told you. Pastor Yates needs one more favor, Mr. Dunn."

"Policía Federal Ministerial! FBI!" A chorus of shouts and languages came from outside. "Pe-Efe-Eme! F-B-I!" Pe-Efe-Eme! F-B-I!" Sesame Street's bilingual episode, "Aprendiendo Mis Cartas! Learning My Letters!" had come to the desert.

"Dad, you go with Bob. I'll handle this–"

"No! I can't let you do this, I–"

"¡Policía Federal Ministerial! Tiene diez segundos para salir con las manos arriba!"

"FBI! You have ten seconds to come out with your hands over your heads, and your nose pods disengaged!" Larry gave his father strong hug as Bob opened the trap door to the basement.

"C'mon, Mr. Dunn. I guarantee you'll see Larry again soon."

"Dad, I'll see you later. I promise."

Dunn went down the dusty steps into the cellar of the adobe hut first. As soon as Bob was in, Larry threw the trap door shut from above and placed the small rug and table over it. From below, Dunn heard the door blast off its hinges and crash to the floor.

"On your knees, Mexican scum!" yelled an FBI agent. Her Mexican counterpart echoed the order with a south-of-the-border twist. "¡De rodillas, pedazo de mierda americana!" Look it up.

"I surrender, I surrender! Please!" Larry cried. Dunn listened in horror as his son's plea was cut short by the rapid fire of an AR-15. The FBI and Mexican PFM tore apart what little there was in the hut, and presumably moved Larry outside, though Dunn didn't hear his voice again.

Mr. Dunn and Bob waited in the cellar for two hours before daring to push open the trap door. They startled a curious boy standing near the space in the wall where the front door used to be.

"What do you see?" Dunn demanded.

"Nothing," Bob said. "There's no one."

"Is there blood?" Dunn was frantic. "Do you see blood on the floor or anywhere?"

"No."

"You're a liar, you bastard. Your Pastor's a liar!" Dunn dropped to the floor, his hands scanning the dusty floor for signs of his son's blood. "Is this the 'last favor' I owe Pastor Yates?" he yelled. "My son's life?"

"I'm sorry. Here, let me help you up."

"Leave me alone!"

"Please, Mr. Dunn. Faith Alone, brother. Trust in your god," Bob counseled calmly.

Dunn scrambled to his feet and located a chair, swinging it in Bob's direction. He heard Bob gasp and back up. Dunn lunged at him with the legs of the chair, backing him up and trapping him in a corner; Bob couldn't move. The choreography of this fight was exactly like one he'd had during his first week in the SuperMax. Dunn pressed the rungs of the chair against Bob's chest.

"You go back to your church now, Bob the Rap-eest," Dunn spat. "And tell your pastor he'll pay for this."

* * *

"Your buddies will be glad to see you back, Dunn," sneered one of the four FBI agents assigned to make damn sure Lawrence Dunn. Sr. was delivered in shackles back to the SuperMax. "But you won't see them for at least a year, what with solitary confinement 'n all. Oh, I'm sorry—you can't see anything can you?"

"Agent! Remain focused on the task," barked his superior. "No talking to the prisoner."

Larry ignored them both.

Through the tinted windows, he took peeks at the spectacular natural beauty of the Pacific Coast 3,000 feet below. Near the California-Oregon border, the helicopter banked inland to pick up the Pacific Crest Trail north, to the SuperMax. They passed over the rim of Crater Lake, dropped altitude suddenly, and headed toward the helipad on Wizard Island, the volcanic cinder cone at the west end of the lake.

As the two agents hurried the fugitive away from the helicopter, the furious, chopped air blew Larry's chest-length, ZZ-Top beard horizontally into one of their faces.

"Goddammit, Dunn!" yelled the agent over the noise. "You and your filthy, fuckin'–"

"Agent!" The senior officer opened the metal door of a small brick building for Larry and the other agents. The room had two exits; the one they just entered and the elevator with one stop 500 feet below Crater Lake. One agent held onto Larry's arm and pushed the down button as the senior officer reprimanded the chatty agent across the room. The fourth guarded the door.

The elevator pinged. Just as the doors began to part, Larry violently sneezed the dark glasses off his head and across the floor. The agent holding his arm released his grip and moved to retrieve the glasses as the elevator doors opened wide. Bending to pick them, he glanced back at Larry, who nodded, took two steps backward into the elevator, and disappeared in a spectacular flash of fire and fog.

Dunn 4:2.2   **November 1, 2026 A.D.**

"I see now, Lord, as I have never seen. I was as Saul, persecuting your poor and righteous supplicants to such a degree that you Lord, reproached me saying 'Saul, why persecutest thou, me?' "

After 40 days, walking and hitchhiking the 1150 miles from Boquillas del Carmen to the outskirts of Oaxaca, Mr. Dunn was stuck in Barrio de Xochimilco, less than five miles away from Black Shade's Saint Lucy Enucleation Clinic. Several times he ventured onto Carretera Federal 190 to beg for a ride to the clinic, standing in the middle of the treacherous highway, but the people did not recognize him as the blind abbot, even after he'd traded his Crater Lake SuperMax uniform to a shopkeeper for enough burlap and rope to dress himself in a Black Shade robe.

He was surrounded by a hellish urban chaos foreign to him; prior to surrendering himself to the FBI in 2011, he and the Black Shade monos would regularly minister to the poor in this barrio and, despite its open sewers and occasional cholera outbreaks, he cherished his time here. He was invigorated by the people's struggle to survive in the face of hopeless odds. Many of their children would die before age three and those that lived could only hope to follow in their parent's intractable misery. But the people abided their fate, and daily renewed their faith in God.

But everything was different now. After days of standing and sitting and sleeping in the middle of the highway, he began to wonder if he was even visible to anyone. He received no kind words or offers of assistance; no one bothered to blare their horn at him to get the fuck out of the road. No one even tried to steal his white cane.

"I am mistaken, Lord! Please forgive my ignorance!" Dunn threw the sunglasses from his face, and yelled at the scorching sun. "I am not Saul who you blinded for three days and nights, as he entered Damascus. You cannot blind me Lord." Dunn stared into the sun's yellow noise, eyes wide, and felt its heat on the backs of his empty sockets.

"No Lord, I am Job and you are testing me! I see that now. Yo lo veo, Dios!" A speeding car knocked the cane from his hand; disoriented, he reached out to nothing, Frankenstein-style. "Strike me deaf Lord, and make of my legs, bloody stumps. I will hear your whispers and run to your loving embrace. Deliver me!"

He whirled away from the sun and continued to turn, full circle. And again. His robe flared as he twirled again faster. "Oh Job! What evil have you done to bring God's wrath upon you? ¿Qué mal? Job?" he accused himself. "Do you hear me, sweet Lord? Help me!" He raised his arms and continued to whirl, each turn punctuated by his pleading mantra. "Do you hear me? Do you hear me? Do you hear me?"

"Do you hear me?" The voice was not his; it came from somewhere else. Dunn listened as he whirl. "Do you hear me? Do you hear me?" It was God's voice. Yes! God is asking me if I am listening, he realized, rejoicing in his deliverance. God was listening!

"Dad, do you hear me?" Mono 72 stood in front of the Abbot, gently shaking his shoulders. "Dad! It's me. Do you hear me?"

"I hear you, Lord!"

"No Dad, it's me. Do you hear me?!

"I am your servant, Lord!"

Abbots of Black Shade 4:6.1   **November 25, 2026 A.D.**

"Welcome home, Abbot," Clara Barton Fafáfa embraced the man who had so suddenly left Black Shade's Saint Lucy Enucleation Clinic in 2011 and had not been heard from since. He'd appointed her abbot, and Galen Ram Dass, clinic director; together, they'd nurtured the organization they'd grown to love. "I trust you're feeling better."

"I am, thank you," Dunn felt his old office around him. "Mono 72 tells me that I've been here for three weeks. Thank you for your kindness."

"This is your home, Abbot," Galen offered. "You are our brother. We've been worried for you."

"I know. I apologize for not telling you where I was or when I might return, but it was necessary to save Black Shade." He chuckled. "How dramatic that sounds, no?" He felt for the chair in front of Fafáfa's desk and sat down.

"It would be helpful to know where you've been for so long, so we can assist with your recovery and help the monos and followers understand what has happened," Fafáfa said. "There have been rumors about what happened to you, and–"

"I committed a great sin against a young man, a child, almost 20 years ago," Dunn said abruptly. "It was as a rock thrown into a pond; its effect rippled in all directions causing lifelong pain and suffering to the boy's family and friends–and myself."

"Why did you commit this sin, Abbot?"

"Because I was a singularly hateful man, full of anger and greed, which makes the sin even greater because the very act of hurting this boy put me on the path toward righteousness. He was blinded and I was rewarded with the grace of God."

"You blinded him?" Galen asked. "Was this before Black Shade?"

"Yes, many years before."

"But why?"

"Because he rang my doorbell," answered the old abbot matter-of-factly, leaning forward in his chair. He hung his head, wringing his hands. "He and his friend kept ringing my doorbell and running away." He paused, reaching out to locate Larry. "And they and their friends teased my son and made him weak– that's why."

Fafáfa and Galen exchanged glances. As Black Shade Abbot for the past 15 years, she'd regularly received the confessions of the faithful. Galen too, had heard heartfelt confessions of nervous zealots as he prepared to remove their eyes, their faith vacillating as blindness loomed like the grim reaper. The two confessors listened quietly to Dunn.

"But you know of this, Galen. Or should I say, Dr. Phelt?" Dunn paused. "But what you don't know is that I've been repaying my debt ever since, to God and to that boy, struggling to make amends by leading the world to God through the peace of blindness."

"And then for 15 years, I sought redemption in the Crater Lake underworld," said Dunn angrily. "For most of that time I thought I was dead, that I had unceremoniously transitioned to perdition, my eternal damnation. Of course, I thought that because that's what I deserved; it was my penance."

"But you didn't know all of that, did you Dr. Phelt? How could you? You were dead. As I recall, you killed yourself less than a year after that freezing night in February 1999. Remember, we all had lasagna? In the basement?"

Galen ceased to be Galen as the taste of Elvira Yates' lasagna and all the smells and textures of that night before the double-dodge tournament returned. Jake looked at the man who had, thirty years ago, discovered a vulnerability in his young son, and cruelly exposed it for all to see. Mr. Dunn hadn't understood it as anything other than a tool to punish Peter, Jake Phelt now realized–and for what, ringing his doorbell?

Jake felt rage and penetrating hatred, emotions he'd long ago shaman-ed away from his purified spirit-self. Dunn had been the catalyst of everything that had gone wrong in Jake's former life. As surely as Rube Goldberg had meticulously designed each cause and effect, Dunn's ruthless bullying had tipped Peter's emotional balance that night, prompting his attack on Aby the next day at the tournament causing head trauma and blindness, which triggered Jake's divorce, psychosis, a fake-suicide and who the hell knows what else!

Jake felt his body launch itself at Dunn, arms outstretched and hands at the ready. His fingers clamped around Dunn's neck, his momentum crashing them both to the floor. Jake scrambled to gain the advantage, straddling Dunn, now disoriented and barely offering a defense. He tightened his vice-grip around Dunn's neck, reared back, and smashed his head against the tile floor with all his strength. The force of the blow caved in Dunn's cranium; the back half of his head disappeared into the floor. Bloodied and gratified, Jake relaxed his stranglehold.

Dunn sensed an expression of pained disbelief on Galen's face. The reassuring hand of Mono 72 on his shoulder calmed him as he awaited Galen's response to Dunn's monologue. "Dr. Phelt?" There was no answer.

"He's in another place and time, probably strangling the life out of you. You are a colossal ass, by the way." Fafáfa said. "Famuelita?" she said to the office door behind her. "Please take care of Galen." The young mono she'd positioned in the hall entered the office to escort the expressionless Galen out of the room.

"Galen Ram Das is a master of creating alternate realities to cope with difficult situations." Fafáfa explained. "It's a gift really—he thinks it's genetic. This isn't the first time he's killed you in his mind—not the Abbot-you, the Dunn-you."

"Of course not," Dunn said. "So, you know about the—"

"Cut the skubalon, I know what I know." Her deference to Dunn was over. She'd grown impatient with his self-serving account of his tribulations. "Where have you been since 2011?"

"In the SuperMax under Crater Lake, as I said. I turned myself in."

"For the embezzling charges?"

"Yes."

"Why turn yourself then? Why at all?"

"That's what I've been trying to tell you. It was my atonement," Dunn said. "Pastor Yates told me to turn myself into FBI Agent Dunkin under the clock at Grand Central Station. So, I did. It was the only way to right the wrong for blinding him."

"Who is Pastor Yates? Is he related to the boy you blinded?"

"He is the boy I blinded! Arlen Bob Yates, Church of the P-Free Sabbath." Dunn said, exasperated. "Jesus, haven't you ever heard of the Church of the P-Free Sabbath?"

"Black Shade is totally off the grid, Dad, except for the IT monos who manage our social media," 72 explained.

"DAD!?" Fafáfa erupted. "Dad?"

"Yes," said Dunn. "Allow me to introduce my son, Larry–"

"No names," she stated firmly. "No birth names. That serves only the past." Fafáfa looked at 72. "So, when were you going to tell me–?

"You've done well in my absence," Dunn interrupted.

"I've done well in my presence," Fafáfa corrected him. "Does the FBI know that you have anything to do with Black Shade?"

"No. I don't think so."

"So, when you got out they just let you cross the border to México? Aren't you on probation or–"

"They didn't let me go. I escaped."

"You escaped." Fafáfa studied Dunn and 72.

"Yes, with the help of Bob the Rap-eest." Dunn explained. "We disappeared."

"Okay." Fafáfa said flatly. "You escaped from a SuperMax prison with a rapist, and then what?"

"He's not a rapist–we went to junior high together." 72 interjected.

"We didn't just escape. We vanished." Dunn explained.

"Look, I don't care if you machine-gunned or Tinker-belled your way out of there. Cut the disappearing crap. All I need to know is: are a bunch of jack-booted federales going to bust my door down looking for you?"

"There's no way they followed me," Dunn answered. "But God works in mysterious ways—"

There was an urgent knock on the door. "Abbot?"

"Yes?" Dunn and Fafáfa answered simultaneously.

"Come in, Famuelita!" Fafáfa glared at Dunn. "What is it?"

"¡La policía está aquí, jefe! ¡Ellos estan aqui!"

Mono 72 quickly knelt in front of Dunn and grasped his hands. "Dad, we have to go!"

"72, what are you doing?" Fafáfa yelled over threatening police commands in the hall. "Everything will be alright. Don't do anything stupid."

"Stand up," 72 instructed his father.

"Sit down!" Fafáfa implored them. "This is a legal sanctuary. You are safe here!"

Dunn felt 72 grasped his hands firmly in the familiar double handshake. "You ready?"

"Stop this!" Fafáfa yelled at everything. As the door burst open, 72 backed his father up two steps and together they disappeared in a spectacular flash of fire and fog.

Sixty-Second Sermon   Circa 2026 Y.O.S.P.L.

Cyron Furm and the family Furm heard a very special episode of the CPFS Sixty-Second Sermon on KXDT-AM at 3:30 a.m. At the time, they were on their way back up the mountain to look for the Furm family cat, Melvin. Mrs. Fanny Furm tried to convince the children and Mr. Furm that bringing Melvin on their annual camping trip to Chimayó wasn't a good idea, but no one had listened.

So, they'd gone camping with Melvin and managed to keep him safe in his carrier until the last evening when Mr. Furm decided to take him on a walk through the campgrounds to show off the clever cat leash he'd invented during his Wi-Fi-less evenings in the Sangre de Cristo Mountains, north of Santa Fe.

As Mr. Furm wrestled his cat into the body harness, Melvin had an epiphany. No human had ever successfully walked a cat on a leash; sure, there are claims to the contrary, but none substantiated. Allowing this to happen even once would forever relegate his fellow cats to be no more than dogs. While Melvin didn't particularly like his fellow felis catus, he truly despised the pandering canis lupus familiaris. For that reason, Melvin decided to take all necessary measures to ensure that his species would never be tethered by the neck, like a pack of dogs.

When four-year-old Cyron Furm Jr. counted the bloody gashes inflicted by Melvin on Mr. Furm's forearms and hands, he came up with 43. His sister Furgi said they shouldn't count the ones that didn't bleed a whole bunch and she came up with 39.

"How many do you think, Popi?" she asked as they left a Santa Fe minor emergency clinic. "I don't know, honey, it feels like one big scratch to me, but it really doesn't hurt," he said, turning the minivan north on US 285 back toward Chimayó to look for Melvin. In the darkness, Mrs. Furm sighed, knowing it would take more than her advice to turn Mr. Furm, the children and the minivan around; she reclined her seat and turned on the radio. Through the A.M. crackle, they heard the familiar voice of the CPFS announcer, the one with the unconvincing Hoosier-Hindi accent.

"Tonight's Sixty-Second Sermon will be delivered by Legacy Dianic Wicca High Priestess Bast. Her sermon is titled, "Poof!" The scratchy signal cleared.

"Poof!" said the voice. "And now I have only 59 seconds, 58, 57. Fifty-six seconds now, until I disappear. I'm told by our Pastor Yates that millions of you will hear this sermon. From my perspective, each of you will disappear when our minute is up. I sense you now, but you'll soon be gone, and that's fine.

Many people you know in life will disappear from time to time. Some of them you will want to re-locate, others you will not.

I am High Priestess Bast. My name comes from the Egyptian War Goddess, a guileful feline who protects us in times of conflict. When there is peace, she disappears and we do not seek her out because she abides only in a world of cat fights and bloodied arms. Stumps! Goddess Bast thrives in mayhem and evil, amid monsters lurking in dark closets and under children's beds."

"Mama?" Furgi Furm trembled. "Is Melvin a cat god?"

"No, sweetheart, Melvin's –."

"Me-OOOOOOWWWW!" shrieked High Priestess Bast. And then louder, in piercing rapid succession, "Me-OOOOWW! Me-OOOOWW! Me-OOOOWW!"

"Turn that down, for Word's sake" yelled Mr. Furm.

"I'm trying!" Mrs. Furm frantically fumbled with the radio. "There–it's off now." The car was quiet for a few seconds. And then, softly, the High Priestess' voice came from every speaker.

"We love Bast, the war goddess, yet we rejoice when she disappears. This is how it should be. POOF!" The radio was silent.

Mr. Furm looked in the rearview mirror and saw Cyron Jr. and Furgi, shivering and silent in the back seat. He pulled the van onto the shoulder.

"Uh, that makes sense to me," he said, almost as a question.

His wife stared into the darkness surrounding them. "Let's go home."

Escape from Oaxaca 4:7.1   November 26, 2026 A.D.

Fafáfa, Galen and Famuelita narrowly escaped the federales in pursuit of Dunn. The cloud of smoke from his and 72's disappearance gave the trio time enough to slip into a trap door behind the abbot's desk, constructed in the '00s for exactly this sort of occasion. With Famuelita in the lead, they felt their way along the walls of a pitch-black subterranean tunnel for the length of a Mexican fútbol field until they emerged from the side of a hill. Famuelita oriented herself and motioned to the others to follow.

Being the most resourceful person Galen and Fafáfa ever met, Famuelita surprised neither of them when she located an opening in a chain-link fence surrounding a car repair garage, hotwired a 2010 Honda Fit with 999K miles on it, and whispered "¡Vamonos!"

The only place to cross the U.S. border on such short notice was Falcon Lake, a 17-hour drive on the back roads from Oaxaca. A decade ago, the US president attempted to build a wall the length of the massive international reservoir–on the water itself–but gave up, blaming Dwight D. Eisenhower and his Mexican counterpart who partnered to build the reservoir in 1953. That was a bad deal for the United States–the worst deal ever.

They arrived in Nueva Ciudad Guerrero on Wednesday at midnight, just as Thanksgiving Day began on the other side of the border; it was a perfect time to secret themselves across Falcon Lake into Texas. Famuelita messaged her cousin, Jesús, to meet them northwest of town on the rocky shore where, as children, they fished for alligator gar and picked wild olives to make jelly. When the three arrived, the headlamps of a large pickup flashed once from the shore. Famuelita slowed the Fit to a nonthreatening 20 km/h and turned off her headlights, realizing the waxing gibbous moon would provide plenty of light once her eyes adjusted–that's right, she knew how to hotwire a car and the phases of the moon.

Recognizing her cousin, Famuelita stopped the car and ran to embrace him. As he had as a child, Jesús would take care of his pequeña primita; on the water's edge was a small skiff with an oversized motor, stocked with food and fuel. With a promise not to mention he'd seen her, Jesús pushed the skiff away from the beach.

Galen and Fafáfa clumsily rowed the boat far enough to lower the propeller of the ten-year-old Suzuki outboard into the water. Famuelita looked to the shore, saw the brake lights of the Fit and heard its engine start. The tiny red lights disappeared into the distance as she pressed the ignition on the engine and guided the skiff into the night.

* * *

After the last harrowing 24 hours, the rhythm of the boat gliding through the calm waters of Falcon Lake was a blessing, as were the snacks, fruit and drinks provided by Jesús.

"What the–?" Famuelita spit a slimy orange blobby-ness onto the deck of the boat. "I thought Americans had better quality control in their Cheetos manufacturing facilities! Gross!" This was by far the most complex, colloquial English Galen or Fafáfa had ever heard the young Mexican woman speak. She reached into the cooler for a bottle of water. "What gives?!"

"I never really thought about it," answered Galen. The three watched as the small orangey wad puckered and shuttered, crackled and popped, and then slowly un-crumpled itself. Famuelita reached into the Cheetos bag for another puffy cheese treat and then picked up the orange paper.

"BDAVM 00:00 Sat," she read.

"What?"

""B-D-A-V-M? 00:00, Sat?" She handed the paper to Galen.

"Saturday? Midnight? Do the letters mean anything to you?" Fafáfa looked at Galen.

"It's Dunn," he said, incredulous. "Jeez, he's–"

"What?" Fafáfa asked.

"Nothing," he mumbled, as a stained-glass pattern of assorted Goshen sounds and images flashed through his senses. John Lennon glasses, optometry boards, canned oyster stew and the woman clad in whit¬¬e, mistaken for–he thought at the time–the Blessed Virgin Mary. "He wants to meet us at Big Dick's Adult Video Mega-pleXXX in Goshen. B-D-A-V-M."

"Charming," Fafáfa said. "Indiana?"

"Alabama."

From the stern of the skiff, a light shown on Famuelita's face as if she was holding a brilliant candle. "That's only 966 miles from where we'll ditch the boat. No problem making it there on time."

"What is that?!" Fafáfa and Galen asked together.

"An I-Phone," Famuelita said. "A lot has happened since you came to Black Shade."

"That's a phone?" Fafáfa asked.

"It's not just a phone. It's the I-vanka Phone 6000," Famuelita explained. "Black Shade IT staff gave it to me to monitor the InterMess for potential threats to you and Galen."

"That thing will do that?"

"And anything else you want. How do you think we kept the enucleation clinic stocked with the scalpels and razors? How about the drugs? Where do you think that cool bloodshot-eye wallpaper in the clinic came from? And how about the Thursday night Popi Juan pizza deliveries? Did you ever wonder about those?"

"No. Not really," Galen said.

"You can order anything you want on this thing," Famuelita said, thumbs dancing in the light of her I-vanka.

"Why didn't you tell us about all of this?"

"Sorry. 'Need-to-know basis only' and you didn't need to know," she said. "Besides, you both shunned technology at every turn; all you know is landlines, analog televisions and fax machines. We needed technology to sustain and protect Black Shade, but we knew you would never be okay with that. That's why we didn't tell you."

"You're right," Fafáfa pursed her lips, wondering about the world she'd shunned over the last three decades. "What else have we missed?"

Famuelita scrutinized them with a grin. "You sure you're ready?"

"Absolutely."

Right before their very eyes, the arms of Famuelita's nose pod emerged from the center of her face. Galen, wide-eyed in disbelief, passed out and phased into an alternate reality to do a little coping.

"I gotta get one of those," Fafáfa said

* * *

Famuelita and Fafáfa shared the driving from Falcon Lake to Goshen; Galen, who was liable to "cope" himself into another reality at any time, sat in the back seat as Famuelita updated them on some of the news of the 21st century.

She rapid-fired hundreds of fun facts on world politics and culture, the dominance of Arlen Yates' church since the mid-teens, presidential impeachments of note, moon economics, and the 2024 re-emergence of the Soviet Re-Union.

"Just in time, if you ask me," she offered. "The Cold War has been in full swing for the last two years thank God. It's put a stop to the real wars in Africa and the Middle East, not to mention the Icelandic/Greenland standoff that was on the verge of going nuclear. The winter was coming on that one, for sure."

Galen and Fafáfa listened quietly, aghast, but somehow not surprised.

"Now, all we have to worry about are the corporate proxy wars."

"The what?" Galen sputtered.

"Oh, look, your son was elected governor of Texas!" Famuelita said. "And there's talk of secession." Galen's eyes disappeared behind their lids; he slumped across the length of the back seat, unconscious.

"He's kind of a weenie, isn't he?" Famuelita adjusted the review mirror to see Galen sound asleep, the shiny beginnings of a drool at the corner of his mouth.

"He's sensitive," Fafáfa smiled. "It is a lot of new information. We've lived in a virtual blackout since before Y2K. How did that work out, by the way?"

"Let's see here, it says it was a great year for t-shirt sales. Here," Famuelita handed her I-phone to Fafáfa. "It's time you started using one of these. Ask it anything you want."

"Okay," She awkwardly held the magical device in front of her face. "Ivanka, who is the governor of Texas?"

"The governor-elect of Texas is Peter Phelt. The current governor is Levar Burton," Ivanka said.

"Kunta Kinte?" Fafáfa asked.

"Yes, Kunta Kinte!" Ivanka answered cheerfully, adding, "I see you're near Houston, Texas. Would you like to purchase some Astros gear, or a nice down pillow for the man passed out in your back seat? Or, you might prefer a stylish sackcloth robe for the Abbot of Black Shade who is waiting for you in the parking lot of Big Dick's Adult Video Mega-pleXXX? Or perhaps–"

Fafáfa looked at Famuelita, horrified.

"Quiet, Ivanka!" Famuelita said. The phone was silent. "Sorry, I should have warned you."

"Oh my god, it knows–"

"Everything," she said. "Somewhere along the way, the world decided it needed to know everything. So...our phones know everything."

"Everything?" Fafáfa asked.

"Yeah–well, except how to make a phone call."

"Oh." Fafáfa put the phone in the center console and took a deep breath.

"It's a lot of to take in, but you're doing well! Better than most people would in your situation, Abbot."

"I'm not an abbot anymore. How about you call me 'Fafáfa'– better yet, just call me Binky. That's my real name."

"But you've always said that birth names only serve the past," Famuelita protested.

"Well, that's where we're going, right? Back to Galen's–Jake Phelt's–past and my past. Dunn's too, it looks like. We all have too much past and too many names."

"You have lived a life. That is to be expected." Famuelita said. Fafáfa looked at this twenty-something who was proving to be wise beyond her years.

"How about you? How many names do you have?"

"I'm just like you and Jake Phelt–as many as I've needed to get by." The seams of the concrete on eastbound Interstate 10 gently rocked the car at 90 beats per minute. Galen mumbled a shamanic incantation from the back seat.

"While we're changing names, you can call me 'Fam.' "

"We're changing names?" Galen asked groggily. "Why are we changing names?"

"No worries, Jake," answered Fam. "We're just resetting a little bit of our world. Oh, look!" she said, refocusing on her nose pod. "Cool! Here's a video of a play at your son's school in Indianapolis, Fiddler on the Roof!" she said excitedly.

"How the hell did you find that? What–?"

"Relax, Jake. Don't pass out again, for god's sake?" Binky scolded.

"I won't," he said, indignant. "And you should know better than anyone, Fafáfa. What I do is not 'passing out!' It's a metaphysical transporta–"

"Binky," she said. "Call me 'Binky.' "

Just hearing her name, rendered Jake consciousness until Saturday night as they crossed the Alabama state line. The traffic had bumper-to-bumpered at a mind-numbing pace ever since leaving Houston, and showed no signs of thinning out. They would need a little luck, or a miracle, to make it to Big Dick's by midnight.

Jake's head appeared in the rearview mirror. He looked at Fafáfa, the one constant in his life since Finna Galen Himlen that would never change–but it had. Of course, he'd known that she was Binky from their first meeting, but she'd never spoken of it and had simply become "Fafáfa."

Emerging from 18 hours in his own never-never land, he yielded to the truth that "Fafáfa" was yet another precious gift from God he'd been unable able to hold onto, like Phyllis and the boys. And yet, as he looked at Binky in the mirror, Fafáfa was still there.

"Binky," he said mustering a slight smile.

"Jake, good to see you back."

"I think I am back, finally," he said. "Let's see some of that Fiddler on the Roof."

Fam flared her nostrils, projecting the video in front of each of them. It ended with the flash of Mrs. Greenhaw's disappearing act.

"Amazing woman." Jake said. "I've been working on that since '99, but I can't even fade."

"Larry–72–and some his friends from junior high can do it," Fam said.

"The ones in the play, right?"

"Yeah. He doesn't think they all can. Just the ones who've really needed to at some point."

WHOOP! WHOOP! The syncopated BLAT! of a siren shrieked behind them. Flashing lights across the top of the large vehicle strobed red and blue noise at them. Fam realized it wasn't one but two Humvees, as one passed them and the other stayed behind. She increased her speed, keeping pace with the leader as the gridlocked mass parted.

"There is an urgent message for you Fam, from the Humvee following your vehicle," Ivanka said. "Would you like to hear it now or would you like me to direct you to the nearest Starbucks where you and your friends, Jake and Binky, can enjoy a Chai-licious beverage and perhaps a–"

"Play the message!"

"Alright," Ivanka responded with a tinge of hurt. "The message reads. 'You are being escorted to Big Dick's Adult Video Mega-pleXXX. Please keep pace with the vehicle in front of you. We will arrive in 24 minutes."

"Shhh." Fam put a finger to her lips. They rode in silence as the lead Humvee weaved around groups of vehicles stopped to let the convoy pass. They exited the highway one mile after the historical maker sign reading "Vatican Miracle Commission-BVM and the OMG. Next Right." Moments later, the leader took a sudden sharp left and then an immediate right into the side parking lot of Big Dick's. They stopped in the center of the empty lot; the escort vehicles extinguished their lights and muted the sirens. Ten seconds later the Humvees unceremoniously exited the parking lot. Fam, Jake and Binky scanned the dark shadows of the parking lot.

"There!" Fam pointed at the far corner of the building. "There's 72!" She opened her door and ran to him. Jake and Binky cautiously got out of the car. It was eerily quiet, especially for a weekend nightspot like Big Dick's Adult Video Mega-pleXXX which had, against all odds, leveraged the lucrative niche market of Alabamians who prefer to enjoy their porno on Betamax, even in 2026.

Dunn emerged from the darkness across the lot.

"What the hell was that?" Binky strode across the gravel with purpose. "You send us a super-secret note in a Cheetos bag telling us to meet you here? And then you send your paramilitary goons to make sure the entire world knows we're here?"

"The feds and Mexican cops are after you," Jake added. "Did you forget that?!"

Dunn was uncharacteristically silent for a few seconds.

"Do you hear what we're saying?!" yelled Jake.

"Yes, I hear you," Dunn said calmly. "And I believe you."

"Thanks, but we don't need you to believe us," Binky said. "All we need to know is what the hell's going on here–."

"I believe you because the exact thing happened to 72 and me, after he disappeared us from Oaxaca to College Station."

"College Station, Texas? Oh my god, that's awful," Jake offered sympathetically.

"Everything happened so suddenly. I didn't get the destination coordinates quite right," 72 explained, disengaging from Fam's hug. "We re-appeared on the 50-yard line of Kyle Field in the middle of Aggie Yell Leader tryouts."

Jake projectile vomited on the wall.

"Exactly," Dunn said. "We snuck off the field and made our way off campus, not knowing where to go or what to do. We stopped by an Aggie health food store and got some beef jerky, Dr. Pepper and Cheetos, and–"

"No way–" Fam exclaimed.

"Way, Fam." 72 said. "Here's the note we found in our Cheetos." It was identical to the one almost swallowed by Fam on Falcon Lake three nights earlier.

"72 hotwired a car and we drove to Goshen," Dunn said. "Thirty miles out, we got the same treatment as you with the Humvee escort. We got here 20 minutes ago."

"And what?" accused Jake, "We're supposed to believe that you figured out what 'BDAVM 00:00 Sat' meant?"

"That's exactly what you're supposed to believe," Dunn said, "because if you don't, and you insist on believing that I orchestrated this meeting at this Vatican charade, then you're more lost than I thought you were."

"Who, then?"

"How the hell do I know?" Dunn shouted, pounding the metal tip of his white cane into the asphalt.

"Excuse me, sir," Fam said, momentarily star-struck. Having joined Black Shade while Dunn was in prison, she'd never laid eyes on the mysterious abbot until four days ago. "If we don't know who, then maybe we can figure out why."

"Ah, a problem solver. Perfect." Dunn said sarcastically. "And who are you, señorita–?"

"Famuelita, sir. I been with Black Shade since '21."

"Five years? Good. Very good," he sneered. "Plenty of time for the deep-state puppet masters to install you as a mole in my organization, become invaluable, and fuck my son while you await your orders. She looks like a sweet piece of brown ass, son. Good for you."

Larry observed the angry racist who had raised him; he put his arm around Fam's shoulder, and said nothing. Jake looked at Dunn in disgust, but considered the possibility of there being a long-term spy in Black Shade–he hated himself for giving Dunn's words any credence, as his mind raced, examining all the implications. A spy? Spying on what, who? Dunn? Sure, he was an escaped felon now, but he'd been in Crater Lake for the past 15 years. Spying on Binky and him? They hadn't broken any laws except for smuggling eyeballs into the U.S. Is that important enough to install a Mexican Mata Hari in Black Shade for the past five years? Then he caught himself. Fuck you and your bullshit, Dunn, he thought.

"Go ahead, say it, Jake" Dunn said. "Say it out loud."

"Say what?" Jake barked.

"I don't know, whatever you're saying to yourself in there. Was it maybe, 'Fuck you and your bullshit, Dunn.'?"

"We don't have time for this," 72 interjected. "We have to figure out what we're going to do now."

"You know what I'm doing," Dunn said to his son. "I haven't got any choice. I'm here because Yates told the feds I was in Oaxaca–why, I don't know, but who else could it be? I went to jail for years to make amends to him. Then he sends his rap-eest to spring me, and my son ends up going to the SuperMax in my place. To top it off, I'm forced to disappear from the only place I've ever felt safe, and now I can't even eat a bag of Cheetos in peace!"

"He's right. Remember when the CPFS 'good will' delegation visited Black Shade in '17 or '18?" Binky asked. "They sent two legacy-faith ambassadors–the Nothing-Matters Relegationists and the, uh–"

"The WowNon Binaries," said Fam.

"You're right, yes. I did enucleations on two or three of them." Jake recalled. "What ever happened with that? Didn't we talk about working together on some border contraband-transit projects?"

"Is that what you're calling it these days?" Dunn snarked.

"Yeah, that's what we call it." Jake wished Dunn could see the scorn on his face.

"Yes, we talked about that and other things," Binky said, ignoring their exchange. "They were very excited about the prospects, but we never heard another thing from them, did we, 72?"

"Uh, well, not officially," he said. "I did get a couple texts from one of the WowNons after they left."

"Why didn't you tell anybody? Which one?" asked Binky.

"The cute one," he confessed, glancing at Famuelita. "It was way before you got here."

"Nice, Romeo," Dunn nodded his approval. "Please tell me you didn't talk to her about the–"

"It was nothing," Larry protested. "We chatted for a couple weeks and then I didn't hear from her again. That was it."

"Did you tell her who you are? Your name?"

"Shit." Larry covered his face and shouted into his hands. "Fuck!"

"Are you ready to help me destroy Yates now?" Dunn approached his son. "He's been fucking with you since you were kids; they threw you off a goddamned house, for fuck's sake." He reached for Larry's shoulder. "And he used whatever information that WowNon sweetie got from you to destroy Black Shade–your home. My home. They burned our compound and torched the enucleation clinic. We have nothing."

"Damn him." Larry's body shuddered with anger. As a child, his father had been the embodiment of wrath, modeling for Larry how to embrace rage and use it to hurt others and get even. Try as he might, young Larry could not live up to his standard. He knew he should hate his schoolmates who teased him, but the only person he truly hated was his father. Still, years of indoctrination by his father bore deep into the boy's psyche, leaving impulses of fury that came to the surface—not often, but whenever they damn-well pleased.

"Do you remember telling me they called you a nigger?" Dunn pressed. "And I said to you, 'Don't you ever come to me without bloody fists and tell me that somebody called you that'?"

"I remember, Dad."

"It's time to get your fists bloody, son."

Down Under Deep Eddy 4:8.1   December 14, 2026

"My people tell me there will be a bumper crop of SWORB this year," Arlen whispered.

"You can talk out loud, for god's sake. We're in a bunker, 100 feet below Deep Eddy." Governor-elect Phelt said. "The transition team gave me the keys yesterday—there's another one under Dan's Hamburgers on North Lamar. We're perfectly secure here."

"Good. I don't know what the budget looks like for the 90th Legislature, but SWORB presents an opportunity to put Texas in a strong financial position for the secession."

"SWORB," Peter said. "SWORB is good thing, I take it."

"For Texas, SWORB will be the ticket to independence."

"Excellent. What the hell is SWORB?"

"Spelt, wheat, oat, rye, barley. SWORB. Matzo grains. Follow?" Peter still didn't get it. "It's the only kosher grain-blend certified by the Boston Urban Rabbinical Provincial Council."

"BURP?"

"Exactly. There are two facts you have to understand. One, over eight million American Jews eat nothing but BURP-Certified SWORB matzo for Passover, not to mention BURP SWORB pastries, spirits and beers. And two, the Borneans have had a monopoly on SWORB since 1406 B.C."

"I hear they have a pretty good soccer team," Peter said.

"Do you want to hear about this or not?"

"Wait! Don't tell me, you know some Borneans who will–"

"Of course I know Borneans," Arlen said impatiently. "A lot of them. CPFS has over ten million members from Legacy All-Faiths Caliphate of Borneo. So what?"

"Sorry, brother," Peter shook his head resolutely. "I appreciate what you did for me during the election, but some of my team are concerned, suspicious. And, frankly, so am I."

"You should be suspicions–I wouldn't waste my time on you and your 'team' if you weren't smart enough to be suspicious."

"Okay," Peter said, "but how the hell are we going to make any money when the Caliphate's got a monopoly? What–a little market mumbo-jumbo and then short-sell? Is that your great idea?"

"No," Arlen said. "This is not a short sell and you're not buying SWORB.

"Good."

"Borneo will have a bumper crop this year by design because they've partnered with several maquiladoras looking at value-add artisanal BURP SWORB salsa and ice creams." Arlen flipped open his Big Chief tablet to a hand-drawn map of the U.S. He drew circles on the Mexican side of the Texas border across from Eagle Pass and Laredo.

"These two facilities will be up and running in eight weeks, each with 1,500 Hasidic Jews processing BURP SWORB in highly regulated manufacturing facilities. That's just the start, though. Add on three more kosher maquiladoras in México and four in Canada, and we're in business!" Arlen drew three more circles south of the Rio Grande and four more across the top of the page and smiled. "Well, almost in business."

Peter sat back in his chair. Arlen had been explaining his schemes like this ever since they met at the quarry off Keystone Avenue in 1996. He'd start in the middle, add in the backstory and then–finally–get to the point.

"Mr. Governor-elect, do you know where all of those BURP SWORB products come into the United States?" Arlen asked.

"Let me take a wild guess. Texas?"

"That's right, even the Canadians are required by law to fly anything made from BURP SWORB into México and import it from there."

"Would it surprise you that, as Governor-elect, I am aware of that?" Peter glanced at the wall of digital clocks, noting that it was already tomorrow in Borneo; or was it yesterday? "Where are you going with all of this?"

"Beard nets." Arlen flashed his trademarked smile.

"Beard nets," Peter echoed.

"Yes, beard nets. And thanks to the bumper SWORB crop in Borneo, there will be over 60,000 male Hasidim working in the BURP SWORB maquiladoras in Canada and México and they all have to wear beard nets–a new one every day. That's 60,000 beard nets a day."

"Okay, so?"

"So, what if there if there was a little public health regulation requiring them to change their beard nets every hour?" Arlen asked. "Better yet, every 15 minutes?"

"I'm fine with that, if I'm a beard net mogul," Peter said with some suspicion. "But I'm not."

"You're not now, but you will be. Because, the State of Texas will buy $500 billion in beard net futures."

"With what exactly?"

"With this." Arlen gave Peter a piece of paper with teensy print and the innocuous title, Transfer of Funds-Recipient Acceptance. On the bottom was a signature line for Peter Phelt, Governor of Texas. "As soon as you're inaugurated, you sign on the dotted line and $500 billion is transferred from Singapore Branch of the Famularity Bank in Bangkok, account #3.14159265359 into the state's Diverted Funds Fund."

"But that's where the legislature puts all the money it diverts from other funds, so it can be diverted somewhere else."

"Exactly," Arlen said. "Money goes in and out of that fund with zero oversight. It's a giant cluster-fru, totally out of control; just like the foster care system."

"And who's giving us $500 billion–and why?"

"Let's wait on that, I'm on a roll," Arlen said, on a roll. "You must have another question."

"I do. If this scheme is going to work, the price of beard nets has to go up, right?"

"It does, yes." Arlen said encouragingly. "And, so...?"

"So, what makes you think the price of beard nets will be high when we need to cash in, right before the secession?"

"Excellent. That's the question!" Arlen flipped to the next page of the tablet and scrawled a John Hancock-sized "E.O."

"Executive Order, baby," Arlen circled the letters. "The mother's milk of do-whatever-the-hell-you-want, Mr. Governor. Forty-eight hours before the secession announcement you'll issue this." He handed Peter what would become Executive Order PP 27-01. It was formal and concise, containing only three "WHEREAS" sections–not bad for an E.O.

"WHEREAS, a beard hair in your food is the grossest thing ever; and

WHEREAS,

　　1) I do not know Rick Perry,

　　2) this executive order has nothing to do with the human papillomavirus vaccine, and

　　3) my chief of staff is not also the chief lobbyist for the beard net industrial complex; and

WHEREAS, the Lone Star Dental Association estimates that 11.2 million Texans will discover a foreign whisker or pubic hair in their teeth during the 2029-30 biennium;

NOW, THEREFORE, I, Peter Phelt, Governor of Texas, by virtue of the power and authority vested in me by the Constitution and laws of the State of Texas as the Chief Executive Officer, do hereby order the following:

　　Any and all employees of manufacturing facilities producing flour-based products, including those unleavened, imported into State of Texas shall wear an OSHA-approved, sanitary beard net for no more than fifteen (15) consecutive minutes, after which interval, said beard net shall be replaced with a new OSHA-approved, sanitary beard net which shall be worn for no more than fifteen (15) consecutive minutes, after which interval, said beard net shall be replaced with a new OSHA-approved, sanitary beard net which shall be worn for no more than fifteen (15) consecutive minutes, etc.

This executive order supersedes all previous orders on whiskers and other pubic matter that are in conflict or inconsistent with its terms. This order shall remain in effect and in full force until modified, amended, rescinded, superseded or otherwise fiddled with by me or a succeeding governor.

"I like it." Peter nodded. "The Perry disclaimer is good."

"I agree. Unfortunately, I can't take credit for it–it's required on all Executive Orders these days."

"Oh."

"But I will take credit for how you're going to fill the meager coffers of the State of Texas, just in time to fund a glorious secession."

"Not so fast," Peter said. "I need to know where this $500 billion is coming from."

"Actually, that's exactly what you don't need to know, Peter. And it's not even about 'plausible deniability' or protecting you from future prosecution; by the time you're banking the $1 trillion in beard net futures contracts, Texas will be a sovereign nation. Who's going to prosecute you?"

"If that's the case, then what's harm if I know who we'll owe $500 billion to if the whole thing goes south?"

"Exactly that," Arlen insisted. "You'll know, and knowing changes things, consciously or unconsciously. Knowing could impact decisions you'll be making as governor, how you interact with the press, how you deal with the legislature, and– how you fuck my wife."

"Agreed, but–wait. What?"

"Do you think it could affect that?" Arlen asked calmly.

"I don't know," Peter was lost in that surreal moment known to all sexual interlopers when confronted by the cuckold. "I'm sorry, I–"

"Relax. You seem to forget that I believe in everything. I am the embodiment of the anything-goes doctrine," Arlen said matter-of-factly.

"I know, but–"

"But what? You can't accept that the Church of the P-Free Sabbath embraces and cherishes all faiths, all beliefs? Even yours, whatever they are exactly. I, and everyone in the church, believe in ritual sacrifice and the inviolability of life, concurrent darkness and light, free bonobo-love and the sanctity of marriage. I worship these and all other things."

"You're right, I don't understand," Peter looked around the room, nervously.

"And that's fine. You had a youthful dalliance with the Jesus movement–and Missy–back in the day, after my accident. The infatuation ended, so you came to Texas to make your mark, just like Davy Crockett and me," Arlen smiled. "I get it. You're a wondering agnostic in crisis, looking for anything familiar to lead you back to what you think you've lost. If your path includes a little of the 'in-out' with my wife on the CPFS boardroom table, so be it friend."

"Yeah, uh–"

"Agnostics wonder if god is anywhere," Arlen said. "CPFS believes that god is everywhere, alive and well in all the blessed and evil corners of the universe. We also believe that god is dead, and that it never existed. Faith Alone sustains us."

Arlen had Peter exactly where he wanted him; he patted his hand across the table. "You can stop looking for the truth now, brother. It's all true."

Capstone Light 4:9.1   December 15, 2026 Y.O.S.P.L.

"Welcome to the third meeting of Capstone Light on this, the 15th day of December, 2026th year of some people's lords! Any old business to discuss?" Pastor asked.

"If you're talking about your meeting with Peter yesterday, yes." Sister F'nA asked, walking into the room. "How did it go?"

"Great, if I may say so myself."

"You always do," she muttered, taking her seat.

"I gave him the 'You can stop looking for the truth now, brother. It's all true.' line," said Pastor Yates. "He ate it up."

"Of course he ate it up. It is the truth. It's our sacred doctrine." Cardu said, annoyed. "It's not a slick con you pulled on somebody. It's our core belief, for Word's sake."

"It is our doctrine, yes." Pastor paused. "And it's not our doctrine, is that not correct Brother Director Cardu?"

"Will you please–" Sister said.

"I asked the brother a question, Sister F'nA," Pastor stated.

"It is our doctrine, Brother Pastor," Cardu said quietly. "And it's not our doctrine."

"Thank you."

"Are you done now?" Sister F'nA said exasperated. "Is Peter good with the beard net futures plan, or not?"

"Yes, he'll sign the loan papers from Famularity Bank on inauguration day."

"What did you say when he asked where the money was coming from?" she asked.

"We decided he didn't need to know," Pastor said.

"That's not like him at all," Sister F'nA said, puzzled. "Why would he do that?"

"I don't know. Greed? Steely-eyed focus on a successful secession? Guilt? You tell me." Pastor couldn't believe Cardu and Sister F'nA hadn't pressed him themselves, on where the money came from. For whatever reasons, they too had decided they didn't need to know. "Okay, so we're good on that," he said quickly. "What else we got?"

"Just a couple other items," Cardu said. "About that Capstone Dark document you showed us in 2023..."

"Y'know," Yates explained. "That document is history now. It doesn't really matter anymore."

"Matter anymore?" Sister F'nA said. "Was any of it true?"

"Well, sure. But–"

"But what?" she continued. "You convince some 'high-value fugitive' friend of yours to go to jail so you don't have to pay your delinquent taxes?"

"There was the jaywalking charge, too, don't forget," Yates smiled.

"Quit being an idiot," she said. "What's going on, here? I'm Sister Finance and Administration, if you care to recall, and I file those Word-damn IRS forms every quarter and have ever since the three of us founded this church. I've never seen anything from the IRS about delinquent taxes."

"Well, it wasn't exactly a church matter."

"I'm also your wife. I'm the smart one, and I do our taxes. Same thing, no problems with the IRS and certainly not with the FBI."

"Okay, okay," the Pastor said. "You're right. All of that was part of a 'motivational exercise' designed to uh, motivate some people–one person actually–to do some stuff."

"What is that nonsense supposed to mean? Do you ever listen to yourself?"

He sighed. "Look, that's all I can really say right now."

"What do you mean 'That's all I can say right now'?" Sister said. "Do you have a secret master who forces you to keep secrets from us? You said you would never lie to us again. Are you being blackmailed?"

"No," he answered.

"What, then?" she insisted. "Who is the fugitive?"

"I can't say. I can't tell you."

"Just tell us the truth," encouraged Cardu quietly.

"You can't handle the truth!" Pastor yelled dramatically, his words ricocheting off the Carpathian Elm walls. He snickered. "Man, I've been waiting my whole life to use that line."

That was it. That was that. Cardu and Sister glanced at each other as Cardu reached into his layered robes, produced an envelope, and slid it across the table at the pastor.

"These documents certify that all CPFS funds–all six trillion dollars or so–have been transferred to a numbered account at Mel's Hole Bank in Kittitas County, Washington," said Sister F'nA. "You will note that this is a legal transfer of funds because two of the three church founders, myself and Brother Cardu, have approved it with our bona fide signatures which have been duly notarized by Sister Chief-Chief."

"Not to worry, Pastor Brother," Cardu added, "There are still several billion dollars in our operating accounts to carry-on the day-to-day obligations."

"But I'll need that six trillion for–"

"For what?" Sister asked.

"I can't, I–"

"That won't work anymore. We're done listening." Sister said. If you want that money, you're going to have to tell us the truth." She and Cardu turned and walked out of the room. The third meeting of Capstone Light was over.

The Third Teller

"The voice did not tell me you would be quite so handsome," said the all-gender, part-person but mostly-beluga whale. It was careful not to capsize the small boat, in its excitement about meeting the Second Teller.

Dvau Vatkr's pampered hands gripped the gunnels to steady her ride, just as she had the sides of the precarious sedan chair during her procession through Kaziristan on the first day of her reign. In exchange for a boat and paddler, the beach merchant had received a priceless pink tourmaline she'd carried from Kaziristan. There was no bargaining; as Queen of Kaziristan for the last 37 years, she'd not had to bother with such things. In any case, the gem was her last possession and she would use it to secure the means by which she would complete her last task as the Second Teller: passing the scroll to the Third Teller on the blue land.

"You're very kind." Dvau Vatkr grinned at the whale. "Is the water deep enough for you here?" They were only 1,000 goat lengths off the shore of what would one day be, for a short while, Da Nang, South Vietnam.

"It's very deep here, thank you."

"What else did Voice tell you? Are you still hearing it?" she asked.

"No, it's gone I think. But it told me to say 'hi.' " As massive as the whale was, it was able to stabilize itself upright in the water so that Dvau Vatkr and it were eye-to-eye.

"Is it the same voice I knew years ago?"

"Yes. It told me to tell you not to worry because it's learned a lot since it last spoke to you."

"That's good. So, you understand that as soon as you touch the scroll, the Third Teller's tale—your tale—will be made known to you in an instant. You will know everything...almost." She watched the beautiful creature nod and grin.

"That's what Voice said, yes."

"Okay." Dvau Vatkr reached into her pouch for the scroll. "How do we do this?" The whale gave her a full-on, toothy smile and then opened wide its octopus-hole.

"Are you sure about this? You're just going to swallow it? What'll happen when you need to give the scroll to the next one?"

"I'm not certain, but I'm sure everything will come out in the end," chuckled the whale. "Sorry, bad joke. Truth be told, I asked Voice that same question and it said 'You are a friggin' talking whale, taking the Queen of Kaziristan's scroll—that will determine the fate of humanity, by the way—to a place and time that is unknown even by the gods we've not yet created.' Then Voice asked me, 'and you're worried about a little shit on a scroll?' "

"Hmmm," Dvau Vatkr said. "It does appear Voice has gained a certain perspective over the years." The whale nodded, opened its large mouth and gave Dvau Vatkr a double-wink, the universal sign for "I'm ready for you to throw your scroll down my throat now."

Dvau Vatkr tossed the scroll into the beluga's mouth and marveled at its path around the whale's shiny tongue, past the uvula and down the hatch amid undulous folds of throat flesh. The whale backed away from her boat with a look of terror, as the truth of the Third Teller's tale was revealed to it. The sea quaked beneath them as the water glistened with a bloom of bubbles, forming a turbulent circle around the Third Teller.

Like barnacled tongs, the gargantuan jaws of a transparent sperm whale suddenly broke the plane of the water and swallowed the beluga whole. Its momentum from the depths carried it 20 goat-lengths into the air, but it didn't crash back into the waves. The translucent giant effortlessly performed a pulsating figure eight pattern above the boat. Inside its fifth stomach chamber, the one for passengers, the beluga laughed for joy as it was tumbled-twirled in the slimy belly like clothes in a dryer.

Had her virile, young paddler's hair not immediately turned white and fallen out, Dvau Vatkr might have thought this was a common occurrence on the blue land. How was she supposed to know? She was an inveterate landlubber, on the water for the first time in her life.

"Gibberish! Gibberish! Gibberish!" the paddler yelled. Dvau Vatkr waited for the words to be translated, as had the countless exotic languages she'd heard since she met Voice long ago. Her one hope was that it wasn't another channeled message from the aliens about some new scroll. She'd already accomplished everything asked of her; she was done with scrolls. The only thing she wanted now was to go back to her little hut on the beach and, when no one was looking, disappear in a spectacular flash of fire and fog.

"That's the most amazing thing I've ever seen!" Dvau Vatkr listened to the paddler's translated words. "Can we please get the hell out of here now!?"

After a few more aerial gymnastics, the sperm whale crashed into the water and disappeared beneath the sea. The shores of Borneo were several million goat-lengths away, but the distance was of no concern to the sperm whale or its passenger, The Third Teller, for the scroll they carried need not arrive there for another thousand years.

BOOK FIVE

Pugnare parabis.

Let's get ready to rumble.

State of the State 5:1.1 February 9, 2027 A.D.

The mid-speech firestorm in the House of Representatives chamber of the Texas Capitol was easy enough to ignite. A tiny drone with a remote-controlled BIC lighter, like people once used to light real cigarettes back in the day, hovered inconspicuously above one of the four large brass chandeliers hanging 250 feet above the chamber. With 182 Texas representatives and senators in the closed room, there were plenty of methane and other unpleasant natural gasses wafting high in the fouled air to create a nice little explosion. Add in a few ounces of military grade C-4 and you got yourself a nice big explosion.

Governor Phelt's 2027 post-inaugural State of the State address to the 90th Legislature was similar to Massachusetts Governor John Hancock's 1793 New Year's Eve speech in all aspects, except for one. As the careful reader will recall from the preambulum of this tome, John Hancock would have been three months dead when he delivered his remarks. Governor Phelt, on the other hand, was alive—but just barely.

Both great men recounted with passion the devastation of the previous year. Governor Hancock's oratory featured volcanic eruptions, reigns of terror across the globe, and the great yellow fever plague. Governor Phelt cited the injustices imposed upon Texas by the so-called "United States" and how

Texans fought glorious battles in the Supreme Court to uphold its right to enact the law against certain individuals sharing the same toothbrush, and defend the state's Harbor Master Baiter bill.

"If Texas wants to require its own harbor masters to inspect every piece of bait used by commercial fishing boats, it's no business of the United States!" the Governor proclaimed to the uproarious applause of the legislators, all of whom were keenly aware of the benefits of master baiting. A Harbor Master Baiter law would shoot significant liquid assets into the Texas Diverted Funds Fund through license and registration charges, inspection fees, late penalties and fines.

"No new taxes!" shouted the governor. "Fees good! Taxes bad!"

Larry and his father had visited the capitol on a public tour the previous day. As the guide led their group from the public balcony overlooking the house chamber, Larry lingered behind the group long enough to unpack and launch the drone without notice.

The next day they were first in line on the south steps of the capitol to make sure they got seating in the balcony. The Capitol grounds were immaculately clipped and trimmed, a masterful edge-up worthy of the occasion. Each of the 47 statues and monuments were festooned with Lone Star banners, and oversized Texas flags lined Congress Avenue all the way down to the Rick Perry Bridge.

Larry breathed in the cool February morning and closed his eyes as they waited in line; he clasped his hands behind him and stretched, filling his lungs. He wondered where Famuelita was and how on earth he could have made the decision to abandon her and travel with Dunn to this moment. It had been almost three months since they'd left Binky, Jake and Fam in Goshen to take their revenge on Arlen Yates.

With CPFS no-doubt tracking them, they rid themselves of all technology, electronics and IDs, and began the 750-mile trek to Austin. They would have disappeared themselves to Texas but decided they couldn't risk re-appearing again in the middle of Aggie Yell Leader tryouts.

They arrived in north Austin on December 22, 2026 walking most of the way and accepting only one ride—one they had asked for. Once, a car stopped and offered them a lift; they politely declined and then hid in a cotton field the rest of the night, suspecting the driver was a CPFS agent. After that, they decided that it would be impossible to get to Yates at his church or anywhere in the P-Free City of Light. It would have to be at the Capitol during the governor's speech; Yates was bound to be there.

Over the next six weeks, the two acquired everything they needed for the bomb, shoplifting batteries and wire, and stealing a 2017-era drone from the Radio Shack Historical Museum on Parmer Lane and MOPAC; it turns out, security guards don't think blind people steal stuff. It also turns out that Larry Dunn was eminently qualified as substitute high school chemistry teacher, the kind who works for a couple weeks and helps himself to a little sulfur, charcoal, and potassium nitrate. Finally, they stole a BIC lighter from a sleeping hobo on the Cap Metro North Burnet-Southbound Flyer. They knew he was a hobo because he was wearing his "We're all Hobos on this Bus" t-shirt.

As the day of the speech neared, Dunn worried about where they'd acquire the C-4 and a detonator. He ridiculed his son for his inability to get the explosives. The Sunday before the big event, Larry slid a small baggie across the table as they were finishing up their two-for-one turkey and dressing special at Jim's.

"What's this?"

"Feel it. You tell me," Larry said.

"Feels like the fuck-you finger of giant. Wait, Play-Doh?"

"Exactly like Play-Doh, except it's not."

"This is it? The C-4?" Dunn whispered excitedly, grinning through his beard.

"Yep." Larry said, patting Dunn's burlapped arm. "Plenty enough for our purposes and then some."

The line moved forward as the doors of the capital opened. Larry looked at the old abbot, his father, reconsidering for the millionth time his decision to follow him to Black Shade after high school. At that point, no one had heard from Dunn since he'd literally walked away from the Indianapolis courtroom with 10 million embezzled dollars after being sentenced in 1999.

That would forever be the saddest day in Larry's life. His dad was gone and, despite years of abuse, he was the only one who'd ever told Larry he should be strong; that he could and should fight back when people teased him. And so, when the sombrero-ed blind man brushed against him after his packed high school graduation ceremony and pressed a piece of paper in his hand, Larry decided to seek out his father. The paper contained an address in Oaxaca, México and a scrawled "I'm waiting for you." When he looked up to ask the man a question, he was gone.

His 2,300-mile bus trip from Indianapolis to southern México had taken him through Effingham, Muskogee and Waco, all of which looked like pretty good places to just get off the bus and disappear–like his father had–but he didn't, propelled by a son's hope that his dad would somehow have become less mean, less violent.

"Are you different, Dad?" he asked aloud as he'd drifted in and out of fretful, anxious dreams during the four-day trip to Oaxaca.

Vernon Purdy snapped at him from the top deck of the riverboat "You want a blindfold or do you want to walk the plank like a man, pussy?"

"Please don't push me!" Larry pleaded. "Please!"

"It's your friends that keep ringing the goddamn doorbell!" His father's angry voice bellowed and then faded.

"They called me a nigger," young Larry explained, weeping. "They called me a—"

"Lazy nigger!" The thunderous accusation came from everywhere. "NIGGER!"

Larry was startled awake, panting; drool soaked the front of his shirt. Brushing at the dampness, he looked across the aisle at a crone who smiled and stared. He sat up straight, wide-eyed, determined to stay awake for the remaining 13 hours of the trip.

He desperately looked around for something to keep him alert. Anything. And then he noticed it. Could it have been there for the entire trip, right in front of him, pressing against his knees? A thick, black, dog-eared book in the seatback pocket. This was surely a divine intervention to deliver him from his torturous dreams; yes, God was watching over him. Larry relaxed into his seat for the long ride, and opened the book that would sustain and protect him during the rest of his journey: *Debbie Does Dallas*.

When he stepped off the bus, Larry recognized the huge blind man with the gray, foot-long beard as the one who delivered the note at his graduation, but nothing suggested it might be his father. The man made his way across the large room and stopped two feet in front of him. Taking a deep breath, the man said with a familiar voice, "There is nothing about me that has ever been worthy of you, son." He waited patiently for a response from Larry. When there was none, he added, "we will talk about everything soon. Thank you for coming."

Larry was welcomed by the Black Shade monos into their order as an unnamed apprentice. He worked hard, and was thankful to be around people who respected him simply for that. As the months passed he was astonished to find himself gaining confidence and making friends. He was becoming a valued part of something larger than himself.

The next five years passed in the blink of a sighted eye. Larry took his sacred vows, becoming "72nd Black Shade Mono of the Sacred Order of Santa Lucía del Camino." He and his father never had the talk promised to him at the bus station –the one where Dunn would explain why he used to be a crazy, angry racist and then beg for Larry's forgiveness. That was fine though, because every day since his first, 72 had seen only a great and empathetic leader in his father, easily judged by his good works to be a righteous man of God. There was no need for the talk.

"Here, you do it, son," Dunn whispered, handing the crude remote-control device Larry had cobbled together to ignite the explosive. For a quick and fast exit, they'd positioned themselves in the standing-room-only section near the east door of the public balcony. "Do it now, before the governor stops speaking." Larry held his breath and pushed the button. They both looked above the chandelier where the drone hid. WHAAAAASH! It burst into laser-thin fluorescent orange-red flames shooting from the center to form a perfect circle engulfing ornate ceiling. Dunn was heartened by the hot air against his face, elated by the smell of sparklers and burned farts.

And then, it was gone. What was to have been a deadly conflagration was simply a spectacular, but harmless, burst of fireworks. Below, on the house floor, legislators applauded and cheered the celebratory pyrotechnics.

"What happened?" Dunn yelled over the raucous cheering. "Larry! What the hell happened?!"

"I'm sorry, Dad" Larry said. "I just couldn't do it."

All-Faiths Caliphate 5:2.1   August 8, 2008 A.D.

Pastor Yates hadn't taken notes during his first meeting with the All-Faiths Caliphate of Borneo but he could replay every moment in his mind at will. It took place one week after the official establishment the Church of the P-Free Sabbath in 2008.

He was flabbergasted when he'd received the invitation to Borneo. He couldn't imagine why such an ancient and venerable organization would take even the slightest interest in his fledgling central Texas church. The only conditions of the invitation were that he come alone and not tell anyone.

The flight from Austin to Kota Kinabalu on the All-Faiths Caliphate corporate jet was less than 20 hours, arriving just in time to be chauffeured to his meeting with the Caliphate Latitudinarian Council. Minister Bint-X and Melvin Schleinmann did most of the talking. X was an up-and-coming 20-something Muslim woman from Crown Heights, Brooklyn, and a converted Hasidic Jew. Mel wasn't quite sure what side of the faith-fence he fell on, being an old-school spirit head.

"Namaste, effendi," Bint-X smiled from across the circle. "Please sit." Yates and the dozen Council members situated themselves on yoga mats arranged like spokes of a wheel in the circular room. The group included men and women dressed in a variety of what he assumed to be religious garb. As near as he could figure, there were two Muslim sects, a couple of Jewish varieties, a Buddhist, one Priestess Confectionary, an Ojibwe Jesuit, a red-eyed ancient from the sun and moon crowd, a Thible Bumper with great hair, and one Bushongo, easily identified by the ceremonial vomit on his tunic.

"With your indulgence, we will share a story that has no end–yet," Bint-X offered. "Mel Schleinmann will tell the tale."

"Thanks, X," Mel jumped in. "Yeah, so Arlen–can I call you Arlen?–you're gonna love this one. It's all about Famuel leading the Israelites to Borneo in what, 1366? B.C. Or was it 56? X, can you help a brother out?"

"Sixty-six, Mel."

"Right. So, after travelling across the far-eastern lands and seas for 40 years–that's in addition to the first 40 years of wandering around the desert–the Israelite ships crest the final blue horizon and sight land in the distance–Borneo!" Yates appreciated Mel's telling of an ancient story using the present tense. He made a mental note to consider doing the same in his sermons, on occasion.

'Promised Land-HO!!' yells Famuel's great-great-grandson from the crow's nest. It wasn't the actual Promised Land that Moses had taken the rest of the Jewish diaspora to, but this would be the place where Famuel's group finally gets to settle down and grow some decent matzo grain," Mel explained. "You with me?"

"Absolutely," said Yates.

"So, they're all jumping up and down cheering at the sight of land, when they're slammed in the face with this horrible smell—some serious stank! We're talkin' like the '87 New York City garbage strike, brother. The stench is ungodly, but all the ships drop anchor a quarter-mile off shore. People with bloodshot eyes dry-heave off the ships, bellies to the gunnels, trying to make sense of what appears to be an enormous bloated jellyfish beached on the shore.

"So, they send a couple dozen Israelite anosmiacs in rowboats to investigate. As they near the shore they realize that it isn't a jellyfish at all; it's a goddamn translucent sperm whale. Didn't see that coming, did ya?!" Mel said and then paused a beat for effect. "Those anosmiacs didn't smell that coming either! HA!"

"That's a good one, Mel," Bint-X commented.

"Nearing the beast, they see through its cloudy tissue—wait for it—another whale!" Mell said. "A beluga whale inside a sperm whale! The Israelites marvel at the sight of it—I mean, who wouldn't, I ask you?! Both whales are long dead, but there are teeny ripples across the taut outer skin of the sperm whale."

" 'This has got to be Biblical!' says one anosmiac."

" 'Man, this thing must stink to high After,' says another."

"From the main ship, Famuel yells and waves frantically at the shore. 'Don't touch it! Get away! Get away!' "

"Y'know Arlen, anosmiacs can't smell a damn thing, but they can hear just fine. Even so, they don't hear Famuel screaming bloody murder from a ship a quarter-mile off shore," said Mel. "One of them pokes the bloated whale just a little, and then another pokes it harder. A third anosmiac pokes one of its big bug-eyes with two fingers. From the ship, Famuel's going nuts, waving his arms and screaming.

" 'Famuel wants us to quit goofing around and get on with it,' " the eye-poking anosmiac says. So, she picks up a sharp piece of broken oyster shell and walks to the middle of the whale.

"Now, if I was gonna write a novel about what happened next," said Mel, "it would have to be a graphic novel, for sure. A very graphic novel. I gotta tell you, Arlen, she barely touches that bloated whale with the business end of that oyster shell and that thing–along with every anosmiac–explodes into smithereens. The force of the blast blows all the Israelite ships a mile out to sea, but that doesn't save them from being covered by tiny bits of stanky whale and anosmiac flesh. Can you imagine how gross–"

"And what else fell from the sky, Mel?" X asked, politely.

"The Tellers' Scroll, al-hamdu lillāh! It fell into the blessed hands of Famuel," said Mel. The room fell silent as all heads bowed.

"But the deliverance of the scroll to the Israelites is only the beginning of the tale, Arlen," said X. "The story continues with the All-Faiths Caliphate–and you, if you so choose."

The Priestess Confectionary beside Yates handed him a 10-inch-long brown stick, the diameter of his thumb. Wrapped around it was a legal-size piece of thick animal hide. To Yates, it looked like a Waffle House Pig-in-a-Blanket Special (he'd hadn't had a chance to eat breakfast after the long trip). He took the scroll and held it carefully.

"Don't worry, it's not fragile–except for scroll-eating Baluchistan ants, nothing can harm it," X reassured him.

"This is the actual scroll?" Yates asked.

"Yes. Go ahead, look at it," she said. The Council members watched as he unrolled the scroll. "Those are the Ten Concepts of the of the Tellers' prophesy—"

"Actually, there are only seven," Mel interjected. "The Fourth Concept tells us that the Third Concept is false, and the Seventh Concept is only a place holder."

"Thank you, Mel, for that clarification," Bint X smiled. "It is our practice, Arlen, to chant an ancient invocation on occasions such as these. Will you join us?"

The Bushongo elder initiated the supplication with a deep, sustained tone that made the Arlen's innards vibrate. He prepared himself to experience the most sublime, eclectic spiritual enchantment ever heard on this earth—an ethnomusicologist's wet dream, as it were.

Unfortunately, no one else in the room could hold a note, much less sing or whistle, or make any sound that might be considered a musical accompaniment to the Bushongo's E-flat, two octaves below middle C. Yates tried to hum along until the thing ended several minutes later, thank Word.

"I've never heard anything quite like that."

"You are very kind," said X. "We wish we had more opportunities to sing that prayer, but scripture tells us to do so only when an earthbound soul is inducted into the Caliphate Latitudinarian Council."

"Well, that makes sense. You wouldn't want to sing that song just any time."

"Welcome aboard, Arlen!" Mel said.

"What, me?" he asked. "Why—?"

"Look at the scroll, Arlen," X instructed. Yates scanned the Ten Concepts, wondering if they were the Other Ten Commandments Moses forgot to bring down from Mt. Sinai.

1. There will be Happy Matzo.

2. The five grains shall be as one.

3. Five grains will be cast down to the earth as mammon; Four Grain will comingle with One Grain in dreadful coition. Five Grain shall beget the sad matzo.

4. But wait! Number 3 is not true; verily, it is fake prophesy.

5. One Grain (with a little help from the other grains) shall immaculately beget the Happy Matzo.

6. The Happy Matzo shall bring forth unto the world, the Cleansing.

7. Place-holder for future Concept, if needed.

8. Tellers and the Fams shall be the guardians of the Happy Matzo and the Cleansing.

9. A great nation of souls shall be delivered.

10. Oklahoma shall be as Canada.

"As a religious scholar, you know the story of the Exodus and how Famuel left behind the one special grain to make matzo. The first two concepts of the scroll you hold in your hands foretold that story, millions of years before it happened," X said.

"And number five, 'The Four and the One Grain shall immaculately beget the Happy Matzo,' " said the Thible Bumper, "became God's truth in 1797 when the Far East Massachusetts Matzo Trading Company journeyed to Bornean shores with all the grain-seeds to grow the SWORB. Embrace the SWORB!

"Come again?"

"SWORB, Arlen," Mel said. "Spelt, wheat, oat, rye, barley. The Five Grains of the Happy Matzo!"

"For three thousand years," X calmly explained, "our ancestors made matzo from jungle greens and sand. It sucked, but they had faith that the Five Grains would be provided eventually. All members of this Council can trace their lineage back to the Israelite diaspora that sailed to Borneo 1366 B.C." X said. "But you, Arlen, why are you here?"

"I don't know, I–"

"The Happy Matzo shall bring forth unto the world, the Cleansing," intoned the full Council. "The Happy Matzo shall bring forth unto the world, the Cleansing."

"Well, anything I can do to help, I suppose." Council members nodded their approval to one another.

"Thank you for that, Arlen," X said. "Bless you. While the hatred and vengeance you hold for your childhood friend–and future Governor of Texas–are not qualities we look for in new council members, they will serve well, the prophesy of the Tellers' Scroll."

"We do not judge your intention to destroy Peter Phelt's life," said the Bushongo minister reassuringly.

"Yes, about that. I really didn't–"

"We know all about that, Arlen. We have known about that for thousands of years," said Bint-X. "It is the catalyst for the Cleansing."

"The Tellers and the Fams shall be the guardians of the Happy Matzo and the Cleansing," chanted the group, under her words.

Yates had a million questions but didn't want to insult the Council or challenge their beliefs; after all, they'd just made him a charter member of what might be the oldest and most exclusive cabal in planet history. He decided to go with, "What's a Fam?" There were polite chuckles around the circle.

"Let me get this one," Mel said to the group. "Arlen, Fams help predictions come true. Revelations don't just happen because some scraggly, pony-tailed dude in a cave says they're supposed to–you gotta make it happen! That prophesy's not gonna come true by itself!"

"Makes sense," said Yates.

"You bet, and that's where Fams come in," continued Mel. "Hell, we wouldn't even be here if Famuel hadn't forgotten the matzo grain in Egypt."

"That's certainly true."

"And, how about Famularious K. Perdue?" Mel continued. "You don't know him, but he was a very talented three-ball hustler in Baltimore the day you and Peter were born. He made sure your and Peter's dad arrived just late enough to the hospital to cause the chain of events that led to the baby-switch."

Arlen's mouth formed an astonished oval shape and his eyebrows raised higher than they'd ever been; this is what surprised cartoons must feel like, he thought.

"Do you remember Pastor-Lawyer Famulonomous Agane."

"Remember him? I'll never forget him. He brought the $1.6 million insurance check after my dad–Peter's dad–died. My mother hated that guy–he was always poking his nose into our business."

"Yes, that Fam has been working this prophesy since the beginning, we think. They're damned hard to keep track of sometimes." Mel turned to X. "But it's all about making sure everything's in place for the Cleansing in 2027."

"So, the 'Cleansing' is what?"

"We don't know, exactly, but the date has been re-confirmed by generations of religious scholars," said X.

"So, prophesy is our destiny. Period?" Yates asked. "Or ..."

"We do not apologize for being the business of prophesy. We have long-term goals, strategic initiatives and quality controls to meet our objectives," said X with a little my-way-or-the-highway attitude in her delivery.

"Don't worry, Arlen," the Confectionary smiled. "You've always had free will. And you always will."

"That said," X added, "this is a partnership and we both have obligations to meet. Your responsibilities are as follows. Mel?"

Mel's word-per-second count increased to 10, about the pace of a legal-disclaimer at the end of a pharmaceutical commercial. "One: tell no one about the Tellers' Scroll, the Caliphate Latitudinarian Council or the Cleansing. Two: do not pay any inheritance taxes no matter what. Three: create a liquid cash account in the amount of $6 trillion by 2019."

"Did I hear something about $6 trillion?" Yates asked.

"Yes," Mel resumed his normal speaking pace. "That's for the Cleansing. We've already set aside our $6 trillion, as the prophecy says we should," explained X. "You have until 2019 do yours."

"That's good to know, but there's no way in this world or the next I'll bank that kind of cash in 11 years—or 1,100 years. We just established our church last week!"

"Faith, brother," said the Bushongo minister. "Faith Alone. You will have that and much more by that time."

"And besides," offered Mel, "with inflation, we're only talking $4.5 trillion in 2008 dollars. Save a little bit each month, and you'll do fine—compound interest is your friend."

"Thanks Mel," said Yates. "And why am I not paying the inheritance taxes?"

"Sorry, Arlen, but that's need-to-know only," said X.

"And I don't ..."

"...need to know. Correct," she said. "Let's just say that doing that will get us where we need to be when Texas leaves the Union."

"There will be a secession?" Yates asked.

"Something like that," X said.

"But, I want to make sure that—"

"Don't worry, Arlen," counseled Bint-X. "You will have your revenge on Peter and we will have the Cleansing."

"Alright then," Yates said. "I'm with you."

"A great nation of souls shall be delivered," droned the circle. "A great nation of souls shall be delivered. A great nation of souls shall be delivered."

"Ahem," ahem-ed the Ojibwe Jesuit across the circle. "We mustn't forget the last Concept, Bint-X."

"Yes, thank you, O.J.," she said. "Arlen, this is a little embarrassing. We pride ourselves on the interpretation of prophecy but..." X hesitated. "Well, about the last Concept..."

Soft encouragements came from the circle. "Aktu boweja." "You go, girl." "The One-Who-Is." "Al-hamdu lillāh." "Oh-wha-ta-goo-siam."

"We don't know what it means," X confessed for the group. "Do you what the hell 'Oklahoma shall be as Canada' means??"

"Not a clue," answered Yates. "But neither one is going to be happy about it."

SoCo Four 5:3.1   February 10, 2027 A.D.

Larry woke up early the next morning hung over, leaning against the Ten Commandments statue on the capitol grounds adjacent to the Texas Supreme Court. The last thing he remembered was his father yelling at him from the House of Representatives Chamber balcony. He hadn't looked back, making his way out of the capitol to lose himself in the jubilant inaugural crowd. He was soon offered a bottle Antonio Cruz de Mantanzas Handmade Vodka; he didn't know what it was, but it damn went well with the tiny cigarette he wasn't familiar with either.

"Time to get up now, Senator, you hot thing, you," Ivanka cooed to man snoring next to Larry. "I-vanka is waiting for you. Oh my goodness, sexy boy, it appears you've been having some very naughty dreams about your I-I-I-vanka." Coming out of his stupor, Larry realized what the voice was and reached into the man's damp pants pocket for the I-Phone; Ivanka was right about the dreams.

He pressed the honorable senator's thumb on the I-Phone with no results. He then forced open the man's mouth, gently pulled on his tongue and placed the I-Phone on it. Nothing.

"Dammit." Larry positioned the phone against the man's right eye and then left, as he held up his eyelids. Were it not for his snoring, Larry would have assumed the man was dead. He wracked his brain for other biosecurity measures to try.

"What would you like for breakfast, Sweet Cheeks," Ivanka purred. "Coffee, tea, or m–"

"That's gotta be it!" Larry said to himself as he pulled down the man's pants down and pressed Ivanka against the senator's ample left cheek.

"I love it when you unlock me, Senator. Nobody unlocks me like you do," Ivanka said, admiringly. "But you've been a bad boy. Are you ready for your punishment now?"

"Deactivate voice," Larry ordered.

"But, I–" the phone protested.

"Deactivate! Call 011+52+951+589-3475." As the phone clicked and chinked, struggling to connect to the Oaxaca number, Larry quickly walked off the grassy knoll toward the Texas Historical Commission; the last thing he wanted was to be chased down by a horny, hungover Texas senator chasing after the man who stole his Ivanka.

"Hola?!"

"Fam? Is that you?" He hid behind a line of bushes against the Price Daniel Building.

"Larry, mi cariño!" He could hear the smile on her face. "Where are you? Are you okay? I've missed you."

"Yes, me too." He held the phone hard against his cheek. "I'm at the capitol, in Austin. I have so much to tell you. I'm so sorry, I–"

"We're at the capitol, too!" she said. A man sneezed nearby; Larry froze and looked through the bushes for any sign of the senator.

"Bless you," said Fam, away from the phone.

"What?" Larry whispered. "Did you hear that sneeze?"

"Larry, where are you exactly?"

Not seeing the senator, Larry crawled on the ground to the end of the building and peeked around the corner to see Jake, Binky and Fam. "I'm right here, Fam."

* * *

"We should go," Larry said after a brief, happy reunion. "There might be somebody coming after me, and I'm starting to believe all my dad's paranoia about Yates tracking our every move." He threw the Ivanka on the ground and stomped on it. "Not to mention, now there's a crazy blind cleric who's pissed off at me. Let's go."

"There's no way anybody knows about us here," Jake offered as they cut over to Lavaca Street. "We've been holed up in Oaxaca for 20 years."

"I hope you're right." As they walked through downtown toward the river, Larry recounted his last two months in north Austin with his father. "He was hell-bent on a real explosion, with that C-4, but I couldn't go through with it. I don't know, maybe I've finally come to my senses. He never really changed; he never will."

"You're right," Binky said. "I'm sorry, I–"

"He's dangerous," interrupted Jake. "He's always been dangerous."

For Binky, Jake and Fam, the trip from Goshen was a 10-week hitchhike. With a lot more hike than hitch, they'd walked most of the way, depending on the kindness of strangers for food and the occasional shelter. They'd arrived in Austin the night before the State of the State speech. Having little money, they decided to sleep on the soft, well-watered turf of the capitol grounds; it was the safest, most comfortable night of rest they'd had in months. Their wake-up alarm had been Larry's phone call.

The four now stood on the corner of Riverside Drive, thankful for the elevated walkway above the eight lanes of traffic. Ahead of them, District SoCo stretched to Oltorf Street featuring, among its many historical landmarks, the famed Austin Motel on South Congress Avenue. A popular by-the-hour, no-tell motel during the latter decades of the 20th century, its clientele of prostitutes and johns had been replaced by out-of-town 30-somethings who eagerly paid very tidy sums to stay in the heart of SoCo.

The district's well-preserved one- and two-story 20th century buildings were surrounded by towering living communities thoughtfully developed for well-healed transplants. While each skyscraper prided itself on its tailored multi-media marketing to potential customers, they all seemed to feature this as their opening pitch:

> *Welcome home. Our community is nestled in a vibrant enclave of upscale retail, unparalleled dining and pristine promenades. Luxury accommodations exude stylish comfort and nurture your (insert "active" or "slacker" per target-demographic) lifestyle. Granite countertops by Dornschnoggle, White Ebony burl flooring, and adjective-defying mega-closets are standard features. Entertain your guests poolside, and take advantage of our on-site fitness center, natatorium and next-gen surgical center—everything you need for the SoCo life, you SoCo-deserve. Nose-pod today for an appointment.*

Jake read the tiny personalized billboards projected in front of him as they walked down the avenue. One was for a deep-tissue massage by a shamanic master channeling a long-gone Austin named Leslie; another announced a sale on burlap sacks from Callahan's Hardware. Although he'd experienced some of the InterMess on Fam's phone, Jake began to feel nauseated, disoriented. Anxiety filled his chest as images of his pre-fake-suicide craziness in Indianapolis flashed. He sucked in rapid, shallow breaths.

"Feeling upset? A little overwhelmed?" asked a soothing voice that reminded him of his mother's. His billboard showed a water fountain-like device at the entrance of the Austin Motel. "Relief is just one block away and it's free from the Austin-

Travis County Behavioral Standards Department." Jake broke away from the others and ran up the street, despite his shortness of breath.

Fortunately, one of the 27 water dispensers was unoccupied. He bent over what looked like a sink, gasping; his eyes were drawn deep into its center. Squinting, he saw his sons as small boys in Goshen, Phillip pushing Peter on the rope swing in their front yard. He looked closer; was it a picture, a video? The boys waved. "We miss you, Dad!" they yelled to him. Jake smiled and mouthed, "I love you." He took in a deep breath, watching as they played and wrestled in the lush Bermuda grass. He felt Phyllis' hand on his shoulder; his eyes watered as the tension flowed from his body.

"Are you feeling a little better, Dr. Phelt?" No one had called him that since 1998. "Your rooms are ready, sir. May I help you?"

Jake was steadied by the strong, young arm of the Austin Motel concierge. Ze led Jake into the trois-retro lobby, offering him a seat on the wall-length, chrome-framed couch. The psilocybin-inspired green, raspberry and lemon vinyl cushions recalled to Jake the décor of his first optometrist's office.

"Thank you." Jake was still a little confused, but the panic was gone. "This couch is more comfortable than it used to be. The vinyl used to get so sticky and hot in the summer—I mean the one I used to have did."

"We're glad it suits," ze said. "Unsaturated Hydrocarbon-Radical Chic. Ah, here's the rest of your party."

"We almost lost you," Binky sat on the couch beside him. "Are you alright?"

"Yes, yes. Everything's fine, I think."

"Your rooms are ready whenever you are," the concierge said. "Your son has prepaid all charges. He left a number for you." Binky felt the tension return to Jake's body.

"Well, I guess I can stop worrying about telling Peter that I've come back from the dead," he said, managing a smile. "You didn't even know I was dead for a while, did you, Fam?"

"Oh yes, 'Famuelita' I believe it is," interjected the concierge. "Did I pronounce that correctly?"

"Yes. Thank you."

"Excellent. Do you have a pronoun preference?"

"Not that I'm aware of," Fam smiled.

"Very good. For you, Larry Dunn?" ze said, checking the registry.

"I'm fine," Larry said. "Thank you."

"And Binky?" the concierge raised zir eyebrows in Binky's direction.

"Let's see. 'Me,' uh, 'I,' 'we'. The 'me of us?' What else is there? 'Hers?' 'Co?' Ze?' 'Zir?' "

"All are noted." The concierge bowed elegantly. It was an Asian/English-butler fusion curtsy-bow with a SoCo flourish. "Welcome to the Austin Motel."

* * *

Fam leaned her back against Larry as the warm shower rinsed the suds from her body. She reached up and brought his mouth to the nape of her neck. He caressed the softness below her navel briefly, gathering her close.

"I'm sorry, I think I missed a spot," he said, massaging her breasts in a new lather.

It was almost 2 a.m. This was their second shower; they were both exhausted but made love for a second time before trying to sleep. They spooned and managed to think of nothing but each other for a few precious moments–and then the rest of the world returned.

"What will your father do now?" Fam whispered.

"He will do whatever he needs to do to get at Arlen Yates."

"Will you go back to him?"

He turned to her, holding her beautiful face in his hands. "No. I will be with you forever." He kissed her eyes. "As soon as I stop that old man.

BOOK SIX

Non est his similis Mater.

Mama's not gonna like this.

Capstone Light 6:1.1 February 10, 2027 Y.O.S.P.L.

"Welcome to the fourth meeting of Capstone Light on this, the 10th day of February, 2027th year of some people's lords." Pastor said. "I know there is much old business to discuss."

"Last time we cut off your access to the church's $6 trillion and now you want it back," Sister F'nA said. "I don't know, is that old business or new business?"

"It's urgent business."

"Okay. In that case, we have some 'urgent' questions, beginning with when did all of this start? When did you start lying to us at every turn?"

"When I got that $1.6 million inheritance from Mr. Phelt," Pastor said stone-faced. "That's where I got the $79,000 to buy the church."

"You said you got it from some crazy uncle," said Cardu.

"That wasn't true."

"So, you did this because you didn't want us know who your real dad was?" Sister asked dispassionately. So far, she wasn't buying any of this.

"That, and–" he hesitated, "the taxes."

"And why didn't you just pay them, for Word's sake?" Sister asked. Pastor's stomach began to churn; thinking he might vomit, he noted the location of the wastebasket in the corner. He'd not been compelled to tell so much truth—or lie so much—in decades.

"Because I shouldn't have to! I was Jake Phelt's son and I wasn't going to pay. As far as the State of Indiana was concerned, I was just some kid who got a bucketful of money and they were going to get their share. Peter got the same amount but paid next to nothing because he was his 'legal son.' I was nothing."

"How much were your taxes?"

"At the time, $288,000 in state taxes."

"So, you just couldn't bring yourself to pay that amount, and walk away with what, $1.3 million?"

"No," Pastor said emphatically, "I couldn't."

This was sounding a little more plausible to Sister F'nA. "And then?"

"Well, I didn't pay the taxes and I didn't fight it either. I didn't do anything," he said, "except spend it all on CPFS during the first year. And then I didn't report the inheritance on my federal tax returns over the next couple years, and the IRS got involved. There were late fees and interest, prosecution, threats to seize church property and even rescind its non-profit status, for Word's sake."

"Why didn't you just come to us?" Cardu asked.

"Because you two would have paid everything off for me. I couldn't stand for that," Pastor said.

"Then what?" Sister asked, exasperated.

"I went to the IRS in 2010 to make a deal. I told them I would never pay the inheritance taxes, but said I could get them a Top Ten fugitive for the whole thing to go away. That's when the FBI got involved."

Sister F'nA shook her head, trying to process all this the new information and the possible veracity of it. "Was there ever a Capstone Dark group? Or is it just you?" she asked.

"Just me."

"How about the CPFS moles in the governor's office. Are they real?"

"Yes. They're waiting to hear from us."

Sister F'nA flipped to the next page in her Big Chief. "Who is the fugitive?"

"Dunn."

"Dunn? Who's Dunn?

"Mr. Lawrence Dunn," Pastor said. "Embezzler, re-relapsed-reformed racist, federal fugitive from justice and father of our old pal, Larry Dunn."

"Wow." Cardu tried to recall everything he once knew about the Dunns. "Mr. Dunn. Yeah, the square-dancing party in middle school?"

"Right," Pastor confirmed. "And the one responsible for bullying Peter into whatever psychosis led him to attack me at the double-dodge tournament. At least that's the way Dunn saw it, back then." He paused. "Remember? Everybody was having dinner at my house in the basement and Mr. Dunn–"

"Are you still telling the truth, Word dammit?!" Sister's stare across the table was condemning. "Swear you're telling the truth! Swear on it!"

"I swear on–" said Pastor.

"On what? What do you swear on? Word? Our church? I don't think so–nothing means anything to you," she yelled.

He couldn't meet her eyes. The room was as quiet.

Sister F'nA stood up and circled the table, considering the possibility that her husband purposefully ignited the conversation to avoid the real truth, whatever that was. She settled back into her chair.

"So, Dunn went to prison for you because he misbehaved at a dinner party? And it's all his fault Peter went nuts on you? That's–"

"Crazy and insane. Agreed," Pastor said. "But yes, he thought what happened was his fault and felt horrible about it. He was there the day I came back to school on the last day of eighth grade. I never forgot his words: 'I was the catalyst for Peter blinding you. I will make amends.' After that, I just thought he was a certified psycho. I was afraid of him because I knew he had it in for me and Peter for ringing his doorbell; it was all ridiculous, but we were just kids. I never forgot what he said, though."

"So, when the IRS came after you...?" Cardu prompted.

"I took a shot in the dark, contacted Dunn, and told him that turning himself in to the feds was the only way he could repay his debt to me," Pastor recalled. "To my utter amazement, he did it and spent the next 15 years in the Crater Lake SuperMax."

"That is psycho."

"Where had he been hiding since he escaped from Indianapolis?" Sister asked.

"Oaxaca," Pastor answered. "México."

"Don't tell me he joined Black Shade," said Cardu.

"He is Black Shade—the Abbot of Black Shade."

"I thought Abbot Fafáfa was–."

"She's been the Abbot of Black Shade since Dunn went to prison in '11, and still was when the feds raided the place and torched it last fall. Dunn blames me for all of that."

"Back up. When did you learn that Dunn was the Abbot of Black Shade?" asked Sister.

The Brother Pastor cringed. "Twenty-five years ago. Word, I'm sorry. I was wrong to keep so much from you."

"So, where is Dunn now?" Cardu asked.

"Off the grid. No sign of him," Pastor said. "We assume he's hiding somewhere in México."

"You are useless," Sister said.

"You're right, I'm so sorry about all of this." He paused and added softly, "this may not be the right moment for this, but I think we have a once-in-a-lifetime opportunity here."

"Oh! And what is that, pray tell?" she asked sarcastically.

"To establish true homeland for our church."

"A homeland," echoed Cardu.

"Yes," Pastor said, energized by the notion.

"I guess we'll need some 'homeland' security." Sister F'nA snarked.

"No, really. Think of it," Pastor said. "Why shouldn't the CPFS faithful have their own country? The Jews do, the All-Faiths Caliphate does. Even the No-Cow Hindus do, don't they?"

"I thought all this was just a vendetta against Peter," Sister said. "We went along with it because we support you and believe in you–plus, the church is going to walk away from this whole thing with a couple trillion, right?"

"More like three," Pastor said. "Jeemaneesus, it seems like everything used to be in billions. When did billions turn into trillions?"

"Late teens. Don't you remember?" asked Sister F'nA. "The Federal Reserve over-eased their quantitatives." Pastor looked at Cardu blankly.

"Look," he said, back on point. "We're thinking too small about this. What will there be when Peter is ruined and Texas is bankrupt and abandoned?"

"Chaos," Cardu ventured. "Violence, rebellion–poverty for sure. It will be awful for the children."

"And what do starving, desperate masses look for when all is lost?"

"They look for a leader," Cardu responded.

"And the church will be there for them," Pastor said.

"The secessionists won't give up without a fight," said Cardu.

"Peter fight? Wage war? Peter? That's not his style. He doesn't have the stomach for it. He's a peacenik like you, my friend," Pastor smiled. "But that doesn't matter; we won't have to fight–we have what the people will need. Food, water, shelter, security."

"He makes a good point," Sister F'nA agreed.

"Yes, we'll have leverage. We'll have everything," Cardu nodded.

"We'll have the future!" Pastor added, as a juicy quote for future historians.

"Did we actually just agree to this?" Cardu asked.

"I think so." Pastor and Cardu looked at Sister F'nA.

"Okay, I'll start the paperwork with Mel's Hole Bank in Kittitas to transfer the $6 trillion back into our regular accounts," she said, and then added, "You better not be fucking with us."

Pastor nodded. "Thank you, Sister. Brother Cardu."

The triumvirate sat in silence. Pastor's mind filled with glorious visions of the future. This would be the moment recorded for posterity as the true genesis of the Church of the P-Free Sabbath. A nascent revolution had been given voice this day–another good quote for the historians.

"Oh, by the way," Pastor said, not looking up from his papers, "thinking you might agree to the 'new country' thing, I went ahead and set up a CPFS Nation Naming Committee–y'know, to look at branding, marketing, naming rights. So far, they've come up with P-Free Sabbáth-istan. I asked them to go back to the drawing board; I think it lacks a certain je ne sais quoi. You?"

Cardu and Sister F'nA looked at each other, blankly.

"Well, no rush there." Pastor said, cheerily. "Plenty of time to discuss that later. "Listen, we can't meet in person like this anymore. We'll have to go dark," Pastor donned a furrowed brow. "We'll need secret names, we should never meet in the same place, and uh, keep it very low-tech–Big Chiefs only."

"Dark? Like Capstone Dark?" Sister asked.

"Not that dark. Capstone Dark was 'dark-dark.' But 'dim' definitely."

"Capstone Dim it is, then," said Cardu. "I'll handle the logistics. Don't worry. I got this."

Spies 6:2.1　　　　April 24, 2027 A.D.

Texas Railroad Commissioner Ozmana Zelotes would remember until the day of her death, less than two months later, that first wall-shuddering pound on her office door. Actually, it was more of a battering-ram sound, she thought, right before a battering ram blasted the door from its moorings and laid it flat in the center of her office.

A dozen body-armored Capitol police yelled orders and pushed Zelotes, Texas Air, Field and Feast Commissioner Tomasina Thomas and Health and Human Services Enterprize Executive Commissioner O'Nathan Obel face-first against the wall.

General Jane J. Primo strode into the room followed by her son Lil' J Primo, Director of the Governor's Security Detail. "Turn them around!" the general ordered.

'What's up, Ono?" sneered Lil' J, smiling at his urine-stained pants. "You and the ladies having a little wrestling and relaxation time? Looks like you might have shot your wad there, buddy."

"Doesn't look like any of them have much fight left," the general said, surveying the room. She looked at the broken plate glass window and traced with her eyes, the path of the shiny steel ball as it must have travelled across the room with force enough to bury itself in the wall. "What's this, I wonder?"

She turned and stared at Tomasina Thomas. "Commissioner?"

"I don't know."

The general nodded at one of the officers, who walked over to Thomas and placed his large palm against her forehead and pushed it against the wall, just a little.

"Oh! Ouch!" Tomasina said, surprised that so little pressure could be so painful. "Please. Stop it! Please!" She tried to move her head, causing the man to push her head harder against the wall. "Ahhh!! Stop! Help me!!"

"It was a note!" yelled Zelotes. "Stop! Stop hurting her!" General Primo nodded at the guard. He pressed harder for a second and then backed away from Tomasina, letting her head slump forward.

"Show me."

"There it is, on the floor." Zelotes pleaded. "Commissioner Obel was reading it when–"

"Shut up," Lil' J snapped, picking up the tiny piece of paper. "Faith Alone. Keep your shit together," he read.

"Sounds like something the good Pastor Yates might write," the general opined. "He's so sweet and encouraging–always knows the right thing to say."

"I gotta agree with you on that, Momma," Lil' J said. "Ono, are you by chance a spy for the Church of the P-Free Sabbath?"

"Yes!" Commissioner O'Nathan Obel said, staring fearfully at the guard with the big hand.

"And these other two?"

"Yes!" squeaked Ono.

"I can't believe we were actually worried about you three– such a confederacy of dunces," the general scoffed. "But there is one thing that's a puzzlement to me, commissioners. If y'all are Church of the P-Free Sabbath spies, why on earth did your own pastor rat you out?"

Capstone Dim 6:3.1   April 25, 2027 Y.O.S.P.L.

> ID3: You said you were the only one who knew about those three. So why were they arrested last night?
>
> ID1: I don't know. Nobody else knew about them, except us.
>
> ID2: And the three commissioners, themselves–they knew it.
>
> ID1: Wait, what? You think one of them is a double agent?
>
> ID3: Or, Triple maybe.
>
> ID1: But that would mean–

ID3: I'm kidding for Word sake! I really wished you'd planned this whole thing out a little better.

ID1: Did you set up the 99-cent payment to the Mexicans, Two?

ID2: Yes, I just finished the hack. The transfer was made from their account at 11:59:59:59 a.m. so they won't have time to correct the error.

ID1: Okay, it's time to sit back and enjoy the fireworks of the day.

ID3: Any news about your old pal, Mr. Dunn?

ID1: Still in Oaxaca. No worries.

Prison 6:4.1　　　　**April 25, 2027 A.D.**

After his son sabotaged their attempt to firebomb the capitol, Mr. Dunn realized he needed to rely more on his innate skills of manipulation and deceit, and less on other people. He should have known better than to rely on a weakling like Larry. As a boy, he'd been useless; the man was no different.

As students of better-government know, there should be an agency with the responsibility for knowing exactly how a person like Mr. Dunn first contacted Attorney General Flip Griff-Raff at the Bastrop Federal Correctional Institution and further, why Griff-Raff agreed to add him to his visitors list. However, there is no such agency and no one knows the answers to those questions. That's that; please don't raise the subject again.

The two men met in the prison cafeteria. The hard walls and floors amplified the ear-piercing goings-on of too many toddlers and their whiny older siblings. For Dunn, it was a walk down memory lane; the cacophony conjured images of the children he held so dear at his federally-funded daycare facilities. For Flip Griff-Raff, it was the reason he had very few visitors.

Sunday, April 25, 2027 was another in a succession of historic days. It was four days after the failed Texas secession and its ejection from the Union, three days after Puerto Rico was accepted into the United Nations as "Texas," and two days after three CPFS spies were arrested in the governor's office and Treasury Secretary Judy Real informed the cabinet that Texas was broke. Griff-Raff couldn't be bothered to remember what the hell happened yesterday. He was exhausted but, more so, frustrated at still being stuck in a federal jail nearly a week after Texas's break from the goddamned federal government.

"You shouldn't be in here," said the Abbot of Black Shade calmly. Dunn had re-assumed his clerical identity to facilitate his visit to the prison.

"Thanks for that, whoever the fuck you are," Griff-Raff said.

"I'm just a man with some information and advice."

"Are you really blind or is that part of the 'Abbot of Black Shade' thing. It's a nice touch, in any case."

"The whole thing was a setup, Mr. Attorney General," said Dunn. "I think your people should have followed the money a little closer. Isn't that how you wound up in here–prosecutors following your money?"

"I don't care what you think you know," Griff-Raff said. "Your note said you had proof."

"How about a little of both?" Dunn retrieved a large manila envelope from his frayed burlap man-purse. He placed a stack of papers on the table. "On the top is the proof-of-bank-ownership document for account #3.14159265359 at Singapore Branch of the Famularity Bank in Bangkok."

"Wow, this is earth shattering," scoffed the A.G.

"I don't know about that, but it is informative," Dunn said. "It's not in Braille, unfortunately. Can you tell me the owner of the account please?"

"All-Faiths Caliphate of Borneo."

"The next document is the ledger of Appropriated Fund 0847–Texas Diverted Funds Fund," said Dunn. "I know you're very familiar with this fund, Mr. Attorney General. Look at the revenue entry on line 1066 for January 20, 2027. Inauguration Day, I believe."

"$500 billion from that Famularity Bank account," Griff-Raff said. "Look, we knew the money to buy beard net futures was coming from anonymous deep pockets, but it was perfectly legal. So, what if it was the Borneans?"

"It's no problem at all if it came from the Borneans," said Dunn. "I rather admire them–and Pastor Yates, of course. Would you care to look at the other documents?"

Griff-Raff snapped up the papers and rifled through them. "What the hell?" he asked, "what the–?"

"Hmmm," said Dunn calmly, "do some of those papers make it look like the Borneans were betting against beard net futures while the state of Texas was betting beard net futures would soar?"

"And Yates, too!"

"It appears so," Dunn said, enjoying every second of this. He loved watching the moment when idiots like Griff-Raff finally realize they are idiots.

"These are short-sale contracts–shit!" Griff-Raff said between his teeth. "So, when Texas lost hundreds of billions on beard nets, Borneo and CPFS made–"

"Several trillion." Dunn held back a smile. "Each."

Griff-Raff buried his face in his hands. "How the hell did they pull this off? What? Is there some way they knew in January, that a typhoon would wipe out most of the South Pacific matzo crop four days ago?" Griff-Raff stood up from the table, yelling. "Do these motherfuckers control the goddamn weather?!" The room was hushed. Four guards took several steps away from the wall they were holding up, toward Griff-Raff.

"Sorry," Griff-Raff announced to the room. "Apologies for my language, I..." He sat down.

"They do control the 'goddamn' weather, as a matter of fact," said Dunn. "Not often though; only on special occasions." Dunn slid a binder across the table.

"That's full of photographs of secret prayer vigils across the world, all date stamped April 15. There's a copy of the actual prayers and chants that were repeated over a 24-hour period by millions, all summoning the April 21st typhoon that devastated 60 percent of SWORB matzo crop worldwide," Dunn said, almost cheerily. "I have recordings if you want."

"No."

"I understand that Borneans and Pastor Yates are well-positioned to make a tidy profit on the soaring SWORB matzo prices, too. Up 26 percent this morning," Dunn added, nonchalantly. "More than enough to finance the minor infrastructure damages in Borneo. Those people really know how to prepare for natural disasters. 'Don't Mess with Borneo!' I think is the slogan. Catchy, huh?"

Dunn waited for a reply but got none. "But I guess everything will turn out just fine with that $7 trillion loan from México, last night," he said. "Thank goodness for that!"

"You bet your ass, preacher," grimaced Griff-Raff.

"Absolutely," agreed Dunn. "So, I guess with that and your admission to the UN as the 'Republic of North México", everything's copasetic. Is it really true that you'res now, officially, a Tex-Mexian?"

"It's Mex-Texian, fuck-worth," growled Griff-Raff. "That's just the stupid politics of the deal and we're going to have to live with that for the foreseeable future. But I wrote that goddamned Mexican loan contract myself. There's no way Yates or the Borneans can screw with us on that. Every dime of that $7 trillion was wired to the Treasury last night at midnight."

"Good terms, I bet." baited Dunn.

"You're damned straight we got good terms. Every day at noon, we wire those Mexican bastards $1 and that's it," said Griff-Raff.

"Well, that's terrific," said Dunn, feeling his watch for the time. "I guess you feel pretty good about having made your first loan payment at noon."

"Whatever," said Griff-Raff, dismissively. "Look, I have to get back to the governor with this information. Is there anything else?"

"Yeah," said Dunn. "One more thing."

"What is it?"

"Your $1 didn't quite make to the Mexicans today."

The Cabinet 6:5.1   April 25, 2027 A.D.

"How the hell didn't we know about any of this?! And how is it that this Black Shade person DOES?! Goddammit!" Governor Phelt grabbed a cheap, hollow bust of former Governor Greg Abbott and threw it against the wall. "I've been wanting to do that for years."

"Yes sir!" General Jane J. Primo responded crisply.

" 'Yes sir' what?" He glared at her.

"Yes, sir. We've all wanted to smash that bust."

"Not that, for God's sake!" the governor screamed. "Why do we have to wait for some blind priest from México to tell Griff-Raff that Arlen Yates has totally fucked us? Isn't that your job? And your son's job? Remind me PLEASE, what his is job?!"

"Director of the Governor's Security Detail, sir."

The Governor picked up Rick Perry and smashed him against the wall, too. "They had to have been planning this for months. Years! Even before I was elected!"

"That's our working hypotheses, sir."

"Great, that's just fabulous," he fumed, eyeing the bust of Ann Richards.

"And you!" He looked angrily at Department of the Treasury Secretary, Judy Real. "Somehow, our first loan payment to the Mexicans–of ONE DOLLAR–was not made at noon today?

"No, sir. The payment was one penny short."

"And?"

"And we are in default, sir." The Honorable Governor Mark White flew across the room, and shattered against the wall.

"I trusted you to secure the state's finances, at all costs," Phelt said without a scintilla of calm. "At all costs. I trusted you! But no, you let Yates and his church bankrupt the state not once, but TWICE!!"

The Governor looked around the room at the other members of his depleted cabinet. "Famulus B. Redux, the eminent Director of Prisons, Pharmaceuticals and Economic Development. I can't remember a time when you didn't have your fingers in just about everything going on in Texas–and that's exactly the reason I wanted you on board." He gave Governor Richards an ominous pat on her head.

"Now, I appreciate you keeping Griff-Raff tucked away in Bastrop all these years; God knows what damage that clown would have done on the outside, but I wonder about–"

"I've always made my recommendations to you based on the facts at the time."

"Yes, of course, Famulus," the governor nodded. "I assumed as much, when you supported Griff-Raff's insistence on not accepting an outright grant of $7 trillion. What was it he said? 'It's gotta be a loan, otherwise we look like some third world backwater taking a handout.' "

"I wonder," Phelt continued, "do you remember when I called you last December about the beard net futures investment?"

"Yes sir. You'd just met with Pastor Yates."

"I listened to the recording of that call today. It was interesting; at first, you balked and laid out the 'substantial concerns' you had about investing. Then you made a masterful pivot, skillfully addressing each of your initial objections and leading me to the decision to invest every dime of that $500 billion in beard net futures."

"Yes sir. That was my thinking process. Again, based on the facts at the time, I thought it was a wise investment with acceptable risk and high gain potential. As I counseled you, the

Borneans are shrewd business people and if they were involved, then–"

"And that's the thing; on that call, I did not tell you that the Borneans were involved." Governor Phelt didn't pause to enjoy this Perry Mason moment, but immediately turned to his Chief of Staff, Mary Levi.

"You are the biggest disappointment of all. Everyone else here is either incompetent or crooked–they are strangers to me. But you're a trusted friend, I thought–one of my oldest. I think I'll miss you most of all." He walked across the office to the ceiling-high window and looked at his reflection glazed upon the darkness of the capitol grounds.

"All of you are more useless to me than our double-agent colleagues who were arrested last night. You don't know what the hell happened, what's happening now, or what's going to happen." He turned to face them. "Secretary Johnson, you stay. The rest of you, leave. Now."

There were no protests. After the last cabinet member left the room, Governor Phelt motioned to a chair.

"Sit please, Cyrana." He wasn't given to manspreading, but on this occasion he sank into the couch exhausted, legs spread a full 90 degrees. "That was a bunch of crap, obviously. I never trusted any of those people and Mary Levi isn't my oldest friend." He sat in silence for a moment. "You are, for god's sake–and Missy and Aby, Charlie and Faith."

"I haven't thought of her for years," she said. "You and Faith were quite an item in what, seventh grade?"

"Yeah, I was head over heels, for sure."

"Ever wonder what she's up to?" Cyrana was trying to gauge how much small talk about the past he wanted to have before getting down to business, whatever that was.

"Not really," he said. "Not until the Abbot of Black Shade contacted me through Griff-Raff a couple hours ago. The abbot knows an awful lot about us–and he's got a score to settle with CPFS."

"Who doesn't?"

"Yeah," he smiled. "Evidently, Arlen's responsible for him being in jail for fifteen years."

"For what?" asked Cyrana.

THWACK! The Abbott of Black Shade materialized in the middle of the room, his long burlap sack-robe concealing first-century sandals. He stood facing a 40-something woman, each grasping the other's hands with crossed arms. Both remained still as death, until the abbot slowly turned his head toward them.

"Embezzlement," he said, winded.

"Excuse me?" asked the governor.

"I was in jail for a minor misappropriation of funds. It was nothing, really," the abbot said, gently flexing his hands to disengage from the woman's grip. The two moved slowly, as if they'd been in repose for years. "I think you all know each other."

"Hello Peter, Cyrana." Faith Bountiful was smartly dressed in business casual, light makeup. She sported the same stark but fashionable hairstyle as the replicant in Blade Runner, who–spoiler alert!–escapes with Harrison Ford at the end.

"Hello" was all the governor could muster.

"It's good to see you, Faith," said Secretary Johnson, without a beat. "Governor Phelt and I were just discussing old times."

"Well done, Peter," beamed the abbot, "Wonderful job, keeping this one around. She's first-rate!"

"I don't believe I've had the pleasure, Abbot," Cyrana stepped in. "I'm Secretary Johnson, Republic of North México."

"Enchanted," said the abbot. "Please, call me Mr. Dunn," casually removing his sunglasses. Staring into his ebony sockets, Peter re-experienced the fear he felt years ago in Larry Dunn's kitchen during the eighth-grade square dance party, backed up against the wall by a towering man whose only concerns were the "nigger in my house" and who the hell had been "ringing my goddamned doorbell."

Cyrana's diplomat-self prevailed. "Why don't we have a seat," she said. Dunn felt his way to the one chair in the room, as the others sat on the couch.

"He knows all about you, your office, beard nets, the Mexican loan–everything –from me," Faith said, anticipating Peter's first question. "I can thwack in and out of anywhere." Peter wondered if this was a nightmare and if so, could he dream it backwards to right before he decided to run for governor–and decide not to.

"And she can take a passenger!" Dunn said, almost giddy. "My first ride-along was with Bobby Rappaport when he disappeared me out of Crater–well, that's another story."

"Our Bobby Rappaport?" Cyrana asked. "From Mrs. Greenhaw's class?"

"Yes," Faith said. "Some of us can thwack and others can't– or don't."

"That's–" Flummoxed, Peter blanked on an adequate adjective to describe thwacking. He settled on "Wow."

"I can thwack," Cyrana offered. Cricket. Cricket.

"What? Really?" Peter asked, looking at Cyrana anew.

"This conversation is even more entertaining than I thought it might be," smiled Mr. Dunn. "So anyway, while Faith has been popping in and out of here and there, we've also been strategizing on ways to defeat the church so you people can get on with building a new uh, 'La República del Norte de México.' Is that how you say it? How's my accent?"

"Excellent," Cyrana said without a hint of sarcasm. "We're always open to innovative ideas."

"Good," said Dunn. "First, we gotta fight fire with fire, Peter."

"We?"

"Yes, 'we.' " Dunn confided, "Listen, just between us, I could give a fucking Hosier-honk about Texas or whatever you call this hell hole. We aren't 'we' because we love Texas. We are 'we' because we hate Yates and his church. It's that simple."

"Fair enough."

"Good," said Dunn. "Yates and that P-Free gang of his are terrorists, plain and simple. He terrorized Texas out of existence and me out of 15 years of my life."

"And they have terrorized a generation of One-God believers practically into submission," Faith said, forcefully. "They are heretics and need to be eliminated."

"Eliminated?" asked Cyrana. "I don't think that's what God would want, I¬–"

"It is God's will, Cyrana." Dunn interrupted. "He gave you that brain of yours to implement His will, not to question it." Dunn double-tapped the metal tip of his cane on the floor. "First, we'll demoralize them."

"And then, deliver the kill shot," Faith added.

"Well, I'm not sure we..." Peter hesitated. "What's the kill shot?"

Faith and Dunn smiled at each other. She was the one to answer. "Prayer."

Capstone Dim 6:6.1   April 25, 2027 Y.O.S.P.L.

"The Seven Sisters Reverse Enucleation Clinic," ID1 said, looking across the CPFS boardroom table at ID2 and ID3. "Two, what's the latest intelligence on them?"

"Word Almighty, can we please dispense with the Capstone Dim cloak and dagger crap?" said ID3.

"If you insist, Sister," Pastor nodded. "Brother Cardu, please continue."

"The clinic's in Ferrum, California on the Salton Sea. For the last 20 years, it has surgically restored the sight of refugee kids from Black Shade; they all get new eyeballs.

"Refugees?" Sister asked. "But they work together?"

"It's a scam," explained Cardu. "It promotes itself as a sanctuary for Black Shade families disillusioned with the blind thing, but they're in cahoots with each other."

"Now we're getting to the good stuff," Pastor said.

"Yes, the Sister's Reverse Enucleation clinic is a fail-safe to make sure Black Shade never actually loses its followers, especially those parents who had their own children's eyes removed. They think they're escaping, but they're just moving from one loony bin to another."

"But the families are no longer with Black Shade," Sister F'nA said.

"Right, but they've embraced the Seven Sisters, which might as well be part of Black Shade," Cardu offered. "They all believe in the One God and that's the most important thing. This way, they're all under the same tent."

"Makes sense," said Pastor. "Those fanatical monos and crazy-pots defect with their kids from Black Shade to the Seven Sisters, but that doesn't mean they're not still fanatical. They need to channel that mania somewhere."

"And the Seven Sisters deliver?" Sister F'nA asked. "With what? How can you compete with removing the eyeballs of a three-year-old? That's powerful stuff."

"With Unified prayer," Cardu said solemnly.

"Shit," Pastor said. "How far along are they?"

"Not sure. We had someone on the inside but we think they ate her."

"Ate her?"

"Sorry, not exactly. We think they removed her eyes, crucified her, and fed her to the dogs. So, technically, the dogs that ate her." Cardu paused, then added, "They have rules–and being a spy is against the rules."

"Of course they do," Sister F'nA said. "Who knows what awful things would happen without rules?"

"Look," Cardu continued, "these uni-God zealots think CPFS is evil incarnate because we believe in everything under the sun."

"They aren't the first to hate us and our legacy faiths," Sister said, dismissively.

"No, but they're the first who can hurt us—destroy us, even."

"What? With their "unified prayer" whatever that is?" asked Sister. "Can their prayer cause a typhoon to wipe out the SWORB matzo crop?"

"That's child's play for them."

"He's right," said Pastor. "A focused and unadulterated unified prayer can be unimaginably powerful."

"But we have hundreds of millions praying," Sister countered. "How many pray-ors can they have? Five, ten thousand?"

"Seven," Cardu said "and they all pray to the One God. They aren't the Church of the P-Free Sabbath where everybody believes in a different god. Creating the typhoon took us weeks of preparation and a full day of prayers."

The argument was convincing and frightening; Sister yielded the point, although she wondered if unified-praying to a turnip might work just as well.

"Are Faith and her sisters still Howdy-Doo! Resurrectionists?" she asked.

"Evidently not. That Father-Son-Holy Ghost spiritual scheme didn't fit their business model. They needed a new entity with zero baggage to make unified prayer work— something that everyone could pray to." Cardu explained. "They call it . . . ."

"Come again?"

"It doesn't have a name. Names have too much history," he explained. "You're just supposed to pause for two seconds instead of saying its name; it kind of slows down a conversation."

The Blinding   **6:7.l April 26, 2027 Y.O.S.P.L.**

Pastor Yates stepped through the wrought-iron gate and closed it behind him, stepping onto the elevator platform that supported the massive wrap-around obsidian pulpit that would emerge from center stage and then rise another 25 feet, seemingly suspended in mid-air.

Yates penned that sentence after his first sermon in the renovated Church of the P-Free Sabbath in 2013. It would go nicely in the fifth or sixth chapter of his memoir, giving readers a tantalizing glimpse inside the magnificent ecumenicon that was a testament to all he, Sister F'nA and Cardu had accomplished since the founding of the church in 2008, and a reminder of all they had to lose.

"_astor is in the shaft and on the rise," Director Brother Cardu said into the ear phones of the 40-member CPFS stage crew. "Camera one, when you lose light, _an left and down slightly," "Ready camera two, with your close-u_ of _astor, ready mic, ready cue." Yates donned his smile and extended both arms to the masses. "Two, mic, cue."

He emerged from the main stage floor to thunderous applause and music. He looked up at the suspended megatron screen boasting images of a standing-room-only crowd. From the sixth-floor media booth, came Brother Cardu's weekly personal encouragement. "They're all yours, _astor Brother."

A piercing crack filled the arena, darkening the screen and all but the emergency lighting. Then again, CRACK! Dozens of 240-watt LED high bay lamps burst into fine dust 90-feet above the main floor. The megatron spat bursts of nonsense-noise and light; then, in a flash, then the omnipresent human-like KRNM news anchor appeared in 5,000-pixel-per-inch clarity. Anchor's appearance changed, depending on the occasion. Last night a Jim Swift clone did a charming piece on aspiring Austin rockers snorting pulverized Stevie Ray Vaughan bone in hopes of being remembered forever, when and if they died in a fiery helicopter crash. Today, Anchor looked like an Ever-even Ivan/Quita Fulfeffer hybrid.

"We're outside the Travis County Courthouse in downtown Austin, awaiting the arrival of–oh, here they come! Get that shot!" Anchor said. The camera swung 180 degrees. Ozmana Zelotes, Tomasina Thomas and O'Nathan Obel, shuffled along the sidewalk from the county lock-up next door, just like Paul Newman in Cool Hand Luke. Surrounded by heavily armed Republic of North México Rangers, each former-commissioner sported a fluorescent urine-colored jumpsuit, a waist chain with handcuffs, and Smith & Wesson Model 19000 leg irons.

The prisoners were led halfway up the wide, marble steps of the courthouse and halted. El Presidente de la República del Norte de México Peter Phelt emerged from the courthouse and stepped to the mic, flanked by his one-member cabinet, the Abbot of Black Shade and the Faith Bountiful. He looked down at the trio of traitors and motioned to the Rangers to turn them around to face the crowd.

"These miscreants are Church of the P-Free Sabbath scoundrels and conspirators!" he announced. "They were recruited as children and groomed to infiltrate the Texas Governor's cabinet with the sole purpose of destroying the State of Texas!" The angry crowd surged against makeshift barricades.

Everyone in the CPFS ecumenicon stared up at the megatron, mesmerized by the perp walk and accusations of el Presidente Phelt against these people who were evidently their brethren. They were appalled, but weren't quite sure why.

"Lies!" yelled Pastor Yates into his dead microphone, shaking his fist skyward from the podium. No one in the church heard or even noticed.

"They will receive justice, you can rest assured," Phelt continued. "Even as we speak, our own spies are infiltrating their church, to undermine the very base of their heretical doctrine and legacy faiths! We will deliver justice to the Church of the P-Free Sabbath!" Over the cheers of the growing throng, Phelt added, "We are a forgiving people and we wish the innocent no harm, but our standard bearers are the One God and His messengers!"

Phelt glanced nervously at Dunn and Faith Bountiful; they had been persuaded him that the "kill shot" was simply a metaphor for healing prayer. He'd agreed to go along with their plan, as long as there was no violence.

"It's about killing the hate in people," Faith had said, "and replacing it with unconditional love." Whatever the "kill shot" was or wasn't, Phelt had no choice but to join forces with Dunn and the sisters. Meanwhile, he thanked the god he didn't really believe in, for Cyrana.

"Abbot, will you share a few words with the people of la república?" Phelt asked as the crowd quieted. "Ladies and gentlemen, please welcome the Abbot of Black Shade!"

Dunn took Faith Bountiful's arm and slowly approached the microphone, acknowledging the polite applause. He looked like an ancient, round-shouldered goat herder, head bent to the ground as he walked.

"I am but a weak and blind abbot of humble means, but I will not yield until I see this church and its so-called 'pastor' destroyed," he said resolutely, quietly. "This righteous woman here with me, is the harbinger of triumph and grace for the republic. She will be our sword." His voice intensified as Faith's sisters materialized in a circle around him. They appeared so slowly that everyone watching ignored the question their brains were asking: "Hey, where did those women come from?!" They were just there.

"We will confront and destroy this false prophet and all who follow him by whatever means necessary!" Dunn proclaimed. The crowd was warming up to him now as he stood taller, stronger. He raised his arms heavenward, like Moses on the verge of parting something. Around him, the sisters clasped hands and began to chant.

"Right now, in the P-Free City of Light, the infidels are in their pagan coliseum watching us and fearing us!"

"Okay, thank you Abbot!" Phelt said, hoping to move Dunn away from the microphone. "Let's have a big round of applause for the abbot!" He approached the circle of sisters, extending his hand to touch the youngest sister's shoulder. He felt a strong electrical shock surge through his body; it simultaneously knocked him to the ground and, 30 miles away, caused a total blackout in the Church of the P-Free Sabbath.

Pastor Yates banged on podium and knocked on the microphone–nothing. His earphones crackled; Cardu's unintelligible words sounded like a disembodied spirit with asthma. "PRAY! Pray to your gods to spite this devil," Yates screamed into the deafening noise. Not one soul, devil or god heard him.

On the courthouse concourse, Dunn ignored el Presidente Phelt lying on the ground. He stretched out his arms, crucifix-style and turned in a circle. "These are OUR Seven. The Seven Sisters that will guide our prayers against our enemies." The sisters remained in formation around Dunn, chanting.

"And here are THEIR seven!" he continued. Nose pods klarted and charped as they unfolded from faces in downtown Austin, the CPFS ecumenicon and all over la república neuva.

"Scripture demands that we name the demons!" Dunn bellowed. Regaining consciousness, Phelt looked up at Dunn as he held up 12x15 wanted posters, one by one. "Pastor Arlen Bob Yates! Sister Missy Bradford! Brother Cardu! Mono 72–Larry Dunn! Famuelita de Oaxaca! Former-temporary Abbot Fafáfa - alias Monica Binky! And Galen Ram Das–alias Jake Phelt!!"

Anchor's googol-bytes promptly algorithm-ed the named 'demons' and thought it best to use its whispering golf-match-announcer voice to share its analytics with the viewing audience. When the abbot next paused for a crowd reaction,

Anchor whispered, "Jake Phelt, the dead switched-father of el Presidente Peter, is apparently not only not dead but is also fighting against his switched son. Now, back to the action."

At that moment, Jake and Binky were enjoying a local artisanal brew in the lobby of the SoCo Austin Motel, where they'd been holed up since the inauguration. For the past two months, they'd enjoyed talking with the concierge and smelling the wafting aromas of food truck fare through an image of an open window on the wall. Late April evenings offered the last of the cool breezes before the Austin summer. It reminded them of better times in Oaxaca where they were blissfully unaware of such things as secession kerfuffles and high-stakes Texas political rumpi.

"Turn on the screen!" Larry said rounding the corner into the lobby, clad only in a thin, white bath towel. Similarly dressed, Fam slid in right behind him on the handcrafted Italian terracotta flooring, shipped to SoCo on negative-emission ocean transports.

"We're all over the news and InterMess!" Fam said, turning on the viewer.

"This is crazy! Why does the government think we're with CPFS?" Jake yelled at the screen. "Peter's been footing the bill here since February for God's sake. Why–?"

The concierge politely interjected, "As you may recall, upon your arrival I simply indicated that 'your son' has prepaid all charges. I don't believe I mention a name, per se."

"We have to leave Austin before my father and those women find us." Larry said.

"Where do we go?"

"Where else? P-free City of Light," said Binky. "That Pastor Yates son-of-yours is probably the only one in the republic who really knows what's going on and what to do next."

"_RAY, WORD DAMMIT! _RAY!" Yates screamed from the podium.

"Brother _astor?! Aby! Can you hear me?" Cardu asked urgently through the earphones. "Aby, it's okay, now. Deep breaths, brother. Calm."

"Okay," said the pastor.

"Okay?"

"Yes."

"Okay. The generators are working now and we're getting our systems back on line. We'll bring u_ the show lights, megatron and your micro_hone in two minutes. We've dis_atched CPFS counselling teams to calm the crowd. You still with me, Brother ¬¬_astor?"

"Yes. I'm here."

"Good. Listen," Cardu said, "Scholar Jäger is here in the control booth. She's offered to deliver an inspirational message to congregation that she thinks will give them strength and calm the waters."

"Yes," Pastor said without hesitation. "They love Odede. Thank Word, she's here."

At the courthouse, Cyrana helped el presidente to his feet. They stepped away from the circle, as Phelt managed a weak wave and half-smile to the crowd.

"Your president, Peter Phelt, is a strong leader, and he will lead us to victory," the Abbot said. "That little shock he just felt was a tiny fraction of the power these women will yield against CPFS!"

At the P-free City of Light, Jake, Binky, Fam and Larry exited the driver-less Roy's Taxi at what they guessed was the entrance, though there was no sign of a door or gate. They'd been thoroughly scanned as they approached the City, revealing every mini-me of their existence. No doubt the terabytes of data on Binky and Jake included details of the moment they and Benjamin Yates crossed their Rubicon to forever reside in Switched-Baby Land.

A small entrance opened in the wall and waited patiently; it figured that any concerns the four might have about walking through a hole in a wall that might close on them halfway through, would shortly be outweighed by the RNM drones approaching rapidly from the west.

"C'mon!" Binky saw the flyers first and corralled the others into the entrance that turned out to be more of a transport than a passageway. They felt the centrifugal force of it speeding around the city's perimeter, inside the massive circular wall. Seconds later the transport dissolved one of its sides, and the four disembarked into the backstage area of the CPFS ecumenicon. Stagehands stood at the fly rail for their next cue as deck managers and technicians busied themselves in the dim light.

"Our church and community have just been attacked by the pretender government in Austin and their sorcerers," Pastor Yates proclaimed from the pulpit. "But our prayers sheltered us from their incantations!"

The response was deafening. Jake, Binky, Fam and Larry were startled by its intensity and vitriol.

"But we are safe now," he continued. "Our gods–each and every one–have protected us. Word has protected us. Look!" Pastor pointed to the rear of the arena where a spotlight shown on Scholar Odede Jäger. "Our beloved friend!"

Cheers of "Odede! Odede! Odede!" drowned out the rest of Pastor's introduction as Scholar Jäger made her way through the throng and up to the pastor's podium. They embraced and raised each other's hands in the air, and Pastor Yates yielded his personal podium to Scholar Jäger.

Despite her protestations, Scholar Jäger was obliged to accept another ovation from the CPFS faithful. She was their loving mother, come to soothe and protect her children. They yearned for her understanding of the chaos and assurance that everything would be okay.

"Shalom, my family! Shalom!" Scholar Jäger, called into the microphone to quiet the crowd. "Shalom! Peace is with you! All is well in the blessed light of Word!

"I must tell you a story, my friends! Do you remember just two months ago, I told you about the Israelites' exodus from Egypt? And how Moses took half of them to the Promised Land and Famuel took the rest to Borneo to grow BURP SWORB, the five matzo grains?

"I mentioned Moses' autobiography, One Hell of an Exodus–did anyone have a chance to read it?" Scholar Jäger asked. Many people raised their hands eagerly, hoping to please their Odede.

"Good!" she said with a broad smile. "You understand then, that Moses was a true seer! He prophesied the jubilant crowning of the Bornean-born Miss Universe in 1963, the 1774 arrival of the armada of cargo ships from the Far East Massachusetts Matzo Trading Company and, of course, the introduction of pygmy elephants into the jungles of Borneo in the 1826.

"These are all pivotal moments in the history of mankind, so I ask you one question here today," Jäger's voice quaked with emotion, "Why?!"

"Why?" she yelled from the altar, glancing at Pastor Yates. "Why didn't Moses tell us that our beloved Pastor Yates would betray us?" Yates smiled, recognizing a tried-and-true rhetorical method he often used himself: an outlandish mis-direction of fact to later demonstrate a salient truth.

"Why didn't Moses bellow from the top Mt. Sinai that our Brother-Pastor would collude with politicians and foreign governments, sinners all, to serve only himself, and–"

"What about Harvey?" a man called out from the rafters.

"Yes!" Scholar Jäger answered. "Not welcoming the victims of Hurricane Harvey into our church ten years ago was also unforgivable! But these things that Pastor did not do pale in comparison to what he will do!" She thrust her finger at Yates as if were a lightning bolt. "J'accuse!

"This man will bring the world to the brink of destruction and blind us all to the love of Word in the process!!" Horrible, discordant reverberations came from the upper levels. Screams. Shouts of "No!" and "Stop her!" echoed among inaudible cries of distress. Yates looked away from the podium, scanning the high, dark heights of the arena.

"Arlen!" screamed Sister F'nA as she buried her face in his shoulder. Scholar Jäger stood on the podium with steak knives buried in her eye sockets; and she was smiling. Everyone watched in horror as she pulled them out and shoved them back in with maniacal force.

The ecumenicon welled with revulsion and shock as scores of people mimicked Scholar Jäger's every action. Knives in, out, and in again. Yates frantically watched the mayhem, unable to take it in. The lights went out. In the pitch dark, he instinctively looked up at Cardu in the sixth-floor media booth but there was nothing. He hugged his wife tightly and listened to the deafening chaos, helpless.

Suddenly, every light in the building was on. The congregation shielded its eyes from the sudden glare. The noise subsided as, one by one, people strained to see the podium where Scholar Jäger stood, and locate the countless others who had bloodied themselves blind.

Surrounded by a murmur of confusion and fear, Pastor Yates stood and scanned the crowd, willing his eyes to see what was not there. There was no blood; there were no knives or self-blinded congregants. There was no Scholar Jäger.

Negotiation 6:8.1   April 27, 2027 A.D.

On the CPFS boardroom screen, el Presidente Phelt, Cyrana Johnson, Dunn, Faith Bountiful and Scholar Jäger sat on folding chairs around a dingy wood table in an even dingier room. Yates thought they might be in the antechamber beneath the Santa Rita rig where he'd had his reunion with Phelt less than a year ago.

"You wanted this meeting," Pastor said to the screen.

"Yes, to give you and your people an opportunity to stand down," said el presidente.

Standing in front of the huge screen, Pastor Yates, Cardu and Sister F'nA looked at each other, incredulous.

"You want us to stand down?" Sister F'nA.

"You have no choice, Missy," President Phelt said. "You've seen the power of the Seven Sister's unified prayer and–"

"What we saw yesterday, Señor Presidente, was a power outage and a parlor trick. Nothing more," Sister F'nA said. "Whatever magic the sisters used to trick us into seeing that bloody spectacle doesn't matter. Or, are you talking about the sisters' unified prayer that led Odede Jäger to betray her CPFS family–the family that cherished her, only to be terrorized by her deceit?"

"Deceit?!" shouted Jäger. "And what of your church and your pastor using the BURP SWORB matzo as a tool of destruction against the state? Matzo is the holy sacrament of our delivery from bondage, not a commodity to be traded and used as a political bludgeon. Shame on you!"

"You've already lost your Alt-Israelites," said el presidente matter-of-factly, "and it's not looking too good for the Alt-Pharisees or Sadducees legacies either."

"And we have commitments of all the traditional Uni-Godders to destroy your CPFS believe-in-everything charade," Faith Bountiful added. "It's a movement: Anti-ecumenical Dis-establishmentarianism. Our crusade will reclaim the truth on the ashes of the Church of the P-free Sabbath."

"We are aware of the movement and support it–just as we do everything else. In fact, we welcomed the Legacy Alt-Anti-ecumenical Dis-establishmentarianism believers into CPFS this very morning," Sister F'nA informed her.

"And the Worldwide Confabulation of Congregated Uni-Worship?" asked Faith.

"Them, too." Sister said. "They're now one of thousands of Legacy Alt-religions supporting CPFS across the world."

"Your point is taken, Sister F'nA," said President Phelt. "Please, can we talk terms?"

"Sure," said Pastor, "How about you open the Rick Perry Bridge to south Austin, grant landing rights to U.S. cargo planes delivering critical supplies to our people, and STOP FUCKING WITH MY CHURCH??"

"Aby, please. We can work this out," Peter cringed at his almost-pleading tone.

"I told you he'd pitch a hissy fit, Peter," Dunn sneered. "And then you'll pitch your own hissy fit when you don't get your way, right? Both of you are still a couple of schoolboy shits, ringing doorbells and hiding in the bushes."

Ignoring him, el presidente nodded at Cyrana.

"I've just messaged our unconditional terms for surrender to you. As stated in the document, the Church of the P-free Sabbath and its affiliated Legacies and Legacy Alt-religions will vacate all holdings in the Republic of North México. Further, all members of the church shall travel east through the Bosque de Pinos–formerly known as the Piney Woods–and cross the Republic of North México/United States border into the State of Louisiana."

Pastor's systolic blood pressure spiked 23 millimeters of mercury with excited anticipation; this would be the modern-day Exodus and he would be its Moses. From the former-Texas high plains to the Rio Grande Valley, his followers would converge on the City of Light to form the soon-to-be P-Free diaspora. Only he could lead them through the desert of the once-green Bosque de Pinos to the shores of the mighty Sabine River. With the army of the Republic of North México in hot pursuit and the Louisiana Promised Land beckoning across that great divide, Pastor Arlen Bob Yates of the Church of the P-Free Sabbath would summon the gods of all the Legacy Faiths and command that river to–."

"Arlen!" Sister F'nA whispered hard. "Say something!"

"Let my people go!" he said, emerging from his daydream.

"There, you have your answer!" Sister F'nA said. "You have no right to herd our people from their homeland, onto your trail of tears."

"A poetic mix of metaphors," said Dunn, "but you have no choice. It's settled. Tell them, Peter."

"Perhaps we should adjourn for today," Cyrana interjected, "to give both sides an opportunity to confer internally."

"NO!" shouted Dunn. "No more talking. This is not a negotiation!" He glared at Peter and Cyrana.

Without looking at Dunn, Peter said, "We are adjourned until 9 a.m. tomorrow, at which time the terms of surrender will be finalized."

"Could we make that 9:30, Señor Presidente?" Yates asked, nonchalantly.

"NINE O'CLOCK!" Dunn shouted. He stood up, walked to the camera, and put his face six inches away from the lens. The CPFS boardroom screen was all nose, nostrils and mouth. "NINE O'CLOCK or nothing, you pre-pubescent sack of–"

"We're sorry. Nine's not good for us. We could do 9:30 maybe, or perhaps another day? Yates offered congenially. "Say, sometime over the weekend?"

"Phelt! Do not let him run circles around you like this. He's–"

"If I may make suggestion, Mr. Dunn, Pastor Yates," Cyrana interrupted. "How about 9:15?"

"NINE O'CLOCK!" Dunn bellowed. And with that, he stepped back from the camera, summoned a substantial exorcist-green hocker from the depths of his chest and spat it at the center of the lens. Pastor and company couldn't help but stare at the screen for the five seconds it took for the connection to be terminated; it was pretty gross.

"I think that went well," Yates smiled at Sister F'nA and Cardu.

"It did, actually," said Cardu. "We stalled immediate action on their part."

"I almost feel sorry for Peter," Yates said, "Dunn and the sisters are pulling all the strings. He's just a figurehead." There was a knock at the door. "Our visitors are here."

Jake, Binky, Larry and Fam entered tentatively.

"Hello, Dr. Phelt," said Sister F'nA.

"Missy, hi." Jake said. "Uh, this is Monica Binky, and Larry Dunn—you know him, of course—and Famuelita."

"The SoCo Four!" Pastor announced. "Welcome!"

Missy gave Fam and Larry warm hugs. Cardu followed suit. "It's good to see you Larry, truly. Welcome."

"Hello, Monica. I don't think we've ever met—forgive me if we have. I'm Sister F'nA." Missy extended her hand, but decided on a hug. "It's a pleasure to meet you."

"Nurse Binky!" Pastor said, staring as if she were the rarest of ancient artifacts. "I am fortunate enough to have met everyone in the world I have ever wished to meet except for you."

"Pastor," she said confidently, masking the guilt she still harbored for the decision she'd made on December 16, 1984.

"You are hereby marked off my bucket list," Yates said. "Welcome to the Church of the P-Free Sabbath. Oh wait! There is one more person I haven't met," Yates cartoonishly put his finger to his temple. "My new sister!"

"Bella, our daughter, is on Tesla Land," Jake said.

"And, oh look, the long-dead Prodigal Dad. Hello, Dad!" Yates said.

"Hello, Arlen."

"Y'know, I've been thinking about our little saga," Pastor said. "The book is one thing—best seller, no problem. But, I'm not really thinking feature film on this. No—more like a five-season HBO series. Thoughts?"

"I don't know," Jake said quietly. He felt Binky's hand beside his and held it. "Whatever you think."

"And Famuelita—may I call you Fam?" asked Pastor, with a grin.

"Why are you being this way?" Jake asked. "I used to like when you were a kid, but now, you're kind of an ass."

"Excellent, Dad. Keep that angry edge, because we're going to need it," Pastor said. The screen-wall flickered behind him. Dunn's mucous was being cleaned from the lens, around and around until the hand doing the cleaning was visible through the slime. A blue spritz covered the lens as the cloth labored in circles.

"Hello?! Anyone there?" The voice came from beyond the Windex. "Arlen?" The cloth made its final lap around the edges of the lens. Peter came into focus as he backed away from the camera. Pastor motioned for everyone to leave the room.

"Arlen, you have to stop this. There are bonfires on the south shores of Lady Bird Lake, from the Stevie Ray statue all the way east to the Longhorn Dam. We can hear them from the Capitol for God's sake, chanting, praying–whatever the hell they're doing. Your people are–."

"They're not my people," Arlen said. "They are the people."

"We'll they're in SOCO and East Austin. They're sure not my people!" Peter said.

"Look, is Dunn–sorry–are you ready to meet tomorrow? At 9:30?"

"Nine o'clock," Peter stated emphatically.

"Peter, you and I, right now–we'll schedule a meeting for 9:30 tomorrow morning, and I'll see what I can do about those crowds on Lady Bird Lake tonight. Otherwise–"

"God dammit!" Peter said. "You know as well as I do Dunn won't agree to 9:30. That'll never happen."

"Alright," Arlen said. "Then something else will happen." He terminated the connection.

Battle of Lady Bird Lake 6:9.1   April 30, 2027 A.D.

Battle of Lady Bird Lake
From Wikipedia, the free encyclopedia
For other battles of the same name, see Lady Bird Lake.

The Battle of Lady Bird Lake, fought on April 29, 2027 in Ciudad de Austin, La República del Norte de México, was the first battle between the Republic of North México formerly known as Texas (RNM) and counter-revolutionary forces lead by the worldwide Church of the P-Free Sabbath (CPFS).

RNM forces led by the founders of the Seven Sisters Reverse Enucleation Clinic and the former Abbot of Black Shade hurled thousands of unified-prayers across the lake onto its southern shores, only to be rebuffed by a multitude of pray-ors launching their own invocational sorties. The clash was observed by non-combatants in the middle of the lake from the Legacy-AquaFest and Legacy Alt-Armadillo Forever faiths, as well as a phalanx of plaintiffs' attorneys waiting to offer their services after the battle.

As reported in El Hombre de Estado de Austin y México (formerly The Austin American-Statesman), the 18-minute battle was a stalemate. No territorial gains were realized by either side and injuries from the bombardment of prayers were limited, including:

- six RNM Catholics sent to purgatory;
- three CPFS Legacy Buddhists returned to the first realm of rebirth;
- one CPFS Legacy Alt-Hindu Brahman demoted to a Shudra; and
- an entire family of RNM Jains forced to kill a bunch of ants.

There were also unconfirmed reports of a plague of snail darters in the South Congress entertainment district (SOCO), and a bizarre account of the Ku Klux Klan Holy Rollers of the Real Jesus delivering gifts and food to the Miss Jane Pittman Descendants of African Slaves Nursing Home in East Austin.

The battle followed a declaration of independence by the nation-state of Austin on April 28, 2027, which was immediately recognized by the Queen of Kaziristan and the All-Faiths Caliphate of Borneo.

Contents [hide]

Gathering Greenhaws 6:7.2   April 30, 2027 A.D.

"RNM has already started to build the wall at 15th Street on the east side," Cardu said, looking over his shoulder at the bolted CPFS boardroom door. It was 3:01 a.m., one minute past the witching hour in central Republic of North México.

"I know. Peter is bat-skubalon, wall-crazy." Cyrana was alone on the wall-screen. He guessed she was in one of RNM's not-so-secret bunkers.

"We need to take care of Dunn," she said. "Can you move your Greenhaws east and then north to Williamson County? You should be able to swing back south into old North Austin through Pflugerville from there."

"I think so," said Cardu. "You'll be with us, right?"

"I hope so. But if I'm not, you have to do this."

"Of course."

"He's living above the Bump Stock 'n Mani-pedes Salon off Metric Boulevard," she said. "It's in a run-down strip mall, so it shouldn't be any trouble getting to him."

"Okay. How many Greenhaws have you located so far?" he asked.

"Just me, sorry. Trying to organize anything more than take a coffee break is suspect over here," Cyrana said. "Tell me again why you think the connection we're on right now is so secure? What's it called, the–"

"After-Future Deletion Protocol," answered Cardu. "It destroys every yeet of digital data before it's created–what I just said was vaporized two minutes ago."

"Yeet," she smiled. "Listen, thank you for risking everything to get in contact with me."

"It wasn't a risk. I knew you'd feel the same way I do. Peter and Aby will destroy everything if we don't do something. I should be thanking you."

"You're welcome then, if you insist," she acquiesced. "How many Greenhaws you got?"

"You won't believe this," he said. "Turns out there are eight former Greenhaw students living right here in the P-Free City of Light. It's amazing."

"Well, she taught for 43 years. There have to be at least ten, fifteen thousand of us."

"So, with Bob the Rap-eest and Larry and me that's eleven, plus you."

"Larry knows he doesn't have to do this, right?" Cyrana asked.

"Just try and keep him away. He'll be there."

"Good. Now, what about the 'How about 9:15?' demonstration."

"Everything's on track. Binky's an organizing savant, and Jake's got the P.R. and logistics handled. Ten a.m. tomorrow. We expect three or four thousand people from your side and ours, including Benjamin Yates."

"Mr. Yates will be there? That's perfect. Peter will be so pissed," she said.

"And you think Arlen won't, after he figures out what's going on?"

"Too bad–if they can't agree on a starting time for the meeting that'll determine all our futures, then they'll just have to deal with their daddies marching up Congress Avenue."

How About 9:15? 6:9.1   **May 1, 2027 A.D.**

The How About 9:15? demonstration was attended by tens of thousands RNM and CPFS supporters from all over the Republic. Flusses and bladder-cars transported Mex-Texians into Cuidad de Austin from El Paso to Naranja, Eagle Pass to Paint. El Presidente Phelt and Cyrana marveled at the spectacle from the catwalk above the south entrance to the capitol. Through the uncommonly cloudy sky, they squinted to see six miles south to Bulevar Benjamín Blanco, where thousands of How About 9:15? protesters waited to join the procession northward.

Dunn and Faith Bountiful appeared behind them on their rickety perch. "You've probably never seen anything like that before, have you, Peter?"

"Jesus, man, quit sneaking up on us like that!" Peter said, steadying himself on the narrow, iron walkway. "This thing can't hold all of us. Nobody's actually supposed to be up here, anyway."

"Relax, Peter, we're not up here at all. Faith and I are "imagined" here by the will of the One God and—what is it called dear?" Dunn asked, turning to Faith.

"Unified prayer," she said. "We pray as one to the One, and miracles happen."

Cyrana turned to look at them, annoyed. "So, you're not here?"

"That's right, you're seeing things. We're not real," said Dunn with a saccharine smile. "Just like all those Church of the P-Free Sabbath fools who watched each other stab out their eyes last Monday. That wasn't real."

"And neither are they." Faith pointed at the thousands of How About 9:15?-ers marching up Congress Avenue.

Peter swung the length of his arm through Dunn and Faith. They disappeared. "Dammit!" he shouted. "What the—?" He and Cyrana stared at the throng and their banners nearing the capitol, waiting for them to disappear. "There's no way—are they telling the truth? Is that real? Why would they make us see a peace demonstration, for God's sake?"

"He's just screwing with us," she said. "He does it because he can."

"But why? It doesn't make sense."

"I don't know," Cyrana said. "I'm not even sure I know how to know anymore."

* * *

The next day, "How About 9:15? Demonstration Fuels Hope for Peace Talks" was the headline in El Hombre de Estado de Austin y México. Cardu and Cyrana finished reading the article on their nose pods and looked at each other via the After-Future Deletion Protocol connection, wondering what they hadn't said yet to each other, that was erased for all time two minutes ago.

"Did you see the live feed of the demonstration from CPFS?" she asked.

"We think we did, but ever since Odede Jäger was here, nobody's sure what they're seeing," said Cardu. "I'm not even sure that Binky and Jake organized the demonstration, even though I watched them do it–I think."

"That's it. That's why Dunn is having the sisters create these illusions," she said. "He's making us question everything we see so that–"

"···we're all in the dark. We're as blind as he is," Cardu finished her sentenced. "Trouble is, he's great at being blind. We suck at it."

The Abbot's Chifforobe 6:10.1   **May 2, 2027 A.D.**

Famuelita and Larry arrived early. They stood in the shade of an expansive southbound overpass below the newest 24-lane toll road, this one leading to the fifth largest city in the Republic–Pflugerville. It was barely 10 a.m.; hours earlier the sun had set about its business to raise the surface temperature of the asphalt acres above to 136°F.

"I can't stay long," she said.

"I know," Larry said, resigned. He kissed her hand and looked into her beautiful eyes for what he knew would be the last time. She'd been distant and quite since they'd arrived at the P-Free City of Light and met Pastor Yates. "Why do you have to leave?"

"For the same reason you have to stop your father. It's what you're supposed to do." They hugged each other hard and long.

"Who are you?" he asked gently.

"I don't know," Fam confessed. "I think I might be everyone." She touched his cheek for the last time and walked away.

Larry watched as her silhouette on the eastern horizon was replaced by ten alumni of one of Mrs. Greenhaw's end-of-year musical extravaganzas between 1978 and 1998. Twenty minutes later the group entered the shade of the overpass mid-conversation.

"I say we disappear the bloke, straight off to his own special 'ell-'ole," suggested the star of Mrs. Greenhaw's 1978 production of Pygmalion. "That'll teach him!" she said, as Eliza Doolittle.

"I think that might work," Larry offered, as if he'd been part of the 13-mile conversation from Nagaswamie. "He made me 'disappear' him into lots of different timeframes and locations– he travels well, so he could make the journey to wherever we decide."

"He's a conniving curse," growled the mean old lion from the 1992 revival of the Wiz. "We have to go in there with some serious intension. Unified, like those Word-damned Seven Sisters."

"You're so right, man," said Bob the Rap-eest.

"I think I have the perfect place for the Abbot of Black Shade." A thin muscular woman stepped forward, wearing bib overhauls over a dirty white t-shirt and a gimme cap with Atticus Rules. "I say we disappear that sorry bastard to Maycomb, Alabama right into the body of Tom Robinson."

" 'You come-on in here, boy, and bust up this chifforobe,' " Cyrana's impression of the white temptress in To Kill a Mockingbird was a tour de force.

"Exactly!" the woman said. "We'd have to change the story a little, but we could have that racist bastard bustin' up chifforobes for eternity if we want!"

"I must have read To Kill a Mockingbird ten times," Cyrana said. "It rang awful true in Jasper County, where I grew up."

"I hear you, sister," the woman said.

"I wish I could have seen you. I bet you played a kicked-ass Jem."

"It was way before your time, honey–1979," interjected the once-Boo Radley. "But you're right. She took no prisoners."

"You think we can really disappear him into a book?" Cyrana looked at Larry along with the rest of the group.

"I don't see why not, as long as we all have the same intention, like Lion says."

"In that case, why not disappear him into Titus Andronicus, as Lavinia," suggested the erudite lead from the original 1989 production of Shakespeare Kills, the Musical.

"I say we disappear him into Melania's Inferno," suggested Officer Krupke, Westside Story, 1987.

"I gotta go with To Kill a Mockingbird," said Gertie Cummings from Black-lahoma! which received rave reviews in 1968. "It just seems like the right thing to do." All heads nodded agreement.

"It's settled then. You say he's at the Bump Stock 'n Mani-pedes Salon?" Lion asked. "I know exactly where that is. I can disappear us there if you want."

"Shouldn't we physically travel there so that we conserve our energy for Dunn's disappearing?" Cyrana asked.

"I don't know, I've never done this before," Lion said. "Should we?"

"Once, I disappeared my dad to three different places in one day," Larry offered. "But he wanted to disappear with me; it's not like he put up a fight or anything, and they were all short hops. Still, I was wasted after the third one."

"But there are 12 of us," Jem pressed. "Surely we all got enough giddy-up to disappear ourselves up to north Austin and take care of Dunn."

"I agree. It'll be a six- or seven-hour trip in the pre-noonday gridlock. It's 15 miles away, after all." Charlie said, glancing at the 24 lanes of motionless traffic above. They all knew this was not the first or last time Austin traffic would re-route history.

"We're agreed, then," Cyrana said, nodding at Lion.

"Alright, circle around me," he instructed, stepping into the center of the group. "Now, hold hands in a daisy chain" Without further direction, they closed their eyes, and slowly began to move counter-clockwise as Lion purred the GPS coordinates, "30.416041, -97.695189. 30.416041, -97.695189. 30.416041, -97.695189. 30.416041, -97.695189." The twelve THWACKED! into Dunn's second-floor apartment.

"Who's there?!" Dunn scrambled to reach his cane, moving away from the sound into the corner of the kitchen.

The Greenhaws silently filed into the kitchen and re-formed their circle, leaving a gap between Cyrana and Jem, for Dunn to enter.

"I know you're there! Who is it?" Dunn demanded. "Yates, is that you?" He swung his cane hard at the room and hit Lion in the back. "Ha! Take that, you–"

Lion grabbed the cane, broke it in two and threw it across the room. Jem turned the top-burner knobs on the old gas stove next to Dunn. The electric ignition clicked three times, followed by the SWOOSH of the blue-hot flame. Dunn felt the singed hair on his forearm and bolted forward into the center of the circle. Cyrana and Jem closed the powerful ring, the force of it pinning Dunn's arms against his sides.

His curses and incantations were ignored as the Greenhaws chanted. "Kill a mockingbird, kill a mockingbird, kill a mockingbird." With each repetition, they felt a swelling of energy in the room.

"Kill a mockingbird, kill a mockingbird." It was working. As one, they envisioned the hellish, monotonous future of Mr. Dunn, doomed to 'bustin' up chifforobes' for eternity. They were almost there.

"Kill a mockingbird, kill a mockingbird." And then it stopped. There was no common vision, no chanting. They could not speak. A renewed strength coursed through Dunn's body, as he freed his arms and swung his fists at his captors.

The Greenhaws shouted encouragements to each other to maintain the bond of the circle as they leaned back to avoid Dunn's blows. Cyrana shouted the mantra, trying to regain their advantage. "Kill a mockingbird! Kill a mockingbird!" The others joined her, desperately trying to control Dunn, but their ability to vision as one was gone.

"Great Walk Stand, Great Walk Stand." Another mantra met theirs, enveloping the circle in a four-dimensional headlock. Macabre images of the Seven Sisters appeared deep in the psyche of each Greenhaw. Lion suckled, as a baby, at the teat of a 90-year version of Rachel, the Second sister. Officer Krupke wept as his wife, Bathsheba the Seventh, sold hats in a Jerusalem market, oblivious to their stillborn child, dead on the ground; Delilah, the Fifth, gouged out Jem's right eye while trimming her bangs.

"Great Walk Stand, Great Walk Stand." The opposing chant swelled around them, through them. Cyrana felt Charlie's wrist in her hand as they watched Rebekah, the Third, hurl a double-dodge boulder to break the bond of the circle. "Kill a mockingbird!" Cyrana screamed. "Kill a mockingbird, Charlie!" In their shared nightmare, he looked at her and struggled to say the words.

"Kill a mockingbird."

"Kill a mockingbird!" she shouted, squeezing his wrist, as if giving it CPR. He squeezed it forward to Boo Radley's wrist, weakly at first but soon reaching a life-sustaining rate of 90 beats per minute.

"Kill a mockingbird!" Boo hollered like a razorback-doggin' hogster, celebrating a kill. Their intention was slowly rejuvenated around the circle. And then again, as their chant found its strength. "Kill a mockingbird!" "Kill a mockingbird!" Their renewed energy coursed through the circle's voice, dissipating Dunn's strength; the other chant waned and was finally silenced.

In their minds, the Greenhaws heard Lion begin the countdown. "Five, four, three¬–" They all crouched into a deep knee-bend. "Two, one!" As one, the group jumped up, flinging their arms and Dunn toward the ceiling.

It happened in an instant, but they all witnessed it in slow motion. Dunn's head, arms and torso disappeared through the ceiling, on their way to an everlasting life of bustin' up chifforobes in Alabama. But the process suddenly stopped, just as his knees were about to follow the rest of him. His gnarly toes wriggled in black and white-striped, calf-high socks. The Greenhaws looked at one another and then at Dunn's sandals on the floor, left behind by the force of his sudden upward motion.

Lion pointed at Dunn's legs. "Really?" he asked the universe, exasperated. Then–a la the Wicked Witch of the East after Dorothy's house landed on her–Dunn's toes slowly folded back into his feet like a neatly rolled sleeping bag. They all gawked as the roll consumed his ankles, calves and finally the kneecaps, until all of him disappeared into the ceiling without a trace.

The Greenhaws sank to the floor, utterly exhausted, hopeful that their soul-sucking battle with the Seven Sisters was over. They closed their eyes and slept. And slept.

Cyrana awoke. "We have to get back to Peter and Arlen," she mumbled, sleepily. "They'll agree to meet at 9:15 now, surely— once they learn that Dunn has been disappeared."

"Oh my god, that was almost two months ago!" Larry said.

"What was?" Cyrana asked.

"Check your nose pod," Larry said. "We've been here for eight weeks."

"Word Almighty," said Charlie. "It's June 17."

The Great Walk Stand 6:11.1   June 18, 2027 A.D.

From the steps of the capitol, el Presidente Phelt regarded the grandeur of the Great Walk, the black and white diamond-patterned pavement leading south across the stately grounds, to Congress Avenue. Weathered bronze statues of Texas Rangers, Alamo heroes and sainted Confederates framed his view beyond the Great Walk Gate where Pastor Arlen Bob Yates and 50,000 Church of the P-Free Sabbath faithful gathered, loaded for bear.

Phelt had chronicled the coming events of the day in his diary the night before. He'd named the decisive victory he would most assuredly have today, the Great Walk Stand. Moments before emerging from the capitol he read aloud the ten-page journal entry, as would Peter Coyote narrating another Ken Burns documentary. It was poignant.

This clash would not be another Battle of Lady Bird Lake, where the weapons were prayers of mass destruction and the generals were the Abbot of Black Shade and the Seven Sisters. They were gone now, as were Yate's faithful Cardu and Phelt's number one, Cyrana Johnson. Rumors and accusations about their disappearances had raged their way across the InterMess since early May.

Phelt repeatedly stated that Dunn and the Seven Sisters had been extraordinarily-renditioned by CPFS to a U.S. lab in True, Nevada where their amygdalae were being weaponized. Yates appreciated the originality of the allegation and scolded his staff for not coming up with something equally absurd. He was forced to simply denounce the claim as just another skubalon-for-brains distortion of whatever-was-passing-for-truth-these-days. In any case, that and everything else mattered little now; the die was cast and all the gods' children were ready for an old-fashioned guns-and-bullets showdown.

Both sides had struggled to secure suitable military equipment for the occasion. U.S. military bases left nothing behind as they were evacuated in the dead of night on April 20, the day before Texas was expelled from the Union. Texas hadn't maintained much of a military force, and the airtight embargo imposed by the United Nations was actually working, leaving the two wannabe armies to appropriate arms wherever they could.

Opposing patrols fought gallantly over museum-quality guns, cannons and munitions, some dating back to 1836, from the Bob Bullock Museum; a midnight raid on the National Museum of the Pacific War in Fredericksburg garnered a smorgasbord of bayonets, cricket noise makers and pineapple grenades for CPFS; and, several hundred loyal Texas Parks and Wildlife Department game wardens occupied fireworks stands from Brownsville to the Red River. (The State Auditor's Office later questioned the efficacy of the $13 million operation, noting that the wardens could have simply purchased all the fireworks in the Republic for less than $5,000 at the Memorial Day rate of "Buy 1 Get 1,000 Free.")

Amid the scramble to secure armaments, RNM loyalists and CPFS faithful alike were grateful to the 90th Texas Legislature for passing legislation to amend the mandatory open-carry law enacted the previous session. The new law passed in February 2027 required all K-12 students to strap on a weapon, right along with their parents and, by March, every Texan kindergartner had a real gun to play with, to the great chagrin of Texas toy-gun manufacturers. Except for them, everyone thanked their god for the divinely inspired legislation–otherwise there wouldn't have been nearly enough guns to conduct a proper Texas battle.

With the slightest of nods, el Presidente Phelt ordered the first two volleys from the restored Confederate 12-pound Napoleon cannons positioned near the Capitol steps. The cannonball issued from the 1864 field gun barely made it out of its barrel, dropping impotently to the ground. The shot from the other cannon veered off to the right, obliterating the entrance to la Mansión del Presidente, formerly the Texas Governor's Mansion. The CPFS rank and file laughed uproariously and spontaneously mooned the thousands of RNM Mex-Texians, who responded in kind.

Women and men on both sides of the Great Walk Gate exposed and widened their cheeks at their former friends and kinsmen, laughing and baiting one another like only family can. They stood inches away from each other, separated by black wrought iron fences surrounding the capitol. It was a final, raucous farewell before they got down to the business of killing each other.

What happened during the next several hours is much disputed by the Washington press corps, *Popular Mechanics* and *Highlights Magazine*, but they all agreed on one point: it was bloody mess.

Without warning, CPFS faithful thrust medieval lances and swords, liberated from a travelling exhibit at the Blanton Museum of Art, through the iron fences. After piercing random lungs and hearts, the priceless weapons were thrust into other torsos. RNM fighters responded with stilettos and chains commandeered from the West Side Story revival at the

Paramount Theatre, WWI German stick grenades, and scores of 300mg cherry bombs and M-80s.

Machetes from both sides chopped at enemy arms daring to scale the wrought iron barrier. A CPFS surge of bodies toppled the main gate, followed by the collapse of the entire fence on the capitol ground's southern boundary. No immediate advantage was gained by either side as hundreds of civilian troops dropped dead amid fevered hand-to-hand combat, replacing the iron fence with a human one.

Stationary guns from gone-by eras fired rounds on the capitol from the Austin History Museum before they were silenced by the Longhorn's touchdown cannon. Three blocks away, 500 RNM regulars, stationed beneath the Trinity Building the previous night, quietly moved south to Sixth Street, flanking the CPFS force. Their attack was little more than a nuisance to the 10,000 CPFS-strong rear guard, who cut them down like so many crusaders at the hands of Saladin.

Three hours earlier, before the sun dared rise, 150 CPFS undercover agents and their families created a diversion two blocks east of the capitol at the Visitors Parking Lot on 12th Street by arriving in their minivans all at once, thus creating a strategic parking brouhaha. Many RNM militia members, thinking they'd arrived in plenty of time to secure free parking before the battle began, were livid. Long guns slung over their shoulders, they walked the line of minivans stretching down the hill to Red River Street and beyond.

"Minnesota? New Jersey?! Indi-fucking-ana?!" RNM regulars called out as they read the license plates.

"Land of Lincoln?!" roared an old dude with a ponytail, right before he bashed out the rear window of a van, igniting an all-out street brawl.

The diversion worked. Most of the RNM military police guarding the west entrance to the Capitol's underground parking garage were immediately dispatched to the Visitors Parking Lot. The remaining three RNM officers were easily overcome by two dozen CPFS science teachers who'd been blowing things up since they were teenagers. They streamed into the dark garage, broke into in their assigned teams, and began drilling holes and placing explosives and detonators into load-bearing columns.

As designed, the explosion would not produce the symmetrical implosion of the Capitol, but would immediately destroy the west wing, its subterranean extension and the cavernous underground parking area. If it were the will of Word, the rest of the massive structure would collapse into the gaping hole, destroying the Supreme Court Building in its wake.

THWACK! Charlie appeared on the tiny pedestal supporting the Goddess of Liberty atop the capitol, 308 feet above the slaughter. A cannon shot obliterated the gold star held high by the Goddess, knocking Charlie from his feet and off the narrow ledge; he desperately grabbed the statue's waist as a 187-year old arrow first shot by Comanche Chief Buffalo Hump in the Great Raid of 1840, nicked his ear lobe. He felt his blood drip onto his neck, staining his brand-new KEEP CALM AND DISAPPEAR t-shirt.

His nose pod vibrated as he struggled to regain a foothold on the Goddess's base. He pulled himself up by her neck and the nub of her shattered arm. The pod opened to a 12-screen communication, one panel per Greenhaw. Each was stationed at a strategic location around the border of La República del Norte de México, at the highest point possible to report on local battle conditions. On the southern border were Larry in Naranja, on the coastal boarder with Louisiana; Eliza Doolittle in Corpus Christi; Jem in Brownsville; Bob the Rap-eest in Del Rio; Cyrana in Ruidosa; and the old lion reporting from the roof of el Banco de La República del Norte de México Plaza in downtown El Paso.

"Jesus," said Cyrana, from her perch on the belfry of the Sacred Heart Mission; behind her, motley contingents of the CPFS and RNM militia fought gallantly for the one square mile that made up the entirety of unincorporated Ruidosa. "The war is everywhere," she yelled.

"It's spreading to the other side of the border, too." From his vantage point, Lion trained his camera across the Rio Grande, to Ciudad Juárez in flames.

"Same here!" said Officer Krupke from the top of the Professional Wrestling Hall of Fame and Museum in Wichita Falls. "The Oklahoma National Guard crossed the Red River at Burkburnett, and now there's goddamned three-way battle."

Charlie captured a 360-degree view from the capitol for the others to see. As violent as the close-ups of downtown Austin were, they paled in comparison to the devastation in the distance. A Dresden-worthy firestorm consumed the horizon, the conflagration masking periodic explosions. He looked down at the historic Texas Children Monument on the northwest side of the Capitol and silently apologized for placing the future of all that was once Texas on their shoulders.

The Greenhaws were silent as the rest of the world raged. Their resolve to act surged from one to another as if they were physically connected. This was the cleansing, the moment of reckon foretold by the First Teller before the Big Bang banged.

"We have no choice, now," Cyrana said. They all looked at each other one last time and deep-breathed their eyes closed.

"Reach out for the one to your right, and the one on your left," Lion said. "Extend yourself. Reach out. Feel each other's hands and draw them near. Closer." All 15 million feet of the once-Texas border tickled the universe, as the fingers of one Greenhaw met another. As one, they took two steps forward, and all that Texas ever was or would be disappeared in a spectacular flash of fire and fog. Just like that.

Omega barada nikto.

The Last Fail-Safe.

December 16, 2056 A.D.

The nursing home's circular driveway suited infrequent visitors who never stayed long and valued the easy escape it offered back to their own lives.

It had been another hot, dusty trip into a brilliant sunset from Nagaswamie to north Austin; the worst drought in 99 years that began a decade ago now aspired to be the worst in 100.

He parked, turned off the car and sat. If he'd kept track of his visits over the years, this one might mark an anniversary. Two hundred, three-hundred? Maybe. It didn't matter–he was here.

Inside was his lifelong friend. Sixty years ago, they'd imagined boundless adventures beyond outer space with their girlfriends, filled with life-and-death battles and even more daring moments of fantasized middle-school intimacy.

He navigated the craggy peaks of the sidewalk that reminded family members not to ask if Grandma or Abuelita ever got out for a nice evening stroll. That was the language of health and freedom, not of this place.

"Evening, sir," the nurse said to the man, as she double-checked the rate on the IV drip. The room's linoleum floors and sanitized surfaces glistened under ancient white fluorescents, belying the abiding smell of urine. She drew the curtain, halving the room and hiding a sleeping, old blind man in the other bed.

"Hello Mrs. Famstone. How's his book coming?" The man managed a weary smile.

"He was working on it some this afternoon, it looked like. It must have been an exciting part 'cause he was mighty agitated."

The man made his way to a wheelchair at the foot of his friend's bed. "My word, I think I may be needing one of these myself, pretty soon."

"I don't think there's any rush on that, Pastor– you still look pretty spry to me." A comfortable silence lingered in the room.

"How long you think he's been writing it–whatever it is."

"Lord, let's see. I've been here since the early '30s. Back then, the therapist would give him one of those Big Chief pads and he'd scribble in it for hours," the nurse said. "He must have gone through a couple hundred of those things through the years."

"We all have a story to tell, I suppose," he said.

"For all I know, he's been working on it since he first got here," the nurse added. "Back in the '90s, I think."

"Yes, it was a long time ago," Pastor Phelt nodded. "He was just a kid, praise God."

The frail, elderly man in the bed pursed his lips and groaned softly. Mrs. Famstone soothed his forehead with a cool cloth, as she had for as long as she could remember. "Don't you worry, now," she said. "We'll take care of you."

ACKNOWLEDGEMENTS

I am indescribably grateful to my wife, son and daughter. Each, in their own way, willingly gave me the support, time and space I needed to write *Skubalon Storm*.

Karen O'Halloran honored me with her rendering of the Texas State Capitol on the stormy eve of secession.

Kathy Hill brought her considerable talents to bear on the cover design.

Jeff Carmack, *Skubalon Storm's* fearless first-reader, proofed the manuscript and, in the process, provided good cheer and encouragement to me after four years of first-draft solitude.

I am humbled by the tireless work of those who care for and preserve the history of Texas, including archivists, librarians and conservators across the state, and those who buff the floors of our capitol and trim its grounds daily. Thank you.